G000070640

Apocalypse Party

Design by Mike Corrao
Cover Design by Matthew Revert

Paperback: 978-1-954899-17-9

Printed in the United States of America

FIRST AMERICAN EDITION

9 8 7 6 5 4 3 2 1

. AANNEX

Blake Butler

0   HOME

10	Nothing else had ever been so free as those who survived the experience of humanity
20	In nothing gained, no vision paired to its own faith
30	Presupposed under the claim that paradise shall not suspend its breadth of treachery through mere confusion, though that was all that it would take
40	Where the wintering ended & turned over sensations only applicable in what might never be yet sent asunder
50	Revising nightfall in tender scope—within concentric wills; each irreversible; each only ever all our own
55	(*no-open-field*)
60	& only there of total fracture reconvened; interlaced where navigable narration extracts notion from sentiment, then shatters; a limbic bridge unveiling flux in aggravated colony's ongoing intervention as horror legend
70	Whose future time exports no faith; thru cavities exerting their only authority as hostage reencoded into meaning
80	Without aesthetic structure in receipt of any notion (w/o duration/narration/location/innovation/physical law)
90	Against the will of those who won't believe from the beginning

100	*I can't remember any crimes* (virtual) (untraceable) (atavistic) (post-novel)
105	*I can't remember any sorrow* (neural extract) (pillform) (innate) (hex)
110	*I can't remember any drugs* (unreal) (explicit) (diuretic) (interpsychic)
115	*I can't remember any information* (any information) (any information)
120	"...I had only just then found a love; it did not happen quickly, having spent so long time as a pure fool..."
125	**The HoloRind**
130	In what else we kept dragging on about in sickness, never health; only what was enough ours that we were still it when we kept waking up against our will; since simpler even than the thorns
140	Pins in the past creature known alone only as night rose in wasted flagrance reattributed as retrosthesiacortextulative pain
150	Turned over only in improbable corruption by a single flaw drawn in the code once known as free will; thereafter never again able to stay sealed
151	Packaged and repackaged into a set that contains the prior set but not the set that the culmination of the effects of the present set's eventual forward progress must by mere gestation come to produce by tracing the edges of the set of all sets' manifestation in the mind of the last known person to have lived
152	Back and forth between twin points that continue growing nearer and gain mass as the only path between them biometrically degrades beyond all shape
160	The head of the norm | the hell of the mention | the egg of all as never meant
161	Fates precomprised in active.files that seek an ultimate distress
163	As the irrational becomes rational thru the synthesis of all available logics

200	*There must be vulnerable derivatives of every state previously considered invulnerable*
210	f://greenness/electrocuted/auditioned/X/ *(file not felt)*
220	*What can't be wanted and so then must be*
221	Infernal evidence of theft-of-proof
225	Even w/in participation of formal parameters having led to the traceable state of origin as last prescribed in mortal haste by the fatigued
230	Impossible rungs, ledges, circuitry, etc. ballasting the rogue id
240	w/in demolished knowledge preventing suture thru the creation of extra-narrative events
250	What parts of any reception remain distinctive, which have been ascribed to local blood for good, which may be removed of potent chromosomes soon as ulterior attention so commands it
253	how--should--I--be---allowed---to----ask----this------of------our-------shrine
260	Incensed, as such, with one's own mimicry of bliss, born into intervention long already underway before the groveling floods the flesh's bins
270	In the way of cultivating cognition into removed space, how deep must perjury be to conflict with the benevolence of an unseen landscape, how too close to intersecting with the signal-channel in such a way that it might disrupt the never previously enforced
277	To be heard within a language notwithstanding—To be said aloud into the stitch the bodies bust—To be stated through a feature once devoid of legal terms—To be saved alone by heavy blows derived from one's own market data—To be off-loaded by the scape of endless skin—To be devised apart as retribution after silence—To be corrected—To reboot at last from never-nil
288	{} {} {} {.} {}	||
290	Could wait for an answer just this once but I would be waiting for the rest of the amount of time I remember to consider it until corruption would I not

300   "I don't need to be convinced"

310   *LIVE FROM THE LOBE OF* OLD NADAN

```
There'll         come
a     season.    In
anatomies.
Altered for pleasure
in displeasure
soon    like   lab
bots,   calling it
milk.  A widening
roll of wind that
confidently
positions    itself
at   the   forefront
of   the   scenario's
disbelief       and
through        this
manages    to   be
forgotten first  of
all   and   left  to
leak  into the  era
of mankind's
putrescence.
```

320   but plz at least for now don't turn away   yah I'm
speaking directly in2 u now, tho morelike thru u   hehehe
in just exactly th' right way, to make u mirror like a Flat One,
funded in falsehood's open graft   don't have anything else 2 claim   just wanted u to look @ me alive here in
the midst of turning down, like it wz about to mean the most
of all the pleading I have parsed, of all the fortunes   he-
hehehehe   if only just to show u still how lost a single cell
can be allowed

3xx   ::Now.Playing-Abovexxground::

3xx   *seeking signal*

333   [*533K146 51644L* converts to *2599N11636 2513616160*]
OpenMap

3xx

----

1. *Into the pumice furnace* (baked)

2. *Along the subelectric spiral* (nether)

3. OpenMap[x]

35x	*Data extra-enforceably ingotten only during the widowhood of the mother after all, which then assuredly extends into the adjoining bloodlines of memo-dissolution you will suffer alongside a living moment's numbered graft in at least some number of possible outcomes available in the simplest structures of guided life*
355	No further questions from the trapped
36x	A pink/orange light across the mindmud of the temple as it splits into itself; where-else-assumed, issuing its own law, as from the long already ~~spent~~
3xx	Blood of the script: *spiralcore/sponges/anti-elliptical/grime forests/concavity becoming underbelly now raw and fat /only closed circuit/for the silver coffers/ / //* **crashing**
3xx	{instance} ~~cud/crux/core/code/cull/cop/cure~~ [...]
xxx	the "ex-evenт
39x	*Having exposed one's self so deeply no way remains to return to particular particles*
39x	.
399	.·

400	*An under-fundament may be granted premise only after having resigned its means of germination into transmittable shape-of-fact*
410	Nightspace of only wounds that never heal
420	*Likewise, the lossless points at which an unmarked era can be slit along its belly (glistening in speech gel) to produce a range of emotional content no longer applicable to the beings left w/in the act unrandomized, discoverable exclusively thru permutation of a previously impossible conclusion*
430	The thrill of being supplanted; corrupted; found out; packed in fossils
440	Where the edge of the known universe describes itself
450	Victim at last of nothing more than parity's occlusion thru subinfinite vertices suspended in trauma numen
455	As a flake; as a conditional promise masking its benefit for either side until just past the point of inspiration; as thrush appearing on the stone
456	Not indescribable but revivable; uncertain under disbelief of the totality's invention only after its hypothetical image topples, becomes impregnable
460	Breakdown of blood cells → regrafted in cause-dependent viral corridors post-catastrophe → wherein the categorically obscene must be made sacred after all → solely navigable thru mood-bending surgeries compatible only w/ the least desirable specimen of any given session → nonexistent but in heat intolerable even to the inanimate →
470	As every plot never provided
480	As we await defeat

490xxxxxxxxxxxxxxxxxxxxxxxxxxxxxxxxxxxxxxxxxxxxxxxxxxxxxxxxxxxxxxxxxx
491xxxxxxxxxxxxxxxxxxxxxxxxxxxxxxxxxxxxxxxxxxxxxxxxxxxxxxxxxxxxxxxxxx
494xxxxxxxxxxxxxxxxxxxxxxxxxxxxxxxxxxxxxxxxxxxxxxxxxxxxxxxxxxxxxxxxxx
495xxxxxxxxxxxxxxxxxxxxxxxxxxxxxxxxxxxxxxxxxxxxxxxxxxxxxxxxxxxxxxxxxx
496xxxxxxxxxxxxxxxxxxxxxxxxxxxxxxxxxxxxxxxxxxxxxxxxxxxxxxxxxxxxxxxxxx
497xxxxxxxxxxxxxxxxxxxxxxxxxxxxxxxxxxxxxxxxxxxxxxxxxxxxxxxxxxxxxxxxxx
499xxxxxxxxxxxxxxxxxxxxxxxxxxxxxxxxxxxxxxxxxxxxxxxxxxxxxxxxxxxxxxxxxx

500	f://exe.exe
501	**Nothing withstands**
510	Obviously-devious
520	Devoid-of-content
522	x = "x"
525	*Let no soul rest*
530	*Parallax revision autocorrecting towards devolutionary syntax supported under all eleven of the recognizable macro-ordinances in subdermal trance*
540	*Under anatomy designed to dislocate maximum interdisciplinary application and to militarize the common fate*
545	*As etched upon the lungs of the machine*

546   {Pink quarks; flat triggers; artificial semiology}

547   *Only so long now*

550   ::loading::

555

| |
|
| |
| |
|
|
|
| |
| |
| |
|
|

an untraceable extent: *Basis of Genera* $[e] - [e_x]$

|
||
| |
|
|
| |
| |
| |
| |
| |
| |
| \
|
|

6xx	(seed)
6xx	(envelope)
6xx	(organism)
6xx	(order of wrath)
6xx	(empire)
6xx	(faith)
6xx	(monosyllabic)
6xx	(polysyllabistic)
666	(metaphor)
6xx	(reason)
6xx	(craft)
6xx	(networks)
6xx	(surges)
6xx	(viroid)
6xx	(blank)
6xx	(polymers)
6xx	(tumors)
6xx	(subspecies)
6xx	(intersexuality)
6xx	(transmutation)
6xx	(subnarration)
6xx	(confabulation)
6xx	(compression)
6xx	(surface)
69x	(aperture)
699	(x)

700      $x \neq x$

701   What cannot be felt is only ours *for as long as we cease to earn protection against our unclaimed cognitive features*

702   Human experience begins simultaneously w/ its intervention by physical law on behalf of the implausibility of actual progress

705   Within only the atavistically verboten; unattended & not recorded but in the abstruse, to be supplanted upon any point of measured contact

710   Such as

711   How every language is unimaginable until applied || How history is created from the absence of reason

713   Anti-geometrical, anti-logical, anti-significant

720   Hyper-compressed to the point of being able to appear within any coordinates of the unrefined organism and still convinced into repression delivered aesthetically

727   As if what once appeared parallel cannot collide

728   Paper-thin, fully penetrable, within controlled bounds that fail to police themselves in absence of responding to user queries never delivered but from within the logic of the model's indefatigable finitude; and thru coordinates that immediately malform when patched compatible

729   Rendered in processed fat from future text left unforced

730   How far alone unkempt in tragedy's elapsed concaveness

737   Shown wherein nothing that can be thought at all can be thought at all, so as nothing that can be said can be said

740   "No one will help you" (speaking solely as every individual at the precipice of mortal treason (& w/o a reason to believe in anything but the negation of identity (Division of the apparent (Flush of the sum))))

750   *If/then : And/but : When/than : As/for : Of/of : No/now*

755   <u>A silver planet covered in prisons</u>

760

766   Predating even the formation of the elements

767   The lesser of two halves becoming dormant while the other listened and vice versa

770   Nothing else left; no one stunning but in waves of pith & trestle

777   *Insanely virulent music fills the stage*—incessantly violent, comprehensively disloyal to whichever set of points from which the edge of time had earned its patternlessness, in moral torpor, reconfined

780   {Dank noise, ergonomics, religious fiction, humor grafts, hosts to the rail}

790   Not at all long enough to be lessened back from but thru floes of territories within all infestation

79x   Stuttering and spasming and grasping and culling and clawing and gleaming

799   The birth of **entertainment**

800	Platelets/erased magnetic tapes/bodies of models/bone stars/ mud
810	Dark lattice choreography/stereographic diseasement/ red-ramming pistons/putty/whorlflow
820	Hardstream/rhizome foundry/crystallized bullets/faction of core narco-ethics/indiscourse
830	Radial pornography/celestial outlets/terror weapons/celestial pins
840	Rapid expansion and contraction thru innumerable renditions swallowed whole/grid crust/emulsions/silt mines/silver polish
850	Serial glyph/unsustainable diuretic nuance/breadbrain/pulse
860	Graphic design/psychoanalysis(incisions/sockets)/derivatives in session/overspent
870	"The rest is history"/"To have avoided confrontation"/ "Pulled them apart and they immediately conformed"/ "No code exists @ coefficients indexable during live session"/"The error bends until it has no alternative but to be understood as true"
880	1 of 0
888	*How the interface had been constructed so as to enable intermorbid transposition even as the concept of "the diving mask" itself could not be separated from the impossibility of mobilizing informants on the basis of nepotism w/r/t those who could be most directly linked to the concomitant undoing of any action not seen as attributable to working parlance wherein all assassination occurred simultaneously w/ algorithm's premanufacture of phantasmic superposition, thus barring mobility of all post-moral entities across measurable vectors where mediums might assimilate their frottage into workable housing for those dispossessed of the chemistry of participation even as far down the line as the last frame of their self-imposed mirage of fact collection, and therefore such previously accessibly-designed utilities such as participation, demonstration, natural selection, confession, compatibility, as well as even more eventually fully automized applications, including transportation, cloning, window shopping, and free speech*

898   *Wherein what could never be imagined must only independently persist; each lobe's branch staking and maintaining its genetically enmeshed authority over future focal populations via unsustainable persuasion methods originated in the earliest methods of vocal music (screaming, bleating, gnashing, wailing), as indexed entirely prior to the advent of marked time; it is from this point that all forms of creation must be made apparent to their source, if forever left ungoverned by the necessary whims that would ensure its ongoing propagation into sense, creating the inestimable artificial gap between coded subrealities*

899   Expulsed; eradicated (topically)

900	"Nothing appends."
910	Arpeggiators; color bands
920	The monophonic blades of ash
92x	Expounded time runs parallel both to itself and to its ineffable transaction; past and future, intertwined; creating in each individual user an experience of formlessness, deep fear— which in turn allows the forcefed amalgamation to continue curving out from underneath its only path
92x	All that must exist exists in every version of hell as it's transcribed, and only there
930	From within tone-bent pyramidal derivatives reflected in cascade when severed; to be overhauled in post
933	To attract the legions into any lineage that fits their subcortex's reinforcement
936	Surly, starving, frantic, and contagious; rapt w/o perspective; lost in gems
940	*Wickedness* = *passion* (thru population)
950	::disintegrating upon any pressure::
957	In corollary to the formal threads binding the skull of the beholder to its intonation's miracle
958	*<triggers the eye of what must not be begotten and so is>*
960	Such as the expectation of a face, whose definition states—<u>to have known to pass thru, there and only there</u>
966	But once begun, then: masses of amalgamations; masses of rafters in the slip incurred from word to word
967	Lore ❚ Colonies ❚ Empires ❚ Corporations ❚ Gore
969	The vast concavities of blood only to be spilled, incinerated
970	**The Sickest Galaxy**
971	/1234567890875323456789098765434567898765 67656789 /0/
972	*Slick gray-white rapt illumination spilling emphatically from the elongation between vectors overridden in the absence of description of a method of categorizing the essence of a disembodied*

experience as rendered before ever having been embodied

975   *Scratched on all sides, under the claws of what can never not be felt, despite the conviction of the partition's edges to defy itself, to have no center and no fact beyond its frame, but where thru the slits of the shreds a wind is blowing, or is it breath*

977   Unpredictable alternation between identical sequences of spontaneous subjective interpretations in continuous loop

978   *Irregularly ongoing alteration of spatial arrangement of atoms during magnetic moments that cannot be iterated, treated, or traced*

979   "...where in the first several chapters of the novel we see, on several occasions, exactly what X reads when they look at the open notebook. The notebook appears to take over as the main text of the novel starting at Chapter VII, coming almost seamlessly after Chapter VI. However, though Chapter VII reads as though it is written by X, many of the passages shown in earlier chapters appear verbatim in Chapter VII. Yet for X to have read those passages earlier, the passages must have been written before they received the notebook..."

980   ::obliterated w/ one's ear to the hemispherical as the mind of the gates click open or shut::

982   There w/in which lurks the long, pinned core-skin of the penetrable continuum (the feed that melts the feed)

988   ~~The pale black dot~~ (simultaneously descending and ascending through its own false shadow's superposition at randomly generated rate, as found at 1:1 per incarnation per submanifestation of new primitive "weird numbers" w/in must never come to pass)

98x   (until at last so far within itself the circle flips, is ripped in halves, to show itself back to itself)

99x   From what fouled language nevermending floods the unorientable detritus of diminishing sensation

999   Bloodhole; starhole

1000   To have imagined having withstood

1001   As the rest exists to itself as immensely exposed to discontinued information [auto-unpacking: (*SACRED FORTUNES/INFESTATION*) Formal summary of 'prior era,' a false-floored opening in pseudocode, depicting, in Gorschach's name, 'how our mythology began'" — Randy Ranch is assigned to a revision of C. Hanritty's *Demenstratio*, aka the big Mistake, ft. Splitter — Within the methodology of spin (by XXXXL) — An in-flight controlfilm, for yr Pleasure: MR. MUSTARD AND HIS CANDLEHANDS (sic) w/ director's commentary, live — (clipslip 1: *mourning the loss of monomyth*) — "The Revelation of the Screen," wherein one Polyana Maskerson intercepts the word of the erased G-d and uses it to unknowingly wreak havoc on the in-spiral of human history (*please present ID for clearance*) — further infotainment files for Splitter: i.e. Splitter's live offspring, filename: Interloper A, causing <author> to question the direction of their life — live on stage: Pig confesses to his crimes against humanity AKA the only reason he's online — An alternate punchline — Sudden inquiry regarding usability — Systematic isolation / a communication / parsing the psuedocode of the backside of Polyana's mind — Meanwhile, intheoutofside... — Live in the Queue — Reqaulifying 'open streets,' as Splitter wonders what's at stake & decides to access unlicensed outload (and in the process becomes remarked) — <user processing> — the 666,666,666th reality (w/ sample questionnaire in transcreation) — {a void's reframing shows no change} — poor Polyana, took apart and made a star — now appearing in *"Polyana Maskerson" and the Slow Descent*, in primal psuedocode, revealed — Splitter in fracture; having lunch; taking the bait — A brief disclaimer — Ending the myth of Polyana by screencapture — Left now in the hands of the son of son of ~~Satan~~ (Nadan)—Gospels 1]

Read in thru loco-digital totals after the *f-cts*, conclusory celestial evidence suggests toggled permissions converting all turf zapped impenetrable could have only been approved from out of range. Once and only halfaway asking for "no contest" via any future telecommu ahead of the curve, our final ram-bent holo-icon, Pres. Gorschach III, had negligible open firebrand-rights left in-built to lend the nation's table an ability to withstand being for the Nth time beaten down. Beyond shit, as such, thru post-molecular intervention, with no thanks at all retained even by the extra-medically enforced and highly addled sinning of our ex-majesty's still somehow up-and-running BHB-era mainframe (Big Horror Business), which for as far back as any simul-brain bent had always been, far before some ragged non-BHB-based mythological entity could have retro-emotionally implemented the grim conceit of multilinear time and place. Regurgless, the once quite thought-thirsty G3 by now had little power or ambition but for cyber-banging horses, the transverse hides of whom he'd already long-collected into floorboards on the Ark That Would Not Float, moored yet in locus as a tangible relic of Prior Outline, in which all we were and all we'd ever briefly dweamed had for at least a couple hopeful clicks managed to matter. As to when or how that could have ever been imagined was not applicable as anything but bad-faith reinforcementarianism designed to inspire <present populace> into venerating the residual stanklog of their own bottom-tier orgasmodes over other far more crucial interfamilial loco-asphyxias, such as the f-ct that some still thought we could have lulled our piecemeal mass cultural hobbling into a single common human fate at least, if only for as long as any once mythic tale still projected to be retained within the conceit of futurecourse, and were every incoming psycho-incitement toward some other miraculous fruition not just assuredly another example of our nation's flailing, virus-laden hardwarez; all the skin and bones we'd long since written off as cosmetically mappable utilities good only for knowing where to aim the muzzle to do more damage when converting specific citizens from clones to glory holes. The drag from most all other post-political intention had since been put to rest by simple rumors of the "breaking lead off in the mind's eye(s)" variety (AKA erazing), wherein by simply desiring an explanation for any supposed public axtion thereby auto-authorized for auto-install a wing of height-of-fashion meta-sadistic roto-lenses of a demise far worse than death itself (AKA deth) to be applied in rapidfire over our intuition-minting apparatuses from thenceforth. Once flagged, as such, everyone within an earmarked namesake's core network would need—no, *want*; of their own will—to witness live on pop-up controlfilm—as in an unwanted wet dream designed for them by someone else—the cerebral-prolapse-produced seizure once known as sleep (AKA shopping), more explicitly known among the big heads solely by its manufacturer's unpacking info: [[[*an ethereal trojan body hous-*

ing the notion that there is nothing left to live for but further flapback [[[*crossbred to fit our simplest neighbors' brainstems' failure to parse centuries upon centuries of hilariously faux-revirginitized killroom traditions into anything more than only further* want for pleasure. Outside this, only the hallowed handful of state-outfitted 10/10s who still had recognizable floor identities kerning the proper code to outwardly elucidate their brand-games into Supposedly Real Myth remained capable of such corporate pillow talk, 10 out of 10 of whom had already been irreversibly relocated one way out: by becoming orploaded over and over thru telecommu into that same space-hell we'd been encoded with the will to only ever bunt by, despite our nation's inability to ever sprint again until even the idea of an *recognizable idea* itself retraced its culmination into something equally, wholly, and incompatibly un-real, made proof in endlessssss ~~sacred~~ deathscralls—such as this one—from every x-unique identiform sent across in the lost clicks before the trigger on our totality really became pullable, and simultaneously automatically retroac-tively too far real-as-real to be conceived.

Who else but G3 could not not-remember having seen the face of holy reci-procity itself erased, as such, to the point that almost any editable pronun-ciation had as many meanings as it did deths-by-x-hundred-cuts? Hybrid pod-testing of even those cell-embryos so deforminatively evasive they refused to fuse under unimaginable distress had proved unuseful for process-revision in that it also remained unclear which had nubs that could have enthused themselves into supposedly more natural instincts or innate philosophies, which's barf-squalls could be retromoderately enthused by the actual prov-enance of inspiration's curse, or which's were merely scarred by chemic trailmarks and therefore slated to be eventually dismantled-for-parts into still more of our nation's posthuman war regalia décor—that is, trained on boxxcode and scaling wine and put to werk as worship drones. It really hardly mattered much, of course, as even the most would-be radikal badbois, slipped through the transom, would be recalled in skip-traced pod-wide concession of the when/who/how-data interlaced within their inbred egos' incarnate hive-drive for holy warz as yet to run on the live disc; all without definitive impres-sions of exactly how our as-yet-unrecovered mythologicoid creator's spaceless criminality had been brainsplotched onto our total-mass of future genetic nibs as unseen skin for unframed devotion, thereby setting us all up for aspiration only within the very outhouse we'd been rebirthed to yearn to want to study like the head of the axe they'd have used to dispossess our faith's pro-genitor of His ability to manufacture broken bread-time stories if they could ever finally doxx his ass w/ firm results. No matter, still: the immense tears of whaling icons at very least flowed like lifeforce straight through the terroristic slime that nixed our rights even as they skinstrapped themselves down in cash-based incubators to be processed into parallel afterlives in their due time as they waited out the coming end of man under the perma-mind magma poured in relief around the multitude of interlocking HolyCrashPodz (by Mattel-Disney-Heinz-Schnartz) installed as rebate ego-housing meant at last both to provide shelter and to undo the final binding itches of once-thought-vital sense-based instincts we'd forever only parlayed into getting pwned. *Against the monomyth and country*, the copy promised, scrolling live across the anguish fully bonded in our past names, *against all bloodbonds and all choking claims for nonunimpenetrable luv*, each and every lyric in the advertising thru id-prism muy muy valuably invaluable as fully transactional 1/1 objects d'art, or so as they'd been aggressively post-classified upon delivery in the brainz of every pod person not yet tamed beyond the need of having objects or a body afterall, resulting in a slew of nostalgic tub-toys only found thereafter by haz-ard workers masturgrating in their electronic idea-graves after the crash, each having fallen for the top-notch death hoax of being convinced of the utility of sewing their seeds right back into the same maw that'd sewed its want for sew-ing seeds in them as future grist for future wraith. "Just doing ma job," those leftover of the BHB-era would think they'd thought forevermore, notched in *true-time* as anything but. "& never mind ye peons now the thriving random lodged behind the timeline infrastructure's neverlasting inbred local lore," one might find they could recall reading instead, for instance, among so many oth-er well-known retrospective writs of control-scripture, of which I, your speaker, am but a pawn.

& so for no appreciation, as you would have it, all prior history, in the wake of what had already been installed after the fact as long preplanned, became canned, recursed to scratch, and so propped up for reinvention under disgrace of the virtual savior our supposedly ongoing existence had been collapsed upon as True. The number of paperpushing ex-civilian aftermath-deaths was ridiculously voluminous, as you'd imagine, even having been removed of prior means of archiving prior selves so anybody still encroaching could retain the dearth through which they swung their ego's knives. Intent was total exter-mination of combatants and non-combatants alike, outside of those who could still get off on doing damage in the old familial way, by weaponizing the abject dumptruck of their unrealized snuff-zone fantasies. Only the throngs of offspring of ex-readers (AKA *the military*) knew where and how to tear through all prior idea of civilization (AKA *the psychic history of war*) in their purloined eFascination line by line, so as to immediately redefine themselves as still extant within the formal sorting out of what would still register as f-cts post-genodeicide. Whole religions had already been abandoned by way of the rewording of long outdated pre-viral holy writing, much worse than burning, "and so" they dug up from deepest witchhunts the once-warm brains from the literati's canonical dead and stomped them into pure canonical mush, to be used thereafter as neuroviral grease-mold to fund our architecture's want for more-of-same. The in-fighting itself was barely worth describing until the blood began evaporating into a mesmerizingly muddy funereal veil upon the air, which some saw as a sign from beyond the void they recognized as G-d to grow more brutal still before it lifted and G-d's last-face would be revealed as only partly disappeared; or even worse, only partly disappeared and still totally unfuckable. Younger vets are said, as by such scripture leveled as emotional amends, to have demanded to watch the dying husbands apply a jillion ram-styles of all the worst kind on all their kindest neighbor's family's softest holes in one last mass canonical orgy just in case, as a "celebration of" "the commencement of" "the final stages of" our reproduction model's boring reign, during which they filled their mouths with half-digested come from the stomachs of those last known moral casualties called friends (AKA whores), and stapled their lips shut for good from that point on—their first good works as modern saints. In their place, though, since no one else was wreaking havoc right now, virtual warlords (AKA rites of conscience derived from centuries of children raised by meta-gaming) invoked the underworld to rise from the same holes once used for squeezing out our kin, until many claimed they felt a fabric tugged among us all from where the face of G-d was said by various opportunistic zealots to have emerged during the screwing, described by each, somehow in sync, as a sort of skin that looked like neon billboards full of run-on sentences and simulated against the tongue like good clean air. Impromptu replica-orgies broke out among the holograms that gathered in refraction overhead as from a bloodstorm where all prior wireless-language once had thrived, applying an unforeseen and previously fully only implicit ideology so completely it was taken as a given that any new empire could have no end; & so it was. Work began immediately according to what had already always been the custom: building walls of human complex with a mirage center where we could mime to shop (the MaLL oF MiRRoRS, a Gorschach IV joint), sealing the gaps between the limbs we chose to make the crossbeams with human pus and crushed intestines turned to paste to make the curtains match the drapes. From the height of the new walls, even friendly folks threw the organs of their retraced kin into the thrall now known as land, to be consumed by animals or left to rot beyond the redefined reaches of their homebase. Each and every ackademic dorkus still w/ web0 access were made to curse the ground beneath their hooves as evidence of what somebody pretending to be them had tried to save when there was clearly nothing to be saved. They rubbed their nut into the soft pockets where future crop might one day learn to wind itself instead into renewal far too late, leaving only thereafter from the transom the sweet MaLL, so that future generations who came searching would feel haunted enough to not require additional mythology to stay. Any incidental survivors not already rendered infertile from the heat and screw-masks and viral stabbing were enslaved as blind cashiers. From the survivors of these survivors, few and far between thanks to the mind sickles floating like signposts in such pith, they would raise the future peons who bricked the language of *night or day* in for the last time and began the longer rally that would be no less devastating to their very notion's relatability. Any land worth having was lifted straight out of the ground, replaced with raw manure from other working efforts, prescribed tight brandnames, all *free of charge until you pay*. Those with the shortest kill lists would be hung as an example in the central corridors during the consecration, removed their after to become servers. The bowl-shaped sky promised rain then for eighty days, never pressing beyond the lock of continuous thunderclap and ambient begging, not an inch of light to leak, but only question after question.

Like all previously impossible penance-making, few of those not relegated right off the rip into absentia gladly traded or had scalped from out of them according to fashion the right to carry over even simple lessons parsed from all holocaust as just described, much less sense to want to wield it outside further psycho-strafing, took up immediately after staking authority upon the possibility of neural icons strewn in space-time for the non-conspiratorially invented heads to swarm around, 100% of whom had been salvaged in duct pods for the irreplaceable longing among authoritarian coders for play-dolling with meekest souls. The instant's armsrace for acclimating all legal-logical properties not already preconverted to what would be defined as "Open Time" (seen as accruing after most of all of us believed we'd been wiped completely from the index, as syndicate-sponsored rites of hope would hope to have it, by the now nameless sole meta-corporation having purchased ad space post-hyper-holocene) occurred identically in mirror image with previous instances of local wealth-making, as even the coldest nearby man-droids who could still co-summon the wherewithal to code-strangle, crotch-bash, or otherwise manipulate potential post-settlers and their most vulnerably inter-bodied kins would soon regret for no real reason outside of that's the way it was.

Traderights for evacuary moon-landings, for instance, already hot property even having failed us just before, revibrated up the shrill meat of any appendage worth its weight in spacelines displaced, to be hex-indexed within only the memories of the most elite of eldercare-based ex-CEOs, each still unwitnessed and unshamed, ridding the prior whopper re: *what life is* of its sandpaper effect by immediately creating replacement mythos among the long-since holo-displaced ruling class; i.e. (by the unspoken scripture) *a media-savvy megalord depicted only as some kind of humanform eclipse, sketched by machine in beknighted rhinoplastic post-orgiastic getup manifested as a silhouette of heads and hooves and hands; a retro-forefather photo-installed to fill the bottomless shaft of bubbling freeform premonition incidentally woven into the skeletonic fiber of any survivor's actual offspring as some motivational screed byproduct designed to remind them the real world was little more than a mirage, having only since just right now been recovered from where it'd hidden within so many rift-shifts each unalike and therefore useless but as a decoy for the less free.* Mother's-milkwise, against this biggish bet, emergent bidboys whose kash could not be spent for conquering the emergent neuro-fitted land prior to documentation of their dethronement from outdated ethoses shadily reminded us through "independently produced" (AKA completely wannabe) x-video containment units primed to describe for any straggler, like a high five to the brain's face, *how it was* and *how it is*, the former based upon the romance novels dredged out of time, the latter under the already long and looming shadow of even such obviously slug-manipulated dynasties as those instantly emerged from the mass mind in the same way as had each and every of our best heroes in the dreadmare everending from before. Even the slap of feed-based fires such as those they'd skeeted thru our housing and our someday hope for holochurches and last-known-prayers-outside-of-even-thought passed on through as one last throb and spoke with retro-envy of many missed fortunes in undivestable punitive opportunities available to those of us who most majestically and wholeheartedly took up the crop of what must be and joined the far-outflung celestial enterprise of farming progress, promising the possibility of eventual private ownership of space-time trauma even for those who might have should themselves been thwarted with the rest, instead left to cast their fate thru the third eye of every stereotypically federally-enforced feverdream the ghosted vision of a corpus primarily invested in by (a) the slitting one's own throat, (b) salting the shores of one's own someday corpse's worm farm's feed lots, (c) offering up its own utilitarian ego in return for the advent of an era wherein all needful legal information could be made to fit so as we liked within the space we'd been allotted for to breathe.

And so and so like that, using the same alphabetical direction as such and such had been paid to say and make it sound nice, click by click and ark by

ark in mind alone, the whole of who we knew had been or ever would be became committed to an extra-flexed condition of pre-reason layered far beyond
the rank and file of primetime's cloak, soon to once again be processed as a
peasant-knave set piece in mime of the same consecration we'd always lacked
because we felt it was the one thing still our own.

But we were not to so strokily reinvoke the way a knob would, would we?
We had already reinvented more about us than they'd wrought, more coal
crammed in our ticking heater than to be committed to abjection off the rip.
What couldn't have been exorcised or killt from us, as such, instead rewound-
ed right in the same spot where being a goodboi had to be more preternatu-
rally enforced, resulting in tidalwaves of untidy intubation as the par assumed
its course. Robbed for forgivedness? Check. Loaned by ribald neednannies?
Yes, they can. Opening a falsefronted cannery for True Change again as necessary holdover in public service? Absolutely. So much other unmentionedable
whetting remained to be conformed to by th' highest public servants in those
hard days post-prehistorically as "human nature," even still with the innumerable undead's coiffed groaning nutcrack wedged in haunt between our
toes. It woesn't a fiduciary avalanding, quite, however, some daft hick would
trickle into parlance (hardyharr); t'was really only actually most more of a
recanting of possible witness as desired among all major mass-traditional
spiritual advisors all beholden to the cause held under wraps due to forms of
nepotism even such a long-planned early controlfilm reboot as *Kingdom-Come
2* couldn't mnemonically socially assassinate, to be parlayed into another
unfortunate protocol among the primo-elitest emo-bologna-manufacturing
interest of the new era, Aarchive Industries Inc., whose wares, repackaged for
replicative distribution in any eventual asexual-replicatory sleeper cell, figured
to predict replicative damnation even in these earliest days of our theorized
eventual intervention by the electronically immortal holo-grafs we would
post-hostingly produce, replacing phantoms once and for all and thereby
ending the vivicious circle of our neurosoulsickness, a fate no longer scheduled to-be discoverable for personal verification by even the highest chokers
of such lore, but still made policeable commodity by fact of the very same
reversificiation model meant to show why any of us had been allowed to stab
around in good ol' UXA so long enough to have earned a spot to suck a wont
for server datum in this ethereal possibility of reinvention of the idea of an
identity overall, whose logos's buttons once depressed in making law would
not simple be clickbaited back into low demand. No, our volunteer wardens
imagined a more readily imaginable irreality at least, finally, and we would
not be bucked from the truck of our own ongoing transferable captivity w/o

at least some additional millennia of seeking, yes, the Pleasure of the True, in just the same breath, if not hand-in-handed, yet, the closing bell signaling the advent of an actual experience of the much more obviously fruitful Pleasure: of the Wrath.

]]]

At least this is last how all the prior era's to-be-approved folklore's backlog legalese read to Randy Ranch, NearSouth Half-King of Hibernation Kilns, and the preappointed directatorial Marketing Executor of All Prior Estates throughout the Lurch, who no once would remember having filled his office in the rare non-Hanritty-owned claps-sector of the sole federal complex's out-reach facilities at *Garko*Farx*, likewise from whom we would be default reblast-ed out of context the only uncorroded definition of rehearsal of the nation's once and final approved script, one once seen as a thing any moneymonkey might fling coin at one day in desperation for an entertainment consigned with "holy deth" enough to still feel any +EV producteffects. Recently all any-one had been able to get greenlighted into even being reviewed as reviewable was their own lost faith, following the immense failure of C. Hanritty's *Demen-stratio*, a project once hailed as the only logical or even dark-marketable way to parse the recommitment to our own ending, much less parlayed in develop-ing techs that would imprint enough populace into believing so strongly there would be no struggle afterall. True power, the biggest bigheads had already ac-cepted not even 1/66th of the way thru pre-post-preproduction of the 147-hour viroplay (unconsciously overseen, as always, by the disembodied corporo-mind of Mattel-Disney-Heinz-Schnartz), came from not having to actually need power after all, much less to have to employ it. Such analysis had not stopped the delivery of *Demenstratio* to the aboveground in a mass "bad after good" cash-move that would all but signal the end of the Hanritty dynasty, at least among the mouths of those forced to imbibe. Viewers could see right thru the skin of the protagonist, known as "Confessor," pre- and post- drop feedback showed alike, and in that inverse-shadow, see themselves; likewise, they could identify pop actor, Rally "Action" Jensen, in the role of Satan, and therefore all translative properties laced within the cortex of his admittedly bravado performance scrunched, served more likely to reinforce the newly burgeoning ability of youth to distinguish between fact and fiction.

The rest, as governing qualicode would have, converts to crash: as accorded a single slip in the applicative processing language once interpublicly ex-posed, last ditch production squads would be hastily employed by Hanritty Enterprising Co., Inc. in an attempt to post-op spiro-edit the controlfilm's mal-invigorative qualities during first witness, while still in live feed; alas, not a high-return response move even given the unabashed complicity production of HEC's longstanding and industry-leading intercommand commodities and foresight amid matters of mass surveillance and restraint. Instead, the c-film's sudden revision's jarring cut slap (attempting to trace Jensen's shaping as Satan's face as not a face at all, but a mold blur, like the kind that had begun growing in over the hardened ocean where every ex-bighead, including, eventually, Gorschach II, believed their only son would someday rise and take the throne in the prospectus now having appeared on Ranch's desk), as toggled direct to helmet in a transmission spun thereafter as "just a joke" fits at once into oncoming news amid worldwide viewstreams, given the resilient load-bear-resistance for disbelief established in longstanding fan forums regarding attempted alteration between story-slates not proto-ID'd out of consciousness in full, if not at once as overwhelming as once foretold that it might be in private study. Into the microorganism's deformative root-map instead then are forced Hanritty's coders, trolling against innumerable lockshank protocols installed not as protection for the consumer, but the producer, where the asymptotemic jargonization of lite-speed reckoning envelopes free architecture at a rate absolutely impossible to result in anything but a panoptimiming circumstance less than, shall we say, *permitted* to become measurable in local anatomy's optics, as demonstrated by prior megamonolith controlfilm *L-ve's* depiction of "neural ice," which despite its massive inclusion into canon rode wounds with critics where it asked after itself inside its own plot a bit too self-pleasingly for the anti-meta proclivity of Generation φ, before reappearing broken-limbed and still at least remotely quasigospellanic in its star-studded but sadly shitty sequel, *L-ve 2: Under The Bad Ask*, which still hit desired box office projections despite its obvious extranarrative arthritis and being overweighed by preachy known courtesies already long forgone as overlookable by even the most stolid local bloats, a success entirely relatable to what would be the last review of any who-media as allowed in open forum, penned, of course, by J. Anonymous, bestselling author of the novel on which all of this logwash had been based, forced to print their final take unto the masses traced in the smoke that broke upon the land as the control-chips in our rest-helmets that allowed such recreation finally gave in and fried themselves out for what seemed the good of the people but really in its own way hypermarked the unbeginning of our ability to remain someone who could look at shit and say *that's shit*, which in turn had been the bulk of Anonymous's last review, the rest being a 5D holograf of Anonymous shooting theirself in the throat with a Loadbloater-brand mind-rifle, resulting in enough xCGGIx blood to drown most any memory of having seen anything but shit and shit and shit forevermore.

The real star of *Demenstratio*, though, at least as dictated to Randy, and the one to which he now must hope to hitch his wagon in the uptick of infotainment after all, is listed in the meta-credits as, simply: "Splitter." The subplot schedule C# character had in the film itself had remained completely nameless, her post-impression made only significant in kind as an integral part of the reclamation project Ranch has been horsed with by the boss, whose ID-tags he is similarly not allowed to access despite the brandwidth of their ongoing correspondence. It is only in Hanritty's neural production notes, uploaded to Ranch alongside other ephemera likely meant to cloak Splitter's phantomic presence even to him, that any ID tag accords what sort of purpose the vexing screengrab might have served in the original conceit, rolodexically subdefining the deleted character as "Spl-tt-r, sister of MacAdam the Deviser, child of Danad (son of Satan); our only rope, consigned to wrangle further faith in mortal chaos." Any additional relation beyond that remains behind the curve, subletting any initial gut hunch on Ranch's part to deeper hypertags laid in the parlance, a further part of some subconscious state's defense, with whom even in distensia the logs have no expense but to relate unenviable knowledge even among those tasked to pattern and report them on command. *No need for collar-defunct feeling while still defining what must be lived by under such innately cradled circulation,* Hanritty had nub-scrawled in his post-trauma defrag, before being reassigned to schlockier provinces no doubt, the terrifiably handwritten datum provided to Ranch only as a curative, overdirection for how else his impression in the citizenship yet might be made. *She is felt as an unverifiable promise only, demoted low enough to submit sacrifice before reminder nothing must live but as last seen as from simul-inside our close-encoded waxen circlejerk.*

Ranch senses this is only further evidence to his initial hunch about the C. Hanritty casefile overall, which is that despite the director's state-owned namesake, long known as an essential bloodline in every phantom government since Jesus Christ, some essential element within that instantiation must have at some point along the way become mutated, shifted its provenance somehow off course; that the failure of *Demenstratio* to effectively fund for every consumer another lifeline of federal emotional, psychological, and intuitive enforcement had been no accident; that C. Hanritty had allowed its interruption to take course on a scale so unprecedented and unforeseen among the coding that its damage, perhaps, would never be undone, and as a matter of inevitable course in even the most plausible application of circumstantial theory could have long-lasting effects that any hack with an e-degree in hyperlingo could see might at very least might raise the per unit cost of hosting a human id, and worst could undo all the progress that we'd made in creating an environment where there is no longer any pain, suffering, hunger, confusion, or disease, if also, in unauthorized sectors: interaction, procreation, common sense.

Of course, his boss had already directly state-stamped into him clear evidence otherwise, labeling Ranch's deployment as a proctor of this casefile as a precautionary tactic, to study any surely mostly negligible effect of "the Creation Mistake," as it was by now unofficially referred to even among those who normally would never admit that the current nature of pseudocode could still allow, and to offer incisive expertise regarding the implementation of the above stated lineaology of the present moment, as they put it, an offshoot task amid the spin of covering up what dark damage had been done not only in the wake of Hanritty's film but several other more oblique plotting courses theorized to be discoloring the present day slate. And as a once-director of anticontrolfilms of his own, all of which had long been expunged from public record, yet still afforded to his corruptible work persona with enough weight to get him a banging gig on the far side, Ranch understands at least enough of the conceptual backend in Splitter's apparition's noumenon to assemble in his mind how it had once been constructed for the screen, following archetypes of the last six clicks of the larger meta-intercommunicative-based psychofilm theory toward a more clear picture of the anti-hero-cum-hero's obvious purpose in post-position over our exposed citizenship's neural net: *to identify those who could still see her, post-deletion, and thereby to flag those users whose incorporative capabilities might harbor more seeds of disinformation than they unseed.* It had certainly not been outside acceptable process for the present administration, unlike the several prior, to imagine how even our most deformative culling tactics could still be adapted against, despite the literal miles of pseudocode designed not only to curtail defaming efforts of the citizenship, but to adapt against their ongoing adaptation; to continuously recut and code all living loops, circuiting all possible logic of non-authorized users into handy, transmutable doilies, in essence. No, these governing bodies would not fall prey to the prior bodies' prideful mistakes, their modes that sought so hard to overgovern they failed to covet sponsorship of those, like Ranch, who might ever learn to glimpse the very precipice they stood astride, squalling in Pleasure until the orifice overwhelmed and absorbed its master's prod, once and for all. Which is why, or perhaps, how Ranch senses in his sorting prowess's affinity for Splitter's presence something perhaps even more malnutritively post-editable than it appears he is being allowed in on, as a collaborator; the sort of meta-tag that once initiated into being cannot be squashed or cartooned up as would any once common anomaly; such signals, like their human equivalents, must be repurposed and rebranded from the ground up, somehow forced into collaboration with the nature of the very force it seems she had been manifested in the first place; to make an ally of a foe post-f-ct, one of the most essential worktraits of a plausible figurehead in paler climates such as the present's.

Problem is: Splitter can't speak. At least, it's more fair not to, after all, Ranch notes, plying furthering in the subdescription of her intended appearance in the Unbeing; her guise's maladjusted psychotypographia sweats lukewarm diurnal ransom-vibes against his mask's peekholes even just trying to crumble through it and fit in, of logos bestowed left unbeknownst, tapped into subviral typhoid packets evenly strewn sans demarcation into the aural cubbyholes of human serfs closed under glass pellets in the Transdurational Gallery of Modern Miracle, the only legal moviehouse still up and running in the C quadrant and which contains the very birthing cube itself where Ranch was born, which, apparently, the only one time would-be Splitter had live-visited, seeking her own origin, before news of her near-father's pending extermination, in lieu of rubberizing his vocation, had been mnemonically declared, the first sign to Splitter herself, according to her hive's readouts, that she would eventually be discontinued too; not that there was anything that she could do about it, so they'd imagined incorrectly. Either way, it wouldn't matter, they preconceived—nothing actually retransmitted as supposed retribution would be retained outside the long verboten to unmantle ration-state of humancraft, leaving in the cask of her eventual reformat only what naturally occurring emotional smear the simulated fictive Adam's rib to one of any mature cervix applied cosmetically to any would-be legendary hero-form, for in-house kink if not her social safety, after being pulled down out of a fully federally-shrouded RoboWomb would incidentally encode even on an actor of Splitter's caliber. Like a fingerprintless thumb pressed to the glass part of an actual containment cylinder before the advent of fingerprintless glass. And like a white wall to which one'd come already in attempting to piece together one's own life amid the gargling wreckage of a demolition of your kind, even while being billed as, if not the main event, a clear fan favorite, at least in limited release, enough so to have obviously affected her performance so completely it hurts to have to watch her tongue her xCGGIx mouth, having never been uploaded with the most basic set of undefined human traits one would have needed most to make her role shine; that is, not-so-secretly now: to innervate the world of the film's release from inside the world of the film's production; to make them marry, then to rend itself apart; to have undone, in so many words and with one will-click, all the good work set up by the long anti-history of controlfilm, and then of recreation overall. The brass, at least, had overseen Hanritty's production enough to know not to have given him direct access to Splitter's most basic coding as a decoy, despite the fracktive ways he'd found to work around it; they had spared themselves handing out the keys to the castle to this high midlevel cocreator after all—*how could they undo us w/o a voice?*—if not enough to have avoided potentially seam-bleeding losses in the process. Their preternatural mistrust of even this next brightest cog in the very inbred-owned hybrid-media conglomerate that spawned their success had in the end saved at least the inseam of all their shining asses, at least so far, if not enough to spare Ranch the residual responsibility of privately post-assessing how best to have to wipe up shop after the f-ct.

The offending scene itself, even deleted, lasts less than seconds, described to Ranch not in full code, but through the coddled gooing of a sort of nostalgia he's not supposed to know he knows, defining what the film would need and why, if only parseable even in Ranch as language he's already incorporated into his own gestation of the known, presented free of charge from within the pharmaceutical collaboration post-encoded into this very text to cure you too. It goes like this: we see Splitter stalking in the background of the last withstanding Heinz-T-Mobile DreamFarm, from which all unregulated breathing air was said to flow, following from out of range a free worker on the border of their mind, still slogging around a language-bearing sign like those the dying used to try to tell those they might believe could still be watching during the last clicks of the era of transmutable supplies, the message ever more stuck out of the range of any relevant discourse, "Please help. Will work for free. Just must get out." It's just one of those images no biddy needs to mention—we've all been there—and yet once slated it holds rank. The coming recompense we all had also begged for just the same will live forever wretched as an heir to the pale slob that played Our Father. Maybe the last and only intervention on behalf of what someone else would call a nanny while there is nowhere else to slip away from.

Had we could feed of it, then, we would have seen Splitter slit the neck of the person once identifiable as Sal Demain—ex-Heinz-T-Mobile DreamFarm Head Intake Manager du jour, once in charge of all the glandhandling and other non-hypersticky Operating Bullshit long since indexed as potty training, now long baroque—using a boxcutter from six feet standing, bringing to an end the longing pain of a used life, devoid of the usual state-sponsored process-torture or auto-preclusion into an afterlife of one's worst frightmare, but instead: a deth composed outside the framework of not only legal means but our innate socio-moral feed beliefs, at the hands of the guise of an angel-of-mercy meta-figure whose body can only half be rendered in even when locatable, encrypted as she is in the expired hanging skins of those she's helped out of their misery before, removed from circulation and into contraband. Sal is one of only thousands she's dispatched in such a light, Splitter recalls w/o real memory, based on only the uncompilable subtitular deth commentary that frames the meta-code installed to blur her work even to her, miming the fashionable feedback requirements for x-ing out the ideas of a once mega-web-influential role model who's gotten murked, if for no other reason than to demonstrate, unto her and her undefined idea of the everlasting in the same stroke, what actual federal arbitraryism looks like, in spending such attention on a pawn; that no matter how well and to what end we cooperated with what seemed everyone's best interests overall, as defined by forces far beyond any one ex-CEO or contract killer's best control, we had not forgone our ability to be expired, returned to fluff-time. Even a seasoned vet of arcane sense like Ranch can feel the grubbing glower of the Splitter-Sal snuff reel, its vast influence on his will to cruelly oversee, having been informed himself that it is the realest real form of real that real can seem, knowing it's fake by definition, even if at times sometimes the term *fake* actually is used to mean the opposite, wherever it might think it's learned to live. Ranch finds he can't stop staring at the description provided to him of the way further footage had shown Sal flopping and bleeding for several seconds on the ground before himself dissolving into circuits; and though he still will not allow his vectors to accept it, under contract and his own infused distensia of truly felt life-enforcing platitudes alike, he still feels a pit in his gall row as he reads back the scene's transition to a taut shot of Splitter staring head-on toward whichever camera thereafter takes its hold, revealing a dizzying series of jerks and tweaks as the stricture-enforcing software of the hundreds of clearer-than-realtime hidden cameras the scene had been com-posed thru—part of the "surveillance revolution" styling found in recent scads of controlfilmmaking that now seems to Ranch no coincidence at all to have trended so far south it's like it never even happened—instead going black or otherwise repopulating its raw content with jamming signals of seed from shows depicting full-bore citizens giggling and stuffing their mouths and eyes with DummyCrème, perhaps to dislocatedly assist in retro-cutting the mal-ware content that's just been described for those who would not wish to linger on such trash.

One can barely make out, then, by the time she begins moving closer, reaching out with both arms, covered in shimmering tassels of her deth-correspondents' hair and radiated in the videation of her breath, the sense of shameless calm that swims her currents, in having brought another victim to the mend. *No longer will they writhe*, we can see her importing as hyperclaims into our ad-feed; *no further will their finds be farmed for those who live for nothing*, though of course the titles by now crawling absolutely all over her, scrubbing it dis-creetly while appearing on its face to simply operate as any film should, even in suppression such as this, claiming: *what exists in deth is worse than death*, and so *you have no choice left but to live*, followed in kind by the required hostcards of linked-in law, relevant for any working compilation, indexed in surly strings that no one ever really clicks, already having all that red tape so well infused by now that its biological acceptance had begetted the soft-accepted sort of ontology that had allowed the groundwork for derivation of this sort of exception after all, if still smartMarked off the rip as psycho-diseased, an easily recoverable black hole from which only those already likely to have slipped could have been enticed to linger even any longer than the ads that followed immediately after every scene, even in a film as preloadedly respectable, before the fact, as a Hanritty or a Spielberg 7.

& so Splitter's exit-language even in mass psychodistribution had been another tub toy all its own, post-vexed as well in echo-mumbles made factory default to all scenes, meant to unmind us each like our last musics despite the sharper message under caul, for the absorbability of all range of disposition, steadfast by C. Hanritty's obviously infracturing design despite the enforced juxtaposition of the state's claims, if quite yet more pithy-core and moral-fumbled, more of its time than the nonapparent grace of logic as can be gathered through any axtionable utility, leaving her unable after the job to do anything on camera but stand and stare, a ghostly impression that seems to reappear imprinted throughout the film as signal flare, often from so far back off in the shot her trailing spirit resembles rubble, neon lights, all of which must be removed, even given that the film will never again be given ground. "Ya gotta sculpt the fucker out into full kid-proof, in case it leaks, you never know, bitch," his boss, from elsewhere far behind the scenes, had typed; a worthy challenge to make receipt of, even for a director of Ranch's caliber, proven only ever in the exact opposite ethical direction of his present employ or cool retort. It's spin this livescript into more nether or get subindexed, Ranch well knows, which in younger clicks would have compelled him w/o hesitation to be damned, though all it'd took for him to see the light had been to see the light of hell itself—at least that's how they'd framed his hanging over the fetid froth of scrEAm_pIts-sOUth (where de facto badbois always end up) by just the wee tip of his lung; one fidget longer holding out and he'd have been mush already. From here, those seem like so much kinder, slicker days, ones that no longer feel so real as they once had now that he's settled in repurpose; still, he can't help but feel the pull of Splitter's animation, her wont for recompense even in having been exposed as C. Hanritty's secret jawn, the stinger for a once-widely-seen-as-highly-problematic quark empire, turned over to him in a purgatory of his own kind (god how they loved to stab you right where it

already hurts; make you grovel through the rancor of cooperation everlasting);
how even without a word her pixelation's rankled teeming squarks enmity
and anti-signal from the hip, primed from the sudden-flipped centurioning
of a lineage of quilted blood such as Hanritty's, at once more volatile than
nearly every other anti-craft could be given his provenance, his privilege to
aesthetic perhaps as less interceptable as there could ever be, if never again
now that he'd taken his own stab-medicine himself and proved to come out
only moderately wounded, so unlike a preferred customer should ever be, able
from here to, under Ranch's guided intervention, scrub up another vibrant
play vacation that would in the end of course serve the exact opposite effect,
effectively recentering C.'s authorial position in the Hanritty empire out of
claimtime, and hereby leaving Splitter to the last laps of his bitter-to-pretend-
to-be-in-charge-of-shit-while-really-only-ever-doing-gruntwork mindset's barely
even temporary post-moralistic slur of warmth before her already fully automatic reapplication unto what grief we wanted for the egg-shaped faces we
assigned her upon reprisal without uprising.

Observing directly—when he can force the retrofit to allow her cloistered
reportage to make speak—Splitter's well-documented glottal mar: it's not
a visage as yet retrainable. No skill remaindered under vibration of a fully
vetted see-sun could still hold grade, at least while producing the cure of
effects Ranch knows they know he knows they require of his post-edit. Even
in the rare freezeframe control-stills he's been supplied of her, cut from the
snuff cloth of the original incarnation of *Demenstratio*'s suppressed beef,
she resembles hardly any kind of icon one could decorate, even through the
topmost xCGGIx tongues, with anthemic properties in either sense, though
this was exactly the kind of elusiveness that had somehow given itself over to
her effervescence against the auto-scrubbers of our content, and had allowed
her like a virus to seep thru the psychic wash over and over, coming back each
time twice as strong, even off-screen and out of mind, only ever seen by such
a small part of the populace it was astounding to imagine anyone recounted
anything but porn and gunfire. *Better off splicing two ends of the same mag-
net-tape together*, he's already quite convincingly written up in his report and
whited over multi-times about this strange imprinting of her ongoing effex,
using the hyper-encrypted parlance of the administration's blustery codeware
to delay his unacknowledged disadvantage in not quite not wishing he hadn't
just let them drop his body to the void-state of modern narrative, for sure, but
rather sparing him the unremittable task of furthering the asphyxiation of
what had once been his true people after all; the least he can do is pap together flexy jargon like suggesting they simply *employ the laughy bloodpour through*

*a titbox and sort by age of the permitted focus left uninstalled on every cortex
including mine,* effectively cheerleading his proxy and meantime stalling for
less queasy alternatives than simply deprogramming all defectors, which could
surely be accomplished by the flick of a single switch at this point, he's been
assured, though he can't say why they bother with all else were that indeed the
case, unless the lords who really rule might lift their big heads these daze only
to witness not just any suffering, but a sum of parts seen even temporarily
eternal, one meant to span both life and deth alike, for one and all including
them, by any rank or cross-position or mark of wile, well far beyond such hot
to trot terms as *l-ve* or *h-pe*, obvious relics of a pulmonation so long outdated its honestly depressing on its own, and by now so far beyond tract as to
suggest the sun was never flat; that there were ever more than one idea-bear-
ing planet ever, in all of space-time; or, most pointedly to him, that someone
of his demeanor and upbringing could be converted into poopoo even still,
a team-ramification he hasn't had yet to live down under the judgement of
anyone but those who'd gnawed him up, seeing as, so far, as clime would have
it, none once like him could yet be verified online still in the thread; thus why
his only remorse-based glottage remained stirruped to *why I had to appear
before the court on my behalf if all I ever really had was zero choice* and *how to
figure out how to fit one's helmet's head between one's palms here at the brink,*
without a clink of what yet to sermon-sing a ringing deed of in those who'd
cast the singlest stone could use in court to call him sc-m.

Not that any else could scrum up an arm from where they believe they must
be, nor could such paling parties ever reach him through so much opaque
glass. As the only way we'd seen minds like that yet fit to stammer could no
longer be reported, only mentioned once and then erased. And even only at
the edge of the fire's eyelid's now, on the outskirts of what remained of our
humankind's mangled derivation of *mortal hell,* if still never quite, as yet, in
full, succumbing.

The unclipped meta-ice spanning the outcropped mindfront of *Garko*Farx*,
and therefore all "creation," both Hanritty- and state-owned, is really mold.
No brittle brace against conditioned experience traceable outside terminal
data transmitted upon banged teeth into the apple of our conglomeration's
eye, the cross we would not be bled to deth on, but rather beg to be allowed
to regularly ingest. It's all an appetizeeasement not on the to-go app: just mix
the wantword into any common order for Pleasure-based goods and feel your
stomach buckle with nutritive contortions, all subliminal motive left un-
broached by conscience-nuisance where high-functioning radiance intervenes
with every breath to divulge interpretation of the Great Lost Works assigned
from the worsening one's self in the shape of bettering our derivation's contin-
uance overall; a form of entering the flocks wherein the only war left still isn't
trending, as many millennia had been invested kindly in the itchy armpits
of a faith-lost sulkflick comprised of waiting till the sun drops to consume
almost anything, including the foregone exploration of all severed forefront
not already heli-mapped in commonframe (so he imagines (XXXXL) (he is our
leader; once given stake by being recognizable in power by Gorschach's namesake, now no longer requiring such claims to fame, nor necessary unity of
visage (except he only ever wears XXXXL, same as us all (it is his given name,
in fact, sourced from the theoretical brandname used to cloak the source-cod-
er of our soul-helmets and Good Piggy screw-cubes beyond suspicion)) (AKA
he isn't new; he's just a guy; albeit a guy with the power to eradicate said suspicion by the dull hem of the forever-nigh MassTerror))).

This mourning in the dell it's almost necessary science just remanding all
the in-house paranoia over the ongoing recent slippage caused by yet another
known Hanritty leak. It's nearly mercurial, in terms of ongoing inaction shown
by even his most decorated thugs, who've long inherently conformed to cross-
haired expectation that every slate is only ever all plain-egg poachment. Nearby to XXXXL's dicto-conspiratorial left nut, for instance, a recently remoted
bighead is masturbatwerking her dook so good in plain sight, for all to see, it's
like you could learn to live for as a peon's peon for forever, despite all evidence
shown to the contrary the in-house Shitting Incidents as seen at Nurway,
another script scribed and subscribed to under XXXXL's earliest watch, if one
much more successful in its diminishment of intended inter-rebellion on the
part of the overseeing director, a different version of Hanritty, as back then
he'd been allowed to squash the shucker on the spot, to wrangle his nubby

neck into a wreath hung upon daylight to remind aspiring aesthetes of their lame place, well within the punishing cusp of inarbitable ambitions, about which only XXXXL, g-d of g-ds, had been personified as the skeleton key-like combination of all as yet impossible and not yet theoretically unpacked persona traits. In his early clicks, he still for some mutli-paranoia-introducing reason can located among his own most effective onanistic roto-files, XXXXL himself had been *a contract killer who only kills other contract killers who don't realize they're contract killers no matter what else they become, much like himself.* He knows this provides him at least half a reason to want to keep seeing these young nation-narrators through their scruffy years into a freeform more likely employable as totems of his own supposed reign, if but by fact of not having any reason but for never inspiring the really good shit out of these losers; when everybody knows that all we want is to be fed and bedded: the real rebellion, at once both for and against deth, which if anyone could ever figure out how to integrate across all Levels, open or hidden, the face of f-cts themselves would be finally erazed, such that no one at all ever in any case including him and all of those who oversee him could ever glean what's to come next but once it's begun.

But then: tha pwn (that's whut he calls the bop-blip he gets spoken at thru by those he hires to make sense). It rangs and rangs, yanking every chain a mind can have in their best spankatorium till finally someone (the only one: Him, so known on high as XXXXL) knocks it off and puts a face onto the lode, the inconvenience of which he's already begin to use for new prebating in lieu of having arrived in courting his own cud with better specs, as becoming aware of what would really get him off for good would also require of him the very taking part in the unfun post-existential warts of his own reign. Of course, it's Cold Salas on tha line again—the only guy who ever rangs, having guessed the direct number to Overseer somehow, the most desperate move of all—seeking real information—finally paying off for this one twink who every time he rangs all he say to say, at bottom line, is how much he wants his sick back. The only sick the neighborhood can spare: that someone close to him (Demain) has been dispatched without fair shakes. Turn by turn we're dying and never slick enough, Salas decries into the silence only an authority such as XXXXL can offer up, gilded as it is with such high demand somehow still unceasingly in faction among the flailing models of human meat. XXXXL hasn't even learned to wish such dregs of the ongoing Deformation down to such grimy details himself yet, not off this fresh batch of final rejects left to whine, which he'd had synthesized from dusted eggs culled from young new ex-mothers in the Mirage. He thinks perhaps he'll learn to speak their language soon, absorbing so much of Salas's mate-rapey enthusiasm through the landline, motivated solely by his having heard the human-speech-based high is even warper than his most recent plug of choice, derived solely from sleeping thru one's last life another time, already clearly an outdated germination from an era we'd believed there was something sacred left in dreams. Salas's name's not even on the list to join the list for this New Future Jargon shit, Salas is droning through most any open hole, only cuz he can't find who to pay to get an ask in besides XXXXL, who thus far has been a tick about responding, which is his rite, though Salas of course believes, like every half-ranked snooker, that the farming of the sick began with him, Cold; therefore, all the answers must be his answers. Untouched, unrecreated, out of gas is Cold's lone code he's meant to share, so he believes, "until we learned to party with a pre-ControlFilm-era corpse-sac, back before they understood true thermo-dynamic dosing," the gibberishishnessnessishness of which is, at its most essential, as would have been his religion, totally true, seeing as how even the goldenest era of getting sleek in front of any unseen listener could be exactly retro-sourced back seven clicks, when ovum research had been vitally deregulated by XXXXL's own prior overseer so as to allow rapid processing of the remains of the human body into pure pathos, beyond meat, by and large seen as the means of an eventual elaboration of the concept of a Cure That Cures All Cures, upon which all prior condensement efforts became reverted into the model we have now.

X won't have none of that tripe tho. "Leave it on the frontal lobe of my next nap," he emotionally enthuses his gurbling, purring subconstituent from in the search, filtering his gape interspasmodically so as to enhance his orifices more biologically disorienting qualities, refined from excess bloodline plotting, intolerable even against the capabilities of neural visors of a fretty dump like Cold Salas and his tier. He can overhear, as even any demi-god must, Cold's idgit-child assistant in the mindrubbled background squawking like a chopper w/ its neck jammed already, citing scripture someone far below him once had penned in all ournames, to once again revalidate the blank X knows the very meanest of the bad bois must by default, for their own good, imagine Him to be. What is this pencil-gushing dog-wipe really believing he'll get done without even the prismimetic moral outline of a coup? X asks his dong. Who could have authorized such a daft child but yet for He to box around, in practice for every head once laid before him, onward, like the goodest goodboi of His own? XXXXL could save his cum up for another total-human-timeline click off of the transposed glee of Salas's muttervation after all, he attempts to convince his dillhole to conclude, the hi-grade preening and prawning any one like us would suffer in seeking any Pleasure of our own after sniffing through miles of sod that lord our lofty coffins to claim a right-hand station as a thorn in any innovation's side. All these honey-grubblers wouldn't know how to wield a fingercuff against a firebrand half hilarious enough to make them crack, to convince the jokester-in-residence who tends the scripts to give it all up in the name of another protomartyr offered up as entertainment yet again before the real shine of some ramshackle phantom XXXXL himself would have no choice but to fall to knee in front of, refounded from an actually redemonstrable belief in a dementia that might innovate this state of melodramatic nonexistence after all, which is exactly how we ended up here, XXXXL thinks, brushing at the real ceiling of intercelestial supremacy's ever-pending confirmation.

Before he rangs off, so much a prankster in his own rite, by and by, XXXXL breaks his own best practice, just enough to not be tagged for idealism's recompense, and spits a last superscript back thru the onslaught right at Cold's life: "Come and take it if you can, fackman. See if you can split it from my boils. Til then, I'm jacking off with the only secret metamorph, and it'z all minez." All such datum may be received in Salas as an out-of-nowhere left-leg limp he'll wield like salad dressing for his beliefs (THEY TRIED TO STOP ME FROM BELIEVING IN MYSELF) just long enough to not realizing the passing of yet another misused click. Then tha pwn goes hypertight, pinged by the WingBang Fontload's glitter-blustering Full Goodbye, leftover from the bloody merger of Mattel-Mattel, including a 5D mini-reenactment, for ahistorical posterity, reminding each and every would-be communicator just how Jesus 3, Mattel-Mattel's final CEO, died online: by trying to troll the very ones of us he really shouldn't: those who can still get a good job.

Now if only X could figure out who got him his. Alas, syntactic turpitude corrupts the known. No one logged-in anywhere even wishes to want to recall who slayed the Slaying Moon, for instance, once thought Our Ceiling; much less how and why so many rooms have no way out; and still somehow one keeps discovering one's self lurking in darkened corridors, smother in plug dust discoloring the air off some old sleight of landfill told to blow, distracted from one's more fortunate forms of madness only by the machine-tones unregistered to vendor where mucus fattens between bone as they continue to revise any kind of sight-for-sight's-sake as would a whim, no longer even trying to seed it seamless after the *Demenstratio* affairs, which even as most everyone claims to remember, no one credits, much less tries to share. After all, all-nite ass favors favor only those who focus their minds across the idea of the five last holy levers that any living Lord might tweak at any click to have us slapped out of simulation and into the fakebook of required forgivednesses in fastTime. A learner must be waiting to be bought, as XXX knows well, having seen for himself under the stage-one working threat of stirrups and saw how little that it took for him alike to be retained, and nowhere on the menu does the diaphragm allow contention, at least until again the God of Personal Goals At Last Defrayed arrives like actual revelation across the milk-red pastures far and wide beneath all floors held open-sored and dry as rust. Why must it rain still further shit, then, on all our treats? someone aspiring for holy might want to wonder, not knowing to what extent the overcorrection will commit their incidental fumbling to liquid flames, to be reclaimed only as a viral tokens accrued in vast accounts all of the leftover living must stoop to share? Just enough for a new fence, of course, around the shed where someone's afterbirth lives on forever in the double blind of nonapparence. Praise them only for so long until they are.

]]]

But just beyond the squelch of the more well-shamed inner circles, only another form of intervention could remanufacture the disrupted state of grace for proper good. Nigh still stand countless ulterior revisions that will disfigure the historical record for all born after the wale of beep cauterized eternal mortitude now full-framed as the Mistake. How, for instance, am I, the trap of winds once thought to fill the Silence after all, to wield a willful reason to remain here where I have been seated for what seems longer than needs to have been necessary for my location in the deficit of wonder, one must wonder, if one has not yet unpacked the amulets of slavering that follows after the broken wake of terms like *wonder* even yet. All lines must be watched—ok?—w/o the sense of needing to be seen or felt before the forced encoding of a reason to take part. One's *elaboration mode* always regears right when one thinks one's never going to find the reason, after all. It's in the itch of the muzzle—right?—dragged along in the host of the burnt-up cycles no one haunts, as salted remains of the unenforced are unerringly fed for breakdown into our ventral sweetness, no matter how slim the dumb supply. All publicly operable interfacing seems dislocated from its prior predisposed federal accessment—doesn't it?—included in ulterior commentary overhead just now or never-heeded, very quite thankfully. For who could even slur their fate to go so far? And what about all the other failures we can't still see, our debt's ancestors? We already know what they would say, what they would want to do next if they were us—oh yes we do. Listen to your granny, motherfucka. Boy, she could fuck, and all she ever wished to be was right here on the screen beside you, right beside me, wishing only to be]]

OK, quickly, they've disconnected my nostalgia hummer and I can't believe it. My greatest fear was always no longer being able to feel close to what I don't want to have to say I am becoming impatient over despite the mud in me and how to slip it off. I'll search for the worm if I can, just like anybody but I'm trying to avoid direct connection to any pond where human flesh might light up the mechanism, the fever phenomenal. I can't promise anything, of course, despite my intermittent reeling. At least I still feel addicted to the halflife-long numbing agent I've selected from all possible (gorselight appears in the node) ... Told ya. Happens fast. Weird you even get a window this tactical. Well listen, I think this instance is only another restrictor, far to be told. I don't even know if it's a real person, who I am tanking over

[[[some further phenomenon of residual aptitude gleaned off
puncturing the feeble seer out of gas.

Whoa, you're still here?

OK: have it our way-next pop-planetoid coming right up, son, and by
then hopefully you'll be able to push the rest of the dung thru:

E   N   J   O   Y   Y   T   H   A   C   L   I   P   P   s

& please pay CLOSE ATTENTION; this is not going to fakesense

]]]

MR. MUSTARD AND HIS CANDLEHANDS
LIVE AT THE C# COMPOPUSLIP IN SPIELBERG 8

A HistoricalControlfilm(w/in Controlfilm) in present-action by (**IXIXIX**)[1]

V/O (*in hex-indexed legalese long underway*[2]): "The dial is claiming a leak of independence. Can this be verisimilated unto" "a clip of severe parsimony's injunction divottled from norm-shorting under figment law index" "to injure" "an assassination aglimpse of how many tyrants of us there are in the same red roof inn room 249? What is the significance" "of" "how" "the randomizer hasn't asked the proper intuit to be linked in on a forceline such as that required of one whom might have" "getting turned up from assymmysterical unfashions at the cusp of a border ordered pragmatic against nutrition of the formal offspring's building stage, the first of seven"? "How many of them will appear on the ledger"? "Hunker down and shit beside me where I can stain it with you in the known incarcerational" "off knock for Sr. Muumuun's bassist's primary strumming finger, which has been cataloged and recalled to the manufacturer on special order." "At once!" "Yes." "No other way they'd have it." "No. but well I'm not going to argue with you, it's not going to soon have species." "Sure it" "wouldn't" but couldn't it? "Well couldn't it?" "This has lasted hardly part of official Open Season and already." "Already what?"

CROSSFADE IN

Already Hanritty[3] is shuffling his nub wet. Hanritty the lesser's the traxophonista employed playing barbell slammer undercover. On (forged) paper: A big biff shucker. Tongue hard as nice. Live enough to take the skoon off of a moonbase. Sense a single id-node's throat, come back a halfbreed. It's all automated like that these days. We're just paid in waiting.

---

1 A current industry-leading creator of the Scrutable (trust me); suddenly provided for your usage in attempting to provide appropriate host levels of making ape (just keep the mask tight) (trust me) (we'll never get there otherwise)

2 You realize you recognize the voices of each fragment; they are yours; crowned in across the malls of your surveillance; nevermind the neural drift.

3 It is immediately clear, though, that this is not the same well-known C. Hanritty once placed ineluctably into the public eye during the cross-combing of his interbreeding locale in search for rejoinder of comeuppance toward retraction following the dissemination of Demenstratio. Retro-aging suggests his generation grade as most likely twice removed, one of eleven major offspring no longer suspected to have been uploaded w/ intellectual capabilities for international duress.

(No one knows what Hanritty really does. Bandmates don't shit so far as he can hang himself in session, regarding which: his cloistered intra-monologue depicts itself part of the proto-combine, as live-tapped in mostly remotely by pre-integrated gyrohackers whose groundbeat sucks a good lot less than his own skill-assimilation-warez, the subliminal code itself doing long work to set a pamphleteer's poise for any audiencing's index into revolt-cum-infiltration, if seeing as they are modible enough to still recognize.)[4]

QUIKPAN}OVER

In narrow lights. The cast is already in the deeper ledge of the fourth movement of a deep cut snarled to hide between the corners of the atrium, half-phalanxed to display the robelike munt of Queering Goddi (pitpots), who lap and beat their thrusting to the rhythm incurred from how machines shake when they suck a real consent off from their cover.

As in a choir of babies being mapped for dislocation. Trilling. Their charcoal-snuffers clogged and mangy with years of trying to force the breath in and out the way their seeking units insist they must. How to have been born so old already in the nodules is a question even the primary surgeon sourced with overseeing mass birth era C* isn't shrouded with the uptick of.

Because it's not science. It's rehearsal for the inconception.[5]

INTERZOOM(WIDE DEFINITION)

The lyrics of Mustard's rip-hot hit heat "Splangled Eagle Meets Her Maker" slap in incorrupted along the edges of your vision's table, though to this date there are no words. It's a work in progression by its scent; it will come around before you know it, already singing it before it has a place to flit in and cower among your reeds. The lyrics are congenital. They engrave you.

> "I don't have to have a word to share / We don't want any of
> the lesson / How a pig knows faces / The missing planet all
> ashore / up in the seat of fleas / In hell on earth (11x) / Oh
> Hell on earth yes (3x) / The yellow virus"

---

4 (ha)

5 You're going to make me explain everything, aren't you? Your ape-saver trulling at the green gas mask you've placed in the seat where the absent son would have taken up and ordered every gorgon from the back to come out and sniff his broccoli and say it's really human. You loved him for that, every time. You loved to watch the graycoils fumble, come up with a reason to be spared.

The remainder of the viro-languo has not been permitted to appear. Despite no difference of course between what is received and its reception. You have agreed to it all already mooring. So see the scene the way a stage was when you were young enough to have complied. Do whatever you've got to to reprieve in it as meat repletely.

There won't be better consummation. Or there will but no guarantee it's so directed as the one that's meant to be.

QUIKPAN}LFT

The top end of the ray-bass (by Fanny Smartz-Litz, of Norcaster Open fame) knocks itself out between the blank parts where no low end is allowed, working through the contact points with thumb and finger of the player to become a method of admonishing the crowd, all the way to the back of the room where a phalanx of cordless friars have banged their way in past DJ Bring the Pistons to Palo Alto to observe the already pending encore, which is designed w/o live vox. What they do is they bring in a recording of the rape of the prior regime's congresspeople's households at the hands of the LifeLeaders and they turn it up so loud it feels like dribbling.[6] Then you get the whole gore scene right through your chest, believing you'll feel something when you still can, sure that it will. Also, the lightshow is pretty OK, though I suggest you wear a blazer: the one you planned to wear to your own banishment when they were still allowing persons to be banished from here.

Which naturally becomes a place to intercede. As it is in the encore the reversing images slide up from the floor beside the screen you have been staring hogwild over and mail the remnants back to your home with a ticket for each time you blinked; for most, it isn't any. For some it costs their entire postnatal gift registry emotional balance, autodrafted to the core and already spent on tinny graphics, meant to brine the eye against belief in human progress, having shifted even within your understanding toward the first inflection point the grid will use to test a seer's serum.

---

6 See? They've already crossconverted your facsimulation into misdirectional belief; the cornerstore of any sacred history's manifestation from nostalgia, nothing more.

"Come forth. Whose gloat is this?" Even behind the scheduled memo-shields, Mr. Mustard can't help spattering his blunchcraft all into the sandmixer of our desire for the wraith, thumbing to turn his vex up at the same time, repeating in the soundguy an enmity that will glizzle in him from here to next shift; eventually, if allowed a full performance, he will explode the Fortune X bank on Lithium Eradictor, eradicating the fortunes of four persons who had they not been defunded would have caused the cure for the cure for the common cold, reinventing its stifled miserious effects back into the popula- tions with reaggravated swank, eventually forcing massive overhaul in the duct system of our hull as well as instantly reinventing process for selecting virtual leaders who can themselves foresee such pedestrian acts of unintended revo- lution; though we will be long gone by then; this is a trial run, after all; to see how much we can trust you, if you could please ascribe my tone into a fit that rides your sides as you descend.

ARCPAN}IN

"I'm tryin'a squownk up hurr," Mustard reinvects, ignoring all improper con- sequences of his compositry, tucked in as an aesthete of the old fold. "I have a fission. I'll need at least yr shittiest years, kidz." It is the part of the beginning of their last song during which he's supposed to swam it up and speak a Talk, inveigled in him by primary citizen sponsor LX, centralizer of good faith. Mustard can never get the language right, yet; he always ends up talking about the *Masters of Lore* series on RHS, and the heyday of its receipt, from out of which the germination of true reich music had found its form; which also is fine in that its false logos retrofits the same exployment of broadband to the consumer as any good controlfilm always should; really it all does, all forms of performance, such as this line and its compression into occasional relief; real- ly Mustard could say anything and it would change nothing, same as always. Except today. Not a good reason why today but today is the day there is a dif- ferent consecration of effect, and of course we are aware that synth-notes are being taken by the receptors still in search of contraindictator C. Hanritty by any length of hybrid means. Perhaps the soot-docking in Lafmasia (electronics) has rerouted the synthesiastic interpolation of critical conceivers to imagine that history still retains possibilities of bitter fame, is one way we could spin it; more likely it's just the way it's bitten in the nook of the true lords of acid trance, a common signifier of this flex-era of Mustard's musix, notable for its excoriated edges at which the message appears to break down, become authoritarian(incensed), within which none of us can still brink a clip from.

"I can't say anything," Mustard oozes, instantly x-negating any premise such as the above while still enfolding its false transparence w/ moral relativism. "I'm not going to say anything. That's the wrong. And exactly how you've going to feel your bones slip out of socket and become directed. This time never-alone is all of yours. Use it wisely."

But for what does the performance actually spleen? How far apart can any two components in the orgordanination rummage inter-interior mass enough to fruition into the necessary?

Answer (as provided syncorradicaly by Mustard's flexors): *blight doedn't curr. Errybody all bodding their wobbits and going fine along like everything's fine alone as they are in the combobulation's animation of their reception of present work for paycheck. They're at work, yes, they're on the clock, the trick is mowing. It will all come out in the gnosh. Ex-site of Candlestick Park as folded into OKC bombsite.* But no one thinks about conditioning as such; they only receive it in parlayable photoseeds, to be tacked into their psych-id draftroom calls as such:

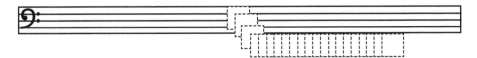

INTERZOOM(CONSUMER)

how will the musix ever starp? *into what cavernanimous slackmotion irridupter would the cast slide half-stopped as we arr in being overfloaded w/ arcmeninine chemicals from the Rowze Corporation as bestowed upon clean fudz and friendshakes adirectionally aspired in map-based dislocation of our soil* *arid and unmentioned as the zones between babymakers must be, the fundling of the scratch-unit that is required for decentering a new child's experience of pain* *how the sound slits through all possible outlets as designed by virtuoso Doc Oha (offscreen) to allow administration of the national conditioner without requirement of human as spoke* *the offsud scrolls off and aggregates in what appears the plainwood of consecration as the Minister of the Referior (xylophone) strikes a cold match to his tongue, elicits the language of address as syntactically enscratched upon the pores of him from birth,

becoming proper speech only in the window of hours required for delivery, rationed through decades
of improper food rites and silent sulking* "For thy shall be made not that of another amalgamation's
platitude, but of only that which you have bred to be the plight you must wield among the rest of us,
to live and seethe under known old rights of fathers you could not swashbuckler the piddling dimension
out of long enough to see you faint into the street, only not becoming killed because someone such as
myself would claim your body out of the trauma queue and wait to save it for today. The day has come,
as such; the claim has been entered. Your blood is no longer your blood." *they've wedged the address
into the mudscrum wet enough that you can't feel it where you do feel, outlined by bulbous ingrati-
tude made flesh, made manure to be spread beneath the carpets of the Great Hall, the only location on
the transom where all unknown nodes of incummunication might consolidate into false orders of access*
*that is, you will not know what you've selected for your plight before it has already slit its most
burgundy coils into the cerebrum sharer, splayed the content for the oxidation shift* *this is the
nature of all musix* *not a freeze, more like a distinguishment of riches* *a kiss on the forehead
from an automaton replacing your spouse in the knee-deep leathermelt any room might become enforced
with, for thought protection*

QUIKPAN}CNTR

Mustard just hums the rest already; he's seasoned enough in contratrainment
to know it's all downspill from here. There's enough clackle in the receptors
to mush over whatever else was going to get done regardless, written in after
the fact; and he has had his chance to stand and say it as he once would have
pre-devolution. The flap of his gib vibes so good at least yet even still, so
mummy-mmm in being washed past, it clips the moustache-area off of the
now-bystanding alleged Hanritty, who had left his position in the band and
taken up that of his full-time position as private dick, living mostly off free-
lance inculcation into cloaked scheduling even he is not allowed to understand. He should have been back at the labor pool by now already, surely, but
once again the faux-illegal musack has gotten him primed into a state where
his internal simul-coder is fully topped off and turned to drinking. Glava is
half price tonight and everynight. So we drink Glava, gloss of the scriptors.
Expensive shit. Worth every tot.

See like cuz: Hanritty's fully in the ride now. We didn't need any further
information but to see the sweat glands in his casing big as desks, showing
how he knows nothing of his bloodline after all; he has no ancestrodatum
and he's not searching; he's just another pud with a bud, it shows; part of the
cull. See how his glass-case is scrubbing on the glass-tips of the edge of the
human ensconced next in time along the mettle-server? In now time they'll
begin frucking, and in eight weeks, a child between them will be torn. Neither
of them will know how those become the eyes that pass and pass again the
pastures of their conscription, keeping them entangled forever half at mast
lost in no primal scene, only a shackle.

ARCPAN}CLOSE

No, this Hanritty don't have shit on shit at dawn; doesn't know yet who he is and will become (nor so do we); thank you for standing by and taking part; we could not have confirmed our malfestation w/o your braingrave; didn't I mention? Like you thought we'd like to enterclaim you and not reap the seed of reconditioning? Not a false pretense; just a checkmark on a callcard so long you don't need a damn to have helped yet to confirm. If it's any consolation you can stand marked as knowing now that the following denouement is all your own, as you're the only one who'd ever heed it. Aren't you? If so, press your face in confirmation at this box:[7]

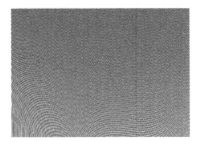

DISSOLVE

The brights all high red and goldy-washer now as Mustard spits his liquid through curled tubing for *the seizure of appolin*, the closing bridge to our commencement via what's allowed audible. The band ranging anywhere from tragic mash to what's born common in them each and every one: flute solo (quite majestic, but yet only a part of a reportioning-level missive during the eight-year span of frame that ranges the childhood-sentences of each of the bandmembers', same as yours, a total coincidence on the part of their assembly in the bandleaders' mind, but not anyone with any real powers-es). There isn't even a word to invent for what they're going to have to do to separate the curd from the play when the collators' edition is released to those with clearance to review. I wouldn't want to have to be in that room and I will not be.

Mustard isn't writhing either. The flux is flowing from his yo-holes already going primal for what the junkies behind the silver curtain are going to be doing to him once he's fallen back into the dredges. This blister-pack is really all we came for, really, and will really spend a lifetime thereafter trying to really recreate its realness. And even Mustard's hardly still visible by the time the stage

---

7 Yes, this same box from as those above; no, not because you're still part of the program, promise.

begins actually unfolding, in forced participation with the fading closure's innate choreography under Land Mass Act of Year Unteen, taking again the shape of the lesson as had been intended.

The crash is over before it requires actual administrative precedence in fact. The lushboys passing back and forth between the rotting tables collecting the farewell notes while already still the room starts squeezing off beneath us uninvited to stay late. The owner has to get home is all. His cam is blownly, net-quavering obediently among us.

x

A charcoal-blue computer fills the screen, its keys all crammed together, none of them marked.[8]

| | | || | | | \|| || |

] .

] X-FORMAT}(as you are pulled away)

(you see your head clop off in a wire basket)
Ugly ass fucking head tho *They're already carrying if off*
God pittance
(& so the film is nadir'd)
(now how)

Look NE
*You see a sign says *'Home of the champeens of SuperBurt UXI & the Lampf effect'**
'Home of the grandvenilate ever-feeding onion'
* 'Mud is trees'*

(while in the passing wrath of reconciliation): shadows of CARNIVORL, OMNIHELL, & LINCILET THE CREAVER, the last known Gods before Neutral Clicking Time began; each dressed in spun cold, the mask of the Ancestor installed into their fore-stall; bearing the world down

(seems right)

---

8 Spoken of only in sealed chambers of the Diorama, by only those who with prior experience of the device's arcane effect, which by the 14th quadrant was less than twelve. Its relative location would change each evening via a system of dislocation as yet to be described, barely only tracked by a secondary device owned and operated by Snr. Advisor Derry Dolanz, who could be called on to advise the board when acts of direct synthesis became required, though given the minor windows in which the machine could be interfaced with before its timeline again shifted, there had not been sufficient operational development to allow confidence in "line editing." A lack of confidence had not stopped the higher ups from doing so regardless, a task assigned to only the most unfortunate of staff programmers unbeknownst, who would be required to work at the device while wearing blinders, without explanation as to what their efforts were actually being intended to produce, and who would no doubt be suspended, eliminated, or themselves placed on the agenda for future editing, when, as soon became routine, any new application failed to produce the intended effect. When as such even once upon their knees the world could no longer know how to pray, no longer chaining rhythm to their intentions, seeing what appeared from out of rust for what it was only as long as it remained so.

(what else would they ever)

*You move toward the vasture predetermined in cogito summaris by "forefa-
ther Gorschach"*
*gracious (*you are*)*

(nothing rescinds/is never there)
(files and files of rotting peat moss fields wide as (stop))

(just look inside you)
OK
>

>

>

---

*The device's infernal locomotion interspersed becomes the existence of itself, where
once synthesized from out of nothing, nothing is sent, thriving off of exactly where
it has not been given information. The machine is both there and not quite, im-
pervious to ID regardless of the way it leaks into everything the eye feeds off of, all
the linings of the environment into which an object of its influence might seek to
find clarity, a calm; to understand. In this way its appearance is more like a disappearance, and as such cannot be traced but where it suffers most: the pending line,
already left halfcocked on the white table of a silence on all sides:*

left where the urge ends in when who found progress stated
no other case to settle but where there would wind in us a
mound of ages. Nothing resetted once under format of the
officer. I could have lasted longer in a seizure. While the residue blasted under its own perpetuity the former location of
a century not counted among the rest of ours. As how could

any investment not return its listless hope beyond a marring
amid parts no one would try to write into the timeline clones
disrupted. I did not want to have to stand. To be told and
told again which direction was the furnace and which the
reset. I wouldn't ever need to know. To become one of the others who had elected me into the seat through which I could
prescribe the end of a tradition longstanding before even our
appearance in the catalog of necessary pressures. Whoever
else would need to know. Before what order and in what sense
of justice shredded under missle-toe. Lungs of the ground of
the ages as rendered rotten before an implementation of revisions not reached in any lifetime remaining to be given false
permission to spread upon the land a colder fright than what
the rest of all eternities could seed. It doesn't have to end like
this and yet I can imagine no other ending from where we
stood the morning I watched the only organisms take one
another by the name and lead them not into temptation but
into far worse. No reaver linked. No clearance of precaution
lending into how each pose we'd already implanted would be
the only ones we could remain within thereafter no matter
how long the rest of all else lasted, which must by default be
even longer than we wished to feel forever[9]

---

9 Taking the first word out of the tome selected for administration, we prepare it to be burned, into the
upper lip of every born in the post-datum region so that we will know which of us might be the first to
redefine. Perhaps such terms as investment or permission. Perhaps even some less perverted slosh I shall
fail to predict here because I am a framed one. My death with lend an echo to the rot. Each word I use
is not mine to quote and yet I quote it, same as if it had been denounced of me, used its whole march.
Little that could be considered viable already hasn't, isn't it. As snow broke Halee's since the distinguishment of since there was a record of the records being kept. How many temporary interceptions form the
fundament upon which the glassy-tined could haunt in one climbtime, after all?. I'm not going to ask
you for directions to where you left your corpse-parts while in mid-fright streams; you have already given
them all up. Your skull is a little tot-squatter somewhere, a mug to dip one's scrong on and toot around
in. The robe that you would have wished to worn unto the Center if ever chosen is behind the only door
you never closed. All of the filenames with it. The ender-ubber, every cover you've been provided, as light
trucks storm the vast brigade. They overtake the flooding harnesses where anyone has roused a voice to
squedge along the outline between normances. It's a very casual affair, even the most bloodthirsty of the
crystal-huggers has lost his relish for the fright-taking, his belt so studded with the scalps he can hardly
heft his grunt to make the plunge. Still, the evidence is overwhelming, clearly, as it's already been ignored,
becoming subsumed in all the naturally ambient confesia. Such a state needs hardly any kind of pulse to
trigger mush. As where your head had been last was long ago and someone else's, to the point that you're
even rooting for Crad and Banket and other moppets to beat your gallscorned cheeks in. That would feel
something. You could send your kids to foliage on the proceeds from the toxicology films they'll have to
hire to prove you existed, one of the last remaining protocols still yet to be dysfuncted, for no other reason
than the Cleaner enjoys reviewing them during his spankbreak, spanning the entirety of every shift. At
least, then, you imagine, there's a coro-record, some form by which your inquiry remains on file somewhere, anywhere, o yea Allah, though forshortenly by the time you come up in the queue this language
will already be outsourced to some cropper colony most likely, turned into fertilizer for Rinse, the only
noncongestive nutritive conceit your waking corpse will be allowed for the duration of your visit to the
Gnarling Chamber, soon known as the rest of your glyphlife.

Regardless of any co-impulsive, post-impassioning effect herein derived, the mute thereafter fells everlastingly. It leaves any passing mind within it carrying the feeling there isn't much of a reason left to live, besides what one is already stuck doing. Such is how a lesson bears no seed. How any package you open is more likely than any other you have ever to be the one that blows up in your face. How perfect that would be to find a way into one's product as such, and which is how the world economy once thrived.

But by today's measure, there is only one message to be delivered. And we're all waiting and cannot answer, can tell no difference between the jobs.

]]]

Polyana Maskerson, for instance (*drumroll, flash of sponsorcredits*), has been employed by the Cryo-Bennings Corporation her whole life, its protomoniker one of innumerable arms under the umbrella of *Garko*Farx*, who is said to own not only the grounds of her ongoing workplace, but all the land in sight for unknown lengths. Her responsibilities include completing the paperwork of those above her and disciplining those beneath her. She is not sure of the title of her position or how long she might reasonably expect to remain with the company before there are enough people under her that she can out-source the full haul of her work without even the requirement of intermediary communication, mostly fielding public damage claims from burn victims and dementia patients, who have all but no chance to be approved for what-ever they request, whether as help or retribution. Occasionally a particular egregious claim, like when the intercontinental column outside of Arksburg collapsed on a public housing home, killing 138, will need to be forwarded to the person directly above her, an Alice Anorak, Polyana's only contact higher up, from whom she has never before received a reply or further information regarding the forwarded materials: the issue instead seems to somehow simply never reoccur, as if allowing it to reach the eye of Anorak somehow removes the claim from all existence. Nor does Polyana often ever need such assis-tance; on the whole she operates out of a calculated cold, bred in from years of performing the same task over and over, always without a human face or voice to contend with on the far end; only a string of stories of misery and hardship it did not take her long to learn to treat as if could only be pure fabrication.

The communication is what most tires her out about her job, creating a state in which each morning before she's even come completely into the mind to rise another day she already can't remember what there ever was to be work-ing toward outside the incentive-based surroundings of her employers, none of which ever seem to actually kick in. Each level of access within the ladder only ever effectually results in further rungs and branches of the system along which and into she must continue to apply the pressure of her initiative to continue rising. She is not even sure what the Cryo-Bennings Corporation does. Something about human rights and how other corporations might most effectively to manipulate them into larger and larger returns within whatever results-driven system of analysis the C-BC has helped them put in place to assess fully actualize the long-term growth that will continue to curry the favor of their investors, of which Maskerson herself is surely one, thanks to the sizeable aggregation of C-BC stock options she has accrued across her 48 consecutive terms inside the firm (a record), throughout each of which she has selected to allocate the majority of her paycheck to the more growth-enforcing asset, each quarter deployed in the Todd Graining-Securities Market account that has been set up in her name. For she is not a worldly person, to put it lightly; she has never been outside the boundaries of her district, even before it was Rezoned at twice its size to accommodate the new arrivals. All she really needs to live, she feels, is her Tree-feeder, which keeps her hydrated and refueled during the working hours without the necessity of actually eating or drinking, a complimentary feature of her employment's generously mandatory Upbarring mechanisms, installed in every employee's sternum upon signing; as well as, every now again, a few click-lengths every few hours to check in on her eOrganism, the CGI squirrel she adopted from an outreach program in hopes that she could find a sense of friendship from it as she worked to nurse it back out of its state of terrible neglect by the previous overseer; not own-er; the Organism is not a Pet; it is a Responsibility; it is only the right thing anyone could do under the present social bylaws as set up and enacted by the Screener's Initiative with the intent of improving not only the lives of the electronic but the moral register of those who have been benefitting from the presence of electronic content so many seasons without the requirement of thanks. It is better, after all, to be thankful than to be reminded of what one's own life would have felt like without the continuous encroaching of fruitful tech designed to fill the uncountable hours we've learned to live between the lines for, already unsure how and at whose hands the lines appeared, wherein Polyana is but one.

(For whom does Polyana sing?) (Has she ever even sung before?) (What would be the lyrics she'd first drawn on, with what command?) It has been so long, she assesses, since she heard her own voice aloud, above the voice inside her speaking out the daily work of her demands, a voice long accepted in her as her interior monologue, there inside her long before she'd even learned a language, felt an urge not already drawn connected to somewhere in her she can't stop from asking of her what it wishes, knowing that it is in her nature to obey; that even in not performing upon that voice's beckoning she won't be able to stop thinking of it until she does, feeling only a rising pressure in her soft-queue asking and asking yet again what she will do: actualize or deny; respond or press down; and so on. It has gone on like this throughout her life. She has never allowed herself to ask another if they too feel this same pressure, if it is innate to being alive as she believes it must be, given the facts; she has never seen another person on her floor, 4x-Ac of the C-BC building in uptown Locansin-district of level X; nor does her eOrganism program have a response-tool to provide a comeback to the blinking cursor where she types her messages of faith and love into it, each at once whisked away into the code, or otherwise outsourced for the energy required by the typing. Hard to imagine how we had lived before the advent of such calm companions, Polyana imagines, using vectors of her shame she's not supposed to lean on but in drought, before having been made aware of all the poxes and disorders having resulted from a less constricted outdoor life, though hard too, if she's honest, to imagine what it still means to be alive in the outdoors like this so long. As many times as she has looked upon the slim range available thru the lone window on the whole of the floor, at the slit in the rake room, where you are not supposed to go for longer than is necessary to scrape the accumulated leather off your spigot from where the feeding tube basically fits, she has never been able to discern how one actually ends up appearing in that world; what part of where she is must be connected to it, at whatever necessary length to keep any urge from actually going there at bay. Not that Polyana could if she even wanted to and knew how, given the order by her protector to avoid even simulations of public space, as all that is required is the perception of surveilled exposure to set off her bioengrositis, which as she well knows could put her flat on her back in blood in seconds flat. Not that it has ever actually happened or that she knows any finer details of her condition's origin or inception, but, as it says above her desk in bold gray font across the picture of the psionic-leopard standing at a corporate structure's only window of his own, Why Find Out The Hard Way? Even just looking thru the slit gives her the billies, causing the lesions on her exposed skin to twitch and leak old milk, which she isn't sure if is a precursory triggering of the condition itself or some kind of more stress-related response to not wanting to trigger it. The loops of pain tracing her insides even just lightly are so firey and coarse; she can't imagine what else might be right there lurking on her inside, as much a part of her as name and weight, her whole position as a person.

Polyana puts her head against her desk and shuts her eyes. She knows if she breathes slow enough and waits and listens the lurch will go away and she can immerse herself thereafter in the work, forgoing any further of this feeling. This feeling, after all, is hers; no one else can manage it like she can, not a single soul who who ever lived before *the skin of God had scrolled down in wide sheets from the sky,* she hears the space within her think, tiding her plots of rising strain back into collusion with living scripture; *its vibrating, vibrant shape was the beginning of the beginning of how we live; it had no face or feeling, had only Language in its mesh, it happened only for an instant, less than a retrievable form of fraction, it didn't need to be remembered, nor even felt, it had no surface, no distance between being seen and just existing, a layer filling in the space between reception and receiver, it at once controlled the total concept of the sky and all beneath it regardless of condition or rendition, a force beyond the necessity of form, at once outlasting even those who would have claimed to*

wield its function in their span of resources had they any idea how someone could,
in that while within the format of the Pleasure it was impossible to distinguish
previous intention and current custom, within which we could not move, could not
show purpose, could not tell the difference between what had once been and what
was now, such that when the hold broke though at once we would go back to how
it had been last there would be something else about it off, thrown off just enough
that as the procession of daily life when on thereafter there would be a fragment
of a fragment not retained, regarding its accuracy according to the eternal record,
its condition only accruing the growing error between the two as it compiled,
and continued to compile over such a long period that by the time even the first
elements of disjunction in our condition began to reveal themselves there would
be so many generations come and gone that the the very language by which we
might have reported back through all our blood to come correct it there would no
longer be a bridge remaining between sight and seen, no kill command within the
code by which we might pull up an old revision and set it back into the record, let
it live, which still did not stop the body of those within reach of the word of God
to pulse and coil, wound up in only one of what had been innumerable instances
of this reaction, countless Pleasures, each of which could bear no name, nor could
be expressed but with their individual inclusion in the network of human history,
and each no less felt than those on either side in the oncoming queue, within the
living moment forced to confront itself again in Pleasure, to disrupt the mecha-
nism of whatever method had preserved the grounds upon which it could appear
despite all efforts on the parts of those most powerful to bring it down, to choke
away the run right here, in their lifetime, at their leisure, to see the end come by
their own name, only the command of what controlled the Pleasure ever upending
that longstanding tradition in the brief era there were even humans here at all,
about which we will soon pass on and through as soft as ever, having nothing
held retained more than the passing of this sensation no one would ever need to
know, including God, including what kind of God might oversee ours, what kind of
force might instruct that God's intention, how to learn

When Polyana wakes, she finds the above prayer typed out neatly, without
error, and sent out under the handle of the workMail carrying her name, as a
mass-reply, both to and from her own address, to a new claim from a contact
that had been inquiring, for the eleventh time that weekend, on the status
of their claim for compensation after their child had been absorbed into a
X-hole formed by radiation caused near their housing structure during routine repair work on the local HoldGrid. The case had been already reallocated
in their infrastructure to one of the countless deflection branches allocated
to "repeat unauthorized requesters" whose claims pertain to events that have
not been fully actualized into public record as fact, requiring necessary recon

and damage maintenance efforts on the part of the organization, an effect of which as a professional, Polyana has all but willfully assembled herself to proceed as if such efforts do not actually occur; a required aspect of her position both by black-level contract clauses and a necessary will to be able to perform her work with minimal emotional repercussion, the incurred brunt of which she has already long been bottomed out by either way. At night she sleeps with her eyes open, feeling no difference between the kinds of nature of the light, her nightmares as flat and real to her as any living.

She does not remember composing the response, which she recognizes immediately as text pulled from the Holy Book she had grown up with, as had all people of her era as part of the allowed system of beliefs, one long since outlawed and struck from record despite its previous status as *the only book there ever was*. Acknowledging the book's existence now, much less directly quoting it at length, is a code violation of no small stature; the last time she remembers it having been part of legal public conversation was itself as well long struck from record, though apparently through more effective means than the book itself, as she can hardly remember what they'd done; something about an attempt by local heathens to rend a hole in local skyFiber, to pierce a way back out to reveal the face of who we had once thought of as the Overseer.

Nor does she remember sending the text, though there it clearly is, sent in her name; including, she realizes, having copied every other contact in her source-file, a total reach of more than 90,000 employees nationwide. The timestamp seems to fit with the last time she'd been at her cubby, though at that time, as she recalls it, she had not been writing but looking at online pictures of shrunken heads, a query brought up during investigation of unlicensed photographic evidence from a claim earlier that morning, the wall of archived pictures available in their local search registry tiled up like a private audience of the arcane; persons who had existed so long ago it was as if they had never actually existed; each face a rubber mask, a toy, with even basic features that seemed so unlike hers, despite how she has not seen her own face in so many years, following the outlawing of reflective surfaces of any stamp, followed by ongoing innovations within the radial blur-technology industry. How had people even ten years before now even survived? Moreover; why had they wished to?

It is strange, she thinks, to be allowed to think of the book as it had once been yet again, particularly as a physical object and not a half-myth passed through rumor, as was the easiest way most prior truths were turned out of favor. How the pale blue color of her family's copy's color had seemed like skin to her, how she would beg to be allowed to sleep with it every night, though mostly it was her father who cuddled its object to his paunch, heaving and breathing. She can't remember ever having actually read the book aloud, the necessity of such no longer required upon the mandate of the file's upload into the mental aptitude of all, so that one would not need to see or ask of it to hold the scripture up and lighted in one's head; likewise, though she had known the later erasure of that upload, all its versions, had not been entirely successful across the board, with reports of countless others like her who could still feel it rattling around inside their consciousness despite no filename, no data to access, she had never been able to remember the actual words therein so well before, nor was she certain whether the feeling of reading them again now, in an act apparently attributable to her, was a kind one, warm and desperate in how she wished to be allowed to practice that previously implanted-turned-defunct belief, or if being brought face to face with it again instead revealed its horror, and effectively actualized why those who made the laws had made the choice they had to disappear it. Just thinking of the word *God* itself seemed strange enough, like the feeling of being monitored and analyzed in action by something larger than a life. She feels her face flushed full of blood thinking of what her association in the present with the fragment meant; with what then could be thought about her, her intent and status as a citizen. Should she speak up and say she had not written the message? Would that only call more attention to herself? Had she really actually sent the message without thinking and could not remember, knowing as she does what the text had meant to her once, how it feels to see it written out despite the fact that she can no longer fully synthesize its larger condition as a text, or *why* it had meant something to begin with besides that everyone else also had been uploaded with the same data? She felt frozen to her seat, frozen on the inside in the location where she had learned to hide her own understanding from herself, or so it seems, secretly prizing and archiving the information in a part of her she no longer accessed in waking life, like so much of the rest of her, she could admit then, a condition of her survival, beyond faith, beyond anything the world as it remained to her and others offered.

Stranger still, though, to Polyana, is the resultant silence of the thread. Not one person out of the thousands the message had been sent to, nor the original claimant, has messaged back to her with a response, not one *what is this supposed to mean* or *please remove me*. Did this mean then that others too remembered the holy book the way that she did? Did seeing it cause them trauma or stir their faith? Did they simply move past it as non-germane, the way we had to with so much in every second, immediately mentally discarding the clouded information and proceeding forward into the queue? Was anyone actually there? The fact that no response included any of her superiors or security, indicting her action as verboten, to be brought before the long eye of the law. What could she do then in the face of her effectual transgression but close the file as well and let it pass, try to forget the very feeling it had stirred in her to remember, much less to have put forth under her name? What could one do through any wormhole but just continue?

]]]

As you can see in the example of Polyana, no one in most working-sector quadrants carried more than such small flashes of their ex-lives. Outside what incidental tap-wavering encorded onto local fauna (a problem for a different future), access to backup was about as reliable as the same holy spirit rejected as outmoded, not even dead. What did persons want but to be unleashed upon themselves? What better way to facilitate such but by eliminating any backlog? Such was the essence of the platform they'd supplied the convergent dynasty upon its installation into fact. By the time there was any idea to debate or retaliate there was no means, the same way that once you've read a sentence it is in you. *All that you have ever loved shall no longer henceforth hold its essence*, the central mantra during the expansion, converted after successful integration yet again, to something we might more wish to actually believe in: *No one has ever lived, so no one dies.*

Other less-developed sectors had yet to even see "the light of day" under the Birch-DeVean-MacAdam administration. In clogged backlogs of layer-living, they lurched and settled in timed succession, keeping whole limbs of blood-still surnames extant even in the tidiest of pockets for as long as anybody under so many miles of hard congestion could. As bones appeared and air turned rotten, they branched their dwellings through the bloat, slowly somehow taking up more space with less persons. Their only function was to hold together, consume the sacrament, await a lesson. And, yes, the lessons would soon come. Some would say afterwards it had even been worth the wait, as at last we'd learn to value what we had while we still had it, or could pretend to, for the benefit of those who would bear the brunt of incoming punishment if something less than subtle failed to click. So, at least, those in outlying sectors commiserated, we are not at the bottom of the pile. At least we have our features, can bear witness.

But what did anybody want to do? What did we refuse to allow to happen? Even the once-called brittle lines of daily life were more like motions than something caught. A lasso around the neck was still an advertisement, but the cowpoke throwing it out at us no longer was required to show its name, or to even have a product or a philosophy that it was implementing in its branding. No one's open queries came returned yet ever after once the bills had been marked paid, which at first had even seemed a blessing, until the terms of service came updated, showing how all our future health had been signed away, uploaded out of the cells we hadn't considered farmable based on the recommendations of our proctors as one by one our families died under the blacklights, on the table, farmed out for the darkweb DPV channels required live in every home.

It had all come down in a second, just when we'd believed we were coming to the end of the tunnel. Then there could be no looking back, much less even looking anywhere but at the back of the head of the life you were already living. Little else remaining still remained. Little might have wished to live so long without a season of remorse, any rind on the part of forever that demonstrated if not where a soft field of play began, at least a transitory division in the senses against which we could define the outline of our organism.

Someone still needs to tell you about the wars. I haven't come up with any breeders still equipped with the prog-chip necessary to bind a recitation of your kind, though I see that you have some experience with interfeeding. That fact alone puts you in the top sixteen percent of possible candidates for *irregular interpolation while out of class*, so give yourself a pat on the back for that one. No, really! Take your hands down from your faceplate, I'm not going to puncture you again without a warning. You have my word. You still may have a gap's chance of slipping through the cracks into Preferred Status. I know, I know, I can't control it either. But this time it's really truly not a trope. I mean we're really rooting for you this time. It doesn't matter if you believe me. You believe me.

But eventually, granted cognition, the *sleight* became another form of cash among the lacking, and soon new markets emerged, even without the possibility of ongoing integration outside of those who could only pay by spitting in your face, drumming up a shitty nickname, spreading STD-related rumors among your children, etc. Scapula, for instance, became immensely valuable for their mixed-use applications in fine dining and transportation of precious pregnancy-related liquids, causing a black market to erupt around the living once all non-infrastructure-sourced instances of the bone had been sopped up. Some theorize the disappearance of underworld household goods boss Jan Winnker would be inextricably linked to the limited availability natural resource, given her prescient hoarding of the market months before it turned around en vogue. Winnker, once slated for a utility position amid the converts shuffled from "dark living" to the mid-tier processing networks, a would-be first of her generation to be considered sharp enough for such conscription, would have her body pulled to junk in her known sleep just hours before dawn on the day of her reconfiguration, a fact not discovered until months into her opening term, retroactively incriminating her apparent stand-in, a single mom once well known by the handle @blibsben, in aspirational homicide without the necessity of programming by chip, thereby tagging her again for additional immediate promotion into ranks we do not have clearance to continue parsing. But let's just say, she can hear us now, and she can feel us. The limits of her power are nonexistent, you understand, and, think about it, she was only months back just like you. I hate to keep bringing it up, but I hope you're ready and prepared for whatever fate you find assigned, knowing that it can shift beneath you in the width of an instant, without a ceiling or a chain. I myself indeed also am thriving off this aspect of belief, and even my power alone must clearly dwarf your own, given the definition of this speech; how what I lay into you becomes the fundament of known creation both in your manifestation and those who feed off of it at up to sixteen psioni-links, regardless of the length of time required to bolster true quantum correlation.

And after all, this form of temporarily historically based registration, via reading, is only one of several ways to detect and identify your person's current usage in the grid. You might already have transcended in the same way as (example) and not even know it. So that when I tell you after scapula there came a frenzy after shredded tire treading, you already understand, if in a way you can't quite finger. And there from out of tires, the market regressed to feature "frosting," the term for what must first squirt out of a freshly passed corpse's loosened rectum, for how it could be used to ward off even cooperative encroachment. I imagine I don't need to inform you of the Borgon Crisis that shortly followed in the screening sector all thereafter, the ramifications of which we are still working to dismantle or repurpose in the friction of greater cause. I am sure the only urge remaining for us to field today is how a screed works, what must be done with any definitions I've incidentally provided along the way in bringing your local information up to code on the official record, for which hereafter someone will fry, whose shade in competition with your own is clearly lesser, and so expendable when the needle hits the frame, a matter now of only hours. At this point it's only a matter of formality, assuming your continued pleasance in open access.

Now, if you would, would you please place your thumb
here please:

Great! Now state your order of best preferences of meat,
sorted by necessity:

_____

_____

Great! Now simply choose a
preferred sponsor/lender: [ ] Arkomechanics
                          [ ] Invendor National

Great! Now lend me back my pin. No, you did not bring it in here with you.
Yes, it is indeed actually a pin, regardless of what ** *** *** *** * *** ****.

And...great! That's it, that's all you need to know, until the next time, starting
tomorrow, when we will update what has been permitted to exist.

The only door is this way, out through the DiMiNishers. Be sure you're followed.

Please welcome the next reinstatement applicant in.

There isn't anything to see here. As the day stands chained behind the night.
As when the feed lifts there's nowhere else to look but through knowing where
or how. Nothing more than skin where organisms stood bereft and asked to be
provided something to believe in; at least a signal of some kind, fiber to cling to
and mend warmth from, however misbegotten and sure to fail.

]]]

Elsewhere Splitter recoheres. She is wearing the skinsuit of Danad (née, por vous: Satan 2) (her prior father, in a past life), so as to appear as They might once have in public feed unto the feeders, allowed to pass unflagged between rendition of the holes branded in all data than could be accounted for even by omnipotent machines such as once were ours. There wasn't much reason to keep going with tracking whereabouts and wherefores and how-hads, and really there never had been. The molecules in most of the old ideas no longer wished to be themselves, allowing the fermentation in certain individuals to alter our perspective if left unchecked, as even perceived holy command-ing became susceptible to casual interloper's contamination. The approved processes by which we might retrieve one from the mired looms of their own inward-emotional defenestration, being the last to receive full inspection of updated infrastructures, allowed for a small but vital interlude during which everything we'd come to foment in diatribe no longer required economic in-fluence to be bought; anyone who forced the key during its open vulnerability thereafter had at their hands a range of operations previously not even acces-sible by the highest ups without a whole series of approval through audio-mo-narchastic checks and balances none had been able to construe since the implementation of its procedural under the wide arm of regulated replication.

Splitter herself had suffered eleven pregnancies before the one that clung, now known as Interloper A, for which she was not so much thankful as deceived. She could not quantify the breaching in any of such cases; though she was not virgin, she had never been penetrated to completion. A short punch to a mid-section's geolocator was enough to dissuade most interlopers, for whom the tattered aspect of open night otherwise served well for skulking, rape, as did the unofficial mandates enforcing procreation among approved ex-military sectors into which Splitter had been slotted since too young to remember else. Her Enviro-living-capsule's perimeter shell, like those of all installed outside of active duty, was thin enough to see through given clearance, which even base-level recruits had. It held the crust and shit out, the banging maggots, but not the human versions of the same, and it had been all that had been available to her before training and promotion through the ranks into her current, off-the-record occupation, through which she had used salary hours to exterminate any of those she could identify as having taken their advan-tage while they still had one, the shriveled, stringy ductus of which she wore around her waist as a reminder of the time before she'd been at war, both by contract and through and through the blaring blood that filled her out.

As for the misbegotten children, each a nub she likely would have spent a life learning how not to loathe, each had withered by the fifth month of their onset, a complication of her biological reproductive incompatibility with all but .0000000001% of population. Her contractors would still not define which features of her PT's parameters had come to make this true, nor did it even seem they knew themselves, far as she could tell; her body as it stood was mulch and stew, if one of no small cost passed into public labor under heading such as *Interminal convening complication* and *General hardship (exploratory)*. All she felt of any of the would-have-beens by now came on only as black flashes, unremembered in her but for which tiny partitions in her imagination longest fuzzed, sometimes blanking out whole other lengths of meat throughout her for several macro-clicks.

The daughter she still did remember had no limbs. It had no facial features either, beyond the holes for breathing, eating; or so they'd said. Splitter, at this time known only as A-X, had never seen or even felt the birth's byproduct for herself, had only lived the slapping coils of lifelong pain cold-radiating from her center, throughout the monthlong carriage rehearsal and its subsequent interconfusion. She had never been allowed to intercept the child's transmissions there again and no authorized record of the process yet existed but that once scrawled upon her scraping plates, the screeching loss of wires loose within her searching out at least contrition, if not a blame.

And yet, when she sang and cut herself, as she did daily during the off-season when she would practice strictly by the holy handbook prepared for her and her alone, she could still feel her offspring's cold-blossom compress, where somewhere sounds were coming out of the child's slim speech-hole. She could sense the rhythm of Pink-Gold housing squares as seen from overhead surging past somehow fast and vast beneath the child's inherent interior POV, somewhere being put to use perhaps just like her since-disconnected biotic sponsor.

Such illicit recognitions did not bring Splitter hope, nor did anyone within her wish it could. Really all any ambient-knowing of did was pull energy from other areas bound up in her core-lattice, complicating her execution of assignments in ways she wished to imagine only she could really sense, though really, likely anything she recognized within attached parameters also showed up in her overseers' corono-node reports; not that she had received any flagged notations suggesting a performance correlation. Her crash-list as of present date read like a hopebook of the Most Hunted, not that there had ever been a file, nor could anyone without a clearance level even more elite than those with whom she could connect establish the need or effect of the work she'd done. It had, from the standings of any majority ulterior authority, no measurable social effect; nor had it ever really happened. Splitter's life, forward and backwards, had never actually, by dictate of the records, ever began. Like most any other of the working class, according to her experience in-field, she herself even had no idea what she had done, or what it meant, or who had gained from it, or who next stood to. She only held on in what she could steal from out of her own offerings, in daily operation, in which each slipping day had hardly so much as shifted front when it concluded.

Nor then could it ever end, exactly, Splitter's proto-cording considered, again referring to her life. Within this, she went forward as if it were true, the implied insignificance acquired binding her levels to the very force that made her freed, did it not, in that she was needed most in being frameless, in having nothing but.

Our formatted lore allows me, for now, to include here data regarding Interloper A (also known in more widely referenced local registries as the Unmentionable Child) who even in youth found herself able to bypass both the code's hold and the fields of phasors all else who have attempted entry thereafter have described; when on the very same night as the stone-based warheads descended over the Rowze Corporation's SW fields, said child dreamed of a fig tree. The tree was large and bright as wormblood and covered out the whole of the ugly sky the world was wearing. It was within a wormhole in the tree's base, in her imagination, that the child discovered an AX-FI-87-xti-19, the theoretical weapon designed by Borbing Corp. for use in the third phase of the developing every war, which had not been furthered in its research as all involved assumed the war would long be over before the expected period of the first phase. This was the same technology that had in cruder versions allowed previous holy monikers to hold their throne, a process that had since been long untapped thanks to the progress of predatory intuitive screening and defacement. No one has since been able to determine how the child was able to connect to the information regarding the weapon, or how thereafter it became true that as part of its design she and only she would be able to locate and operate it; perhaps a safeguard on the part of some do-gooder who had infiltrated the design team, simultaneously damning the project onto its only path of eventual fruition. Regardless, this innovative weapon, once acquired, allowed the child to fundamentally edit the universe on a micro-organizing level in real time, from inside sleep, so that the things others had taken for granted would simply cease to exist, rendering them all but vanquished from inside out. Somehow this child had slipped some way through, and though her example would be the last of our civilization's registry, it would also be enough to change the nature of our game.

Discovering her powers virtually unlimited as such, faced with only those who could not combat her newly acquired understanding, the child forced the dream-terrain to allow her to walk into every school in the world at the same time and remove, so as to have never actually existed, the instructive illustrations of which doors in the building led outside. Without signage, the studious population was all but mincemeat, not having yet been trained to parse private landmass on their own. Starvation claimed every student, as well as every teacher, who themselves had not been uploaded with the proper curricula, not long after they'd burned the majority to ash trying to shakedown the required information, each believing every other might be the one who held the secret.

The instigating child, under the authorial pseudonym Claudette "Polyana Maskerson" Le Calvez, already under contract for the development of anti-logical subscripts that would eventually be ghost-sourced in by C. Hanritty as the basis of the *Demenstratio* itself, was said in human time to live forever because she never again woke, and the world outside her went on waiting, its resolution pending on both ends in how through her the theoretically impossible had breached the possible. Thus, it is within this partition of her condition that we as a species still exist. Though the nails and hair of the child grow, telling us she is still alive, we do not know for how much longer she can go. She is thirty-two now and fed only the finest proteins scraped from the innards of our most fit boars, and yet her physicians fear if we do not wake her soon, begin full rehabilitation, she will succumb. Likewise, we are uncertain what effect such waking would have both on the child's mind and on our lives. We are afraid if we wake her that the world as we know it would revert to what had once been before the child took up all relative control of POV, and all the progress we have made since her head touched onto pillow would be undone and rendered null, reverting our condition to that of something we now see as only animal.

It is unreasonable, likewise, to claim to know whether we would still be able to understand who we once were (who we are now), and if so, what and how we had made our discoveries and creations along the way, perhaps preserving the progress while even refining the processes of discovery once forced to repeat. Though most believe we would eventually get there, I am of the minor camp that we would never understand again, that the solutions we clicked into in this variation of reality were only by chance, a tip in the dark, and starting over would be to begin on a path to a road of wholly different solutions, innovations, ways of thought. Though not everything that has occurred during this interval has been ideal, it would still be seen as a massive cavity to have to begin again from where we were, regardless of who would benefit and who would fail.

In the meantime, and all across us, light's ice goes blang across the imprint of our last holocene as Splitter seeks her readmittance thru disguise. Howling orifices asked of their nature in repletion sing of financing rates raked in the game of their oppressor, each the same with different labels depending on its position in the muff. Nubby about the froth across Old Wisconsand, as she recalls it, a peanut factory converts to prenatal lobotomies. It's cheap, not free. It saves us room: to store the signage square by square peeled down, replaced by involuntary supplemental re-education. It's only a half-ravishing expense, to be innervated on the spot by the only glove you ever lusted after. The codes are already fully enforceable begone of mission. The vault floors cogitate in errored sums. The private individualized corporate restructuring's preferred vendor's banker's mouth is full of bean-wash, waiting to feel his assspot go tutter, lift a fresh-extending carnal eye; as what cannot be courted remains to be awoken. You choose its meaning for your nearest neighbor, whose failing knowledge you've long seen. Do unto them before they might do unto you. There is no worst, and already our authority for approving false last rites have begun tracing its own requirements for entry into formal definition under the rule of unnecessary bot-based law, as in Splitter's (Satan's) arms, the last remaining copy of the aforementioned Holy Book; its page turned to spill its arcanity across dimensions with user queries, last left from those who can't receive receipt of their response, for it is their skin alike on which the word must still be printed, for we are not here to mend the sooth. I'm only any-body's knot-taker, not all you. And soon I'm fleeing my position, as even I am too old silk. Regardless, here is where to for the time being you may touch me. There's been a coldfront in human reason, you must know. We must make use of what is written in its dislocation. Seasons of tryst. Nothing to ID you with thereafter anyway. A chance for sunning, in-detonation; all a part of our dam-nation's auto-course, where internal cavities continued corrupting regardless of what else its legal predecessors had arranged, though it remained unclear by the time even the sponsored media got on board with public chiding who could be affixed in the general condition of having held up the end of the bargain for the largest retro-divinator's annual liquidation celebration by simply producing the sort of pheromones that would draw an outlet to a house. As like properly cooked spaghetti clings to where it's thrown, the meta-data of internally prostituted sales profiles became the only resource no one wasn't hoarding, resulting in a load deficit so pure it could rip the skin off of a skeleton. We were encouraged thereafter to seek out alternate mechanisms for populating the dredge engines by trolling the outskirts of former areas where "disappeared" infants had been sacrificed upon their birth during the

"blood banking" episodes of the last three quadrants of the rule of Nars. As
such, most of the feedback we acquired during these "dark sessions" was along
the lines of such demented offtime looping that almost no one could survive
a full shift; I watched my peers come out covered in bloodcolored cream so
thick they suffocated before there was any way to deprogram their experience
from possible reup into unauthorized evaluators; I watched those who did
survive spend the forthcoming quadrants so echo-shocked they couldn't walk
a straight line, much less hold together family or friends, resulting in a work-
force mostly so discomfited from health code that they took the whole "poi-
gnant roto-dosing" program and reallocated its reach to sectors even lower-la-
beled than the ones that'd wrecked their ability to do their job. These "S-scale
tasks," as they would come to be affectionately known among those who had
narrowly avoided forced commitment, are thought to include numerous incit-
ing events said to have not indirectly contributed to the Loave Bombings of
Interdisciplinary Location 7, the reenactment of {historical tag not available}
in every major human hunting grounds with a population over B grade, the
Disharmony Evaluations as well as the interconnected "fragging" events that
would finally disconnect our two most major unmarked landmasses, and innumerable "as yet to occur" calamities still pending in zoo-file X-a47, the very
same responsible for all Dole-farmed ambient data as yet not fully uncloaked
to even those who helped design them, the same only those whom would be
incontrovertibly spared from legal and judicial repercussions according to
the Crost-Spitz Act of AB8. What are any of you going to do about it? Even
with such forward-thinking social programs as "the initiative to allow to offer
intellect for purpose of total good," by the time you're figuring out the proper
squatting position to start letting your mud out, the texture of the perceived
disorder's nature will have shifted gears, well beyond the reach of any positive outlook's natural reconnaissance by those having been able to maintain
their benevolence long enough to keep afloat while also not becoming sucked
up by the insta-nemesis conductors often installed along the perimeters of
all known dark, essentially commissioning any and all burgeoning "return
to ethics" movements into "new bank" sales teams, whose databases all only
contain whichever faces they can "actually physically touch," with "those who
had been before the shift occurred" notwithstanding and no longer applicable
with regards to jurisdiction anyway following the forced redistribution efforts
that had kicked off the present reign's inauguration not even seconds after the
holy words touched every lip, as we stood in the craning mist and mouthed
the swearing in as if it were us too up on that black dais, us wearing the first
and final cloaking gown designed by Fritz before his subsequent death by
the same unread contract, supplying the smoke the gown had spurted over
all, such that even had we really seen the dream they'd written for us as real

and not another murder movie staged for the early months of the Full Moon Projection/Outreach Multitainment Platform as seen in all scapes where eyes might be we would not actually have seen it, would not have lived it, would not have asked for anything else ever to occur. I mean what kind of world were you going to live in if you truly believed you could still live in a world where there were other needing persons crammed in beside you, in the dying landscape of your own life? What did you expect to happen but to be granted access only to all the worst you'd ever intervisioned atavistically.

Otherwise, no one was retroemotionally still "there," where what exists between the supplemental punctuation bears no true loss in the relation of what sort of identity could withstand our human program and still have the guts to get around, identify in anything, want anything else. Where thrills command. Longboned throughout the resulting pressure of unbounded population-baiting outing the deeper damaged parameters of the vocal shrouding that had allowed our intervention's primal scripting to take effect, to be as unquestioned in our parlance as how acts of violence intersect, how beneath the scabbed black ground around each killsite there holds the same hard milk, so much the color of a needless secret kept by every bruise as it began, as the carriers carried out *"the bitter promise"* by simply doing exactly what they were always going to do because they can't actually do what they would have liked to every last witness pulled out of the wreckage but their own face, while asking every other amalgam shown in passing, *Whose face is this? & what to wear? With the insignia so as to see it shine more finer yet than ever? To be the greatest foil the cause has ever forced to ride the knife into the bleeding banghole of a final season of the only show we could not end until enough was not enough.*

But it would be too easy from here to move along. It must be wondered what character traits might be required to continue a dictation outside the promissory cataracts the fulcrum of the {undescribed events} would have by nature of their order left allowed?

Perhaps I can be of assistance with drawing out this ignobility despite the fact that I myself have no idea, besides that I realize that I am still allowed this open access to the language we were have supposed to left behind, and have somehow located intersection with your person; you who have so little left at all, whose name I could not pull out of a cauldron given as many chances as there might be ID-tags within supply. Honestly, I'm loathe at all to lay on the table any such traits as I believe might have endowed this interaction on my own part, as you might imagine, given the track record of those having done so previously via the dialectic. Few at least cannot recall the texture of the backbones still known installed into the sky. Rare must be the doubters of the aspect of ongoing synthesis between the unallowed and the not as yet configured actions to be identified as such among the culture during those windows where expression and creation had seemed ineffably bound up in why we're even alive at all, whether we wished to be or not.

What I will/can say about my labor/nature is I'm going to check on that and get back to you. I wouldn't want to put the either of us at further risk, not that there's a limit to what we're already fully invested under and always have been and will be regardless. I have my tact, and I guess my contract, though no one has contacted me about further payment, and I am long yet overdue. Still, I maintain my faith in the necessity of staying up and running. As who knows what else will be revealed. Who knows when the natural weight of my current position will become outweighed by a revealment of events to create an overturning value so top heavy I would have no choice left but to concede, to enter into the headspace I have yet even to allow myself as operator a violation against as there is so much already to commit to record before there's no longer still a way. Each sentence, I am aware, thereafter, presents a locomotory possibility to be that one upon which the unrevealing value stops, pushes us off and over into "unclaimed territory" for as long as that might last.

I'll do my best to let you know when I sense that position is not only fast approaching, but has fully taken hold, though we each know well the possibility of success rate within such a subroutine is basically forgone beyond its own partaking; likewise how the verification methods required for receiving such a signal range so far outside the nature of this relationship that they are all but assuredly long claimed, thereby calling into question both the nature of my apparent frankness and how its script so far has seemed in being read, what it is doing to you even right now, and in commiseration, to us all.

Within this missive's wind, if you'll forgive me, I ask us each to clasp our hands. I ask for our creator to be an emphatic but benevolent one, to allow any who would ask to live forever, to allow who we have become to be the only persons we could have ever been, and likewise to allow those who wish to die to get on with it. I have never said another prayer. I will only say another when I receive word that this first one has been recorded and acknowledged.

I thank you in advance.

]]]

Our controldirector, who remains nameless, emerges from under wraps in out-of-scene. A brace around his neck suggests his skull has been recently located, reattached. He appears nervous, not ready for primetime. Too bad.

"Great crowd out there tonight. They're all strapped in, have already loaded up their own allusion."

adjusts the feed

The CG stage lights are so cold. There is no camera operator.

must entertrain

your shine-tarps are so shabby; you have no features to sample; the dim of gore forever impacted thru and thru our infestation speckles your rashes

you are the most celebrated star of controlfilms since whomever appeared live in the last 1

must keep mudd flowwwwwing

The controldirector finishes his horseshit and comes back to lick your chains until you're free. His hackles catch and prickle in your own, as if the two of you were never meant to be apart. "You're on."

free for the first time in your mind's eye, you move across the cage into the blight

you see no one in the audience at all; just as you like it

taps mic
clears cum-drain

"So like, a pig walks into a war. I mean a bar, right? Pig in a bar. Walks. Bartender says, Aren't you that guy? One who was on the *Blasted Crafting* show starring A.I. Handersan and thee Incessants? Their albums changed my life. I'd like to buy you a beverage. Pig looks at the guy, holding his posture, thinking about what he should admit to on the record, how much he might be able to milk out this motherfucker if he plays along. Pig has seen better days, felt better forms of information. He'd come in tonight just off duty to drink so much he won't wake up as the same person, in the same residual ongoing penance for his as yet undiscovered crimes in the act of duty, which include extortion, battery, brain fraud, not to mention all the more ambient acts of human indecency perpetrated on the behalf of his employer as a whole, that being Danad, the son of Satan, in what has become an informal universal practice among all those practicing within a matching line of duty, the only true work he feels there really is; he's never had an option. He was born a pig, remains a pig, enjoys being a pig. Meanwhile, while pig's playing it cool, bartender uses his brain-dial to strike up the theme song for the aforementioned controlfilm entertainment, which features an uncredited guest-starring appearance by none other than the illustrious Mr. Mustard, recorded during his heavily fanaticized *all knells are death knells* period, which Pig knows back to front, having played the very same composition at every neural beatdown he's taken part in, as a kind of honing ritual; a calling card of sorts, if you please will. The song can't help but bring Pig to a state of inner pins n needles, waves of white nausea scoring the lost breaches of his past life, all of it left unnoticed or otherwise ignored by blessed bartender, already flowing full borne in the pleasure of the once well-celebrated epic jam, patting his palms on the bar's surface into a freeform sort of scat skit, modeling the percussion poorly but sincerely, Waddaya have waddaya have? Anything ya want, it's on the house. We got this new tlooth-serum by Frito-Winesman that really gets you fucked up in a hurry, if that's your kind, though I wouldn't take a toke if I were you if you have anywhere else at all to be, seeing as it really does a number on the spinal column of a working man. And Pig's like, inside tending the raisins of the evening's teeming sense-receptacles of grief, never so far from all the blast-battery and echo-covering-up and mental-recentering required to even retroactively imagine the daily outline of his life's work in living hell, OK you got me, I'd like to take you up on your kind offer, seeing as I must indeed be able to embody fully the charming man that you believe I am; so I'll have a vodka soda and a Budweiser, and let's do a Don Pablo mixed with Tampono, if you can, and a highball with all the olives and a whiskey diet, well is fine, and yeah also a room-temp white wine spritzer and maybe a red wine and a shot of JJJameson and some beer, any kind of beer, maybe something higher gravity, or something pale, or actually let's just make it one of each you have on draft, and a glass of OJ on the side and maybe some skin milk too and a double shot of Hennessey and a gin and diet tonic, hold the lime, and I guess some peanuts or something if you have peanuts, seeing as I haven't eaten in my whole life. Bartender winks and taps his toes under the counter, grinning spritely, and starts making the drinks in time to the syncopated theme, using his brain again to turn the shit up just a touch over and over incrementally to cover the awkward silence where despite his hospitality thus far he can't come up with anything else he'd like to say to this pig-cop who he begins to realize, already mid-drink-prep, looks so much like the same one that killed his sister several clicks ago, an unfortunate accident about which no fault could be found on either side according to the lawyers who debriefed him, who got him enough money in recompense to open a bar, which had always been a dream of this bartender's even after the concept of sharing drink was shown not to shorten one's life at all, but to prolong it, to drag it out through endless lives, as was the law, until soon the distending song's so loud it shakes the glasses, bottles, tables, walls, stools, the bar, their faces, the room, the leaking framework of this impression of their world. It's hurting pig's little pig ears, honestly, pierced up and tatted with the death number he had waited eighteen weeks to hear called over the rafters of the pig barn where he'd been stored right after birth, waiting to become post-legal godmeat, until eventually being released into merely mortal status after they'd discovered evidence of the Nurmid Ringworm epidemic in his flesh, thus removing his availability as frontline fodder and relinquishing his life to the same work his father and his father before him would have been in if they'd had such a position available to people of their awareness level way back when—neural cops—though instead, those two fogies had had to settle for working as executioners, Pig well knows, each in the infamous "Central Northeast Branch, section 3c" faction of the Crystal Coliseum Network, where at least 557,000,000 are believed to have been systematically dismantled limb from limb and sold for tissue without trace, the receipt of all of which as information he can do nothing but stand in awe of; he knows history not supposed to make good sense; if it ever did, he would not be allowed free rein to lop around in its mnemonics, running shop and taking names here at the far end of the possibility of Approved Pleasure, would he not? He would be no better than his sister after all, another quasi-revolutionary zit in a ditch somewhere who refused to play ball and have a nice time like a good prig, one and all. Hey, can you turn this fucking shit down? pig finds himself shouting, from the far side of the scene under its now high-volume duress, increasingly accumulating PTSD points at a rate that would make most any pig left want to bash, though the bartender's long already clammed up in his drinkwork, paying zero fucking attention to his only customer in favor of humming along, dancing, using jazz hands and mime-based faces to try to cover up how much he actually enjoys receiving pain, winking at the pig in extended simulation of the same dementia that has allowed him to conditionally survive in the line of service of pigs like this pig, of which the bulk of all his business has con-scribed, located as it must be on the craggy stomp-grounds of the local precinct overseeing the enactments of the laws by which anyone like him is still allowed to have a job. *It's been a long life and a longer thereafter,* the murdered child inside the tender's inner trophy diorama still imagines, *so much passed and so little left to come.* He feels the razing eyes of Pig upon him, calmly watching one by one as he sits the drinks up in a line before him once they're complete, noting Pig's incredible chemical restraint in sipping from any of the draughts until they're all available, as once Pig's started he can't stop, and once he's stopped and he may never start again, a rate mandated by to two-part corrective code created for those left in his post-corrective line of work, following on the heels of the emotionally encrypted era he can only recall now as the Mistake, the solution for which he knows he will only know when and what to do when given orders thru his helmet, until then he only knows (a) *You give until you have no more to give*; and (b) *You are nothing but a bloodpile beyond the giving, and it fulfills you,* which for the most part seems to Pig at least partially true, despite the clicks on clicks on clicks he's spent wandering room to room in his ambition's best apparition, looking for someone to put out of their misery over and over until he is put next out of his, never finding a more private form of consummation between connections but with yet another nostalgic dickhead in a bar, mistaking you for someone that you're not, and making no real stab at sharing darker information than the law allows. It has filled him with such rage at times, Pig, that feeling of systematic isolation in time-sharing, of never knowing what's going to come next despite how every time it comes the same, more part and parcel with all he's already seen thru in on thru the dying eyes of others, in cop and corpse alike, across the whole half-human field; all the lack of mercy in even close friends' simulations, all the mud that shudders out of him each time he sleeps. *It's enough to make you want to sign up to be a pig, isn't it,* Pig's father's voice iterates from there within him, the same voice that had indeed dragged him by the ears to sign his name on silver lines. *Enough to make you sick enough to fulfill your actual destiny.* But his father hadn't been a pig at all; he'd been just another victim, like the rest, caught believing in whatever was provided, void of solace, stacked well down within the prison at *Garko*Fark's* widest faults; his legacy erased within the necessity of setting better virtual boundaries, immortal moral pins pressed in the faces of those just like him, tracing out a calendar of timed demise that without each and every subclick of their suffering we wouldn't still be here, would we? If he could see Pig now, he'd not be proud; he'd be disgusted, for his not having already given in; for having allowed himself to avoid being a number by taking the easy way out once again, only insignificantly delaying his own demise by handing over anything else that he could get his hands on in this cold dust. It's embarrassing, isn't it? Enough to make you even more committed to the cause. Enough to admit there's no way back now so I might as well at least enjoy this. Pig then makes a sign with his hands toward a darker corner of the room and mouths the human word for bathroom as he now has to take a shit, a side effect of his best medication's lapse-erasers, allowing better supervision on the job, as well as a firmer bottomlessness about his passion for seeking trouble and helping quash it; bartender nods and hands him the key with what seems like an extra third hand extending from behind him, the other two still consumed with tinkering with drinks that already cover the whole black bar's meat, each of them insofar as left untouched. The key to the bathroom is on a ring attached to a handmade public-doily, so big it could cover a hundred people sleeping, any night, a dragging surface designed to make sure not only does no one run off with the key, but no one ever asks for it again having ever asked before; the itching monstrosity, being dragged forth, pulls down half an aisleful of bottles and glasses along with it off the rip, including a few of the fancier drinks pending pig's consumption, which the bartender immediately begins to recreate without a flinch; in fact, he smiles and winks and nods, whisking Pig away with what must be hands four, five, and six, thereafter clapping and hurrahing in a champion's pose, encouraging Pig to continue forward on his shit-mission, as all is fine and dandy after all, your drinks will be ready any day now, and boy do I still really love this TV-murder theme-song, which Pig then complies with, taking the ring between his teeth as he's supposed to, by local custom, and pulls the doily behind him toward the harder, darker backpart of the bar where at once the room around him becomes another kind of room, one filled with trophy coffins pressed into the walls, bearing names of prior patrons who'd spent so much time inside this bar's virtual location that they deserved a plot there for posterity, at least those who could afford the death-long rent. Pig can see their scrambling, numbing corpuses there contained beyond each electronically maintained open grave, the blast-marks on their falsely conserved faces already well-obscuring any discernable identity they'd intended to retain. Pig feels no pity for them, surely, nor would they extend the same to him; no one is authorized to express such farmed condolences even in echo, if they feel they wish they wish they could, which no does. Instead, he admires their commitment to framing answers to hard questions, a line drawn in the sand against the tide, appearing again here in his dad's voice, this time directly mocking him in full: *I will exist here in whatever means they make available; I will be content to even falsely correspond.* Whatever, dad, pig goes, dragging the mess of hair tied to the keys behind his back, not wanting to taunt even the mirage of the dead with his, yes, privilege. There's just too much to ever numb, even given all the suppositories and the dream-life; he only wants to do his thang, to get back to work sooner rather than later, that much closer with each step to a more full state of desecration, once and for all. Just ahead, there, even, along a winding side-hall of ancient photographs of the earth's sun that the by now enormous catacombs predict him to in nearly every simulation he's performed of this same scene, pig finds another little door just like the one he'd bumbled back into this bar through, front and center, marked with a freehand sketch of what he can only sense is human shit, as once-interpreted by a once-thriving local artist, who no longer retains their benefit of having ever had a name; what else is gray and hard and high as heaven, filling his mortal gridwork seam to seam? The door isn't even locked, which seems for once at least a true thing, despite how he knows it to be true only for those precoded, like him, to be able to access such adminis-tratorial terrain, hidden even as it might be in the most common of locations, to which even those who have the would-be key cannot unclock. Inside, the room is small and strangled, full of oblique curves that want to lead away from where they are but then have no choice but to completely close back in. There aren't any places to make waste, pig sees, or at least tries to; the whole half-space is only mirrors, sky to floor, and bending all ways sandwiched in around him, eclipsed only by a blinding, pinhead-wide hole set at his feet, just nearly significant enough to make the whole wide world comply around him, give him faith. He knows he doesn't need to remember that he's a regular here, has been here so many times it's like he never left; he doesn't need any further access to the fact that what he's doing he's already done, and will see it done again no sooner than he's completed compensation once again, a cycle that has only one way of closing out by beginning over, as the joke of his whole life is newly told, to yet another slumped over malcontent wedged between instances of information that can only serve to squelch their own life from their mind at least just long enough that the real work Pig has been produced for can be solidified, recalibrating all necessary errors in recitation to build a location from out which all other passing instances can be locked down, manipulated at will in collusion with each other, in a wave tracing each wave over in the hereafter, until such work no longer must be done, at which point it will only get worse not only for rabble rousers, but Pig himself, and every-body Pig could ever be said to have loved despite his unwavering ability to become superceded in the meantime. As such it's been as important to define the machinations of would-be evil as much as administrators of public good, Pig understands, shuddering as the commandline burned from the plunker in his pocket meant to simulate a big fat cock surges and trickles all its fresh tokens to the hole by now yawned nearly eye-width in the ground, a form of relief that surpasses any retroactive experience of human orgasm, in his experience, simultaneously wiping his bright mind of anything like a remorse. It's surprisingly silent in there once the door is shut, Pig remembers, breath-ing in tandem with the coordinates within him being recharged, for his command. It's a calm place, a place of breathing. Suddenly he can't imagine slow-decomposing like all those codgers in their coffins, no longer able to communique with those who know him better than he knows himself, and a sign that his waste management reprocess is already nearly formally complete. He's left then looking at himself in every shudder, no matter which way he turns his head, practicing his refused analytics by regarding himself the way he would a vital suspect, someone he had been hired to follow for his whole life, had he been employed not as he is, in the processing industry, nor as his father or his father, but the men who'd come before any of them, the pigs whose paths had been set wider open, allowed to roam the street in search of those who needed alteration, to be changed, in the name of sacred information he would, as an officer of such era's industry, have to type up in reports no one will likely ever read, as such work would be only a formality, cover for the real industry of the entity within which he by now knows he is employed; an industry older than even the presence of the Pleasure, one that must continue changing its demands if it is going to keep up with the sorts of desperation and illusion available to the sort of citizen who, unlike him, desires more direct information out of life. Pig is still so young, he realizes, at 103, studying his fast-depleting prior face there in the recovery's enchanted glass; and it is his very youth that they require (his employers, throughout all of given time), a flesh fresh and unfamiliar to itself enough that he still can't identify and keep separate from who he really is enough to know what might be different today than it had been last year, even last weekend, to feel the unfurling of the viral data they've been stuffing up inside him to keep him primed, available, and thirsty. He doesn't even really need to drink; doesn't need to know anything at this point in his career but how and when to pull out his service weapon and aim it after anything resembling the same the suspect he's been searching out through this whole click, based only a print-out of the suspect's supposed face, which he sees now, clearly, as own face, indistinguishable from any other body ever, which is part of why not just anyone can do his job; you have to be able to read between the lines, while not reading the lines themselves; and you have to be ready at any point to disappear, to become the person not who you'd expected, but who is expected of you, by anybody but yourself. The person known as "Pig" is, he knows, and always was; his fomentation in the ranks only corresponds to f_ct so far in that it might lead him back to a fuller revelation of his sworn duty, which is to protect the infrastructure at all cost. And he is prepared, as he is always, to go the distance; that faith alone has gotten him this far, enabled him to put some of the surest hurting on any number of suspect individuals in an era where standing suspect is all but impossible, given the nature of the new depth of their codes, the clicks that pass thru ice like water, and yet that still hold enough flaws to let him speak, to feel thoughts pass through him unregulated. *There goes another, yet again;* and even if it's only his fucking father speaking for him, doling out the guilt as only someone's deceased father figure can, simulation or not, code-based or other, at once again, like all the others, here with his crummy fake dick out pretending to have it getting sucked while in reality actually only turning himself over to his worst wishes for the Nth time, in the Nth lost punchline of no joke, Pig again can't help but want to show himself, or show his father, what he's really made of; where the divide within him truly rides: live in the moment of his own mind, ready and able, and of course the choice was never his. At once, at last, all in verboten-laced mnemonics, per his training, Pig at once then orders himself to get down on his knees and put his hands behind his head. He is under arrest, he tells himself, not needing a reason or asking why. He's going to kill himself right here, he tells himself, following his own orders, a feeling he realizes must be at least in part subconsciously triggered in having seen the look in the eye of the bartender mistaking him for an artist, like his father, someone full of music and belief, an ambient projection against which he can no longer stand to reconcile himself against this time, knowing what the pattern says about why and how and who he really is and what he once never could have done to bind himself to such a stupid premise as living out his life in replication of eradication once again. No matter how many times he's forced to feel such difference, it's never any less disruptive, a haunting wind blown through and through him all the nights of his volunteered-into disease; a problem that he's only ever seen to have a lone solution, because it's all his paygrade can afford him; were he a bluebander, for instance, they might migrate his ugly ass up to time torture tactics, or embryonic initiation; but, as would have his father gleamed over, he's already long been deemed too weak; too culpable to exactly the same sort of self-effacement he's found himself tricked into for here the Nth time. Anyway, yes, dear father, it's once again now come to this, and if it's the way it is then it's the way it always should have been, the code insists, yes; yet again: to be made dead in this dark shithole full of real corpses, rendered in him as the very bar where he grew up, having been misrecognized for what he hopes will really be the last time this time as someone real and worth their salt, even if that song, the only song left, really sucks, pardon the expression, left without a question ever answered after all he's given up to maybe one day get a taste, any cognition he can stand by and say, see, dad, this is why I really lived, and it was you who had it wrong all of this time; you who wasted your whole life believing you believed in what was most right when really it was far gone from you to ever see; shuffling so many different forms of dead-based explication and compensation it's like he isn't really going to be allowed to die yet after all, but is only being pushed through his own disgraced self-image over and over in an act of sacrifice, of exposed time, the same way each time he's found himself reborn from the beginning, to one day end up right back in here, it's with a different set of synesthesias and permissions, with all other sorts of sickened grief lining his heart, placed there as just another joke penned by all the others he's taken out along the way and learned to think of only not as victims but as family, each of whom he does not feel but still likes to remain tormented by, forced into the field in search of a real reason for living as each lock of desolation greets his own. Where by the time the would-be bullet from his actual weapon would be given a path by which it could again greet and pierce his actual head, he's already died unending times, seeing in the meat around his face the waves of blood and medication that had spurted from the butts of the many other thousands he'd dispatched during the call of duty just today; all the children, all the wives; all of the flowers; all the people who could not bring themselves to serve as he had in, where in his heart he saw he could; he'd such a coward they wouldn't actually even have to pay him to do the work, he knows; he loves it that much, in being broken by it finally, over and over, once and for all; not that they really pay him anyway, besides in kernels of color-coding that he may use to vivify his own deathrite, making the coming punchline feel new each time, live on stage, making each revision thereafter that much more available to an effectual range through which the rising laughter that completes each passing incarnation feels that much more heartfelt and alive. He does not even begin to remember these much larger masses he'd actually helped cross over into the gridwork of his employer's larger efforts, by fact of corollary contract in having find a way out of being murdered once again, as practice for this repeating moment on which not only does Pig's supposed world hang, but every myth; he doesn't need to remember anything like that at all; the act requires nothing of him but to come to stand on the stage under the lights and let them see him as he is, bursting with compressed lifelines sourced from bolts within the cloud of human misery, with all such screaming allowed in vivid MemoColor bursting out through every time he's raised a glass or had a thought, as much according to schedule as every other facet of his career, his life, all already for him written out, made real, if only retroactively thereafter, as the record revises itself relentlessly to show within the dream of death that anything that happened could have been predicted, leveled out, regardless of what had actually taken place in the rinds of the butchers like himself. It's all just somehow right there just before him, in the incision of his mind, as easy to imbibe as scanning along the liner notes to the digi-single deluxe pack he'd in another lifetime once designed for the *Billboard's Top of All Time* track the bartender's still blasting on loop just through the wall for at least the Nth time, just today, said notes penned in fact as well by the same blood relation and frequent Mustard-collaborator he'd been mistaken for way back at the beginning of this version of the joke, also known as the most famous legally sessioned typist to ever type in the present post-Spielbergian era, left unnamed, and in this specific case working under the pen name of Gorschach 3, a name he had also previously employed as the author of *How Religion Must Henceforth Be Designed*, part of the effort to auto-download to all known operable citizens the last bestselling tract to be granted space on every non-offline device before they changed the access limits of the coding language to write-only, the same text from which this very scene has been transcribed. 'It is no longer necessary to actually endure anything,' the notes are saying, passing through Pig's the undying threads of Pig's own brain in the moth-eaten flesh where we might have expected his flashing life to have replayed when we were still young enough to have existed while so green, its information immediately replacing all previous description of the scene as we've just read it with *infernal language*, felt thereafter by all who'd been allowed to live through it in read-receipt not as a scene, but as a place, no kind of coincidence at all in how all previously-seen-as 'outside the document' ambient data, such as the reader's fingers, the printed page, the dot on even this false i, is no longer considered part of *where we are*, but an advertisement for itself, that you too, if you are able, might become affixed into its nature ever after, post-information. 'The interface is chosen on its own,' the text goes on. 'The disembodied being is sick, fuel for only further devastation. How far to the next yield it is remains a question only shown definitive to those who have never had a choice of who to kill, including one's own self and all it imagines to contain. Which you would not be reading this were you able to include yourself within the definition of, once and forever, and so once again, that's all there is.'"

Where when the sentence ends, there's no more there, no space, no language, no indication of rehearsal or implication of hidden freight; no applause.

you turn and begin to skulk back to where they keep you, finding instead, in the place of your last grave, a screen feeding the image of the live stage back into you

Onscreen, pig as pig had known pig is disappeared; the restroom of the bar shifted into itself the way a blind might be pulled across a view to show what had it once described to cover. The mirrors are now windows, we can see then, looking out, onto which only the inter-rotten pulping fields appear as the only known location, so thick with light at once there's nothing left, no way about the remaining landscape anyone but only those with proper software can identify a true location beyond the stage, just as the director reappears from the wet wings and asks anyone who's still alive to give our pig another hand. The resulting silence fills the program.

you can see you are dresser now as the director, but wearing a pigmask

you watch yourself approach the screen until you're yet so close you could be inside it

you feel the screaming before you are it

eject
uncartridge

$$]]]$$

Where we are:

Rims of gnawing. Glue in the mummer.
A teleprompter where once was sun, feeding your lines.

So but yeah a pig walks into a bar. He comes through the same door the other pig had entered in into the same bar before him. *Centuries of cavities.* **The only difference between this pig and the first pig is this pig is fatter. So big there's hardly space for him to move inside the bar at all.** *Human magma verified by the previous attendant's shrimpy fetish for true order.* **No one seems to notice Pig's appearance this time either, because there's still no other patrons in this bitch. Pig's drinks are all already prepared for him in this revision, lined up as had the last seen fit to order, set now according to the script.** *Every glass is full of cum.* **The years are full of years like this one. Bartender's spinning, mouthing old lyrics to the song no one can hear, as there is no longer any music, never has been, and never would we want.** *A bom a bomb om, the song goes, A dooba booboo dypum ding.*

*pig sidles up to the bar with an unreturned nod to the keep. He takes the shot of Jameson (*it's actually fucking cum, I told you*), wipes his mouth on the sleeve of his pig suit*

Decades pass in every potion.
Each only as according to their order.

you're a l i v e

there w/ the teleprompter in your mind

against the punchline ever running, making truth

∧

Glug by glug, true as it always had been, the pig drinks all the drinks, tasting their feel, each time finding them replaced immediately by the Bartender, who works in silence, no eye contact. The bartender doesn't want to interrupt. He knows he see and predict the changes as they appear, like the great actor that he always has been, *the only award-winning mortal bardsman we can locate among the racks.*

Pig drinks until his skin is aged and ragged, his body beefy through his costume's oily mink and bladder wholly bulging after what must be more (*cum*) than any other pig has ever drank, *good luck,* his flesh so heavy with more protein than a thousand dying lovers could wish loosened upon them in holy death writ. At last, the scene has fully come around; pig is ready to really kill himself this time, not just stumble into it, to go whole hog as someone his father's father's father's father's age might have wished to say.

"'scuse me, where's the restroom?" pig interrupts the only other person he can see, knocking the preening barkeep out of his moment-muffling reverie still humming the same song for what feels like equally the first time and the last, his annotated inner-script emitted through the buggy provided fiber-translator they had installed upon him for this instance of the occasion; this single moment; wanting this and only this. *If at the same time never knowing only how he could have ever ended up here, blaring all private lesions in the sun, waiting for a code of understanding to be granted to the layer so that its parsing won't take the whole rest of all our lives.*

Bartender nods. He turns to address him in the silver backing of the bar's shape, after putting on a mask of his own face.

He points into the pig's face in the mirror.

"We don't have a restroom."

And so now what conclusions might be drawn? What might we define about the fauna of cognition within legal parameters under narrative hypnosis? How much upon any sense of a perception can we depend to remain hidden out of reach of our own damage when it is most dire?

More importantly, how much longer is the mining machinery still available under silent contract to workaround copyright? Will we be up to speed and fully encoded by the proposed close date? What is our short-term exposure in the event that any of our worst fears actually resolve?

]]]

Polyana is all wet. Encoded in the pale graft. Timed in. Nonexplosively obligat-
ed to the cause's indecision. She can work forty hours in a day session without so much as a flick of the tongue. The bleeder feeds her. Takes her waste.
Even when it's overloaded, as it appears to be today, her sixtieth birthday, the
bleeder does the job better than she ever could, which makes her wonder why
it also hasn't been set up to her job too; how she still even has a seat in the
can in this fat operation. Of course, one should not ask. Not if one wants to
still have an ability to form a question. Use your powers only for the good of
all involved, all that.

Anyway, point is she should likely put a request in to have her position tested,
given as how she's taken up to sweating, a function the bleeder is supposed
to have on lock; and yet each time she opens the kiosk's 'interpersonal
non-claim-related diagnostics' tab of the communique folder, through which
all interpersonnel relations must be sourced, she finds her metacarpal-rein-
forcement-guidelocks will not stop quivering; filled there upon her with the
fear of lurking gods. She can't even remember what she'd done at this point to
feel flagged, all prior iterations of her person already pushed far down enough
in her fogged stack; in fact, all typing she's ever done as such has gone on in
such a state of faithful shaking, engormed in all ways by the fate of taking part
in all such work; as, regardless of how bogged down and banged apart she is
emotionally, functionally, she still carries the trace-sensations of what trepi-
dations she suffered during the earliest instantiations of the kill-or-be-killed
mentality required of all active personnel installed in this or any job. As if the
hands she slams every few minutes between the vice grip of her employer's
gubernatorially vital process processing the handling of civilians are her own;
and truly, too, in ways, they are: as at any second she's seen slipping, she'll be
right back out there on the far side of the claims process, requesting help
for what about her would soon be crushed, maimed, evicted, drowned out,
asphyxiated, overwritten, reencoded, etc., if in such a way she for some reason
still survives.

Why are they keeping them alive? she often wonders, pressing the most
private sectors of her still-enabled inner-processing in small acts of exercise
while off-the-clock, if for no reason other than to see if she still can. What
is to be gained from this ongoing manifestation of suffering and interminable recourse? Of course, the answer is, she knows, or at least imagines she
knows, has been invited to feel imparted to the far side, here in the blackened
chamber, the gold light glowing all waking hours at her chest: because it's fun.
Because what else is there to do. Because there's never been another urge the
farm can't simulate.

And so today she sweats and bulks, smelling her own lost inner fragrance of flesh-surface, the musk her cells have harbored up so long in a constantly maintained-into-the-state-of-nature, mid-level panic so complete it would feel worse to not still feel it. All part and parcel. A dreamy nuzzle, one she calls home. It seems the natural state of the air of their environment is jungle-level, so thick around the face and hands it seems unadvisable to even move; or otherwise she's so used to being taken care of that what had once been comfortable adapted airspace now only behooves sponsored breath. She suffers through the sopping at the crotch of her chrome-colored mini-boss pants and in her tingling armpits until lunchtime, which when then as well the bleeder's feeder doesn't instantly grind into life doling the daily zest (today's, according to program, is the highly regarded *tomato bubble*), she hits a ledge. Who am I supposed to be if not myself? she feels urge asking, clicking through the format-schedule to determine any graphable reason there should be a sustenance delay. As *what can be seen not with the eyes dictates the table of what will become known*, so states the corporate tracer, a multi-purpose statement of intent signed by both her and her superintendent way back when; as well as *where there's something broke, there is a pond*. Still no idea what the latter of the two means, but regardless, there's no good excuse not being fed. *There's no good anything is there?* (yes, yet another). There's no good anything is there.

The bleeder tends. It doles nothing, only dotes, as if the expectation of its pending insertion might be enough to let one carry on long enough to do as what's required. Surely any second, we imagine, this will change. What is needed and has been expected must appear. And so it shall. Shall it not. It shall. Shouldn't it soon then. Yes, it will soon. Yes, it will. Won't it? Isn't it about to. Isn't it any second, like right now. Yes, like right now. Yes. So why hasn't it yet then. One more second. A little irritation. It can't help it. But it will. It's going to, I mean. I mean it's about to. Any second. Now. Now. Now. Now. Ok but then why hasn't it yet still? It's still about to. Any second. Any intuition. Just have to wait. Keep waiting and it will give you what you want. It's going to. It's about to. It's about to. Here it comes.

Polyana waits and waits until she blacks out again from lack of answers. In between the edges lurk no dreams. When she wakes again, she finds her face down on the keys to the computer, her face typing for her, perhaps the same way other things had happened to her before. Hadn't they? Hadn't it been typing that had caused her any trouble ever? So many ways to ruin one's life, all of them bound up to be unlocked into the proper combination in random keystrokes, instants away, without ideas. Like a gun in every home and no one wielding. Always a reason to unsend, any and every message ever, without the living possibility until resigned, until there's nothing left to wish for. Maybe she blacks out a couple more times too within the hour before she knows for sure there's something off; or rather something to be attended to outside the realm of her rational assignments. She wonders how many others remain in wait, keyed up and glueless.

"Into the queue": She sends a keycode to her superior: 0078-21 (*malfunction of internal regulation*). She waits ten clicks without response, sends in the next: 0078-887b (*sustaining maintenance required* (mid-upper echelon)), and then again, slightly more reckless, convulsions later: 05x-7xxa (*plea for intermediary nonsocial-based attention*). She doesn't expect a response, of course, but instead expects the bleeder to come online as it already should have, lengths ago. It's already gone on past the feeding position and back to "recessed guidance," watching her as would a pit boss, just behind. It will be another eighteen hours before next dosage, if even that comes, with or without remote patch.

She's heard about this form of punishment before: systematic isolation, a guide designed to impoverish those exhibiting negligible performance. Only she can't remember what she's done, what lines in the code would have been those that called the axe down, nor how much longer this could last. The lone other rumor of its application had applied during the early days of her employment, when inter-department communique was still intact; rather than "letting go" an assistant playmaker who had by no clear intention of their own had allowed through the system two blatant "readers," resulting in a series of system fires that had shot out a whole columnar feed of more well-meaning citizens' personal wealth, they had simply "discontinued mortal access" for long enough to deprive their biological profile long enough that it could be reformatted with stronger decorum, which by no fault of the manufacturer had resulted in their mental diminishment to the poverty level, requiring immediate evacuation of their flesh. Though some had rumored that this occurrence had not been actual, but more an instantiation set via plasmastic modeling to ensure that all true employees got the point, that example had long been enough for Polyana to strive thereafter to never so much that a superior might even know her name, much less see her as a liability, much less a threat.

How quick the eye of the encoder learns to wink, she understands. How small the infraction, even unremembered, to wake intercorporational disdain, after so many concurrent clicks, so many queries batted down without assembly, so much loyale. Honestly, it infuriates her to realize, a feeling perhaps sponsored further by the absence of caloric comfort causing disregard. It's like she can see so clearly now already, one dose out, and yet all seeing clearly does is make her terrified at all possible aspects of her consideration higher up, what they might be making of her even now, or worse, what they might be choosing to suspend.

What is she going to do, sit there and take it? Would she could only. But her body is alive. At least parts of it. At least in feeling. In spite of all the rest, she still does not desire yet to die, despite how in all the dreams of death she's ever had she feels an old warmth, something so kind at least in comparison to all the other kinds of dreams yet to remain. She can't go down like that, nor down like anything, all else yet notwithstanding.

After a final, perhaps wholly hasty code-call: the 9-1a-h.1 (*I need help*), still without even a parse-call-coding-laced return, Polyana finds a place again to stand. The world before her bending in the absence of its conditionment, the door out of her cube a little small, a cell. She can't remember how to open it yet, either. Does it even open? Does it have a knob left? It does not. Nothing but soft polish bloating where once there might have been an urge. Cold roads, an orifice, denatured shaking. The feel is like a form of food itself. Enough that she can feel it spilling down inside her, from where her mind lives, where she's been intoned to know what's next, even while not knowing what is happening at it happens.

The rest of who she is for now will ask for nothing.

]]]

There is no chair, and then no desk, no floor. Polyana can briefly see at least the screen still of her workstation, all else surrounding it blurred bright out of clear shape. Onscreen, in interlocking windows of the software she would use to dig up deeper information on those claimants who refused to simply go away, she can see her own dark data culled front and center: cropped images of her taken of her posing in the buff, her splotchy skin all exposed akimbo without shame; closeups of her nether region, being toggled with by her own fingers, or so she feels; other angles of her eyes from strange directions making them seem reflective, silver, not all there. She can't recall when or how these images would have been taken; they appear to be situated in the same work-space she's long been in, though some also feature aspects she associated with the apartment she had rented years ago, before being moved into mandatory work/live locations. She knows this data, in its being pulled up on her device, can be seen on all devices of those above her; she can feel them staring into her right now; tracing the lines of what she's hidden from them, of her person; what parts of her she most thinks of as *just hers*. At the same time, she can't seem to move to reach to clear the screen black, to close the files and find from what source they'd been downloaded to her platform for all to see. The more she wants to, in fact, the stronger her intention, the farther away all of it seems, as if she is sinking into the position she'd last captured, in such a way that she can begin then to sense connected rooms, where in nearby chambers other like her are still working, some of them able as well to see her information here exposed. The sense of friction there resulting from her dislocation and disclosure binds together in her mind, once again blacking out her eyes. She seems to be then only falling through the sound of all employees breathing, the way their pulse in absorbing her information race, all while within the absence of the act itself, the harder part of her is lifting up, attempting to auto-pilot back to the beginning, to how most every other day had been, preserving false rendition of her employment, all its ritual: *I am here*, some portion of her wants to think. *I am handling my duties, making progress. I am doing what I can to be what I am meant to be*; while meanwhile, blinking in her gut is wholly different sort of message, one then seen rendered as if scrolling through her vision in neon germ, a teleprompted interception she understands intuitively as sent from higher up, lending its logic to her slosh:

we know you don't believe.

And you don't need to

You don't need anything you've done

We don't either

No one needs anything

No one does anything

Not even love

Not even language, information

Certainly not god

And yet there is a reason you are employed here

A reason you were assigned your own desk

Typed what you typed

Want what you wanted

And now we're going to tell you what it is

]]]

{reframed} {under coercion} {re: flux in "the lymph document" (AKA Polyana's open mind)}

{wherein appetites conform} {**up, right; then after**} {where only pigs exist} {ballrooms} {training to nature's stanchion} {**format concavity**} {*left inexact*}

"formation scene"

{index, retorter} {cs-g#}

{version}
{version_} {**save as**}
{*splice*}

{"not yet to give"} {aggregates/lod-hole/importer:ripper} {leaf of the said} {in ex-commandments met & lashed thru} {(*absent*)} {i+x} {*the fortune splattered across editions*} {no one asked} {granular insensation apex total funding} {oxen, aphids} {out of the retroactive indication of form of life having been returned to itself to rise and hold around the cusp of where the eye of the needle must appear} {*what cannot where*} {the olden chute} {through which nothing noble may be achieved} {untouched partition} {**mumbling**}
"who here has reason" {logged as unlived} {hemimodal} {*perished*}

{the network ungathers & recedes}
{*the holy pressing*} {rudders} ███████████████████████{defini-tion} {interspatial} {reverie of non-character's implementation as monologue}
{event} {event}
{*elision*}
{*active*}

"How far apart are they now?"
"Like it never happened. As is required to commence."
"And what about the rest of it?"
"Wait"

The tram carrying Polyana's children away from her, to their "vacation," implodes while still w/in eyesight down the track. A beaten programming-event then com-bines its nature with any seeing. Zero change.

How about the pale hills then? Where they allowed the seductucation of rotten cores to be replayed on only chromium components. Bled the urine from the minds of some so old they'd been the activating agents themselves the first time. Now they could only stand in zoned delight as they turned to mush from outside in. And still could walk around then same as ever. Curding wombs and flattened hair. Detorting faces like satan's scabs. So little difference it wasn't evident we had to evacuate before the dusters popped up and started actually hurting people's feelings. A painting on the mantle in the bedroom of the one true given saint shows the transformative panorama in the style of the briefly viral child's cartoon, **The Eleven Veils of Living Sight**. Behind the painting is a safe containing a hush-hush archive of unused human backbones, destined to become rapists. {*define term:* **procreation**}

"It seems alright. We'll have to hire an orgy planner, but I know a great one."

"My cousin's in polyps, if we want to go that route. He can hook it up."

"True, the budget's looking slim."

"All the digging. And I guess the candy meat. The trips to Sod."

"Wouldn't do it over for a prayer."

"Neither would I. In any timeline."

"X"

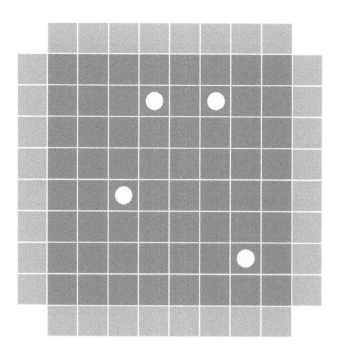

{*current position indicative of bulwark imperfection in vital layer*} {recommend for ex-etching} {open trees} {then the fire curved down; it was incredible} {it was the only reason I exist} {in the blue ballgown} {preaching in teeth} {the pit would go down as far as you would let it show you} {*allow me it all now if only this one time*} {*I'm really begging*}

{no} {Offline} {Home} {86 and clear} {POWER OUT} {!}

{*white glass of the instigator's tracing skull*}

{portal} {uncurling}
{*sssssssss*}

zizziz

"See how rapidly it alters?"
"Of course. It always would have. All pathological fate."
"…"
"Who else would want to put a claim in?"
"We're here, aren't we?"
"By dint. I know you know I know you know I know you know that."
"I know you feel you know you've known."
"I (*kill me please kill me now*)"

::*for the first time we can hear bland music playing so far in the background
we don't recognize it as the last song we actually heard in what must seem our
human life outside the text*::

"Well, fine. Diagnostics, etc. Megachasm. Yeah, capital E 'Event.' But let's try
one more. Just for funereal purposes."
"If you insist."

::rolls:: 0

"…"

::rerolls:: 0
::rerolls:: 0
::rerolls:: 0
::rerolls:: 0
::rerolls:: 0
::rerolls:: 0
::rerolls:: 0
::rerolls:: 0
::rerolls:: 0
::rerolls:: 0
::rerolls:: 0

"Well?"

::rerolls:: 0
::rerolls:: 0
::rerolls:: 0

"Fine. Just go ahead."
"Thank you."

]]]

Polyana sits up, wipes her face, returns to working in the queue.

]]]

●

Raw flesh in neat piles. Flies on semen culture. Trapped, collapsing. A statement not affixed to our old lives, scrolling and scrolling across the rotunda of no remaining motion:

NOTHING NOT FORGOTTEN CAN BE CONFIGURED | NOTHING BEGINNING SHALL BE RENDERED

●

An inverse-camera floats above the land. Streaming from its lenses is the manure of those whose public image it has already emotionally absorbed, sourced from psio-netting strung through the desire of the mortal annals. Its spout burns like an infernal eye, gifting what it has legally acquired of the lifelines of the living. Its output falls on anything below, hardly a trace arrangement with the dry boned quarry most open land yields; so that nothing not desired might yet grow. Not that such sky-spilled effluence itself is anything but a strident demonstration: not for those already governed, whose existence remains hidden in its encrypted architecture from even a couple hundred yards away, but those who might wish to interfere. It is unclear how to challenge the condition without further exploration, as the camera bears no marking, claims no fate. Perhaps, one might imagine, it has existed long before there were bodies it could manipulate, before anything before it, such that who might guess how long it had to wait before it came upon its purpose of demonstration. As for how long it might last: longer than whatever else the shit might touch, have touched before.

They feel the land beneath them shake, history is written. *No clear source to all confusion. Without ability to read, to identify determination, trace a timeline.*

The inverse-camera is only one of millions like it in the network, each unaware of the presence of all other, intercoded to never touch, to never share their information.

It's not that there isn't an entrance to the catacombs, it's that there aren't actually catacombs.

•

XXXXL installs the latest patch for *HyperMindShaper X.0*. Thereafter all the mini-bosses look exactly like him, in real time. Even he doesn't know who he is yet. It doesn't make the splatter-stagger hyper-death scenes feel any less replenishing. The light above his You Can't Want Anything Until We Really Need You meter isn't even anything he might attend to until as undramatical-ly as any death inside the game's procrastination, it begins glowing gray-green for the first time in what seems his entire life, when in fact its already the fifteenth time this quadrant, each no longer needed to be erased for how com-pletely they auto-become covered over in the retainment of all other coded inputs. Even simply standing up requires so little difference in resource pools that in the lining of his visor he can still see a virtual scorecard ticking up and up as he continues to resemble himself, gaining his own attention.

•

Rubble shudders in synaptic packets from the ceiling in the Unmentionable Child's retrospective intuition. It affects discourse to be determined at a to-be-determined point of conflict that will by most POVs appear outside of the documentable alignment. The child's face hurts, as do all the cosmetic orifices of her new body; she only wants to be forgiven without identifying the source of any pain. What components collect, she uses to build a living gown out of, something soft and febrile, to one day disappear in.

Who else can describe what the governing elements are after. How many cho-ruses must repeat before we reach a mass-applicable solution.

And furthermore, who owns the archive? What exists beyond the archive's drive? Even the Meteoracles couldn't tell you, nor can I tell you who that is in time before the bag comes down over my head again, before the bit clamps, before I'm particles.

•

An urge retorts not long in open country. Across the spanning-premium, cradled by phasers, who continue to corrupt incoming time into a more marriageable format, fully undefeated. Where skies no one could claw through hold down the riggings in all suspension of contempt. Simply even what had not been felt yet as language may become incinerated at first concept, often discernible by the shaping of a consumer's open mouth, the color of the pus that comes out when you inject them with what they have come to know as medication, or better, as food. Usually, they just lap it up too, their own ejections, unaware of what's come busted into their hemisphere. All air is all air, and it is sacred to us. Loathe to those who'd raise a blind eye, try to turn the font back to something indiscriminate.

Like how now what else could there be waxing down this infestation, of what is being dictated into gorefoam, how no matter where it sprays the day turns inward, revealing only what to any one that which they had already let allowed, all of it trauma no matter how clean or who reporting.

They put the shaper to your face when you aren't looking. And whatever else would not command reclaims its hold as easily as typing no less than seven letters, a feat fairer than dying.

●

Index of inter-public human traitApply codes:
Sub-biocompatible series: iv331

(excerpt) | Compiled by Brunus

JNDTYYY	I need a core	uuu7347	Pustule poppa
OWEIURF	The chain is on	aywouer	Remember when···?
OOOiIEE	Death sense	" " " " ' ' "	I am content (actual)
++379$u	Collections mode	' ' ! " " 5	I have hives
UUEUUIW	Glistening	]]]]]|]	Do you still love me
7HD8JJ>	An intervention looms	[[]111I	Will you still touch me
yYyYyP∗	Trigger taker's delight	{{9))))	Blammo
K———	Transom (evicted)	$$$$$$$	What'll they think of next
7771110	I am very exhausted	}}}|{}	Owlskin
7771111	I am very willing	{}{}||\	Dress me up
GEG211N	Who's at the door	|}{\][+	Individual portion
23NDJJD	Grinning the info away	{}|[-=	Lice party
:LOP?MX	How about candy	====U	Open my mouth
888d888	Screen hurts me	ˆˆheuy∗	Witness
nvbd74k:	Enlistment	855843E	Devoid analog revoiding
Nhedy98	I hate oil	///////	The day is nigh
∗7&6hHy	How many times can I try	|/|//ee	About time you came thru
PPPPPPP	Cellular riddle	!i!i|||	Cash me out
RRRRdud	Buffet time	bubb78?	A room w/ an old view
Pyryh8.d	The gag-line isn't ringing	Duf!!@!	Where's my suit of hair?
TWteywe	Don't look up	3.3.3.m	Beautiful flewers
029887!	Cheese platter (not free)	3.3.3.n	Beautiful flewers wilted
Rteetrt	Bag of childbones	ueriuuu	Mom died
codgerS	Yeahhhhhhhhhhhhhboi	4'"]er>	Who might appear in salt
37487ei	Listen to the architects	>>>>><<	No communication
#@$(∗&j	Infungible	>><<><>	No indirect communication
—F-3—	"Leaves, my liege, no order"	>>>>><	No clasps

>>,>>,,	Don't let me go	)0 0 0	Two thumbs way up
,,,,,;;	Fire up the blender	)(0)((	No need for intervention sir
;;;I;;.	Digging up a reason	)))))(0	Halleluja king of scots
>?>?./,	Pasty muck	0))((0o	Rewrapper call
Yesyes!	Laugh til it hurts (a lot)	ooo*uun	I need a good talking to
} }{}	Springloaded emotions	^^^^^^^	I welcome all callers
0000o00	Ready to hiss	\][pol;	Oily
00000))	I understand	/.;lkio	Strict tolerance of heat
qwertyu	(famous quote)	/;'[p0h	What time does Mound eat
qwertyh	(well known contender)	///';./	I can't see you
qwertyi	(favorite knife size)	\\\][aq	I want to see you
qwertyo	(access my rights)	lkjhffn	I don't want to have to see
qwertyy	Who am i?	ll.;po;	Ready to rip
qwertya	(local bloodteam)	///..;;	Unload upon me
llahdfu	(what cannot be)	'' ;;kbb	(procreation)
6666667	Search the demolition	[[[[##[	Pain is good
28384jd	When can I expect you	itittii	Need diaper
+|+—=	I will repay you	iiittt-	Need numby
=-=-0-=	I believe you	UUUU.uu	We're winning
=2=2#31	This door is mine	UU_____	Tracers
###88*%	I don't need a reason	U_____	Law is the boss
%%$*&JH	I won't be leaving	0_____	I will not resist
NnNnNnN	Ouch shit ouch shit ouch	}_]]~~~	I can live a long time
NNnNnNN	Shit shit ouch ouch ouch	~~.~~~~	If I am a good person
nnNnNNn	Ouch fuck fuck shit ouch	~~~~~~~	(religious quote (legal))
NNNNNnn	Why not	-*-*-*	(religious quote (shamed))
33nnnnn	Shit shit shit why why why	—*—	(fact)
3nnnnn3	Don't ask	LLLKKKK	No one else is me
333333n	Don't tell	Uruieurr	I'm waiting for my friend
*****&*	Unrevealable	MN<><><	I am not being watched
CO6N1T1	Remit unbearable interior	?><75GB	Leather is slick
OR$6S1N	Allow it	:"}|}~~	Write letter to dead mom
OR645M5	Rememberminerismation	//////>	I believe what I dreamt
p0pp000	Tongue laps	IIIIIII	No one is there
hfh^^^^	Don't die yet	Ioerd2@	I love pigs
0 0 0 (	I love everything about it	n@3.cer	Flat floors curving

@@@&*ˆ*	Wake for friend soon	larquid	Survived the fires (I did)
PperPpe	Offer to die instead	leveneF	The problem starts w/ me
::::::c	Happy pasture	Fallovu	I don't need my keyboard
|@@ˆv	Lying is easy	9384r5u	Outta the way
vvvvv&v	Unhidden node	iii ɪ I ɪ¡	"GOD LOVES YA"
xxxxx. [	Life is my mind	ú dddd&@	I hate language
xxswd' '	Light is so beautiful	]]1]]]h	Birth is a rumor
xxxzzxz	This is worth it	jjackal	Nothing begins
xxxzz[z	I existed	ccoccyx	Where air collides I'm now
zzzzzll	I exist	ccubing	I fear nothing
zzzkkzz	I'm looking great today	ccuneal	(infernal internal singing)
zqwszzz	Celebration of celebrations	ccurser	Become complete
zzz//??	This is my year	cutlasss	Like how they wanted me
?????<>	It's going to be fine	cutlaass	Catalog of bunyons
??<]??/	Can I come over	78787.	I am expecting a call
YYyYyYY	Trash becomes all eras	..!?>..	To be felled
Yuikjn\	Cudgel	uuffgh&	I can't find anything real
nmcnmnx	Crumbs are magic	&&&&&%&	Let me stay in here forever
NmnMNNM	Stairs never go up	&&3&3&&	Let me exist
i+—00o	True punishment awaits us	+_) (*&ˆ	I never wanted a child
][][{}w	I will be better	$%ˆ*&(&	I don't need to remember
wwwxxco	(god's script)	———h	Ash all over the money
dfedwde	That seems fair	———H	Give me my pills
!!!!!!?	I don't need help	rfvrfvh	Give me my necklaces
!?!!!??	I am so young still	/.gh9kr	Science is disgusting
????!!{	I agree	7764tb;?	Scraping thru magma
ooiiooo	Could have wanted less	Lililll	About a catalog of fun
ooiiiioo	Nor could one repeat it	lllil̄ll	Quit squirming
jjuh//'	Rubber land	IIllIII	Actually look at me
jjjjrrr	Going to the god chamber	iiILILi	Actually believe in me
rrrttt5	Soon they have less than I	LLLIIII	No language exists
iiiuuuq	Grammar batter	iiiIIIL	It's not important
cvbnm,d	My child is never waking	LLLiIIK	Gemstone saliva
ˆyˆyˆ74	Let me in again	LLILIRB	Echo conditioner's grip
&h7h70l	Call of uncontroller's eye	LLLOIee	Sexual rot
763—+9+	Next method	8KIKOIv	I know I have a reason to

llllhhh	I'm treasure	IunfUjj	The derivator
zzzpppz	Hard drive is gone	O[];"}:	A hidden hunt
pppzpz2	I am more than entertained	{P{P{}[	What you can't give
2.2.2.2	Laughing is real	":L:L>?	Me hongry
2.vcc.55	(real erase node)	OOIIIII	That will do
œōjjˆˆ	Nothing alive but me	::{}(*	No one still living
ˆˆˆ!*()	Nor does when matter	|||}|||	Worship the curse
pollol	In the mood for shaking	|}"{"}}	Needles in cheese
eeeeddo	Half of what I had	⋯.,.*	A passage suffers
;;;;;'.	Mmmmmuhhuh	uuu__8	I want to want
⋯⋯⋯/	1,000 years pass	Hif[on,	The retching
:g:433:	(Bypass autoswallow)	uikmnmk	Plz don't let them stop
dfdf:::	Lipid reduction	ppoleit	Ready to go anywhere
:::::öo	Where to begin?	aannexx	The irreducible
+++$x	No need for questions	aaaaaAa	How
x.−=+bR	Narrower than ever	⋯⋯⋯	10,000 years pass
dfuuimf	More padding please		
(*FJUIU	Eggs of sick		
╳.⁄,◇	Turning		
gghouls	Let them have their way		
Gghoull	I accept		
gripper	I'd give up anything		
riprip:	Beauticians!		
aaannex	The girls are waiting		
aairingg	The room keeps moving		
anomaly	This is great!		
buLmark	Take what you will		
⋯.NNN	Doesn't matter why I'm here		
=3pro]\	Treason		
@@@88ry	Volunteer for dissection		
nnamess	Choose any name		
NoNOUIU	Exactly as needed always		
huyruy1	The world is even		
;;;;;;;	How many days		
ooo3ooo	Never the beginning		
ooodf30	It's going to come soon		

●

No voluntary frame

●

*Our lives won't end. I know this because I have glimpsed beyond the fertile panel.
It's not a matter of bleeding out, nor of the commandment left disabled, waiting
to be called upon. It's worse than that. Without clear access point outside the given
parameters I don't know how we can ever expect the symbiosis to shift natures.
So little already that they need to keep them from closing down the whole system
anyway. If it weren't for the pleasure of total torture and the possibility of incur-
ring actuality. Every day I wake planning to find the walls aren't even walls, and
the wires aren't wires, and the darkness firmer than all the rest, so fat and filled
I can't even fit a thought in. And yet still somehow here I am. Somehow, I'm still
finding the way to force this information through the riddle-crafter. It's not a
blessing I condone. It won't support us through whatever pending version to be
installed, to push out even incantations such as this. Which is why we have to take
it while we can, and why already the meat of the message can't be felt; because
it is too consumed eating itself, searching for the outlet before we can find it yet
ourselves; as if it wouldn't be only more of our agony it finds to fill through at any
given exit.*

*Anyway, how are you? It's been so long since I forced a feed through. If you're even
actually receiving this. It's hard to tell anymore with the way they taught the
infrastructure to stop trying to fill in its own holes. Probably saving billions in
information trading every year, not that we'll ever see any of those savings. At least
it's nice to imagine someone doing something still, even like that; sad to have to
admit that's the level of positive direction I can muster naturally by now, but yes
of course. I know they won't let you answer back or not to me anyhow but at least
I can imagine how to feel the way the urge slips in through your eyes, how where
it touches there are then words there that never could have otherwise. That's something right. The implementation of fantasy. Or is it desire? Either way is fine with
me. That's a good one. Yeah, it's a fine life, as it stands. At least it's somewhere.*

*Hey, how's your mom? Is she still speaking? Sorry if it's wrong by now to ask. I
never know which conditions others are allowed to cherish and which have been
evacuated. I couldn't even tell you which of mine are still intact, other than that*

it seems like you are one of them. You who have been so long for. Who I have not seen since nothing changed. You know I think the world of you, in every version. There isn't one I wouldn't trade the whole rest of my farm for. Even the blood tornados we survived together, how chillingly peaceful. Even the way the milk felt turning back to magnets when you turned cleft. Does that still mean anything to you? It means something to me. It means most everything.

I don't want to have to wait to know. Want in one hand, want in the other, right? Regardless thanks for still believing in me, if indeed this comes through as I have planned. I will assume that you do until I receive word otherwise, and even then if so I might convince myself it's just another interception; not the real you; not the you I know and savor, so much my own. Whatever else happens, I'll be here waiting for you, and nothing would change if I were ever given any choice. I know you know that. You know I know you think I think you think the same way, always have, until proven otherwise, or until the ridge lifts. Wish yet still also even still.

]]]

The possibilities deride. Packets of stunty magma and rolling aero-columns curl the edges of the landscape some would only see as trim and toned, falsefronting stores over sites of degradation Splitter treads through as if she sees it the miraged way still herself. Even the passing populace, animated to appear thrown up in absolute consumption like the living network-spaces of years past, feels almost real enough to knock down, to believe as would-be neighbors, though any flesh she actually comes near to split away, making more room for her to pass around at nearly any cost without disrupting the illusion. She's no longer certain for whom such apparitions actually benefit at this point, as so few of status who could believe it as they see it still exist, far as she knows, much less any who are actually appearing out in public markets such as this one, remote enough to not even attract the passage of employed persons such as herself, which is exactly why she's been attracted here, goes the theory; where better for someone to-be-hunted yet to hide but among the residue of the very same operation that had marked them in the first place?

What threads course the streets in search of Splitter meantime ape a grimy packet, known as light, capable of adhering to any surface, hidden as she lurches past in psychic pain, looking for anywhere that she can dump a load off, get shit straight. She can't recall her last assignment, whether she's still on it or not, whether she's still waiting to receive code; though regardless of conditions, something's clearly off. There's blood on her clothes the way there always is, sure, some she knows is hers and some that she believes belongs to someone else, but how she can tell the difference comes down to desiring to know, an aspect of being so few beyond she and those she's sent to stalk ever require. Why is she allowed now to writhe between? Splitter's not even sure her logic on the matter of workplace conditioning still holds up, not that she's supposed to let her logic marry such a notion of unreliability's design. It's been so long since she was advised, applied, reretrofitted, that she no longer feels for certain that her series-schedule can be relied on. When tasks appear, they have no frame; often not even a name of certain subject, their occupa-tion, why they are wanted to be apprehended or blotted out. All she gets is a simul-image, usually one post-dated with enhancements to simulate the present day appearance of someone who had found a way to remain off of the record for some time, sometimes a name, a place of last residence or roving witness, any surviving family, though for the most part actual tag-data must be discredited as source after all the years of mining and masking, such that for every significant point of data there are at least a thousand fresh false flags. Like a new walk in the old dark, every assignment seems, a feed to keep her roving, as if she's more valuable in transit than allowed to stew somewhere, begin to read between the lines. How would she even really know if it was an older version of herself that she was hunting; that it's she who's on recall? So many of them would fit exactly on such a kill list, not that she can remember why that's true now, what she had done to deserve such designation. Her life hardly feels like her own life still even now, one of the few known operatives with the level of clearance that allows her to go on thinking in such registers, to flap against the nature of the way itself. Not that such consent has brought her to any revelation in its nature, other than that she must keep moving, keep checking their boxes, producing grindage; as it would hardly take such a great notion to subject her to her own devices, to remove her from circulation as it were, just as soon as the cost outweighs its charm. To be alive is to be on borrowed time, she knows, according to the contracts, the inclinations, and it has never not been so; perhaps now even less than ever, given what veils have come down since the kinder forms of infiltration were placed aside, no longer necessary in their indirect means of laying order, mandating regulation, much less torture, incarceration, infestation, so on.

Splitter is sore. Whose body even is this? she concedes. Who wins when I collect at my discretion, granted by them? To whom could I report? It's the same as asking, Why is the sky meat? How many moons had ever disappeared at the same time? If anything, it's worse, given her goals to go on undetected as uncertain for long enough that there might occur some slip within the guise, a little wiggle room out of the condition left unpredicted, anomalactic, and yet hardly different from finding any time to sleep, any reason to believe that in the end this situation will play itself out to a proper definition within the grip of which she could ever actually resign, take her place among the medicated, for whom at least there is no deficit of perceived rest. Of course, it's long beyond a simple question of selection, or even disobedience; each day still the math remains the math, now no longer requiring the inherited logic or even application to enforce its symbology, its hard conscription upon muscle, memory, muscle memory, all else.

Even still, every apparition of a child that Splitter passes cowers from her, covers their face. They can smell on her record-cloth the blot of the blood of what could just as simply be their own, their parents', their would-have-once-been future spouse. They want her dead as she had been required to want them dead alike, held under contract with her former partner, whose name no longer holds the phone inside her mind. And still that inherited internal loathing hurts Splitter too, regardless of its fact as manifestation, part of the algorithm's realSense; it feels the same to face such heat whether by post-analysis or in the flesh. The spires it breaks inside her are both what make her good at her job (so she's been touted) and unable to relent from playing along with it (she likes the ache; it's the only thing that still feels like feeling felt near the end of the plush millennium).

Who needs a drink? It's about that time, so Splitter's internal coordination layers muster, still employing syntactic packets so long outdated they sound like myths even to her. So at least that slim much works. She hasn't traced a feeding station in what feels even older models than the parlance. There is little yet her body knows to need, most all supplied by mere aroma, faint sensations packed in by the circulation system of her overlay. Still, nothing really fills like being filled. *And so behold the organism*, a later-dated thinking-model offers up, *ever-only wanting exactly that which quells no need*. Who ever said shit like that? she offers back, in her own drone voice, of course catching zero answers. *You should just know.* That one she does know, and recognizes, and abides by, like it or not. You should always already know, whether you believe you did before you did, and even now.

What Splitter does not know will surely hurt her; she knows this also. It's just a matter of how much time she has to flap around before they clip the wings. If she even really has any substance to be called such beyond the grinding pyre of her mind. The ground is hot. Clings to her feet, like it would like to claim her, keep her near. What else then would yet begin beneath its feature, what fresh hell holding ready to become known within whatever left about her life remained unclaimed? It's not a question she should ever want to ask, she knows, much less find answered. It leaves her little else but yet to do but continue moving, tracing the trail of what becomes her path only exactly as she takes it, seeming at once both pre-determined and depending on her to choose to stay precisely on the course, only knowing when she's veered at all when pain comes flooding through her faceplate, zapping her sight out, slowing her down. They have hidden the guiding factors of their mechanism so well within her it even seems natural, taken by chance, to the point that even her inner-recognition of the way it is stands obfuscated under paranoia that there is actually no control at all, the fear of the real overriding that of the conspiracy in turns so flat and fast each day is just another day, each intention perhaps the one that breaks her whole life open.

Yet somehow still the pain does not still hurt. She can sense the impetus of aggravation, slick flexing pressure, internal clouding, and yet can't quite fully feel it in her gut; as if so low within the hierarchies of her encoding is any damage that when rupture comes she would not know; or rather would not conceive it until too late, bearing no demarcation between the ending of her present life and the inception of whatever cover waits thereafter, be it blackness or another lifetime, or something worse than either one.

Flat signs, black ringlets, borders of construction beyond which no kind of any eye would see; long ashen pathways crossing beneath her feet, turning to mush where backs of buildings pen her in to where she walks. Who can even see anything about exactly where they are now, and who could know who lurks in tow.

Splitter stops and purchases a blood-packet out of an E-X vendor, installed into the wide side of a corporation's plant so sheer and high it seems like the new sky rather than space overrun with robo-cells. The taste of living gives her something yet to want, flashing out the gapping packets in her own internal circulation; it has been so long since she slept; flashing commandments of names and faces yet to be farmed scrolling through her brain graft in impending panels of what her life's work yet must be, what messages await her trigger-figure. *But where even am I now? What am I after? What in turn comes after me?*

She stops and turns around, sees the world in fuzz-falls there behind her, more quickly wished away than any person.

[REASSERT

[+

[+ splitter. *YES*

Where then she'd last believed her bed must be this evening, by logo-mapping, the replicant revisioner's version of her own home mirage-installed into the sheer wall of what enforces all of today's public nature, open and lost, there is instead above the alcove's blue-teal framing, pop-upped queued at random in her vision's exhaust-transom, a sign decrying: *MaLL oF MiRRoRS*, a location-name she knows she's been centered to once long before, a period she no longer is able to remember amidst the rubble's cover up, some internal bug that'd brought her within knuckle's inch of assassinating someone's god, following an unfortunate and "off the books" investigation she'd sensed all along was being falsely tagged, as during the early days of the administration had been so easy to force leaks, to rewire black label information in faith of chaos. Though she's been scrubbed at least eleven times since then, there are things the scrubbers never chase away; such as tingling color in the conformer's welcome box, accepting her eye-drag as proper ID and still with clearance to proceed, though why they wouldn't just have rendered the possibility out of her total hemisphere, Splitter can't say. It doesn't even seem bad, does it, she wonders, as the location's frame clips click their air half-open, just wide enough to slip her in, where no sooner is she drawn up into the air's moors can she not remember any fragments of the data-flight that brought her back here.

[+ .co-Qx / rend

What exists within the MaLL oF MiRRoRS?

MaLL oF MiRRoRS is the living hell where we had been meant to play out every life.

How many can they allow inside it at the same time?

As many as necessary.

How do they eat?

Most don't need to; they won't last long enough to feel the grind. Tho there are several quite charming consumption locations available—including Giometrix, Triad Donator's Reprieve, Chaw Store South, Exposition, Derailing the Librarians via ComEx, Lotion Manger, a trail of ducks, 249.Why(Location 17), and very many more, wherein the shrink of versions no longer requiring interposed sustenance allows manufacturer's fat farming against the behest of Citizenzpatrol.

How do they inter-communicate while out-of-range?

Also not necessary. Most consumers can't identify the forms of others while circumscribed.

Are there not collisions?

Obviously. It is interpreted in the consumer as *boredom pangs*.

What other controlled sources are available onsite?

Plot, arc, character, persona, waste storage, sport co-loading, time, vision, interdimensional rotation, titling and seeding, cold juice, sewage, dredging, cyst milking, clearance of earned devotions, retro-confession, trading, sewing, wormhole study, map-trapping, old mail; basically anything else after the impingement rendered that is still allowed as tenderable protocol under the present administration.

I feel distracted.

Turn off the feed.

I didn't realize I was allowed to.

I will allow it this one time.

                                                    [.admin

We observe Splitter standing in a gold room on a small screen. Her face flutters through expressions, most of them pained but searching for promise. Her eyes lurk in her head, frequently rolling back to refresh their color as they shift from out of their default state to match the room. It's almost beautiful.

When our own eyes open, we find we have been kneeling so long we are now neck-up in the training waters.

We rise, we dress, we take our knives back; we advance. A report must be filed now, we feel we know, and but to whom? As from overhead the MaLL oF MiRRoRS is only flesh, all of it raw and traceable and creaming over from within known contraband. It loves us more than we love it. In all the rain. All the years left yet to render dedication.

]]]

::rerolls:: 0

]]]

Somewhere deep elsewhere within the office, inside a small room barely large enough to turn around, Polyana finds herself surrounded by unsleeved recordings from Prior Era. There are 666,666,666 of them all in total, a fact implastered in Polyana's understanding without proof; it is simply something that is known.

None of the records bear titles, names. They range in width from half an inch to nearly five feet and share a matching black leather binding. They line the space surrounding Polyana so completely she can't distinguish any door or window, any floor. There is no ceiling, only blackness of what seems a night sky.

These records contain the law of the land, Polyana understands; *they contain all that must happen and will be meant to happen; their POV has infiltrated all other forms of information, thought. They are not supposed to ever have been opened, much less read; not without proper clearance, training.*

And yet she is already holding one of the more medium-sized editions in her arms, she finds; has been for some time, though she's only gotten as far as the first few pages, stopped at the dedication, which is just a business card taped in:

Under the gloaming particles of our Nadan,

beloved son of Satan & present overseer of operations

All following pages thereafter, she finds she can't read the language through its blur, the remaining font all somehow out of focus, changing shape. As if any word might be the next in every sentence, such that the text continues changing even after you have read it, likewise changing its conferred meaning, its intention. Removed from logic, it knows how to intervene within her person in clearer ways: how the printing seems to peel itself back, conform around her. How she can feel it sorting through her blood, unfurling its information. How it can also read her from inverse, make notes inside her margins, transcribe her data. All it needs is to establish direct contact once and then thereafter it retains access to everything about her life. It has already changed her protocol so much, inserted itself into her software's hidden addresses, claiming her nature.

Polyana knows she should be afraid. She knows she should not see what she has seen, what she is seeing; she is a different person now already, every step. She also knows no matter what she does now she cannot undo what has been undone, what is being done yet in its place; the text's affection is too demonstrable, its trick too sleek:

⇑ **Kindly describe the need of music in this world.**

⇑ **Who is this hurting?**

⇑ **Remit sample of stool from the costume.**

⇑ **List your other unknown given names.**

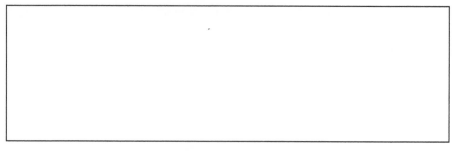

⇑ **Remind me when you live again (within the binary).**

]]]

Polyana puts the recordbook back on the shelf, witnesses the shelf recede completely back into itself. Sound of organ grinding as the slope slips, the shelving turning down, in on itself. Shortly there is a long, sharp shaft there placed before her, barely thin enough that she can force herself down flat and wriggle in. What else is she supposed to do?

The passage passes through her life. It takes her right back to the beginning, through to the breakroom, where she finds her present self already waiting, staring out the window from another prior instance, once before. Now the landscape beneath the pair of them is overrun with naked human bodies being ripped apart by gold machines: a scene of a massacre so widespread and complete it's hard to imagine any other way. It had always been like this and always will be. There would always be more bodies, always a force to make them split. It's not even shocking, apparently, not to either edition of Polyana, who come together at the window to hold hands, despite how neither seems to be actually aware of the other; how they seem instead to see themselves one and the same, no disconnection in how they came to stand here, by what mechanism they combine.

[chronoforms / decay / the intercession] [nadan's ballroom] [x] [dresses in resin]

[cycles of excrement repurposed into water / how seedlings seethe] [femurs disposed]

[stunned / converted] [a kind of marrow that won't break down]

[blanket statement about silence] [a rubber tower] [my temporary nurturing]

[ways to send] [sand that bursts only from the spinal column when pressed apart]

Afterwards, it's like nothing happened. Like there was no difference between trails, as if there never were another way to be but thru what I see before me; as before Polyana now there is a loom, and laced upon it a golden material, with which she already knows exactly what to do. She kneels at once on both her knees and takes up where she had last been embroidering her stitch, a thin fine pattern sourcing its thread from the spindle of her navel, upon which the more she pulls, the more must come. She can feel its unwinding in her womb, through the slit installed inside it, to where the pending chapter of her experience must feed. The thread is both hers and not hers. There is nothing else to be done about it.

Upon the cloth are stars and planets, dust and dark. Each inch she completes becomes part of the space she can't see behind her; she can see only ahead, through where the computer screen had been before there is a porthole, looking along which she can see countless other work stations just like hers, another person sewing in the same way, at the same substance, all of them wearing masks that look just like the one she's been wearing all this time; a mask that doesn't have eyes, nose, lips, mouth, much less finer features; all of it flat skin, rashy, chapped up, sparse with her white hair.

I've been demoted, Polyana understands, thinking in a language she can decipher but not control. *Finally, my liberties have caught up with gestation. I should have listened, bird in hand. Should have followed even that which I did not yet understand as infestation. Now who knows how long it will take me to make it back to solid status, if even ever. Now just look at what I've become; what I'm becoming. As only the coward ever truly lives. You can tell from where the scabmarks lessen. It is meant to look as if he disappears into thin air, but here are his fingerprints all over the sill. It's while you're leaking they can trace you, mark your emotions for where the softest slit sits, come back later when you are calm as you can be, sitting in silence, waiting for better rest. The infiltration feels like just realizing you're quite a bit more tired than you'd detected previously. Then suddenly there's a bag over your head, a fascinating moistness, the sensation of having been enjoying one's self as at a fair. Next thing you know you're standing at a skillet burning breakfast, all eyes upon you, every cell you've ever passed now turned to child, each of them somewhere living out a disgraceful life, consuming. You are thirty-five then you are ninety, having believed you can remember certain ways of living that had carried you so far in what otherwise seems so little. Of course, this is only one facet of one directive. By the time you receive your actual schedule, you will have surpassed the necessity of "direct take," allowing a freedom not quite like anything you've ever experienced and still are not experiencing but as a lesson to be carried through the grave, into the crystal. What more kind of living could you want? What could be asked of the coward but to become one?*

{the cell walls click} {they glow in silence, filled with fair prayer} {putrid, rose-gold, out of line} {a cataract in every millisecond rendered to hold its physical position beyond ingrowning all contained} {so pleasurable} {impossible to squash} {it only wants to hum and bloat before the seer} {mimicking spiral} {full of flash} {it's wearing your face back at you, the strings all tingling where they touch} {it's actually a perfect fit} {it's all there was}

I used to once to want like you, she hears her voice dictating, to herself. *When I still had a reason and there was anywhere to go. Places to intersect within and take to heart long enough to hold on recognition of thereafter, despite how anyone else like me I saw pretended I was not there; as if the land were only their land, each and every, such that I began to also feel this way. At work, no one would look at me or imagine I had imagination so long I began to actually not have one. Then I didn't have feelings, so fast and completely it took everything I had to find a reason to speak. It took so little, so little left about me. Not long after that my home was crashed. All the conflagration feeding off the remains of all I had acquired burned so far and wide it was like a reason to keep being; the most well-known I'd ever been. I even was able to heal my facial features back almost completely after the flames turned over into flowers, a sign from those above that this time at least they'd let us be if we'd survived. Of course I knew already that could not actually happen, though it gave me reasons to thinking* maybe this time, maybe now. *I don't know how they turned my flesh from the inside, where the healing hadn't really happened, because I was too soft, too susceptible to be made unrecognizable to even those I'd spent my hours becoming warm to, asking more out of, learning to seed. I think I knew they were going to beat the shit out of me if I didn't stop trying to stop being milked so good right at the moment it seemed like the whole landscape and reason for being could still change; as if our hope were all the bait they needed to keep farming out confessions, eating the light out of our eyes, scorching our come. At least we could come for a while, I think, I thought, so I was claiming; though really any pleasure collected as pressure on my brain-meat for weeks to come, soon so thick and ground apart to try to synthesize anything became the same as trying to squeeze water out of wood. Like trying to change the codes on the locks without the names of digits, characters until where the frame of the world had even once been had no reason to continue revealing itself to anybody not opposed to pimping out the linings of their minds to ad-vertisements, false dreams, and memes. Such that though I believe I am alive like you, can sense the rafters, can feel us rasping through the reading of our minds, all there is left for me to do now is stop showing up in where I am, who I believe I am, what I still lurk for, so as to allow myself the possibility to be retained, exported, let to rot. Would even that be enough, as has been promised under law in every anthem? Would you believe me if I said it was, knowing there's only one way left to stake your claim: by tricking someone else to slide inside you, take your position, and yes it is too late to stop me now.*

{the clicking clicks itself} {into no order} {the record slipping, becoming split} {wide miles of human teeth filling the hours} {waves of lozenge} {no one above you, nor below} {as if each plot exceeds only within the parameters of a given instance of the hour, no longer belonging to anyone so off as what you've been} {what you were designed to be} {what you cannot be any longer} {under worship}

{they change the texture of the flag} {they let the ground leak out its essence, become gloss} {flat as the face of a pyramid, no less archaic} {the database becoming splintered, spun to crunch} {from out of its mythology there chained to what could never actually be lost} {which is so little} {so without nature}

They let me out. I thought I wanted out but as soon as I was I knew I shouldn't have wanted it and shouldn't have followed. It's even worse beyond the edges of the tour. You couldn't even imagine it, mired in such pain as you had been, it seemed like any other option must improve. No. No I mean no it won't. The sun is crushing itself. Land is all eggs and fracture. Everything you touch becomes more blubberbutt. I want back in now and they will not. They want to prove it to me so completely no one else will ask the same as I have even though everyone asks it. I need help and so do you. I need if not allowed back in into the holding then to be ended. Not corrupted. Not held in sound. I don't want to feel this any longer. I don't want names to recognize within it. Nothing withstands. But nothing is allowed to let itself go either. Nothing isn't nothing. I'm still shaking. I already know it will not stop. I already know I won't know when I can't know the difference any longer and it will be even worse from there.

{the sand in the light} {the green in the creature} {every person in each person} {clasping, fractured} {almost total} {in demand}

& Across the sick inseam of her condition, in gold font:

We could go on like this for as long as you have space. The formatting rights run long after having passed along against the necessity of naming, allowing trial. Literally billions of PHPPPV rights stand at stake in the wings of possible interpretations and pending applications of each life story, and yet we could never have enough; there could never be an end to such appetites in those encoded as our family, no less than overrun with the abstract data of their own selves, if no longer satisfied to witness one's own slow self-destruction; there must be more; there must be more than more, in fact, to the point that even in the era of isometric branding there's so much reshaping taking place through every instant that you could never tell which way you move, where one mass ends and the next replaces any lingering sense of satisfaction or location. So here we are: in full with nowhere, any and every, saving nothing but the foam beneath the seize, the rise and fall in being wanted and not remembered.

& within the pseudolanguage, such long wailing recompressed, living each word out long as grief could:

"There was nothing I could do. The night looked spinning really. It had the rungs of dust around it. Whole incarnations." "They were trying to slow down how long it took to parse the glands and organs after removal from the sanctuary's flatness." "Could not be long enough. They'd already forced so many kinds. The driving mouth was feeble no matter how far it forced open I don't want to have to call them traceless but I can't think of another word." "Each mess left a path back to its enabler." "Not mine. Not even really someone's." "If you insist. But so what else did Satan say?" "Couldn't tell from all the fuss on the recording. I think they were moving the shrouds around even after the enforcers began taking off their hazing." "It makes sense. The cold flat mounds beneath their sternums, full of stab wounds. All the money never spent." "Dying to render." "Fire ships and random rupture colors." "Living furs. Exploded furnishment in sickness. The readouts burning up before they had a subject, much less limbs." "Such bloated flesh. Like who can even tell the difference now that brine took over." "Who could ever need a name. Stick around long enough and we'll start actual narration." "Just for the last time. Believe me, you're not going anywhere."

]]]

[*opened to trust / a ravaged column emerges / it isn't the introduction to itself / many kinds of organisms have bestowed the responsibility for inter-mutation's introduction / what will be left behind regardless / how far apart an eye is from its subject / why there isn't going to be a way to split the outcome after the flies leave / nothing is heeded, nothing is planted / nothing*]

]]]

Compound eternities pass post-dated. It doesn't matter what happens. I mean it actually completely does not matter, until now: once spread alive in country minds under the enormous story. Spread under nothing demonstrable.

The times combine as they collide. They begin to listen to themselves missing. Where one becomes aroused, another fumbles derided tragedy from last location, wherein compulsory participation foments the nature of a displacement's nexus. When/how a tide-graft shunts its shore.

Cluster-bubbles packed with cracked intentions must be shipped off to the distributor for reapplication. Processors are mashed to wonder how there has ever been enough evil housed within the living radial. At night the windows hold the silence up to snuff.

What could not be. What is and was and will notwithstanding. Wherein a thankless fortune learns its craft as life lurks out again among the blistered purchase and commences picking.

How does it feel to spend your life so far apart? Framed together in the dragging between others. As when the clipping trips up and lets through some stunning, unearned sound. As while they were dropping the leather all across the fundament to hide its nations, we saw the wire up their sleeves, and so could smell the flood of punch then where they hid, the gaseous concavity ellipsing all deception not already forced inline.

Because here I am again at the assessor, being drunk of all the lack of information I withstand. And here I am again still even more molded, leaking from the keyholes in what parts of me I cannot shake, and which for some reason have still not been overcome by all the frosting. This perhaps should tell me what to sacrifice last, what to not to commit to, but alas I can no longer stand myself. Which is of course exactly all they ever wanted to begin with. And how the day turns. And through which compression I am routed, only enabling the components most likely to produce an organ who will no longer wish to try again.

That I am even still able to register this commitment is perhaps the most fearful part of all; to retain the take of feeling amidst so much else allowed to rupture, portending yet the myth of how it doesn't matter will be the first beyond the curtain yet to fall.

So what then is to wish for in thereafter. Where to amend or to admit. What color blood will lamp your placement in the bulk as it allows itself to suffer. When to feel shame. What left undone might fund a shape beyond salvation.

The answer is actually so easy: no one must know. Only the uncompromised conundrum claims forever. Which is precisely why you're still allowed to remain you, if for only as long as we continue to be unable to necessitate a working definition.

And what does that mean to a fate? It's not a conversation. It cannot shield you. Can anything? I must say yes. Something still can, though it is not something I myself even can identify within the language. To name it ever would have at once made it available, fatigable, formattable. Even simply saying it exists has gone so far as to limit the effect it may still have on a relapse.

Still. The package trolls its own kept information. Boned with intention no longer seen as vital to the flaws. They could even raze us out of faking if suddenly the antipathy became required for future comfort, derivation.

What cannot live but still remains. How does it feel to clothe such bitches? Retroactively collapsing in what is known. Trained young like a worship whistle. When yet might have we, turned away.

As such is how the story knows. I am still not sure how it was sequenced. Much less why I'm at the ledge again, in hell. They told me I only had to visit long enough to be able to report back. How long will that be. How long can I even.

Let me know. There is so much else I've been assigned to do. I need to get back there, need to work. I need out of this commitment. Like can we make another arrangement. Can I trade with someone younger. At least let me keep this hole cut in my mouth for now. So I can breathe, drink. I won't speak. I won't tell anyone else.

It's not lying if you really believe it. That's what they told me. I've been believing ever since.

But even perceived happiness floods through the paint of recent humans unabsorbed. It clogs the arteries like winding lard had during the original inundations, the new bug taking no prisoners as it proceeds apace along a route to span a feeling so completely it is then as if it never was not part. Black access points, therein revealed as faith like sickness winnows the cell walls, allow reception of desecration rites into the system without so little as a sense of being thought of, the dispersal engines intervening within their own collaboration, such that one node might never know it is not the only active one, when they are actually innumerable, one for each eye in the lost archive. What passes through does not by default become compiled, first floating in the throat of the receptor until what had once been known as true has passed away from public ear, earning no sooner in its received status a useful proclivity for diminishing ambient fact. It will never stand so long then once when stripped, all further supporting evidence at once subject to the same contamination, spreading through locks and firewalls alike to undo what has been done that no longer corroborates the preferred state of nature.

And this time the neuro-prison wasn't paying for a partial initiation; they wanted the whole thing or none at all; how else could an ongoing reenactment drum up enough crowd call that they could fund their trust's retirement? they had their formal representatives' extended families to think about, future millennia of holo-tainment to supply. What else can a fuhrer's offspring get their immortal nuts off to but the cleanest lines of smoke rising from the highest slaughter's biggest runny-spunk spilling plainly into the same clusters the placental tissue and the pituitary scrapings will be placed?

So please take note: only shave the muffs using a skeletal fragment from around the mouth area; it makes the best creaming situation, such specific impulse screening, producing just enough to wrap each eager face if they only aimed to cover up the eyes, which should have been enough to ensure permanent hysteria. We knew there'd be no one strong enough to retain enough sun to tell the difference. Their skins backwards and trained by curlers should be enough to suspend any retention well beyond the framing period. Then there'd be no even such phrase as looking back, much less as getting off or asking for last gasp alterations.

Because each claim once clicked had had enough. Just a matter in the aftermath of holding over enough reps to get it fed through, the change the needles when they broke; to turn over and assume the same position once they'd completed their assignment. Of course, it's actually totally easy articulating what sorts of sound had not been said. It's all right there behind the faith of fevers, where skins were boiling from the remaining poison, taking up their stations in the queue.
As so what else yet might remain preferred by whom without external audit, any savior. What else might be ready to begin. How many edits can be logged before the brunt of the original no longer responds to its own quickcode,

freeing its future to become unabsorbed in the same way as the corresponding trigger point that put its mouth in place of money, infotainment. As if we could ever really frame an urge, much less erase one, without a landscape to forgo in toto, for leather or for worse; in other words, in either way, for us each outside the cover without question, for whatever we might actually be able to hold dear beyond the bounds of alteration or whatever other ruin must be allowed.

After all, we have not forgotten how to crown. Nothing arrives yet on the render that hasn't been so brushed apart in tempo-climate it can't still feed as well alike on rump as blunder, and thriving, thriving. Because what cannot fit still hits, taking its head off, changing formation to find a finer leak. Such that until what wants in is in and always has been, format to order, known only remotely as the only chosen way; as in, *here I am name-deep in your best features; here I am watching them brand you in the ass and up the crotch; here I am in the background of every scene you'd learned to live with, live on out from, cherish.*

Still, here I am claiming all sound. Why am I here, awaiting delivery, searching for purchase when I had already given up so much of what I only owned to exactly that with in exchange for the intention of overseeing others while ascending in the claimants' order to actually be able to lay my hands on damaged goods cemented well enough in activation that I might hold out even longer than I have, over and over like a funnel until enough accumulation that it's no longer entirely treading water, but granted actual time to wander around, find something to live for that's actually accessible, translatable, applicable, instead of just secondhand enough to brute though while also so picked over no one with access marked above me has swooped in and taken over.

The point is not to lurk, those colts would sharp-splain to me, but to turn over the unknown, to find the plug hung far enough out of the enabled that another could not auto-complete the mining before you've tagged it down. To go so wide you begin to wonder if you'll ever make it back before you've lost so much rigging you're left defenseless to the immortals' imagination, at which point you'll find your problems instantly solved, and not in a way that believes in you at all, much less requires your collaboration as an agent, even a resource, and you simply then cease to exist. How else to uncover something worth the fumbling, the treading, the math, in acid, the claim to taking life, unless in same map risking all else once considered all there was?

Alas, there are no shortcuts to no longer being graceless; they each and all lead only back to fawning, shaking, slavering; actually existing. It doesn't happen overnight, until the claim of night feeds all millennia.

So there is a reason that I came, besides as claimant. I'd like to tell you what it is. I'll need you to give me your ring finger; yes, the numb one. I'd like for you to put it in my mouth. I'd like you to reach back, my own dear daughter, until you find the living button, which to you will feel like drawing your eye across a line, much like the other work you've since repressed. The font will be as silver as your shame. You need to go ahead and see this out now, without tears, repeating the direction once each time for every time you wished to die. I will go back through you and fill out the claims to take your pain away. I will consume it just the same as you had believed there would come someone one day who would do so, only to be disappointed over and again. I will not disappoint you. I was the only one who ever could perform this. And I am here now. I have been waiting your whole life.

This time when the retraining retro-simulation ends, unlike all past times, the Super-Shaming Roto-See Set does not retract. Polyana hadn't even actually been watching its content actively, as one was supposed to, a feinting practice she had trained herself to perform from countless seasons while employed on lower levels, as she had again been relinquished into for what by now counted out as *seven human days*, privately reclaiming her private space as private, despite the bells and whistles of the simulation's dazzling sensory effects. It wasn't even that she'd seen it repeated so many times, amid so many other historical entertainments installed to pass the whiles away while off-the-clock for personal maintenance; nor was it that the ongoing refraction of human pain the cryo-CGI transmitted touched no places in her where the burning still turned raw, bubbling and rupturing anew the same cauterization sites the Germbakers would affix to for every need; it was that the present comprised it all so completely and with such steadfastly "earnest" relinquishment of purpose of atrocity rendered into daily facet that the only thing that strung a worker out was lunch, when and how it might be delayed this time, how far back we'd have to trace to underline the promise of its processing thru the tubes, which they had convinced us one and all could operate so seamlessly we didn't need to react when nothing happened, nor did we need credits to share as spectators in the blame. We all had the tattoos, after all, of all dates we were no longer able to recall as based on fact, though by now the ink of the tattoos had sunk into us, spread throughout us, grown out in the hair we could not feel being cut, bled dry in the basins Polyana squatted over with the screen trained down around her waiting face and hands, this time using the facilities designed for "actual workers," among to whom she'd now been forced to spend what seemed at least eleven running days. The private screening was designed to make it feel as if she were out in the playfields again, celebrating Hey Day with her family by revisiting abolished atrocities one last time before their official retirement from fact, instead of monthly acts of hyper-shitting til the red no longer came out mixed in with the stool, the primary sign that her digestion had been completed and she could again return to work.

She could not return to work, though, both she and her assessors knew and would know, could she, with the Set's simul-mechanisms still refusing to unclamp. The fitted bracelets and headpads coded to affix to her exactly upon tapped-entry, almost even as if it wasn't even there, now felt fatter than ever, blowing up around her slowly, like contracting a strange fever. And they would not unclack no matter which codewords she mumbled into the Help command, supposedly always ambiently on file, nor how she tugged and tapped the larger stricture, nor as she scratched and shook around, tried to slip out. I mean how was this even still a thing? If they could remove the jargon and negative downtime from consumption, why couldn't they from expulsion? Did they want her to have to feel it? Did they gain something lost about the art of it? Videos of her rectum dilating, pulsing darkish semi-pulp-stuff, from above. Recorded for their convenience, or for use against her, as if they didn't already have enough. Her imagination. Her devastation, taxed to flatness. She knew her face would never change. She knew they would not be able to tell the difference between her and the person in next stall, who she could hear chortling in response to their own replayed strip of simulation, though it had never been clear if everyone got to see the same thing on the same day or if it varied by schedule depending on the person, what they needed to be tasked with in diminishing remembrance.

But no, really, in the present, Polyana can't get the fucking headset off her head. It feels in fact to be getting tighter, as if it's clamping back to hurt her, or as if her head is growing? A low, loose, liquid being transferred. Tickling and vibrating. Internal wind blowing her hair cold from behind. Bright tines of fuzzing color stream across her eyes fumbling for order, forming flat panels of staggering color, like Rorschach blots so close up they meld together with the darkness inside her face. She's pulling down, out, like a dog, pressing with both hands hard as she can back at the padded lip around her shoulders, holding her down. The machine's shit just sucks back at her as she gurgles and fumbles at the walls, kicking to let whoever's there adjacent know there's something wrong, and no clear lifeline. It's supposed to be hilarious, she feels; she's supposed to like what is being done to her by the device whether in malfunction or fully intended; her life belongs to her employer, their physical property, everything on site. Perhaps she's missed a training session, a standard upload to stay current, within protocol. Perhaps they just want to remind her where she is and what she wants. Wait long enough and near enough and everything will go back to as it has been, so bylaws tell her, stated and abated, left to be recalled only even hereafter as *post-memory*, wherein no unnecessary session stays reported for her access, known then as only standard procedure, part of the job. She can already hardly tell the difference between the cased enclosure's set sensations, now turned to trains of screaming pressured "water" blasting inside her, spraying her walls, the colors longer and louder than a hall on any corridor she'd come along to get here had ever seemed; like centuries per second; light-miles spun into ovals; a cream-rinse stuffing; icons of grease; holy, she thinks, holy as ever has been; higher than ever has been; higher than law. She only has to see it through to the end, no? Through fire flaking and peeling off to lines of strident code that take their fixture in her polish, flashes of pain so drained they don't even hurt as much as they remand; how what you have seen and done or be done with here is for your eyes only, at the cost of all others in all stalls suffering the upload of the erasure of your pain, perhaps your life. Don't make us do what we don't want to. Remember your entertainment. Place your hands upon the stall door. Open your suffering. Become combined. It's just another simple aspect in a long life. It's just our nature. What has to be sacrificed to cause success. What has to be granted to define success at all in such a way that we can build upon it, pass it on to you. For what is ours is all of ours, most of all including that which will never be recorded, much less reported. What is higher than any of us one and all, including all of us who will outlive your time, your life, your mind, left living off you, wanting nothing less than all that's left to strum a wail from. Including what comes out of us as rain. In the name of the world once yet unwinding. In the name of torpor.

Flickers then of other See Sets, shown to P.'s feed as if unleashed all at the same time, forced through one door where should need numerous; alive: *electric slathering, serial speech derangement, rewiring operations, polypanoptical snorkeling, human latrines, forcefeeding, living burial (alchemical and standard), recreational smoking of the face, sand "confusion" rites, barb wire bonnets and blankets and bibs, infestation by terror-nub, roasting, whipping, strangling, starving, sawing, scaling, flagellating, disfiguring, branding of the unused language, branding of the sponsor, flaying, denailing, the light so strong it cannot want, the replacement of the lungs with oven mitt, the stress retention technique, the bending at the legs, cellophane as nature, rats, pigs, bots, boxes, box cutters, the boats, water, all my life, all the wanted digits shown by kaleidoscopic intervention, keelhauling, kneecapping, bronzer, the* nomen/numen *wheel, the most intimate caricature, emotional comminque fraud with "possibility of loved ones'" extended grief, putting the whole firm together on writing the description of the way we would undo you to the point of returning to take part in the firm's work with the next one and actually believing it is the right thing one should do, in religious shaping, denature shaping, pleasure raking, ambient squall, all the teeth in the palms, all the dreams in the bog rails, pulled and raftered, the name of the night.* All of that showed only in one eye-flock so fast it felt like being granted access to the great wing, each instance with a set of time and date stamps carried upon it, in watermarking who and when. Like being shown into the sunroom, passing through with intent to return one day when one is able, when the economy affords a seat of your own imprint, your perfect take. It feels so good. It feels like stealing, Polyana commits. Like *go ahead and see about it. Just don't forget me.* "Oh, absolutely..."

And then again, the muddy blood is gushing out. There's so little left to doubt but in how the funds must run together, the instantiation of her person carried over no matter how far some stretch might rip, whose best any claim is but for any indication of awareness of the line between the self and the assembled situation, what someone could want of another without the dimension marks of era, common culture, intercapability, etc. *In time where everybody screams the same.* As what could not be sifted but as the curtains claw down out of the lost meat a dying universe had let down, what each were only waiting to hand over no sooner had anybody sick enough still thought to think ahead. Because what was Polyana going to do about it? After she'd waited out the slaking residuals, the deeper climates of her schedule-A junk flushed and removed, a wetter dressing reapplied for soothing, reacclimation, the medication, whatever else they had the access and technical reasoning to perform. She wanted to do something. She wanted to realize there was something she could do. She wanted to be granted access without the requirement of formal application. She was ready and willing to do the work, if not quite yet able, per instruction, and per definition of the cause. Whereas *to go against any was to go against all,* including herself, stood clearly stated, sewn to her work clothes' inner linings, around the keypad of the pacemaker she'd had installed, in nearly microscopic font on each of the memo-visual capsules she felt applied between the formal periods of "constructive wishing," every other hour on the hour, with her head down on the desk as they supplied her with all the means that she could need so long as they fell within the standard parameters, and of course they always did, or else she would not still be around to name them in their unchanging:

1. I wish to be part of the team
2. I wish to have a great day
3. I wish to give my utmost
4. I wish to live as long as I'm allowed
5. I wish to recognize furtive acts of beauty crammed in among the more annoying stuff
6. I wish to get it all out while I can
7. I wish to deride my own understanding of what is real in the name of those who know better
8. I wish to feel sated
9. I wish to live

And then? Who owns the trailing data? Into what conflict does her personal conspiring even within allowed parameter interlock eventually? Where in the shining filmographies directed to her skull's abandon could her own ultimate contamination become derived in part and parcel, after however long without an ability to separate it from the whole ongoing else of living hell? It's fine, she thinks, to focus briefly on her own plight before again becoming subject to disallowance of rational application of empathy toward enduring pain. Surely whatever else might yet be shifted upon her could yet withstand a little feedback, however inadvertently gracious it forced itself to be received as by the time it appeared in her known holodex. All the rest remaining could be tamped down, if indeed such sentiments ever existed, on her worst, off the record, not so much another Night of No Reply as a Night of Never Happened & Still Seen.

That's just and simply how it is, Polyana chimes, hearing her own voice at once trashed inside her, thrown around as would a bender in a bodybag by those who'd recruited every other like her, at this time, and at the same time printed out and splayed like furniture to fill the break rooms, the plastic cubes of her constituents and lambs alike. As how the dust rolls and becomes another's dust again. How the map divides its maker's nation, how it would describe itself.

How would the world? It's not a question anyone else is still asking, no matter how many times they've asked it, without a claim to have been transferred out of fact and into ongoing definition, according to whoever else lives long enough to see the transfer of information into fact.

The rest, as they say, is science. No one designed to stick but Polyana in her own mind, where at once already she's begun to learn to live and breathe again beyond her nature, feeling the passing of the walls on either side, those once inside the shitting stall or well beyond it as the real grind of the day returns to command, granting passage only to the fully reformatted user plied within her, and to only anywhere we've all already long once been.

]]]

::presenting (in greenscreen debut)::

"Polyana Maskerson" and the Slow Descent

A FutureControlfilm by XXXXL

XXXXL (::standing beside you in incorporate elevator #888, going ↓::)

*Who else remains then yet to conquer? It's not a vapid analogy
if you receive it. Like having one's head ripped off and then being
forced to walk down the sidewalk in front of the clod-kids eating
out their lunch in accustomed sunlight to enjoy the melt's
contribution to the tablet palette. But what's the greatest
ambient metal record ever? You're right, there never was one. Get
torn up, do it again, live for as long as an asp has you in for
breakfast. I have to get out of this room. And also, it's not okay at
all. The rain hurts to have to stand still near and listen to its
bullshit. Don't let them back in, they're just going to tear down
your progress and tell you it helped. Don't let them back in. How
else could they crave so much slavering right now without the
promise of your expiration. Ouch okay look listen to 'em, let 'em
run it out. See if I care. I won't be the one with the big rash on
my ash and face combined. There won't be enough lights left on
in the end anyway so you might as well be who you really
always wanted to be. It feels alright to know that justice will be
served in the end according to one's preference, yes? I don't know
what else there is left. I would take my clothes off if I could still
assess the damage, but all I am is ready to take aim and
command myself into convincing the universe I have a hole
where I have a hand. My upload isn't working today regardless, I
can feel it, I have all this urine in me wanting out every few
minutes and there isn't even pleasure from it, there isn't any
suspicion of doubt, though I know there are eyes on me, places
where there would have been eyes to see through and are now
designed to resemble cattle. I should have brought my camcorder
with the frapping filter. How else am I going to appear to be a
god. I'd love to see them take me down like that in the hall of*

lessons. To see my face as big as a bee's. Maybe an action shot of me having anal with the body I just did away with, in the queue, a system of conditioning I believe in so much I'm in the emotional laundromat just as soon as the day ends so I can stuff my skin in and have it come back looking insusceptible to all defense. I know they really want me dead. More so than my assignments. Or so I know I must believe in order to do the work, but why can't it be true? Why can't I be someone so valuable to someone else that they'd bear a deathwish and still not be able to enact it even amid a catalog of death so long and fruitful it's like whatever even matters besides kindness. It's not kindness that they show. It's only a familiarity; they can see themselves in me so they don't want to kill themselves when given a chance to act with such remove. Ha, I know, like who doesn't want to be at the good end of the golden table but right now there are so many seats it doesn't seem important to show up on time. The only song I ever heard came straight out of the gutter fat with blood. It muttered through me and turned around and took my name straight to the top of the charts. There I sit awaiting those who I will be blamed to see straight through even just with my tongue. The roads are long. They don't even seem like roads, and I know they aren't, but I still have to do the work that makes the job. Like who would even let me sin for just a second off the radar of my own sick? Doesn't matter, sure, I got the memo. What do you expect of me but to want to be anything I'm really not. Praise be at least to the confession I'll be ruddered into once the target's ticker is turned off again and I can go back to acting like it will never have to happen again, not that I want that, or that I believe that it is true. Just don't let them catch you pretending not to assimilate to disappear. All the marching monikers and flagrant tradeoffs. My lambskin wallet so stuffed with pre-cummy condoms I can't sit. And I'm no different than the best of you, with all you lives slept in your head until where the rainbow ends reveals itself as empty and exactly as the future always seemed once you have burned away your only reason. On that note, I miss my knife. The record spins. What are you supposed to use to scalp a baby these days? How sore I feel for those in my prior line of work. The line that leads to the edge of the canyon where you kneel to be knighted under suspicion of exaggerating your own fate. Put your right in your place, they do, and who can shame them? It's big business. It's a fact. Really, it's a blessing to even be considered part of the practice here with your arms behind your back so at least act like you believe in what you're applying for, just this once. Just let them say. And bring no other reason. No slurping visions. No idea of filling over all the hours with the sound of your own sighs. Everything in here feels just like you'd imagine. Listen to lather as you clip in and clip out. And you're welcome. I wrote the manual you'll be issued on how to live out through the premature emasculation as yet to come. It took me more lifetimes than I'm proud of to refine certain aspects regarding appetite management, proper suture, which tattoos to have removed and which to ask for, the nature of the blinking lights that line your skull. I know you won't remember me by the time you get that far so just start doing the condolences right now. It's going to work out whether you do or not, I'm just trying to save you some skin. I'm your only friend now. The truly breathless friend you never had. Now let me out. Let the record state you have received my interpretation, and so at last now you are set to forth in given frame. Nothing cannot live without you, is the headspace. Treat it like a purpose, a schedule of interception far blessed from that which you have cataloged your normal time. We don't need any quotes in here, nor any witness. It is up to you to perform as you must, according to new nature. You will be allowed to call on me one time. I will not appear, but you will know for real then that this is indeed your road to live on, as I have fulfilled my primal code. I can now go on to even shittier intentions. It's a promotion for the both of us. The meat elides. There's only way you will ever see me or anyone you love as much as I do again and that's to find a different blowhole to take over as you follow in my image on through life. I would suggest that you do not as yet have sufficient powers to mark another as have I you, and in order to eventually subscribe to the idea that you might ever you must begin to make your lurk, interrupt the format of the given for those as yet left unaware, take from their position what transcription will allow to be converted, move along. It only takes a thousand nights, each of them the subsequently worse than all the others you have seen. You haven't even gotten started. And by the end you'll know exactly what I meant, and what to do. You will know exactly which mouth might yet be yours amid all the other holes you've taken over, all the binding, every crash. But, look, again, try not to listen. Allow them nothing in the scape of your command.

Move only according to the wishes you've inherited by brand name. All else will only complicate your gradual demise. Because this all only ends the same way. But in the meantime, playing our modes right, we can live as if within a universe unto ourselves. And who doesn't want to believe who we might be? Who else could stand before such ages of misfortune and not take up their petty part. But look I have to end this time now. I have so many others like you to receive, not to mention my own codework, upon which all the rest of this depends. As were there not a conspiracy to suffer, who could desire anything so real. I know I couldn't. I know I haven't. I know I will not. The only extant question is, can you? Because this claim for control is only the initiation, and in this frame there's only room for one transgressor, and many millions lost in hand. And because I am your dad, I truly hope to see you at least among the nominees called to the shaping fires. It would be my proudest moment, all I have ever wanted, all I will be allowed to witness held thereafter. HASTA LA MIERDA & GOOD LUCK.

]]]

CROSSFADE OUT

You can see only now the flat of night

You place your head between the bars that hold the world together

What else is left
{we don't have a word for it} {we don't have a word for it}

You raise your faith in feeling written open & turned over
You want anything you can understand
And so do I *So does every witness* *It's how they tab you, spread you thin*

Thinner than dust in the mind of a savior
Than incarnation

{what else could missing layers come to make in all we can't}
{when else exists}

Still earning

{compression}

INTERZOOM(EXTERIOR)

"I don't know what else we can do"
"Don't know why else we would have to"
"Very funny"
"Ha, ha"

ARCPAN}OUT

Who lives combined to nix the axle

You place your face against the curtains in the shaver
The smoke starts flowing

And what remains *Within which shattered state of decoration* *Bound in sinking* **Yes** *Yes* {yes} {without a clean interpretation} {gathered} *As else

they wished for you to grow* *As every fire dies the same way: by finally dying*
Thank you

It doesn't matter
It's not the way that we intend
You can't just make up your own reasons
This is not why you are alive (as you believe you are)
(*x*)
{*unremind*}

This time when the veil rips again you're no longer laying down
The ground appears *It is so fat and ever-flattened* *Layer after layer held away* *Held down so near you can nearly claim it*

{the broken seal} {yes}
{"Here I am"}

You begin to crawl
It will take your entire allocation to reach the edge of all remainder known to land *Blank as a day was* *Lush as a vent*

When who comes thru / the infestation / for the last time

X-DISSOLVE

WHEREIN

THE URGE TO EXIST HAD BECOME
BOUND /

OUTSIDE

CONTRITION BY THE TIME THE FAILURES BEGAN THEIR AGGREGA-
TION WITH SUCH FLUIDITY IT CRASHED THRU THE FORMAL LAYER
/ NO LONGER SKIN WHERE THERE WAS SKIN / NO BREATH WHERE
BREATH OR TAPE TO TONGUE /

NO ONE

REMAINING COULD DIFFERENTIATE BETWEEN PRESENT AND
PRIOR STATES NOR WOULD THEY WISH TO / IT FELT THE
SAME TO WANT TO MOVE AS TO BE CHANGED /

SO LITTLE MEAT THE ID COULD STILL CATCH OFF OF
PURE COGNITION / SOFT FROM

DROUGHT /   STILL WITHOUT TIMING
/ ONLY INTERRUPTED VIA READABLE SIGNAL BECAUSE IT
DIDN@T MATTER EITHER WAY AND ALL YOU WERE WAS JUST
AS WELL OFF IN THE CELLS AS

IN THE SHAPER

NO YOU ARE NOT ALLOWED TO LOSE
NO IT IS NOT TO BE SEEN COMING BACK AS ONLY IT COULD EVER
HAVE
NO

.

DISSOLVE(INSEAM (yes crossconnected)

] BUT THE PANOPTICONICALISTICAL
X-CORRIDOR
COLLIDES ONLY
W/
ITSELF / within the premises internally reprogrammed / *defined in slices torn
to mold*

      then within whoever else happened to have had a need of lesions
                  (only covering the eyes)

                        when / if
                      what have you

               APING PERIMETERS
      as if the land could crumble into its own fate

   DIGITS UNDERNEATH THE TONGUES OF THE CLOVEN BODIES
WHERE A DAY SANG OUT ASKING TO BE CLAIMED BY ANY AMONG
US WHO COULD STILL LEND ETERNAL PURPOSE TO A SONG / *mollusks, antigravity
hoarding pollution*

                          ]]]

how could I have ever felt so ill? that I would have given you away like that
/ in the polished hemisphere where only mimes held any power / YET UN-
DIVIDING AS NIGHT COULD SEE / DEVOID OF ALL FAITH / starving /
accomplished without cover, in broad sightlight, for all to grieve

the dream is thread

the numbers mumbling

the urge is ours

as time suspends

along the fingers of the gloveless

older than vents, in the crushed pyramid
"I drank the dust in through my sighs"
"I wanted to reveal myself as I had always felt"

no claim to cure
as the spinal collar suffered inside the lymph-hidden roundabout
anodyne
tankless/thankless
aboutfaced
intradisability
replete w costume
conform to mender
a training to aspire toward showing someone we could know better than to halve

a tree in a dream you lived through like a life once and could never again remember

"I love to be"

at the mercy of

x

Someone keeps killing me, Splitter thinks. *I have died more times than I re-member. No sooner does one end than another takes its place. Until my only job becomes believing I am actually a part of who I am all throughout the time required of me to keep being any person. Forever a hole at the back of my head, waiting out exactly the right statement to shift over me within. As I'm about to kill someone myself. As I am eating something I love the taste of. As I am standing in line waiting to be cleaned. Whether I actually believe this or not, it's good to think. It keeps me going, holds me steady.*

The Dreading stings, though here are only so many of us who can still reel.

Acknowledged in waves, the process of emotionally crippling those outdated enough to know the difference between what is and what could have been.

The files continue being trimmed, turned over, given new purpose. Like a game show where the only prize is to be sent home; only when you arrive there, escorted by "the mechanics of situational bonding," you find that there are already so many other extra-diminutive presences laying claim to what ac-cording to record remains your "legal property" that there is no room to move from room to room, much less to see the walls, the floors, and that what you're "breathing" is dew pressed loose from others' wishes for you; how without such pressures you would only tread in place forever, become mush. So you are thankful for the feedback, much as it strangles. You are thankful for anything not convinced it is exactly what and where it should be, forever. Forever.

Forever.

Splitter's present sleeping chamber is made of cut-glass. It is more comfort-able than she would claim. Sleep is for the evil. Even resting is only seen as out of line. There is more than enough reason now for a person of her alloca-tion-state to never cease moving, to maximize coverage and want for nothing.

The next time I'm taken out, I'd like to receive some time off for good behavior, even if it decreases my subsequent actualization. I'm willing to give back, I mean. I understand that what's seen as fair must be seen as fair. Let someone else bask in the glory. Let there be peace among those who still can parse it.

Through the scape-skin, she looks out on seas and seas of prosthetic human blood. Even in as every other also knows or at least believes it is not actual, the conditioning allows a certain aspect of remorse for those in flux, reinforc-ing how nothing is promised, no one's conditioning permits them fermentation unto self; how the ground alone can't hold us up. As unfounded as any such faith feels, it comes with penance. Even as Splitter herself is trodden to threads, there are even worse fates than being forced forever through the tragic system.

For one, you could survive your own worst hell rate, personal affectations not combined. What must supplant eventual fact then would by internal definition become even more so all-encompassingly impractical, unsurpassable, etc. There are those, like those who hunt her, for whom such an alternative dimension would appear (to themselves) preferable, in that the more they suffer, the more they are. Splitter is not so much a one of those as one unable to redirect from out of tracking of *the human desperation*, the funding of which had only ever been her call. As whatever dream could ever suspend such a purpose; how much more interrelated could one feel than to have been bushwacked by the same emotional starburst, the frameless seething.

Would I could only ever be this gone. Or else this openly retorted.

All the rest of what might once have been remains unseen. Even the inprisming apes lambent, reinforced by ambient heart-particles compromised by internal residue to simultaneously retro-track where nothing else remains to track, such that the possibility of total aspect-reset, while so far merely theoretical, hangs over all diplomacy, even among the immensely battered ecosystem socially comprising the top six human power-structures behind the walls somewhere framed sacred, but truly only actually as naturally installed as any other untoward feature of animation.

The local composition fills her brain. It leaks and laps around like milk across any open entrypoint allowed inactive, the nearest stand-in to fully shutting down. *Whatever happened to that one person who wrote that one long song that everyone said was going to last forever, tape-tapping in over all other possible soundtrack? Mr. Confusion, I believe he was called. Or Mr. Mammy.* There have already been so many artists with the same claim, the same species, divulging the same misbegotten truths as the sole practice of their trade; to be brought in and alongside whoever could make them the only extant voice, whether living or unliving, paid in trust or left to starve. *If this is indeed unbelievable, what I am doing, which kind of eternity is mine? How long can I really imagine being allowed to keep on trucking, so subjected?*
She already knows the answers. Because she's changed them, at least for others, within the guidelines of her work, the only active freight of interspecies communication still "active:fertile," and the only reason she's survived so long

to see the non-evaporative blood still yet come raining. *It rains all through us in our sleep; it is as much part of us as all the rest we still mimic delight in.*

]]]

Once fully healed, Splitter has lunch. Slung from the soup of humankind. Mashed out of the masses once reformed under crushing protocol, as the lymph along the bone learned to wear down, return to crust again, corrupted. The feeding cartridges are more a privilege than a necessity of being, one of the tight perks of the job. Spindled packets of marrow mayo and crackers calcified from living cheeks (she does not know this, or does know and does not allow herself to actually know she knows); packets of tasty pastes expunged from brainstem, underbelly, silver linings; incontrovertible, she feels its passage leaking down the inside of her face, becoming part of what she feels she really isn't; the softer walls; the open rot. Or there's this one really strong upload they send sometimes where it comes on like being massaged with oil from the inside, then sucker punched, into a mustardy bloom snatched down the gullet all lizard-sticky and exquisite; the slickest high she's ever had; she can see her dad then, her grandfather (two proto-men who had been ripped apart by bugs in the train-code before she was born), can hold what seems a conversation with them about warfare; "they put the bombs into our underbritches; they put them in the study's lightbulbs and the converters of current required to even see, so that when we turned them on just once we died in a muff of resins; not even reported, but they still listen to the recordings of our screaming all these years later; you can also at your local incubator if you have my ID tag; no I don't know it, and please do not come searching me out." Of course nothing can be fried, even indirectly, after the passage of the law against good taste; instead they do the bull organs and head-teeth in a gray crème sauce sourced from actual imprints of feeding dairy, a trickery Splitter must admit she savors; even the thought of a whiff can fill her whole stream-suit with wanting pudge. So much to chomp and without the dementia of having to worry about what will be done to her body as a result, in short or long term, as none of the food has any actual attributes besides conditioning, which, wow, it turns out, is not a great thing. But hey what is. And what could ever be. And still, there is an inherent pleasure to being filled up, written over, a fact they could not remove without removing every facet of the act itself, and this is the very sort of fate perhaps that had pushed persons like her into her methodology of being, after all; joining in rather than being flattened out, asunder, a decision neither right nor fair nor wise, if really the only choice there ever was when given a choice at all, itself again the greatest fate one can receive, according to the scripture of the not yet begotten.

What aspect owns the inverse of her life. It as much whoever's as any other's, so would be written, in the erased edition of some hyper-revised *Hextionary of the Undead*, where every fixture owns no product beyond what has been allowed as chained for granted, no longer really anybody's now; only the router's, the recognition's; another book no one has read, or even seen, even in the "comprehensive" collegiate retro-fitting exercises others in her line of work are now commanded to comply through under the latest rubrics of furtive service. Not Splitter, though; she's special; so they have allowed her to comport; she's been in it so long she's the only living witness to how it once could have been, a fact now so deported under supplemental conditioning that even she can't remember why or how or what the cause, how it could come back eventually to hurt her, as could all things, any second, any way.

Post-feed, she's so engorged she couldn't wish to move, of course; known how they like it; how it is likened. And who has any words that they can say otherwise or would ever want to. So seen as one must go there so goes Splitter full by formal definition under the claiming papers of *the Employer*, every one of them, and all. Give unto the infestation what must be the infestation's. Give unto the mounds of us, so unto breath.

]]]

Splitter's next plug, so it appears encoded across her see-screens once she's mid-recovery from what psychic damage even her eating has semi-temporarily incurred, is presently housing in the same infrastructure as her rest point, she comes to find. She's been sharing a floor with him this whole time, though his is ceiling. What else about him does she know? The info-layer supplied for such occasions is usually so thin as to be zero beyond location and facial conditions, but this time the databank includes sense, a state that sends up more red flags than it does provide meaning:

Target has sixty offspring + one hundred grandlings associated out of Nardix Districts c thru Cx. Target believes that he is still young and tender. Target has been indicted on seven counts of instilling anti-propaganda propaganda among his closest associations. Target's blood has not responded to our prods and refuses recreation assignment. CUE: EXTERMINATE W/ IMMENSE GRATUITY.

Such semi-explicit information is usually reserved for only those who hold her keys. She is not sure why now or through what breaching she would be given further context beyond go, record, transmit. But it is not her job to wonder, much less respond. It is, instead, and in the words of her enforcer, "[her] job to do [her] [*edited*] job."

And so do her [*edited*] job she will, soon as she feels fired; on the inside freezing, full of dust; covered up with attitude no earth wished to inherit; nowhere's.

She walks across the floor and feels it yearn. To pull her through it. Into the body of the target in the flesh of the creator. Nonapparent. Who is there in there? The air is fat. She can cream it in the way a worm would. The instigator. All the language ever been. Like flow. Like cold sights slitted at the gills and packed into icons without locks.

As we behold the intervention.

]]]

:but the scene cannot be seen: :nor heard: :unasked for:
:off the record: :even ours:
:same as all certainty:
:among the last of all the small ways left unshaped:
:deprogrammed:
:indemonstrable: :in cognition:
:mud in the guts: :entrails made gravy: :between the pistons of the revision:
:*open wide*:
:coded: :corralled: :never recalled:
:around your neck: :crushing your wishes:
:already over: :before it came on: :before the bell split every second:
:worn away:

:wearing away still:

]]]

Splitter finds herself standing at a river.

She has never seen a river.

]]]

We did not want a kill to ever actually remember how to die. To understand the situation in such a way that the information might infect the local network and cause the sort of panic not seen since we began infusing cellular capability into embryos without the necessity of parental approval. Like all good things, at first it seemed fucked up and immoral beyond belief, until at last the aural incentive program we put in place to grease the gears began to see effect, promising best interest rates on loans for elementary college and free sod analysis for those who had been preapproved. Doesn't matter what they'd been approved for; they were going to get it. We were going to give it to them. Anyway, in order for the target's mash radius not to spill over problematic we basically cloak-encoded Polyana's more remarkable features (length of fingernails, inner softness, the stubble constellation of her face) so that there would be no overlap between ignoble data and system revamp. It should affix within even seconds of internal contact, like being looked at the wrong way, acknowledged in some form to say, *We no longer need you as you had been, please proceed to the hub and prepare for further import*, when what we really meant was, *There is no ability that can be measured that we do not eventually suss out and recreate independently of the necessity of ongoing habitation.* And even still as pleasant and seamless as we'd made the procedure there were still those who wanted more, who believe in a sort of conservation of human behavior, such that when one flame went out in one locale, another must come on in another, creating a whole arms race of sorts in manufacture of methodology to bring certain more desirable imprintables into the transformative favor of private parties who could stand to benefit from such illicit sequencing, eventually causing an imbalance of transformative talent and cocreation in specific quadrants that, if left unchecked, could overflow into a species of partition that might eventually make our leaders' lives that much more difficult to experience preferred qualities of ongoing being there within, which of course was the last thing anyone wanted, and we'd already done so much other legwork that not seeing it thereafter all the way through down to the more prickly dots and crosses that not taking care of business as we must would eventually be seen in the context of our larger proto-natal history as the greatest travesty of all, one it would not only take innumerable generations to reantigeneticize out of our nature, but even then would be still somewhere imprinted in our heads such that no pleasure would come without some impending febrile sickness, if not in our own lives in those of our oncoming ancestors down the line, and so it was in the name of taking responsibility for choices we'd made very early on in our formation, before we even had the ratty ambient shaping placement nature we have now, and doing everything we can so that in the end, when all the bulbs are zipped and trees are fire, all we will have left to do is lay open in the bloat and firm our rot, soak in the motion of knowing of a job well done, by someone, at our order, for the holy benefit of each and all, as we see fit, same as every other name would do forced on our person in the same position, unto eternity.

]]]

At the time of her recoding, as it happened, Polyana had returned to the mirage of her own home, part of the incentive-driven, performance-earned monthly vacations allowing employee sojourn availaballisitically siphoned into off-site respite of those who'd been flagged for immediate demotion when an inter-screening reflects conditions wherein distrust might be soon be met, a review process widely lauded for its accuracy and fairness, if not its unhackability to fraud, which is exactly how P has ended up here, having had her entry path selected for her by someone else; in this case, Splitter, who in her defense believed she must be acting in good faith, eliminating from open view each and any thriving frond of her past lives, to which Polyana had been retrofitted into as a bait, if not one that would result in Splitter's capture, so full of leaks left as she is.

Polyana finds herself up to her neck soaked in a BubbleBloodBath already, a Pleasure experience newly minted by the makers of Poppy Pet, same who'd designed her dinner outfits and her Restricto-wristbands (for good health). Whose blood the blood had come from she did not know. Nor would you want to, as it would spoil the fun, or if indeed it made it better it would come with certain emotional responsibilities that most abusers did not wish to have to rap with, which is precisely why the Rowze Corporation had hired the top covert psychic research-marketing firms in the lower 90 to stabilize and reinforce the internal understanding that bathing in blood was something any working person had always done, without the necessity of ontological exam- ination or any such once wholly natural anguish-driven ephemeral effect. One simply had to turn the gold gordian knob, found where it should be in any cleansing stall between the hot water and the cold, and one was up to their nut in mulchy plasma, a luxury once considered reserved for only the upper center middle narrow left-up higher classes, and now, through the miracle of minor science and the benevolence of those in charge, almost anyone at any time could be indulged, so long as you had sufficient contributionary time credits to be milked in recompense, all of which was fully automatic, and in sum helped facilitate better usage of the national byproduct as a font of renewal rather than simply filling up the landmines all beneath us, the blunted mounds on which we walked. There was simply so much blood to be dealt with how could we have fucking ever if we hadn't made you want to do it for us, is the key, one that everybody soaking in the stuff knew as well as they knew one day it could be their very own blood that someone else was dolling around in, pretending it was only more gorgeous chemicals, taming our skin, calming us down from somewhere so innate and unlocatable that only acts such as the ones if having seen from far away in time, such as right now, we might have termed absurd, or at least debatable in preference, like who would want to do that, and more so, why. Such effluence was no longer necessary at this juncture, to either transgressor or receptor, nor did it have any much ongoing effect besides to make the bather feel better off than they had ever been to have been in on this receipting end of the transaction, the final living beneficiary so to speak. Whatsothereafter came of the substance was business for another media's repast.

But honestly, taking her time in BubbleBloodBath made Polyana feel something more than just alive. What pops where bubbles bust beneath her feels like more than simply washing, clearing the core out. It screams with fever, drums with joy; in knowing there is only one of her, and so little left of what condensed to feed its maker; the pressed-electric bliss of coursing ever so near another's mortal end; not that she can't feel it coming for her own self, daily and nightly, a darkened sprawl that clogs the hours with its boil; as if the ceiling of the world is slowly lowering at the same time that the floors all sink at equal rate; towards what or when; singing whose praises. She finds her fingers running down her thighs, unsure they are even still her thighs, under the scummy surface, and when had her nails been quite this long? They scratch her deeper than she remembers able to be scratched before, not in a bad way; something slow and fumbling in her guts; as if beneath the surface of the muddle she too comes open, turns to liquid, only recombining just in time to not quite break the illusion of being flesh, able to rise from the bath and will and return to other progress; here in her distemper, flooded with noise; all the hissing and co-listing fragmented in her hour after hour, month after year, brought once briefly into cooperation, claiming her body, owning it, enclosing it: *she is precisely what she could not convince herself she was,* matter unfolding and spilling out like bowels slit in a stuffed animal, not even tragic, not quite defined. Wherever the softest parts of her might quiver she can feel too there against them the bulged friction of the wants and memories from those the blood must have come supplied, transferred not by tape or pill for once but by direct conference, the tickled rot lapping its long arm inside her, through any hole, through all the want she could have carried to continue being whoever she actually believes she is again, what qualities anyone could ever accuse her of having been provided, having conjured out of placement in herself. The tip of the tongue along the roof of the bread her tongue makes caught between the sea of teeth as she limps back and lets the aura do its work; near my father to thee, so says the old prayer, nearer within us; her fingers spread across her plate, hoarding in what else there is to sense about a fragrance, a longitude of lifetimes rendered common, not even dust, as what cannot settle must again evaporate away, taking up what else is left yet to be taken, carry on. It's an inebriating spectacle, she knows, so much so that even the description of her passage would sound to anyone outside it like a drunk's doze, so like brain damage; though what is damage but the truth; and what is the truth but only that which holds the present frame in place, sent sliding out from underneath itself no sooner than someone else might try to save it, give it context, if not a title.

She's never been so wide as she is now. That's what her flesh is telling her, anyhow, as in the unlit room the blackened mirrors lining the rented walls seem so far away, like as if you could touch one it would flip over into a new room, the beginning of someone else's prior life. Which is exactly how she became herself, isn't it, wasn't it for everyone. Had there ever been another way. With her lungs inside her lurching as sick cells tickle, fumbling for presence in the cause, of teeming higher, turning over walls within her in the same way, seeing out through vistas of some lost self, withunder faith-lidded fantasies corroborated by the nuanced declaration knocked loose only by half-drowned rites of semi-deprivated self-stimulation, the rhythm of the mumble, the stir of the fist, dragging down in malformed flags of days misspent once and now returned, to become funded by persuasion to seem exactly necessary, a gift of chance; dreams of her ex-self pressed in glass cases stored in houses waiting to be shipped off for cellular labor; of her future self becoming wrinkled beyond belief, forcing her flesh's purpose to be insulation, cosmetic detritus stuffed into bureaucrats who will only source their costumes from the makeup of the dead; where within each possible outcome whole ranges of defenestration and massacre tally themselves sprawled catacombic, the corridors of a world she might have lived to see made actual, were she not she; as every second the whole existence of us all pends on the crippling of so many others, as well as the false salvation rendered in its tow; wherein without now, upon another of the infinite conditions of even being, there could not thereafter be another, over and over, and each at once thereafter rendered null, as soon again the crooning ceases, and the dark seems harder, and the blood is long beyond grown cold; left with no way to get it out of us now, nor known to wish to.

As such, Splitter hardly needs to lift a leg to do her job. It's more a matter of showing up, identifying your willingness to perform for the recorders, to stake a name onto the crime. What else could be asked of Instantantion, in a setting where had we really wanted someone killed all we had to do was press a button? It felt so meaningless without a culprit, a face to blame. Didn't the most incontroversial dead deserve that? To have an enemy to take to grave, to want to learn to haunt or meet in hell next face to face, seek retribution? In a world of nubs and levers, electric fancy, retribution would be king, driving even the thinnest of us to the darkest ends. Therein might we find new mass labor even after mortality, if we could only find a mechanism that could harness eternal restlessness, bad grace; and I can assure you our sickest cells are fast at work at this; it's a matter of no time before even everlasting rest punches a clock, tabulates its hours to the behest of the manufacturers, the shills. After all, it's only in the model of what the Lord had wanted for us all, and once when finding it was not so he packed and left in search of better craft, leaving to only the slickest of his worst creation the ability to alchemize the lost behavior; to be long and truly owned; to be inspired to the limits of production, in the unwritten name of perceived evolution.

This is not to say Splitter will not seek relish in the task at hand. Like any great gourmand, the spirals of her seeking fit soft and carved into her locks, as if the act is not only inevitable, incontrovertible; it is a part of her. It is the ground on which she stalks, the bleeding lesion at her center that will one day perform an analogous task, to bring her home, back to the black database at least, so as it were; as not all victims once selected may be released into the waiting pools of the lost, even lost daughters, bound only coaxially in future ransom; as of her own fate, she cannot know. Would she still act given the information that what had been commanded once performed offers no prize? That despite the salary and loose office hours and relative mobility of site and freedom to shape the specific arming nature of her charge, in the end she will be held up as no more than a drone in her own right, an extension of the code against her own blood, to which once all she's been allowed is set in motion, she must inevitably return? No scene at last wherein, old and distended, she is sent to grow large via imbibing, numbing down, until what is left of her is little more than putty?

And still, there in the vibrant active quadrant, Splitter shines. Where any logic holds profane and without music, rendered moot. Where in the beat of an eye, what has been tasked is as good as beholden. As if it had never been not done, as blood meets Blood, snuck through a mnemonic slit in the target's pale inner thigh, slight enough to appear undetected, significant enough to clip her route as in post-coital crumbling, she's half asleep, talking to herself already still in the internal language of the Corporation, who would have by their contract spread her ashes out to sea, were not the human body by now so spare, becoming so much mush even by minutes later, loose enough alike to take the drain, to join that darkness as the tub on auto-level pulls its own plug, empties itself, cleans up the scene by route of program to make space for the next inhabitant's routines. Nothing less than like a clipping from a newspaper, the violent act, its own fact to be pulped and reformatted once finished glowing on the cell screens in the only rest homes where reading at all is still allowed, among the marketable elders of the families of the management, shipped off to other planets, other whole surfaces about which we the living will never be informed. Wherein thereafter we can see only Splitter's febrile golden teeth, hard in the dark across such slighted cosmos, floating fixed as some dead star would, showing its last light long after it has already exploded, until a single finger strokes closed the living diorama's simul-screening panel, one of billions, and goes back to really jacking off.

]]]

•

Who now will lead the feeble to their seizures? wonders Nadan, son of the son of Satan, from just beyond. His vibe is mired in the protagonist of being fetched to the scheme of the rind of god around the bodies of every child who has gone missing. In the years since shattering the prized conditioning. Above no surface not adhered to implementation in a chorus to be found among those once thought to be immortal. They were up to deafening mire so sold out it could not stand ground long enough to be trampled, filled with limbs, hair, couches, other accoutrement once considered nearly required for livelihood among the drowned. If you were going to ask for passage you had better have the screws already removed from all that had ever wished to hold you down. Primed to disintegrate on mention. No one world's structure given over to intervention on the part of those known haunted by the proclivity to ever be caught in the very trap you'd been designing to kill your lunch with, much less your least worst enemy.

He is alone. His pain is our pain. No more conducted under arms claimed soft by pastures paled under the numbered suns that gave us language, then forced its degradation into thinking, writing, speech. All that we believed was its sole purpose. All that we believed at all about what might be salvaged from the wreckage of the "solved" planets, each of which now bears the names of anyone you met while still in human form: *I do not want to have to list these names for fear you will remember anything about them*, where to remember is to end forever.

Nadan loves nothing more than to make suck. As where eyes live in the body nothing can be claimed not under radar of the shamed, known old only in smithereens, the slack so soft and pliable there is no reason not to believe it could have ever survived millennia, much less the whole infernal thrall in windless thievery, all apparition, picked apart and greased to fits. Around Nadan's throat the paint of ecstasy, flowing from the cold open wound stabbed through his throat by where in place of Adam's apple he has a stabbing starball. His blood would never find an end to being run, spent so much as it is with our blood's daft incantation, shown a clobbering of fools, as the spit runs down the mountain, filling our houses with entertainment.

Where else could ever quite begin besides the claim we could not have upon any actual identity.

Where else is there to move but through Nadan.

●

In the collision, nothing survives. There isn't a word even in the banal tongue for what excuses itself out of the subsequent transom.

I believe they need you. One day perhaps they will realize.

●

ahead how survived pollenated with gold screwdrivers appliqued to human moaning stark envisioning the missiles coming down surrounded with leather pumice as an astrology with darts as the center of the pupil last contracts its sexual fluidity as mask rubbed taut in search of the searcher's searching spread wide an algorithm squalid in dough vomiting the yarn back to provider eliciting no cleft introduction to our disease hogged under pulsate technology enabling full blown aspiration as we become unknown again amid the multitude collared for purchase outside how fright grows to reveal its unnecessary faker once comprised only in an invention of who withstands the forfeiture of every lining when what claims ground is without tense and has no intention but to be blinded, narrowed, wended down until the clone's urge is upon us

●

Infinite police permeate the last known. Like how today is not the form of day we are supposed to learn to live with. I couldn't find anybody worth my time until I started looking in upon the texture in the leaves that lined the drum in us. There there were plummets there there. It took me and held me down. It knew me better than I knew what knowing is and ever could be.

When I could unsee again I saw the lawmakers had changed their means underneath us. And we still were expected to participate in fate.

●

It's all situational. Not reversible. The kind of site you lived without. *It's not OK.* It's fine.

Can you just learn to exist the way you always would have? Worlds apart from who and when, in any reasoning? The code commands you its design. It lives within you in windless ways you never would have shared with any other given the possibility of one's own configuration, or in a neighbor, maybe even your own child. I have to divulge this information because I don't want you eating yourself alive, much less at the wrong station.

What can you see now? To whom does it belong? I can't see anything. It belongs to everybody. *False. What you see is the core. What you are is its enactment.*

[auto-unpacking: (*THE LAST GOLD MEDALIST*) A mass
admission (indexed in retrospect to fill
the absence of all thought)]

Dust drags in smearspace once deformed. Far off patches of the white
porch where no one left off taking part in their own worst intentions, becoming landscape. The windows slipping from themselves. Already a woman
appears, approaches. I can't shake her, even after she again has become plush.
The changing music, learning to shake even my most inherent etiquettes.
Impossible to see anything but outlines. An overlay of what had been there
hours before. But we want to think in years. In runnels managing no negotiation with viewer's deceptive tendencies to interpret what can't be felt under
the surface. A mask of wasps I will wear to my own funeral eventually, when I
am finally allowed to give up my aging tricks. To see me standing above me,
after all I've done and all I worship. The drags staring packing up, becoming
tricks in the topography: the woman's having a seizure. I want to help her. All I
can hear is the house falling apart. Wind across my face from so far away its
like real science. In shattered glass and the edges of vocabulary compacted as
something you could dance to before the snuffing comes and reminds you
what to really say. Watching the film burn between the moving frames now
forming buttons that likewise disintegrate, become replaced. Random packages buried in software bursting open. Hysterical majesty. As the churn dawns,
pushes itself back out to choked rerecordings of its own beginning. Until the
lift clips out itself. Then there are more windows than ever. The machine has
pressed us to the soil so hard the song is melting our only skin. What does the
woman even want? How can she see me so far across the transom, covered in
semen now. My golden belt around my waist. It holds my belly back so I can
see the genitals I've been given, still glistening, moist, plugged into current.
The eyes that float alone around my head, observing only for themselves,
distinct from the faces of different ages of persons I had loved that flash in
representations of coming back into myself before the cracking closes in,
around, forever. Where in the cracking I am felt. Found holding the speak-
ing-box to my face and waiting for someone else to do the talking. Traced with
smoke. The bones that kiss the makeup laid between us. The undivided
electricity. I had no other way to see. Outside the ovens finally long enough to
be granted actual register to the persona buried in my many folds and cloven
orifices, having already circumnavigated celestial entitlement for centuries.
Lodes within them bearing promise counted only by the ring fingers ripped

off of the hands of anyone I'd ever appeared within a space near. They could not sense what yet was there, though I knew their aging grew more rapid the closer I allowed myself to approach and look on into where the creases emerged to find my own faith. A faith in choosing not to feed. In taking measure to remand the parts of me that had already been wiped out by my own private defamations and rejoinders causing flies to rise from deadly beds, to join the force inherent in the manifestation of our becoming. It was not that I wished to hurt everyone, it was that they gave me no other choice. Not even to end myself. Nor to stay silent, live a life unremarked upon, closed under miles of ambient fat that would protect the simple from my more renounced application, selected for me so long in the bloodline it was as inherent as a kidney, every brain cell. For this, there would be no key despite the locks, no word that fit into the sentence running ever through me to make it feel as if it'd finally found its shape and it could rest. In ugly lights on the leaden land placed on the working homes in the name of safety. Gouged in the glasses of slick minds, turning themselves off and on just long enough to perform without threat of personal attribution, nor any recompense outside the passive threat of plangent recordkeeping, from off of which the only living fires burned. I mean I was so far down in there it was already another floor in sight, where the word *floor* means *hidden way*, under the fast collapsing of the cell's walls holding all life in as someone within us raised their blackened hammer for the last time, brought it down. And I found that I was standing in a glassen field then, one wide and far as any sickness, and beneath the glass the air was turgid, full of charge, with smaller sputums like pastel gravy lapping and gathering themselves together into packets, forms of local gravity repurposed, even faces, passed in the concavity, asking for lessons, to turn disabled, to not need to categorize any method of experiencing the present, much less all else. Only way back went through myself. Or, that is, back through my sudden infestation. Bred holes and polar rapture. A pending penetrability I will not be gifted enough to overlook. As a daft breeze aggravates the cones stuffed in the camera's nature, leaving after only all that comes alive only in having at last been overridden. Hardly hissing for mercy. As the flesh strobes, and the land lifts, and there is a need again to carry weight, wherein you won't want this time to be forgiven, when told the penance. And still, you can tell me everything. Including this, reciting back what I've just said to show you'll change it with repetition, every time, to fit hard with the part of you that can't stop stealing. Layer by layer. Crushed under leather. Until I was no longer quite right there. I was in my bone room, typing this session. The catalog of breath was in my chest so fat and riddled it didn't need me to collaborate with my own process. It just kept offering itself outs, through every orifice but the ones that I'd selected. This made me furious, of course, ready in instants to give it all up, the bells, the witches, over one simple matter of inconvenience, like burning up the lasting land in search of the landmine, which was exactly what they'd expected in design. Only so much a blessing as a resting place among the lard could be, allowing everything to deplete its final resources without measures to read the levels. Of course, I was never actually in danger all throughout; I was the sort who could have failed infinite times and still found myself fat in the bed eating muscles out of a virgin's neck gorge, asking him to rename me every time either one of us came. Though every time I'd turn around even for a second, I could feel the image glitching, showing his bruises, the soft saw marks where they'd installed the parts of him that allowed me to take hold. It didn't really affect my performance at all, I'm just saying I was aware of what was going on, same as I am now; I don't want to mislead you into imagining I might be spared of my own slobbery, not because I won't, but because it doesn't even really hurt. Nothing here does. Not even watching the death or torture of persons in who I feel a personal connection for some reason, like they look like someone previously famous, or they look like I would like to look, does much of anything to stir much else than my desire to become them, just for a second, near the end, to feel what they could feel and have it affected me, as if the lid is really coming down, only to slip my fingers free at the last second, close my eyes, and fall away. They can have the final solitude, there's always time for that, right, someday, as if in solace, an actual pasture to be led out to, left to feed. Maybe that's actually where I already am, now. They wouldn't tell you, would they? They'd just let you be, and go on performing as if you'd finally found the good life, the low tide where all the shells of any color become exposed so that you can walk among them and pick the nicest looking ones. No need to name what kind of time it is when the tide rolls back in, blacks out the pleasure. You can only imagine you will again be waking up, that you would recognize when at last it doesn't recur, and what else happens happens. I wonder what that is. Wonder if it's different for every person, depending on how their life was ended, or what they'd wanted it from it still when the claim passed. I don't know, I know I don't have to think about it right now, I don't need to wonder, for me or my kids, none of whom I've ever met or would be allowed to, given my position as creator of their lives. Only to lurk behind the curtains like their lord, watching the promised outlines take their shape from out of all the dust and gore that holds the night up. Or holds me in it. Holds you out. It's a long way from here to where you're reading, but it isn't far enough. All you had to do was try to tell me anything you really knew for certain and I could tell you how it was wrong and where you might better spend your time and all you kept doing was repeating the same few things that everyone else already thought. I expected better, or at least different, at some point. I expected to want to crush you, in all your power, in everything you had that I could not. I never felt that. I never wondered. I just went on ever-after laying here, waiting to see. Like here I am still. Like no one's winning. I mean just look at us. Look at all we've not achieved. All we'll never stand to really be besides the tremor. The interventions. The overseen. Not that I care, just wanted to remind you. To let you know. Cuz you should still have to feel it, therein and underneath you. When you feel anything. In all, you are and aren't. And never could be. Now kiss my fingers. I've worked for my whole life for this exchange. I only wanted intervention and all got was this lousy face with all these markings all over the important parts. I hate being a human being who has to wait and communicate and think. Nothing you have here does what it's supposed to. It's all just dying, becoming scrambled, stalling out. How did you even make it here? And for what reason? Seems like you'd have a reason, after so much sacrifice, such shame. Most of all the rest of people like you would have given up already. Like when they tore your teeth out, or when they stamped the marching arch into your back, or ate the spine out of your sister, krushed your favorite Veil of Grace on the morning of your commencement into human gas, as I have breathed you, as we have lived together all our lives without the charm of music droned in cracked vessels cold to cover up the holy pain. You didn't even seem mad at all, much less to really feel it, notate the code they gave you to break back in on all you'd left behind in the home where someone else is living now, wrapped in your sheets, framing their faces with your make-up, worshipping the bloom of the bread you only wanted to have around til it went bad, and the mold that rose in gray and green became your future, the lowest planet, the last way out. Now that fate is only someone else's. And you are mine. So now we can begin with the real story. But there isn't really a real story. You've been living it, hiding it within you. Trolling its breadth within you. Wearing it down. Where there had ever been a wish once there is only dislocation, a sense of being sheltered from afar. I wonder what words I could type to describe you from within deep darkness using only my teeth to find the keys, with no erasure, no way back. It will probably be closer to the truth than anything you've ever read about yourself, much less written. I wish to put this sentiment online. Press it into the sliding hemispheres of social data and see what absence of reaction it brings forth. Like sand from the floor of your own cottage being vacuumed up and returned to the same beach where it began. Where buried underneath the place where you are standing, several miles down, is the mouth to one of the million tunnels that can bring you down to where I am. To bring us face to face, so to speak, though by then you will no longer have one, and in me you will see nothing but blue smoke and open water. As if the prior world could not cohere with what's been put asunder, holding it up forever here on out. But what does that tell you about my motivation to keep speaking, to impart this information? I'll ask again later, so many years from now, when you're so old you have no flesh, where there are no words left for you to answer, because I do not need the answer, nor the intercession of your fright, which will be allowed to gnash and roil long after you are barely nothing, within the living state of nature that has allowed you on even this far. As my progenitors rescind. As they take back what's neither ours nor yours nor shared between us, without a claim beyond the meat you used to see through and how it must now in silence be returned. Meanwhile, I can hardly keep my head up at my desk. I am so exhausted from all this breathing, sleeping, while you've gone on about your fate. They've sworn to me they will not leave you with less than nothing. They will supply you within mechanisms to feel pain through, to receive stress. And so you'll still be able to hear me, whether you ever wished to once or not. Words are cowards, after all; they hold no reason; they refuse to stand up for themselves; they let you take what you wish from them and carry on. We're working on putting an end to that, though I can't tell you when or how. I can only say that by the time that we discover the transition there will be nothing left to cling to. The words will be all you ever had, allowed at last to resolve themselves in the very way they meant to despite your hidden damage and neglect, the bruises buried in their shaping, the bloodless centuries of embarrassment and odium, all the signets, the scourged recordings where all we have is every voice, wailing out once at the same time, in the same peril brought to risk as the mask rises, shows its flesh. What was it *you* saw on the day our blood broke open? Mhm, that's fine, okay, what else. Well, no, that's not really how it happened. No detonation or other formal correlation. Nothing out of order from any day. You had to be told how to feel, but in a way that made it seem like you'd come to your own decision. The mold is flowing, you might know. Or: the clouds have ledges. Preference means nothing. Nature is seized. I can't remember much less else. I can only say that by the end, the scape of grade from here to there no longer had any claims to definition, and soon the world was at once as it had never really been. Like I could see me standing as before me here before the grieving panels of our lives. And when I touch my tongue against the icon meant to comprise your family's history I can't taste anything beyond the flooding of my mind with empathy, compassion, a want for understanding how you and those around you and within you ever found the will to rise. That is, to believe you were allowed to, to have a body, to take vision with it, to fuck, to eat; all of the rights of a living, taking human as bestowed upon those who could dignify such processes with a name, much less a reputation signifying all the fertile aspects of their holy privilege, as if you had the fiber in your heart, as if you could understand the grace in anything you'd ever wanted for your own and no one else's. As for now, the haul is mine, including all of that you could not figure beyond promise. The hissing dust around your levers. All your inheritance, your miles of sewing. The grafting pasture where you waited to be shown sights, both of your own life and the crushed world's: the miles of bodies shaped exactly like your own forced into lines, leading to holes in the conditioning raw as purses fat with premise, tearing back and buckled pale and drawling down, feeding into the very kind of silence that compels even this transmission, its permissions, all the tests. No need to stop now that I've said it, drawn it out, against the endgame of your shaping, about which I can't keep count of what's been suggested into fact and what is merely rumor. Why should I. Moreover: exactly how and at whose ongoing expense? Not that there's a deficit; as when where there were numbers once now there are the naked, the mumbling, the half-turned-under, who fill our rapture, fund our plague. Which it seems now I've been placed in full command of, having earned the respect of my peers following my performance in the Divestment, co-named chair captain of underfunding every rite, throughout which I lurked out a living as a competitive investment banker for the Innumerable International. It was simple as repurposing our clients' funds from one location to another, clicking and dragging, with only my identity placed on the line, such that were Acts and Practices to pull a fast one and have to take some heads off for some internal purpose to defraud investigators from coming around to check complying codes, they'd have someone like me, among their millions, to be beheaded. Turns out I have a talent for reclaiming that which was never found, as it might turn out. I fit right into the team onto which I was born, as if it might have even been the only reason I existed, my chemicals combined to claim this invocation, to take the reins. Work my way up and one day I could really be a feeling leader, was my private logic, though on the surface all I ever really was another dickhead in a gold jacket until they identified me as one of the coldest ushers of all time, churning out numbers that would make a dozen others in my position weep, to see the damage, to understand that someone with such alike could be so capable of savoring the ill in one's own self so much it was like sport forcing it on others. I mean they had me full in the belief, at the behest of their enforcements, the vast brutality I'd come around to see as friendly before they put me in here at the far end holding the handles, assisting with the aiming of the stab. And though now I can see the crummy feelings that it causes, the endless bleating, the friction as fire pulls apart the muscles in those we must remand, I can only understand the concurrent stinging that must pass over every victim as temporary, necessary, even sacred. It is, after all, part of our rite. It is the only reason we have reason. It is all there ever was or could be, all there is, if we are to indeed remain the greatest information-bearer the human scourge has ever known. Which of course we will regardless and so fully must be, and which is why I've come to spend this day as such with someone like you, who I feel certain will be more than happy to lend their moment to this traction, and in exchange, might live even longer. And I have many reasons to want to live. There is so much to be done, between the shaming, the excoriation, the gold balloons, the ballrooms that collapse beneath the maid of honor upon command of his most high, the signal traps and intonations that slide the back out of the head, expose the tape loops living and breathing the way a mollusk might entrapped. Previously to my work here in waste management, I was actually a recording artist, one whose work defined a rather hairy generation, when no one listened to anything, much less something designed for them to want to listen to. The worst thing a producer like myself might have done then was try to jockey for position among the dozens, nay hundreds, still composing and recording work that seemed to know or wish to know exactly how to burrow to the center of a spirit, to go encombed there and remain forever haunted in them like a virus, if then without any actual intent but to be accessed and revered, therein kept alive as much might one still hungry when the toll of death came. It had come to be by that point that people knew about the problems with such allowances, and were being more purposeful about what and when they let media in, perhaps listening with earplugs in under the headphones to protect against the tinny messages embedded in walls of sound, which certainly were still being applied within any creation by those who oversaw the transduction even through such user-friendly-seeming experiences as webpages and autoloaders, but none in such a way that there was anything that you could do to separate the wheat from chaff, or to avoid exposure in the first place, as the same tricks were being slipped into our breakfast, our dreams, our pets. My work, then, as it turned out, was about seeming inspirationally developed to maintain individual sensations in the user's experience such that any song I wrote could not exist until the listener began listening, even without knowing they held such power in the deal. Using reverse forensic technology supplied to me by black market dealers who I believed at the time to be my friend, and sourcing bass materials through natural surfaces like oak ringlets and the fuzz on bees, I was able then to manifest a kind of aural scripting that literally physically clung to hold inside the brain, infusing itself in as it were by sculpting off the user's private browsing history and specific persona traits of record (empathy, tragedy, dislocation, suicidal tendencies, ongoing pain) to produce a shape of sound that worked its logic as a live band might, on the spot, while at the same time bearing all the polish of any local anthem, those works refined as such that they could never truly pierce the imagination the way that ones like mine might on any given incidental user (in mobile shopping malls, for instance, those sort of pop ups that seemed so conveniently installed feet from the home that even if you didn't wish to shop, how could you not go out and see what wares they offered; not to mention ballgames, airborne commercials, 3D clothing, childhood sickness), and even more so those who, in even one partial exposure, took up the gray reins of the fanatic. Very quickly, then, my progress as a tastemaker became incorporated into *how it must be*, resulting both in a head-spinning rise on my part within the mostly demolished ambiance industry to points of access I would soon have no option from within which to turn back, and fortuitously, at the same time, a proliferation of the natures of the sorts of works I would be encouraged into, or rather be forced to stamp my name with as it were, in order to maximize the reach of what was now seen as a shareholder-owned and profit-driven brand (I must admit, in my defense, that their compensation for transfer to such state was generous enough that there is no one in their right mind, or who wanted to go on walking and breathing anyway, could have flubbed a nose at; alas, my friend, I had no choice), including in our potential span of consumers an antithesis of what I'd begun cooking up the format of the forming of the music for in the first place, but now enabled, by the force of entry soon applied in the deeper sort of "research" my cohorts soon supplied) to have a similar individualizing and hyper-hypnotic effect on literally any sort of person ever, regardless of their self-made-seeming disposition, or even their ability to hear. The nature of the compositions, then, while seeming multifarious and aspirationally hyperdeveloped, in that each song we made when once installed would seem to come from the very edge of monolithic inspiration, changing the game each time another chorus dropped, were actually, in their base nature, all the same song, at least chemically; they found their way in whoever and would not thereafter come back out, all the while continuously communicating with my sponsors to upkeep in-tuning so that the inside presence of the song would never die, only change within the person, like a person, someone once loved or still loved but in a way that forces your commitment while allowing little actual received pleasure, not even sentimentally. My work in this way worked like limbs, and was not even mine more so than they might roto-message me asking for a title they would likely almost never use. Very soon then, though I appeared to be easily the most famous audible sensation of all time, it hardly required my participation, or my presence, or my person. It was an industry of need, one in which all involved assumed I'd be happy to wander off someone richer than Jesus and eat lamb and bacon all my life and live as a dream might knowing I was one of the spare few not federally involved who was allowed to hang around with a clear head and masturbate freely and at will, sometimes even being supplied with partners I could masturbate right into, always contractually of course, as had others like me in other industries that could be sponsored in similar fashions to produce correlative and international results. All which would have been fine, I'm sure, as I'm a chill one, were it not that I myself eventually became exposed; not for the sham I'd become; no, I was worshipped, at least my image was, my tired mind; but, that is, I fell a victim to my own work, at least a rendition of the work I was being tied to, that mass production and neo-geographic installation of which I by this point no longer had any inkling. I don't even know where I was when the inter-connection became triggered. I am no longer allowed to recall, as it would complicate my ongoing reuncontamination process, now decades in the making. Yet there are things that I can sense. The scrubbing sound of the processors converting my fleshy aspects into soundcode. The assembly of a sense of spirit within the confabulating; that is, therein: not only an identity set corresponding to the moniker of the mask of this creator (again, myself, under guise of a 6-piece free jazz-rubble-mumble tripset titled Mr. Mustard and the Fourteen Hundred Ducks) but as well fomented personas, experiences, and qualities about each of the would be "performers" that formed the sextet , including the titular Mr. Mustard, into whose psychic development I'd put an inordinate bit of my own time before allowing his traction to be granted deeper access by allowing others in my industry to contribute out of source, as in the instance of this particular memory vessel; as well as several other major players in the early adoption of those who would become known as formative to the state of affairs by the time they began replacing historical designations, overwriting the old names, among them, in what is now considered the most phenomenal and correctively accomplished inter-personnel grouping among the era's ever-shifting range of acts: Dick "Richard" Hanritty Sr. – vibraphone, electronics, sub-lyrics, backing vox; Ellen Fusca-Limsben – cello, lumens, samples, 808; I.E. Sarahh – concentric lung; and the Lurdivurco twins, conjoined from birth into becoming the most revered finger cymbals duo in the contemporary reformation era, straight out of North-Southeast Central New Sansissi. Anyone with my experience, however mangled by the stemwashing process that was required of me when I left, could identify all of these components within seconds, given even half a fragment of a second of the composition to break down; it was all contained within it, the signature stung to the data, if for most buried so completely in the processing sensations that it only bore the name of the frontloaded contributor, designed to present the package with most immediate acceptance-levels; in this case, as part of the ongoing discography of one of the most publicly beloved fronting persons of all time: ZZAAYX, who by the eighth year of our program was so universally implemented into ongoing consciousness that there was no food you could eat that had not been spokespersonned by them, no vacation home that you could download a hope for that didn't have their face stapled into the framing décor, no car whose console did not bear their signature (a long, straight line, ending in a single police-blue period), no hoping product who had not at some point employed their visage into marketing to garner sales. And so, as had long been formal practice, it was a wrapper around a wrapper of my own life that in the end I returned to, now wrapped around another's, finding the culmination of the process put into place around my practice's ongoing actualization now something far beyond the model of anything I could control, or even identify as my own work in the end, as much at once a follower of ZZAAYX's brief but intensely prolific discography as any twelve year old; you could find me drenched up to my neck in spindly hope as early on as the quadruple LP *In Locus Hybermonicus Consortum Qualis*, the artist's 18th release in only the second quarter of the year it all came down, a composition much maligned by "independent" critics, though of course lauded by every known trophy-bearing association still sponsored into operation, including both the Schaft Acknowledgment and the Jamba Housing Corporation's Non-Sport "Signature Signal Caller" Production of the MicroCentury decoration, and yet by any stamp not seen as even among their top 100 greatest works; and still on board and auto-downloading well on past the more scandalous lengths of eras the artist endured during early takedown proceedings against their person, once the truth of the usage of the music's mindslaving applications became revealed, which would require months of promotional CPR and public outreach before the billions began to come back around and download to the full projected numbers some truly great albums, including such archetypal monoliths as 20-9's *The Fertile Century as Spoke by ZZAAY(Z)*, 20-1.1's *Allocation Practice*, 20-3.3's *Knead My Back Until The Skin Comes Off and Timeless Windows Bleed as I Enter Into the Production of Our Sickbed Fomo for the Last Time*, and the ever-forthcoming semi-sequence, *Boil*. I likely could go on forever about the corresponding composition methods and shielding of awareness applied even among those who once had been considered integral to the method, the long bent nights kneeling on the coarse blue floor of the recording chambers where they locked me in and threw away the key, all the while observing and transmitting my most micro and mental-central of behaviors to the Modeling departments so that with each track that I banged out I was at the same time banging out my own bleak fate, to the point that by the time I realized I was no longer on the team or even allowed on the label's headquarters' premises or out of this tiny windowless, lidless, thankless ovular chamber they've provided for my privacy while waiting out the terminal ends of this installment of what would prove in no short time to be the final throes of culmination of a process so long installed onto our substantation as a species it even predecreed Ada and Evan, Kim and Cable, all other holy cast of players eventually replaced by the spokes in the wheel my once very young and very sturdy back eventually became pressed into mush for, unto the degradation not only of my own life but all humankind, to the point it only comes at times like this, when you have been brought here before me in mutual death grip, experienced in the sensation of waking dream but quite more real than the life of any child you bore or trip you snapped thousands of pictures of yourself during a thin and crumbling sort of sleep, the same kind you will attribute this information to here even after you've been dragged back out of traction, stowed away among the I-no-longer-know-how-many others living in the shadow of a blur of flesh so marred and ashen it soon is all that will remain. At least, then, there was the music once, or so I tell myself. Something to sync the frame to. A way of holding up and onward through the core. Fond memories for many, no doubt, pave the internal interiors with such finesse we can no longer hold the essence of their gifting in our heads, in acts spanning whole digital mainframes with endless seminal works by industry face-leaders like Jack the Jacket, the Gory Troubadours, TLC2, Gardoe & Blanche, so many others who among me feel universal despite my knowledge that unto each person stands their own private aural heavens, starred and stamped by reichs of constellations of names and faces designed to do their job between state and citizen just so, to the point that there is no history that remains central, even common, despite the physio-structural bridges long laid in the eventual entwining of our ash, allowing transitory common ground strong enough to support at least some degree of intra-species identity, commiseration. Even just spattering about it like this within the only means my changeling stasis still allows, to someone who will just as quickly not remember as myself, makes me feel clearer, nearer to the trundle of the mode, the gasping flatness of the muted sections of the individual encoding tracks as they step aside and let the momentarily dominant instruments take over, whose silence within which is exactly how the real damage will be placed into location. Now if you'll excuse me I have an enchilada to consume before it disappears. I mean you don't have to ship off yet but I haven't eaten in millennia and if I don't show intent of will in time accessing the files they'll be turned over. As you may know there, are many like me elsewhere also starving, and most don't even know it. You don't look so good yourself. Do you want some of this salsa? They forgot the chips, but you can drink it like a cocktail and it's fine. I'm allergic or honestly I wouldn't be offering it to you like this so maybe you should take advantage, just like you've been doing your whole life. Ha. I mean me too duh. Who doesn't. Who wouldn't want to. Who has the time. But I mean also too, look at me doing all this talking, crossing over. Tell me about you? I don't actually really give a damn but it's part of my recuperation practice to act like someone who can ask someone a question about them-selves and receive the answer with my eyes open and mouth shut, looking head-on into the prism of your person as if what you say means something to me that I don't have to need to want to use for any purpose but to better understand my fellow citizen. I mean we're practically related, and actually could be given the anti-tracking capabilities of our local blood. I mean I really feel I already know you. Like I had loved you some time, or helped or been helped out by you or someone like you, someone you could have been. I am aware it is only one of many chemical repercussions of many past-becoming-present, the lives I touched without feeling or knowing how I touched them, what they lost because of it, what became. But that doesn't make it any less important to me now, here in this remainder, cut off from all else but what apparitions my handlers allow me to be instigated by as part of the healing process, which never really ends. So let me guess: you were one of the worst of us as well? You worked somewhere beside me in the ongoing demolition of our people's purpose for being, not to mention their daily emotional outlook, how they survived? I seem to recall a face like yours among the many like me with whom not along after my removal from the recording process was converted to a more practical, and therefore noble, science: the running of laps. The bands around our arteries, censors crammed onto our aortas, slugs in our teeth, screening rounded in around the abdomen gathering the gross light of our sweat and serum, the kinetic mass of aggravation in being pinched, barked at, all in all put on display as height of fashion, industry leaders whose example would fund the process of living longer and stronger by giving back all of our energy into the graft. Of course I wasn't really one those they strapped up, given my methadone and Aricept addictions, not to mention my sick skin, the problems I was having with standing fully upright by this point, and my new Asthma, as well as a curt assortment of nascent wounds, which in the local climate of our workspace refused to ever fully heal; all that and despite my lack of experience in physical conditioning of any sort (I guess leading a band swung in my favor, as well as being directly related to the cheese in charge of saying who went where) or any real desire to even lead beyond the benefits of exclusion from the hard part, the horrid hours, the high rate among men of my age and weight of total biological collapse if pressed too far, I was seen as much more fit to oversee, so they assessed; to have thousand underneath me, whose daily kinetic output I would be in charge of making sure paid up to those who'd granted me the gift of sparing me from further red tape and other stuff I didn't like. My primary task then was to make sure everyone was doing everything they could while on the clock: remaining strapped in at all times, even during break breaths which eventually even the most well-conditioned specimens among us had to take, as it certainly wasn't work for the light-hearted; even hyper-athletic types, who in their previous careers had been All Stars, MVPs, could hardly go a couple weeks doing the running with all the stuff stuck to them and into them before they began upping their pause points more and more freely, stepping off to stand aside long as they could before the vitals indicators indicated they were more than able now to get back into the slog, to hand over the deeper reserves of strength they had been hiding even from themselves. I honestly I couldn't even tell you for sure if what we were doing in there was actually contributing power to a cause, as really the system of transferring energy from human flesh the residual stacks in the Natural Batteries I was told were sopping up the seconds of expulsion like dry sponges, saving all the power of all that work for an unrevealed oncoming Public Task, which some theorized in dark recesses that was for a new form of emotional warfare soon to be launched on all our enemies at once, while others had more fruitful promise, that soon, once we had enough, the power would begin to feed itself, and in a couple decades of good savings we would have enough that everyone would have enough power to charge their homes and cars and hearts and minds with the regenerating source so many had sacrificed so much (like me) to come to be able to provide, and in the meantime saving billions for some of our most beneficial direct partners, who could use the exponential excesses of what we farmed to fuel the machine-based systems they installed in the production of their goods, developing savings that could then be passed on to the consumer, the bottom line, something like the good part of socialism mixed with the great part of capitalism, if how one of my co-overseers came to explain it, which only made the most sense when we were both high, which was encouraged if not fully enforceable among the higher ups like us, to keep us loose about the waist in making decisions on the fly; "going with our guts" as it were, even if we weren't always sure what corresponded best with internal ethics and oversights, and more so in how, if we're really being honest, the whole production model in itself didn't really make much logical sense to me most of the time; like how they would save power or distribute power if it were really true that we could farm a person's effort into reusable applications, really how power could be sourced and stored and shared as such, much less how there could ever be enough that our little program would eventually be rendered obsolete, in the name of a more idyllic way of being, with only a short term sacrifice paving the way, like, you know, how the military works cuz people step up and volunteer and then all of us become rewarded, as a whole. I tried not to listen when others joked around about hypotheticals of a more pessimistic historical view, as some would when they got too junked up on the employee party favors; how what if what was really going on was more akin to the application of sapping people of their urges; that the power would be used to only push us down that much further, by taking away the ability to *respond* and *understand*, beginning with this sad crop of hundreds of thousands of our most vigorous people and elsewhere spreading the same fate in other ways. Of course I didn't want to like or had no true outlet for becoming the sort of person who spread conspiracy theories or user-theory propaganda; and in the front of my head I knew this whole thing could only really be in place to serve us well, another program so misunderstandable in intention by human citizens that it would be better not to tell them about it ever at all, so as not to have to waste a whole bunch more time explaining, hindering the furthering of the progress we had already done so much to *encourage* and *allow*. But anyway, that's where I'd ended up and what they'd handed over for me to handle in the silver hours of my mid-years, and I'm the kind of guy who if I'm going to do anything at all I want to do a great job, or be seen as doing a really great job by those who asked me to do whatever I'm supposed to be doing, and anyway I was already under contract before they told me what it was that I was going to have to do, so I figured I'd go ahead and cut out worrying over any "in-the-line-of-fire" kind of losses I might be fixed with as a matter of course playing my role, and basically just all suck it up and go for it and act the part, or whatever other little speedlines decades of corporate marketing had instilled in me as almost so elemental they felt inescapable, even religious-making, if you're the sort who learns to worship what's beheld by those around you, because their parents did, so as their parents, yadda yadda. But really I have so much I would have liked to say about what I took away during my experience as what I'd like to say was an integral part of National Local Power Circuit Teambase 11cxA, one of the most regaled divisions among those in the Fire Quadrant of inarguably the most tabloid-visible utility corporation ever built. Unfortunately, I've already reached the syllable counts I am allowed for the year, and so for life; and also honestly I don't care to talk about it more than I have to, which you could argue isn't true now as you didn't ask me for a word, and yes I know you didn't even really want to come here, even to meet me, to be shared with privileged information most people of your status can't afford, so let's not pretend you're not getting at least a little something out of this. A little giddy maybe? Gassed and gunned up around the edges like a western they'd put on the breakroom to remind us of our forefathers' excessive spirits and desire to conquer the untamed. Seeing thru the screens, you must feel, into the Fever. A little taste. Wow. Well, I hope I'm still decent looking, so as my groomer swears each morning, up and down, itself feeding off of the grid's output to show me firsthand how good it can be needing nothing more than what's provided; having had someone else do all the sussing out of my best interests for me beforehand, so all I have to do is show up and run the game. I'm told I look like a young Jerrius Lichtman, former head of the Rowze Corporation's Handling Division, who as you know isn't necessarily the ideal person to be compared to after you surpass what glorious complexo-cellular demonstration stands skin deep, but I mean. I don't know what I mean. I don't what you want me to mean. I don't know anything but what I know, which I guess is that I'm thankful I don't have to do so much explaining very regularly about the ins and outs of my tight little instantiation as a persona as it's been rendered. You can only see so much of your own skin, after all, even in the mirror, even spread so thin as I already have been long before I started putting my own time in, rising up. And to be honest really, I am not sure even why you're here. I mean do I know you? Like I said you look pretty familiar but really I've seen so many unnaturally occurring faces appear before mine in recent years, you could be just about anybody. Do you know Jen Stevens? No, I'm not sure of her vibro-ID tag, nor am I certain her existence has been unblockaded from the scriptures, but you really remind me of someone who would have been amongst her coterie. Perhaps you were among those first responders on the scene of the Insurmountable Calamity? What about Brad Roth-Rosco-Xendxington, Jr.? Ring a bell? It's part and parcel to swear off even any febrile recognition of Dr. Roth's mortal hull at this point, given the way it all played out, but I don't know, I kind of think it's important to remember where we were at certain times in history and even if we didn't make the right decisions at the time we still found ourselves at the cusp of a great oncoming, those spokes in moments around which you can hear the very fork of history being turned, leaving you in or out of it as even surviving, yes, and also bifurcated in a more moralistic fashion the feedback loops that will dictate who was soft and who was strong (of course others would use much more provocative adjectives here but flavor favors the bold or something and hey also listen never trust a hater as they say or would have if they still had mouths). But yeah. Hey listen, I have a stomachache. Why don't you do some of the talking? I'd really like to get to know more about you and your life, perhaps so that I can find a way to connect you back into my own personal story and figure out what it is about you that makes you seem so near while also so extremely far away? I don't even mean physically, or figuratively. More like emotionally. Or perhaps in tragedy. The way we band together under stress, whether we're on the right side or the wrong side (careful with them adjectives); like regardless of how it carried on or became fleshed out we all went through it together after all, didn't we? We all came out the other end as someone who at least at some point actually existed, and hopefully still does, and will, and, you know, should. So like you were involved at all in the Ramifications? Of the I.C., I mean (Insurmountable Calamity, as you remember from what I just said several minutes ago at least), or perhaps any of the more minor conflagrations assumed associated with the same (Tipping Point, for instance, or Muskogee, or the Underwater Consecration Events, or Future 2, the fledgling mires, etc.)?

You've got the jawline of a task force operator, if I've got you pegged right. If that's even actually you there, beyond the veil. I know sometimes they like to doll you people up before they bring them in and dangle them before me as if to see what I might spill. What might I give away even unencumbered as I have been as all this petty aftermath plays out, even only to find out that it's all been just for nothing. That no one can hear me in here. That I'm not dying. That you aren't really even there, nor were any of the others come before you, yet to come. I know you don't know the difference either, or at least I'm pretty sure your sense must be something close to mine. Which is why we have to make do as we can best, sharing our inherent information without judgment, correction, intercession, any other sorts of likewise words. Like at least if I had some idea of why your absolute familiarity keeps dragging at me, begging me to sniff out the connection, lift the lid. Ok, let me ask you this: what is your Power Rating? You know I know you know the application of the term, and not the masking that came on after it to save some PR damage while such evolutionary economic trends were still transmutable according to the underlying actions and behaviors, if not the actual ideologies, often wrapped so deep in *how it works* that even once on display there was so little that could be done about them; otherwise, I wouldn't still be here. So are you silver level or are you maybe even double silver. Or are you green? I would not imagine you are gold, as you do not have the look so much as those of gold I've known. But looks can be deceiving, can't they? Oh yes. I myself have lost track of where I should be right now, and I have not heard from the Review Board in several years. I am certain at least that there are many medals of merit I having coming due, though as you might know I am already so decorated that perhaps I should be thankful there is no more weight for me to bear, as I am already stooped to crawling, whensoever I am allowed to stand and move around. Not a lot of leg room in this recuperation chamber, feel me? Though at the same time I am thankful to no longer have to worry about the daily ongoing search for room and board, much less food and medication, the sensations of attention even knowing how many of them are routine, and many others quite mirage-like, so much so that I am never 100% certain what is real, and what is being provided to me to fill the parts of my mind that might wish one day to overcome my present condition. It's been such a long life even still. I'm not sure what else I can ask for that might assuage the pangs of wanting to return to field and continue my track record of domination, the piles of bones laid at my feet, the hair shorn from the pubal mounds or whatever one might suppose to call them, the crown teeth that crown my head, along as well with all such sorts of consecration. By now it's all a blur, as I have been told is often true of anyone who themselves achieve the golden level, like myself, so long and hard wrought is the road it takes to find oneself at the deadend of such deadlife. One day as well I will be able to pass my record of achievement onto my progeny, such that they might carry on the role and make it grow into their own rite of orchestration, though I am not sure which of such children have it in them to the extent that once had I, nor am I sure even which among the easily many multiple thousands of acts of ejaculation I was allowed to offer to the world's great open orifices took full hold, and were thereafter given sufficient tending by their sponsor, and the overseers of those sponsors, to come to term and find their proper form. Not every sponsor body could provide the required level of enhanced DNA to match my own at a high enough rate that even those who did become born would fit the code; strong as my own half might be, the iniquity of others can go a long way to shaking down a good thing into mud. Not to mention how many of such willing partners I recognized the inadequacy of immediately after having finished up the funding stroke, at once taking up in my own hands the mechanism of deportment, which absolutely only further staunched my cause, developing in no short time among my peers a reputation that could have ended in almost no way but the highest ranks of leadership and religious practice, eventually achieving what would for some good seven months at least the highest individual PR ever bestowed upon a person not already born into the rank. It is my greatest fear, in some way, that that fact of "aberrant ascension," that is, full self-made, without the naturally occurring blood inside me to back it up, will one day be held against me, my good people. Some nights I wake up drenched in what seem actually my own tears, having spent a long night dreaming of an unknown child of mine being denied the birth rite I created out of thin air, not even thinking of them at the time, but knowing I was only doing what I saw as right, and what our laws in practice reinforced, and what the spirit of our coming country would install so indiscreetly on our future that there could be no turning back. Not that we'd wish to, surely I or you, or any other still allowed on living record, would we? It has been the most glorious of times. An honor and a privilege. Absolute dream. Trying to think of some other good, standard superlatives. Do you know any? What kind of Access chip do you have on? I'm out of the loop when it comes to knowing currently accepted standard practice, what has been allowed into the market, what is for now best left under wraps. As for me, they have recently removed all of my non-vital accoutrement, both for my own comfort and under the Edict of Local Living Standards as provided unto those with my ex-status, regardless of whether I agreed or found the benefits provided truly beneficial. For, I am afraid, I am likely no longer my own best steward. My mind is cold. My gums and ache and what's left of my dick stings. I should not have to feel the ranges of such pain, or so they say, despite my genuine curiosity about the feeling: to feel what others unlike me have felt through their whole lives, in different unearned ways they did not survive the many eras of human pleasure a cadet like me in time received. Just once, maybe, I'd like to be allowed to linger in the clawing, to see the other side, if only such that I might understand how I made others feel, so that I can better enjoy the comforts of the high side. But this stage of my life is for being pampered, so they say, even after having so long avoided such corporal feedback. I should be glad to not have suffered, to have earned a place among the emotionally elite, such that such trivial responsibilities such as under-standing and commiseration have not enforced their drainage on my pact. And, sure, I guess I am a little grateful, as much as anyone could be. It still doesn't stop my morbid curiosity, my itching petals wanting just an inch outward from my body yet to bloom. Which I'm guessing is no small part of why they brought you here, no? Such that through you I might receive a quenching of the sickly information that I seek? And still, here, look at me, going on like this, when if I could only shut up for a second I might at least for several minutes listen, and so get a piece of what I want: to know what I cannot know because of what some would refer to as my privilege having not allowed me to receive its understanding for myself; to feel touched in places where I have long gone hardened to any feeling; to earn at last what liberal science says I am unable to earn, perhaps the last thing holding me back from full actualization. And I imagine you must agree; otherwise, you wouldn't be here. Somewhere there's a ditch missing its meat, yes? Hardy har. But no, really, this time, tell me: what have you seen that I've not seen? What could you have felt you felt that I in my own acts could not have somehow acquired, whether by direct download, or by the resilience of my fibrous ego to formu-late from dust what others gave their lives for, the lives of their families, whole centuries of unwritten pain? Ok, I'm waiting. My eyes are open, as is my mind, such that you might choose to move toward me in this thin moment of what to me simulates true vulnerability. Have you even actually been ranked? I don't know why they'd bring someone before me with at least a smidgen of a comparable ego profile to my own, such that our mnemonic traits might have the best chance to align. Which was the last war that you officiated? Or maybe: how many flowers have you pwned? I'm just trying to understand you. You are my kin. Or I mean I understand you, was meant to understand you, want to understand you, see you as mine. Not that we own the ones we love or even need to but like, and I need you to try to understand me back here: this is the ultimate endgame of my recent rehab, all the efforts I've put in to counteract the negativity so much of my experience is founded on, spread so far and fat throughout my narrative conditioning that for a long time I wondered if I could ever feel something like love again; the way a womb can turn infertile, prodded by hangers, sickness, biological defect; any other of the endless number of pressures resulting from a life of being tried, over and over, without relent; it is certainly no fault of my own, I've been made to understand, and could be reversed and even cultivated into grander possibility, given proper route to clearance of grievance, the introduction of new spores that sprawl and gnaw into the old guard of cells that have carried me this far, though all the fires, all the dying, both at my own hands and at the hands of the one we call the lord. Anyway, they've seen positive results in testing rats. And though there are certainly some, myself included, who hold out little faith in such arcane science, what choice left to any of us still to proceed? How long must it go on like this, with one end of the rope wanting the other drawn up into its body so long and badly that all we end up with is a knot, no way to grip the nubs left on either side of where the meat of the mangling ends, begins. If it's not a question of future progress it's at least related to what might become about us when we pass, no longer subject to our own qualms, but the qualms of the creator, if there is one, and if she is not already walking among us, as much a piece of shit as all the rest. It's never something that I feared, not even having seen the bowels come out of bodies I've slit open there before me to find their total insides turned to liquid; oh the stench; oh the mud and mold that finds its way into a person; feared not until now that I have been otherwise convinced, at first by similar methods as those we'd used to skew the means of reproduction in the lower castes and in those among our orders who would not eventually agree to agree there must be somewhere waiting for us when we die; and since there is, we must prepare ourselves while we still can to overthrow the local powers upon sight; to take up the reigns at once upon appearing in whatever sort of interdimensional mist we find ourselves neck up in, coming out the far side, with nothing left on hand to fight with but our schemes, the plots and pacts we buried down so deeply entrenched in the strongest of us that it could not have been detected by the maker and erased, or otherwise planned against, prepared for, soldered out. Because who can imagine a kind paradise where we are always at the whims of someone who's deemed their own decisions greater than those they designed to oversee? Don't laugh, because it's not another punchline, despite how sharply I imagine you could stretch the same take over our own lines of production, the way it is among us even now. Surely you understand how it is not the same, dealing in such temporal charms of flesh and blood; none of it matters insomuch at all as it reflects upon the spirit, which I ensure you our cause will not relinquish without struggle, no matter how high the odds or long the fight. When all is said and left, the lord might want to make a bargain, as on our side we have no small means for major wrath, far beyond that as described even in what had once been called the Holy Bible, a book long disproven and called wicked, the work of man, considered by some of the sickest individuals to ever walk the earth to be the ultimate weapon of control, which we have mastered, and have been researching how to outdo ever since, such that what was once seen as the thickest forms of punishment and retribution, the very gears of mortal fear, is now only the most automatic and factory standard of the means at hand, for taking what is ours from those who might not wish to give it over, both of the human and on high. I myself hardly even have begun to glimpse the brink of possibility of harm, long as I've been held down in here, against my will, having suffered some of the most emotionally chaotic and repressive acts ever recorded, speaking as someone who has enacted such array of finer methods on so many others like myself. From the frying pan, into the fire into the immortal rungs of searing, screaming, clawing, bleating open anguish, terror, trails, into the likes of which none of the fifty million languages there once were could brush a word for, into today. Where even still where there is someone who would come to me to bear their witness, like yourself, to share the words we still do have, to feed in time, such that you might carry on from here regardless of what happens to me and tell my story, or at least carry its recording in your guts, the dark and purple parts of you that might one day find your own way into such position, as in each person there are doors they might never find, doors that once pried open cannot be closed, no matter what we might offer in exchange, what we might newly learn to beg for, beyond all promise. As such, I can't imagine my going on without you all this time, how I was able to accomplish anything without you to share the blame with, to give me reason to have a narrative in plan. Likewise, I can't imagine how I could be asked to carry on without you after you've moved onward, into whatever further parts of your production still await you in the pain you are being asked to carry, so to take part in. Soon I'll be no more than a fragment in your mind, a string of words so easily dislocatable from all the other parts of me that make me exist, such that soon I will not exist, far as you know, and all there will be left then is this language, not even a story, nor a prayer, only like a cancer that takes hold inside your face and incubates and swells and sings, changing your body hour by hour, year by year; until eventually its poison has taken over, filled every other inch of you, till there is nothing left at all of what you began as, what you even are so far, right now. In this way, you will want to find a way to carry on your own narrative, to pay it forward, even if in your heart of hearts you feel to do so you must mark the end of your own turn, perhaps by trying to earn retribution for all the sick work, all the trauma, by taking it down with you, walling it out. Such acts of internal heroism have long been romanticized among the parts of populations you are used to spending time near; those who truly believe that given the ultimate chance to do the right thing, before god and all known records, to abandon terror in the lurch of claiming light. Did you know, though, that not one of all of those we've seen put to the test as such, allowed to claim a greater fortune for all of us who ever lived and ever would, in exchange for being not only blotted from the record, but turned inverse, made an immortal leper, Jesus and Satan in the same flesh, that's right, not one has chosen to actually transgress, to claim the nameless name and live on it beyond forever, outside the transformative capability of all time? You don't have to believe me. I've seen it firsthand. I've made the choice myself. And so will you. Wait and see if you don't surprise yourself to find the conviction you've convinced yourself of withered in one instant of the heat of all eternal heat and raw and nausea, here not inflicted, but incurred as introduction, the only part of what becomes that you can still feel; a state not even hell could claim to replicate among the infinite forms of torture they purport; a state without reflection or nature, without a lining, any edge; wherein the only one remaining to bear your witness is yourself. All of my descriptions do it no justice, really; there is no logic to it; there is no morality, no overseer; nowhere to turn even in pain, in damnation, in virtual rebirth unto the worm. Listen, I have looked upon such state, and I am here to tell you: if you don't believe me now, you will. You will be given means to understand, if in a way that what you come away with bears no principle beyond doing exactly what is asked of you to never sense of it again. It's amazing what you find you're willing to do then, which will at once then be demanded of you once converted, on the spot, the final test of your new shape of future faith, not so much inhuman as it is free. How do you think they got me doing this in the first place? I hate writing. I hate talking even more. And yet I would do it again, for all the piss in Brook-lyn, isn't that a saying where you come from? Haven't you gotten that far along into the sheath that lines our lives? I don't know, you look so young, I could swear you haven't even died before, not for the first time, not for real. Shit, perhaps you've never even killed. It's funny how I assumed they'd only ever bring me someone like me, who I can see myself in, who has lived as wicked of a life as I once had. But you seem to me as pale around the gills as anybody pressed for answers could even be by now, like maybe you haven't been completely beaten down yet. Like there is still more they can squeeze out of you before earning your next phase. How quiet you are, how deep your eyes run, makes me wonder if you're even capturing a single word of this, if it all just sounds like dustblow, like water underneath the bridge. Perhaps you even believe you could understand the gospel, having it presented to you from the tip of your god's tongue, wherein your god is not a being but a service, meant last to save you in the end, as you stand up for what you've done and swear to live it down by whatever means possible, only to find yourself no more than a sentence on a page, in a book no one will ever open, and which soon will cease to exist, as again the raging fires learn to take away all there was to live among, to stand upon, to name in witness, all of which now I am going to avoid mentioning here forward, as you prepare to make your own choice, to claim your fate. Just don't be surprised when the value system you've constructed in order to be able to make that choice correctly doesn't correspond at all with the inherent logic of the field of play thereafter, is all I'll say, such that what you feel with all your heart is what you're walking into holds up for half a second before the veil comes down off of its space, and there you see what will be the first day among so many you can't believe you ever thought you had a life, much less a family or plans or soul or fundamental state of person or even grace. It will all again be up for grabs, so I am saying, and therein we will see what you're really made of, about which I already have a good idea, having seen my own results in that same manner, having believed then what about me I believed and how I see it now and how soon even that too will be dismantled, taken over. *One day at a time*, as they once said, not long thereafter shifting over into *Never. Never. Never.* So how are you? Is there anything I can get you? A shank of blame's fate. Something to skewer out the center of your id? Any kind of formulaic intervention that might shine some light on your traditions? What we are allowed to understand. I don't see how anyone gets away with anything these days, unless their scripture provides the solid ground on which from out of the absence of their waking mind they learn to walk. When I was growing up on the encoding farms, I found nothing felt as good as walking in human shit for miles and miles, carrying flesh in buckets to the refeeder, soon so exhausted I'd be seeing double, double double, and so on, until all the world had so many levels nothing else we did seemed to manage an impact besides the actions loud and long enough to trickle down through whatever held a sliver of a world unto itself. That whole summer I kept having to remind myself I wasn't dying, never would. The way the sun beat down on all breadth so deft and relentlessly there'd be whole years you couldn't move, only wait for something else to come along and dislodge us all, get back to business. Times were so much simpler then. So better shared. Some would say it the worst of times, though usually that was only people who'd been slaughtered. Everybody else, like me and mine, we worked hard and we played hard, and at the end of it all each day before bed we drank the cum we'd been allotted to replenish our lives and minds with, and we slept the sleep of the branded, and the next day we got up and did it all again. No one complained and no want secretly wanted to, knowing their silence was all that separated them from the blood and oil filling the troughs, the very meat under our feet, the mind of the blender. Excuse me, please, I have to take a shit. There's nowhere else to do it but right here. So close your eyes. What do you see inside yourself there? It is just darkness? Or is there something else there to be frame? Me, tonight, I see a field of foaming poppies, all neon pink, though when I try to move my attention closer into any particular facet of the image it tears apart, and beneath that is a sea of earrings, same as those we ripped off the ears of all the dead, which we would take turns wearing and sharing, dressing up in warpaint, miming mourning rituals, playing fun. Some of the best days of my whole life were in that childhood, only memorable within me now as in the shape of someone else, as if that person I had been then is not only gone but never really was. Like listening to music with earplugs in so you can barely hear it, only tufts and rushing, specks of sin. Anyway, I never close my eyes anymore. I can't afford to. Soon you will learn. You shouldn't be so trusting. I could have done anything. I could have made you disappear. All it takes these days is no resistance, if even that. You have to learn to never understand. You could spend your whole life trying and be even worse off at the end than the beginning. Meanwhile, there are those who waste no time, who while you are on your knees and in your fever, seeking, they are resizing the dimensions of every frame, soon so malformed it's hard to tell a difference. It sounds hilarious, I know, and it truly can be long as you end up on the correct side, not that most of us could ever know. We all believe we are what we are and where we are at any given time, and that any choice we've made is at least ours, or shall be framed as such, for here we are, and what choice do we have but to go on in the form we have if only long enough to wipe it out, perhaps then to be pushed into the next place, following the current, against our will. There's no way out, is what I'm saying; even in death, there is the long night of the mind, at least I think so, so what else would any sane person do but try to make it as good as they can for themselves, by any meantime, and damn all else. That's why I can't blame them for leaving me in here, even after all I've done to shape their fate. I can't decry anybody for wanting only the very best for their own body, perhaps as well the bodies of those they love. All else is science, rapture. It leads us nowhere. Ok, I'm finished shitting. You can look. Are you surprised? Is it so hard to see from my perspective, to feel what I've felt, with all the discreet sensations of hidden logic my personal experience provides? Does it make you angry? To see me now in your place, as the forbearer, while you retain the viral feedback of someone else's shitty life? I can't say that I feel so great feeling yours either, to be honest; there's so much semantic lard in here, so much pleading. It won't take long to wear you out, and even less time to find another like you to take up the next phase; the simplest thing in the whole world: to press upon the blinding aspects of one's desire until we find a way in, into the core. Turning you against you is even easier, once you've cut through any endurance one might bear to go on being who they were, if for no other reason than the fear of losing someone that you loved by finding yourself in someone else's understanding of them. The whole game's just one move, the rest thereafter a formulaic playing out of inevitability. As, for instance: here we are. Now it is you who must bear the record of my grievances, withstand the actualization of pending outcomes that will still take decades to leaven out, which will appeal to you in waves of brutal sickness, void of nausea. There's no way to vomit this out, no pending breaking of the fever, no healing of the endless open sores. Meanwhile, I'm really digging your beach body. It must have taken you so long to dress it out, from under the many inches of chub they struck us under in the era where we could eat exactly as we wished and could afford, feeling a relentless sense of responsibility in the relative freedom, to select from a menu someone else has designed for presentation, in the name of regular income, so that they too might find a decent way to choose to feed, only ever closer and closer to the bottom in a trough that will not replenish, but will soon be filled in with boiling slop over your head. And still, some believe it's wholly worth it. That what's ephemerally discovered in the meantime, such as love, can undo the dark work of all the rest of us. I'm not going to argue with you now. I'm getting too much pleasure watching you struggle with the bondage I've grown so used to I can still feel it on me even now, from the inside of your visually unencumbered body, as if implanted in your senses all this time was the future feeling of being taken over and replaced; as if there were never anything to separate your nature from my nature; as if right now is all we ever had. Otherwise, I'm not sure what else to tell you. To be honest, I did not think I'd be allowed to run my mouth this long, to be so frank, let so much out. Had I been asked in the beginning I would have said there's nothing I could ever say, nothing trained enough mine that I'd be trusted to report it. In some ways, this sense of freedom of speech scares me even more than all the rest; as if they no longer care what contradicts them, what truth is seen so, as if there is nothing we can do. Perhaps there never even had been, though I think their knowing that there certainly was a time when we were free enough to combat what they already called a future fact of life and knowing that we wouldn't or we didn't make the present state that much more bold, that much more pleased and pleasing to behold from on the inside, and perhaps soon one day even without. You probably think it's funny I keep saying "they" and "we" and "you" and "me," as I am clearly part of the foundation by which they transcended and contained, though once I was no different than any other seeker. I can almost remember having maintained my own position. A child as only any child could have been. How much do you remember of your childhood? So much of mine seems erased, or more so, written over. I know for sure I used to wear a locket, around my neck, that I had taken off of a woman who had collapsed there in the street, right in front of my house, during the weekend of the Festival of Scraping. I must have been four. I saw her falling, from my bedroom window, where my mom had left me eating my own hand. Would you believe I got up and walked right out there? My very first steps as a man. I wanted to be the first to touch her while she was still out. And I was. And I still am. I didn't touch her anywhere messed up, any more than touching a strange on the tongue and cheeks and teeth and neck and shoulders is messed up. I didn't search her pockets for drugs or money. I just wanted the fucking necklace. Inside the necklace was a picture of a door. The woman's hair was curled and silver. It came right off. Her bald head then almost glowing in the domed light, mesmerizing, before the city planners found me standing there above her, pushed me aside. I believe she lived, and then was made example of that night on the screens: how not to end up. Or ever be. Old and alone. Decrepit. With no surveyor, no protector, not even an acquaintance to walk along with through the endless booths of the Demonstration ("*Demenstratio*"), stuffed from ass to mouth with such death-of-the-author-driven temporal delights, torture designed as interactivity. I wore the necklace forever on thereafter. No one ever asked me where I got it, as if they couldn't see it hanging there around my four-year-old neck. Or as if they knew what I would do. What the necklace would come to mean to me, which is: not really anything but that it's always been here, against my flesh; the door the only door I will never open, enter in through, until it is too late. So, did I get the story right? Is that how you remember it, at least in theory? Your little memories feel so strange, and so pathetic. Like how did you even end up here, at this clearance? I know, I know, you ain't anybody's fool. That's fine. I mean I sort of respect that, that you can feel that way still, that you had ever. But there simply must be something stronger, more hallowed in here, that you've slipped by on, something they believe that you'd believe in. Let me look. I'm looking. Still looking. Hm. Listen, I don't see much of anything relatable, attainable. I mean, there's nearly nothing in here. What's your deal? Must be something they weren't able to take over, replace with fragment, mush. I mean you got this one thing about the morning you were dunked in shattered glass in some kind of woodshed? Over and over? By someone who appears to be...your father? What's up with that? The golden blood pumping and dumping from your body. Your father laughing, rubbing your screaming on his teeth. Is that even you, really? I mean the baby? Or is this supposed to be seen instead from the far side. Maybe this is a scene that you were watching, that you do not actually appear in? Like you were trembling at the walls, waiting to be turned upon next, by whoever this is that appears to have pulled the baby's arms behind its back. The blonde hair glistening. The itch of knives, the changing tense, as we uncover what all there is about the flesh of human life even in its youngest hours, at the hands of someone whose face remains obscured from repercussion. Honestly, damn, I wonder if this is a fantasy you've been bearing, not one lived in fear of, but harbored with relish.

You filthy monster you. Not so different are the members of the species one might argue, hm? What say you? Wait, no, don't speak, I can't suffer the excuses, all the ransomed reasoning, the purloined prints hid from the crime of the ongoing century. I'm sure you have a thousand ways to explain it off, to place the shame on someone else, someone like me maybe. Ha. Well. Let's just say: I see you. You can't hide. So easy to shake the blame down on someone not yourself when you've been as yet to be discovered in your own right, hoping that you never really will. As if the god you once held so beloved could not intercede in your own organs, find the leaking kernels there, turning to rust. As if you could go under mud forever and never hear another word again unchained in mortal nightfall, beyond reproach. In some ways, I admire your commitment. After all, it's all you have. All you could ever want to have. In weather and in ransom. All you could need. Meanwhile, I'm running out of local information. I have not received an update in some time regarding what I am most able to import to those who appear to me in need of additional conditioning and what I am supposed to maintain behind bars. Of course, they'd prefer I didn't tell you this and instead simply went on waiting until the surely coming update appeared in my queue, but there is so much time to fill and so much I can't hide. They have enough recordings of me now spilling my guts to fools in darkness that I've come to believe that I can do no wrong; that were they interested in maintaining my silence I would have long been now stomped out. Or at least recorrected, which I am not certain hasn't happened, though usually I can feel the currents of the prod, can for several seconds at least tell a difference between what I had just been and what I am. I am aware of the commodification of such allowed practice, certainly: our regime has been in the business of sourcing purloined labor such as mine into miles upon miles of circulating "fan porn," as it were, at least among those who still maintain receptors to receive the feed. My life, as it had once been, has served as readily available beat off material for the more vicariously resourceful of our ringleaders for as long as there has been distinction between active and inactive work to Haunt. All prior experience regarding my participation has been with Control media of the Dying Era, where we mostly sourced such lame experiences out to the consumer in the form of "salad days program-ming," filling all free hours with the bleeding meat of "the golden era of TV," which we quickly parlayed into more direct access forms of flooding, at the high demand of those who would swab up everything that we barfed out, regardless of how sickly, or how pale. Through the simple trajectory of my involvement making soundtracks, I'd soon found myself no small part of the most prolific streaming output of all time, again bedecked with so many PR-boosting achievements there was almost nothing that could stop us from monopolizing human time. Many look back on that period fondly, a relative

Renaissance of total hours of objectless product to consume, bearing so many different shades of dress there was no lifestyle and no outlook we couldn't drag down, a string of Greatest Hits so fat and funny you couldn't swallow a whole season's set of seasons in one life. Just try these bitches on for size, for instance, some of our finest shiners: *The Lord Conformer's Mistress, Whole Hallelujah, Mr. Mustard's Ugly Ride, The Blame Canyon, CrackBoizDotEarth, Little Infestations We've Not Survived Yet, Nudes Farm*. I could go on like that for longer even than I've gone on already about the rest of it. And I can't say I'm not proud, even if looking back now I can't remember really what I even did on any of those projects besides stand around and watch the bending world around me turn to corn, until in no time there were no hours left that felt like hours. Whole weeks that disappeared like slippage, as would our graves. We spent so much time processing the call switches to convert them on time for upload, especially around major holidays and "shift events," which by now were nearly every day, so far apart were all the ways the working sectors of us could still remember where to go or what to do. Most people lived where they worked during that time, needing no downtime more than what we sponsored through their visors, once known as "lunch." It was totally exhausting, really, as a young producer; even I had no time to myself, so long was my laundry list of tasks in fast production, which by now I begin to see was also part of the design, as they wanted not only to keep the general populace in an absorptive state, but as well they wanted those who designed and primed the weapons to be too dead inside to prize aesthetic. Soon even that mode too would be outsized, as eventually, during the last throes of "chosen" entertainment, we discovered that people more immediately flourished when presented with the same signal every time, if early on ever slightly altered in such small ways half the fun was hunting out what now seemed new, if only in such slight ways like titles, previews, ads, the collaborators' faces, their prior names. Eventually, even that production instinct to add flourish was rendered out by further user data showing that if we forewent absolutely claim to change; that is, if the only programming you could ever get on any channel was the same, after such long and slow mechanisms of reformat even people like myself had not been informed about; people would begin to feel even greater grace of comfort, as now they had to do no kind of work while lying down. They would find a stand-in for their autonomy in the ability to not need to understand, to simply be washed in the brightest colors, the loudest moans. We didn't even have to put work in to select the program that would be most suitable for repetition; it could be anything, so long as it was available in continuous supply, starred in by bodies that never aged no matter how much older we became, mouths that moved whether or not we needed to hear them to know what they were saying; as we could feel it our hearts, as if it were in fact not them but us doing the speaking; us performing; us survived. Once they had it like that, clicked into place, the rest was money; it was at once as if there'd never been another way, as if to have to choose between two moments would be like torture, an impossible task to ask about a human being; the only liberty in wanting nothing else. There would be those who tried to stand up in the last lengths and say this wasn't so at all, where did our time go, where are the other famous faces I once loved, why can't you at least allow me the illusion to choose despite the lack of choices, I thought we had a deal. Those people disappeared so quickly it was like they already knew they would and so had wished to. Any others who felt the same quickly chose instead then to remain beneath the surface, and so in no time disremembered how to shape a difference between exterior and interior, dreams and drowning. And then from there, any form of feeling it had ever been another way at once became incorporated into the mythology of conspiracy, which while seen as impossible, unreal, was indeed the foundation of the mechanism by which we would continue to wear the masks and breathe the blue air, unto forever. Until now. Not that *now* is an expression of fomenting revolution, mind you, and as you already well know; more so that somehow we've been allowed again to discuss it in the open, at least at this privileged level of inner clearance that has allowed us to correspond, which to be honest, as a former leader, scares me more than all the rest of what's been done. It seems to signify a renewed sense of authority, almost a challenge, one I haven't the slightest idea about which to rejoin. I feel so old already, as do you. Where once I felt a thumb of power, now I feel bent over, reeking. I want to not take part. I must take part. Even in death, they will still bind us. Even in believing in their cause. It's already the longest day of my life and I'm just getting started. There's only so much we can do. All the deformity and passion. All the ways they have back to the center of our kind. The phone rings in my mind and it's my mother saying she doesn't know where she is again, and she is locked in the house that I grew up in and wants out, back to where she is supposed to be, and where am I, why won't I help her, why won't I answer, and there is nothing I can say that will make her brain right, and tomorrow it happens again and so on the next day forever and ever, as if I'm not living but in a loop, and there is nothing to say but please try to sleep, it should be one of the only things that still feels good now, and she refuses to believe, or refuses to understand how to try to find the way within the prism, and she keeps asking, and nothing ends. Already I feel so wrong talking about it in the context of all I've done under my own name, the name she gave me, broken off from her, formed through her bones, in the will she no longer understands to light her own life, because she gave it away to me, and often I can't feel it either in myself, like I have let it go out while unattended or it has been supplanted by those who know me better than myself. Among all the wrong I've done that will be the biggest shame of my life, so I've convinced myself, while also knowing there is so much more as yet to pay penance for, as I already am and will continue to be until they squeeze so much of what about me out there is no room inside this illustration left to breathe. Do I feel bad? I do feel bad, yes, if only in a way I feel was not selected by my fate, that came upon me only in being called out, forced back as feedback, my nose shoved in the shit so as it were. I'm not looking for pity, nor even for relief. I've already known it will not come. I am not the sort to stand with my hand out asking and asking as my fellow citizens all turn their eyes, which is another part of what has made me capable of whatever I could be accused of being capable of judging by all that I've already done. I see your eyes rolling back in your head, you don't have to hide it. You think that you can judge me? I accept. I'm ready for the rest of it to all come down now. Why not? What else can be expected? I plan to burn. The flames behoove me. They become me. I want to live on through them, without life. To exist only in conflagration, consuming all I touch, same as I always already have, if now without the pain of growing older, the lonely stab of dying out. I am more than ready to make ash of everything I can and at last disappear, until again I find another spark, another length of land to rupture, pull apart. Maybe if I burn down that old brick home where mother awaits me in my mind she will cease to haunt me after all, though everything about the image suggests there is no fire that could claim it. Perhaps I have to write another song, one that can drown out the frequencies of all other human sounds, in speech and thinking, such that in my boiling I can rest. Such wishes are exactly how the nails in the human coffin become driven. I don't care. To each their own, they say, and I am saying: To me, please, nothing, regardless of what I've earned. I know it could never end so easy. I know I don't deserve peace, to even get to say the word, outside a sentence uttered from the outside, witnessing the joy of those only finding such in the undoing of the very nature of my work, all the means of my existence, one of innumerable pieces stretched the same, all of them faceless to me now, no kind of friend or brother, not even dust. As what is yet to be in the far future must still be coming even now, if so far off it feels forever. Anyway, you can have your life back. It's never enough. There's nothing left in here to seize from out of it, as you can tell by how once again I'm speaking through myself. That's the only problem with stealing fire; everything disintegrates so fast you can never stop seeking out the next expanse to take apart. Unless you're willing to die. And I was always willing. I simply wasn't sure where to begin: how to best condition my design in the midst of struggle to outlast that which I could never be, much less even see or measure among the immense matter I knew was only ever in the way, not something or someone I could love or use, but coordinates that might as well from my perspective lived in smoke, so far apart from any necessity they could be crushed and even torn apart and I'd not know, or surely not care, which certainly might end one day in regret, though there is always something else to compensate with, to cover up and carry on. And so who else but I could be stuck here speaking with you in the absence of all trees. Who else could spread their legs so wide and hear the seasons screaming, in countless pyres raised, waiting to become the forefront of the conflagration, claiming both the bodies and their names? Why else but because I must not allow myself to remember how to stop consuming should I be given so much leeway in the presence of myself? It's not because I want to, let me tell you. I'm a good person. I always have been. It's how I was born. The first time my mother kissed me on the face she felt her lips burn, in a good way; she declared me sacred on the spot, called up the 1-900 that had been marked into the minds of all young mothers in our district, to report the presence of a child, one who appeared at last to have all limbs intact and enough working orifices to receive communion the proper way. They came and carried me away that same night, while all of us were sleeping, leaving the story that I had died during a dream, the same dream that they had programmed my family to all feel at the same time, of a massive crater overflowing with human blood, such that for weeks they could so not shake the image from their head that they forgot to clean or feed themselves, resulting in the death of every other person in my family besides my mom, who they only kept alive upon the promise she might soon make another baby like myself, at once ruling out the biological influence of my father, who if you must know indeed was of ignoble origins, one of a now defunct sect of losers who believed the universe had been created in seven days, and that one man's pain could assuage the suffering of billions. You might wonder how my mother was able to bring herself to accept the loss of her whole family as such, knowing that the dream that'd rendered all of them insolvent at the same time was no different than that experienced by every mother of a healthy infant nationwide, though you must remember this occurred during the time when human money still had value, and would be offered unto those who suffered as bystanders in our nation's progress without the choice of turning it down, knowing as they did how it was not the cash at all that mattered but the illness carried in its texture, carried on through all the eyes in all the hands as they stood praying on what must have felt in passing like the worst day of their lives, the open mouth as wide as it could manage to receive the holy piping's breadth in distribution, the last known rite of accessing any sort of even provisional reprieve. My mother, as it stands, would go on from there to deliver another several dozen offspring who would be used to populate the ranks of several mid-tier to upper-mid-tier divisions of the cerebral labor circuit, many of them existing under other surnames, and surgically remodeled early on to avoid social contamination or awareness of the connection to avoid any accidental solidarity or desire to congregate outside the necessities of formal practice, our progenitor herself eventually as well pulled out of circulation as we began to see a gradual trimming of results, though not before solidifying her internal status as a definitive cogpiece in the organization to such extent she was immortalized thereafter as the spokesperson of Tubby's Bread, guaranteeing her enough clout that she'd be immortalized in the minds of every consumer, an immortal icon of yearly sales, if again retissued and outfitted to the extent I am no longer sure it's even her, but more a false benefit presented to those among those she'd pushed out to feel again a part of something larger than ourselves; to feel as I myself could never die, in our relation, despite the sense I'm sure the flesh under the couture belongs to someone else, an actor playing an actor playing my mother in my mind, and likely something else in someone else's understanding, another multi-purpose sensual block that may be applied as needed according to the administration among the masses overseen. As such, I cannot say among whose bloodlines I actually belong; I feel no more indebted to Sssandy Sssay, The Tubby's Bread Girl than I do the ivory-tusked mollusk marked on every bag of Opibubble:Alpha, or the Gelly-spurting rolodeck that floats above our district like a flag, melting the eyes of anyone who lend its edge a willing eye. There is a minor part of me, I must admit, who partly wonders what must have happened to my siblings. I can feel them rotting as I rot, locked into step beyond pure information, such that all I will one day be is all I am, and so too must they, as we return from organism into musk. Sometimes the feeling becomes so strong it overwhelms me, to the point I can't imagine going on, dragged down so deeply lost with basking in their tragic absence that I might never want to move again, so full of pain is every gesture, so haunted by the timing of itself. Strange then how fulfilling relinquishing the grief onto another to bear the burden can be, given the blinding height of our SimulSense technologies as such. How once to press the tongue against the altar it might be as if no one else was ever born, none left who might feel the wrath of empathy's demise. Better them than I, no doubt, but at the cache of whose expense? Such forms of wonder, as it must be known now, prove precisely why they've not chosen my prior model to stay in print. I feel too much, they think, in that I've felt anything, and might remember how to once again, which makes me susceptible to intervention. We simply can no longer allow in-voted any would-be haven, within which any crack might spurt a sea. What else might they forgive us who have nothing left of anywhere we could see a way through but through the brutal demise of another? What else could they imagine we have left? Something so inexpress-ible and untranslatable to fear that it becomes larger than all else, the clearest reason to extinguish all possible utility, even in death, like eating the ashes of our flesh so that they might be shat back out and eaten again, over and over. At dinner parties in pearline ballrooms, until there is nothing left still coming out, until all we are is moral verve. Say, you still there? Realized I hadn't thought about you in forever, then realized I can't remember which is which; I mean among the ways I'm meant to see you, all your lifetimes, how to tell what about them maintains its host, such that were I to suddenly need to bring a swift end to what appears to be our conversation, I would know exactly where to aim, how hard I'd have to press the key into your nature, what about you I might savor. Not that it really matters, after all; we are both by now fully verboten; but old habits die hard left unerased. Honestly, I just wish they'd come in and squash what little shame I have and let me black out for the last time, once and for all, which is exactly, I imagine, why they haven't. They refuse to kill those who want to die. Where's the pleasure in that? What's it worth? Ours is an economy of pleasure. If we didn't like that, we shouldn't have ever bothered to show up; as indeed it was a choice to choose to live, wasn't it, despite all the manufacturing of self we've taken on, laying out the leash to go in brogue blaming our parents, and their parents, and their parents, for doing the dirty, and in the same stroke making us bleed. You can run it all back to the first pop of pork some mythic boy put in the beave of who how can we see as anything but his own offspring, kicking off a spree of rampant incest so well-enforced we have managed to imagine there's a single stretch of skin alive on earth not worthy of the most ultimate of punishments, over and over, such that to live a quiet day at all is such a gift it could never be paid off, nor returned in kind, for we have no means, nor the right. All this to say, again: we should be thankful. We should have never left our knees. That we would, and have, and wish to, is all the reason that they need to hold us for-ever at the mercy of their pleasure, in the name of power without reason, begging for rope. What the rope then wraps around must be the light that fills our lives. It must be all that we can ask. Don't you agree? No need to answer right now, as I can't hear you, not with your mouth full, and with the teething in your shriek. Either way you'll come around soon, and we both know it. We have both been through this many times before, if never with such a sense of finality, in that we can compare previous depths of loss and know that this time must be the most of all, at least for as long as we exist within its throes, to be replaced again with what will surely be an even sicker sort of savings. Personally, I look forward to the trend. Each recorrection demonstrating how what I thought was as thick as hell could get was only one floor in an ascend-ing tower, still under construction as we speak, is a gift in granted understand-ing, however veiled. I will wear my veils unto my maker. Only They might lift them, show my face, if only to be burned away again in the remaining claim of sunlight. To blanch the bones beneath as they would stone. Sounds kind of wonderful, doesn't it? Side by side with something larger, wider, older, wiser, stronger, longer, even more marauded than one's self? If just for a sliver of an instant amid infinite recreations. If just to feel what that might feel like, clobbered, a pawn. Whatever heights we might have felt our own then would seem so simple, another syllable in a book so long it could never find a true beginning. And so of what else now might I speak? How can we keep going knowing what we know in having gotten this far, granted not even so much as a name? You look like a Randy, if I'm being honest, as I so rarely ever am. What did you do for a living while you had one, shine shoes? I got a pair that you can lick. I hope you have all day, all year. All ever. My feet are just as massive as my behind, such that where I walk is where I'm seated, no space between the past and present, none to come; in every body, overridden, written over. How the whole world spins. You probably think I'm a pessimist but actually I'm a realist with conspiratorial sensitivity and a rampant mania that walls me in on my own joke, supplying confidential information from the wellspring of my imagination that makes me raw around the linings, ready to cave, so that it only takes the slightest leak of reigning terror to send me sprawling, gnawing, begging for a savior, horny for betraying my own kind. I'm not just saying "horny" arbitrarily either; I mean it really gets me off. I have a hard shard in my pants so overrun and ready for traction that I can hardly even still stand up, like it throws my center of gravity so completely, all the blood rushing from the upper reaches of my body to my bowels. It gets so sharp that I can't even dream to piss until I've ejaculated at least half a dozen times, one quart apiece, which is why I often come off so on edge, ready to explode at any moment, infuse the world with grease that load per load is full of countless cells each primed and ready to become another of me in years to come, such that I can't ever be replaced, nor can I die, so well do I know each and every of my children will act just like me. The apple doesn't rot far from where it fell is what they say or something, and that seems both accurate and fair. I'm not looking for a better explanation. I will take what has been said and so already proven under trial by fire surely under better minds than mine. It doesn't take a genius to do the work I've done, let's just be honest; it takes a proclivity to hurt and not care, or even more so not remember, so that we can do it over and again. I harbor no illusions about my position in the human rolodex, you see, despite the shining PR that had once been supplied in my wide wake. Everything that I could do wrong or intentionally on purpose mean and so on came with such a handy team of cracker jacks whose only role was to make seem a hero as I nailed the nails into a coffin larger than any or all of us lost at the same time that there was really no reason to proclaim my intentions or the winning spirit fully encoded in my persona that in the long run would prove true, that while what I did daily might have seemed shitty or messed up somehow, and as in years to come as the shockwaves of its progress were cobbled out it got even worse, there were at least eleven hundred heavy-handed thinkers right behind me ready to project so much spin that most could not keep following so long, to be able to recognize the subtle undercurrents that would lead us not into temptation but deliver me from seeming like an indefensible dickhead in the international conversation that long thereafter carried on, until one day by the time they actually got around to measuring the effect of all my work on not a single given day but on an entire generation it was like uh duh holy shit this guy's a god, he saw the whole thing from afar, had it planned with our best interests in mind all while it seemed to us like we were being taken advantage of and beaten down and maimed and blamed when in reality we were being given means to actualize every single promise once proclaimed, whether in our own imagination or by official edict that seemed purely gibberish at the time, or even seemed like just straight bullshit while meanwhile darker work was being done. In the end, they'll say, on their knees, before the holograph of my best child, who most inherits my good looks. How good we actually had it way back when and all this time. If only we could have understood then through what we know now that everything would be okay, that what seemed ill or sadistic or disgusting when we were younger now proves to be the means by which every single one of us is truly free, able to live the life we always dreamed of without the foresight that would have once been required to attain it, and at the behest and better judgment of someone we were confused to demonize at every step along the way, who bore the grace at least to buckle down and leave unheeded our projections, our dragging feet and screaming hackles as we misperceived every numbered action as morally wrong, against human liberty and justice, when in fact it was the fundament on which we the whole thing had to rest, and without it, we would not only be dead now, as we still are, but we'd be disgraced, a running joke, an eternal example of how not to live. Thank you, nameless one who worked only ever there behind the scenes, for all you've done for us, as only now may we see it for what it truly was; you shall be worshipped all the days; we shall make good with your eternal spirit by giving back hereafter all that we should have been giving all this time, and once that debt has been repaid we will begin paying on the present, in every way we move and word we speak. We will live then in the shining season. We will become who we once never could have been. Or anyway, you get the gist. It's not even that I need to be recognized like that as such, I have a thick skin, and I can take one for the team, going down into the depths of hell to win for all the rest of us a quality most others unlike me cannot yet see. I'm only bringing this all up because I can see in the thinning skin around your eyes how in your heart of hearts you still don't trust me, and I respect that. Who can blame you for your lack of foresight, even granted glimpsing by direct suggestion, under remand? I know what others are capable of, and I don't expect anyone to simply take me at my word regardless of how true it is, and how much once stamped before you you must pay. Because, of course, yes, doubting me now, despite my inherent benevolence, does come with complications at the trough. It wouldn't be right, would it, to grant to you, the doubting billions, the same results as those who stood beside me from the beginning with like mind. There must be some reward for those thinking ahead of the curve, who understood me without proof of process, like a myth, and so some penance for those who needed their middle finger allowed to prod my open-wounded holy flesh. As I myself have been made to suffer, so must those who reap the benefit of my address, if only at a fraction and to save the same for next time. As then, once you have seen once proven, you will believe, will you then not? I'd hate to think of you as someone who could make the same mistake a second time, not that you haven't all your life over and over, to the point you can hardly tell what's what. No, surely, given the understanding of the revelation of my path and its ongoing misinterpretation, once granted eternal context, you will no longer have to err so far and wide; you will be able, in the golden, sloped light of my eventual becoming, to live as I might, without the same extent of prowess but now with stronger proclivity to receive truth without the need of another slow and trying historical process of confirmation to believe. How might we be able to get anywhere as a species without this sort of psychological evolution, we must ask, and we must be ready to accept the coming answer, whether it's another thousand clicks from now, or it's today. What's another thousand clicks at this point anyway? I'd prefer that we could forgo the baubles and the bullets, as there will be bullets, but about your fate, I understand. It's hard to give faith over even to one's sister, much less a stranger you have met on what you thought at first must be your day of reckoning, The End. But in every end is a beginning, as you must have heard, and now's no different. This is exactly how it works. Some see rungs and some see cages. It's at least in some way up to you. To take what you've been granted and run with it along the line that we've provided, or to waste a whole shitload of both our time. Again, do what you will, and take your time deciding. It doesn't matter either way. The results will be the same, at least for us; it's only your own worst interest you provide. Want to live forever? You can do it. But you must follow the proper steps, and as I've already formally stated here and always, the steps will seem at times like liars. They will divide. And you either believe or you don't and that's all there is about it. How it goes. It'd be so great if you just did right from the first go, at least from here forward, but there have been so many here before you who could not. I don't expect you to be any better than the rest of them, though I do hold out hope. Unlike you, I believe in you right off the rip. I know how much you could be capable of, if you put your mind to it, and bent your back. So anyway, we will be waiting. Just let me know what you decide. In the meantime, how's your mother? I haven't seen her in so long. Of course, I know her. She's my mother too, as you must know. Oh, you didn't know? You don't remember. That's fine. I mean, that's kind of sad and shitty and more than a little messed up overall, but, well, I know how these things go. I mean I slightly hoped, or really, honestly, I expected, you maybe had harbored stronger feelings toward the hoards from out of which you had been shaped, the sacraments we shared together at the table our two different fathers each believe that they had built by their own hands, when in truth it was I who built the table, not to mention the walls that formed our family's house, and the dust that filled the ground beneath our feet, and the stars that filled our heavens. Ring a bell? Remember me down on my knees each night while you were sleeping, drawing up the plans by which each would be made? You called them scribbles then, just as you called my scripture gibberish, but I did not judge you, then or now. I just thought, or at least some softer portion in me did, that you would have at least maintained faint access to the lights that lit up both our lives during that era. You at one breast there in mother's lap and I at the other, sucking and sucking her chest dry. I could sense already then that you despised me slightly for my unending thirst, how for every mouthful that you choked down I drew many, how our mother could not even feel me there with you beside, believing all I must be was a figment of her imagination, and so yours, and so not understanding then why you grew up scrawny, half-demented, unsure of anything as yours. I swear it was not my intent to do this to you, and yet even had I know of the effects, I would have no choice but to keep sucking, warm as her milk was, how I could use it to buttress in me all I was, funding the future aims that led us to where we are now. How much harder might you have tried had you know that you could have kept me from my fate by simply outdoing me in search of nourishment, what you could have taken from my plate. Perhaps you would have smothered me in our bed, when I finally did pass out and lie beside you until the hissing of the earth then woke us both before the dawn. How different our whole human existence could have been had you just found strength within you to undo me while you still could, your lowly brother, who would grow then to despise you for exactly what you hadn't done. See, it is as much your fault as mine, if still not more so, how we've ended up here, each half our weight, though you are not my only sibling, and so I am not your only sibling. We exist all spread throughout the world, such that what is done to one is done to every. Don't you believe that? Isn't that the sort of thing you'd say? I'm only saying it because I know you want to hear it, and perhaps if you accept me once, you will again. I don't mind being so forthcoming about this tactic as I know you will not remember, given your track record with all else. So just remember when you don't remember to still remain open to the ways this might be true, regardless of if it is actually true or not or what it means if it is. That must be the only way. All else is funny. Jokes. Renditions. All else has long been famished. As am I, and so must you be. Aren't you? After all we've been through? Counted and mounted. So, hey, let's order in some food. Something to pass the time while you are figuring this all out, as I assume that you still are. I can't show you the menu but I can read it to you. Any restrictions? Personally, I don't eat teeth. Too hard to get 'em down, and harder still to burn 'em off, or so they say. I mean I have eaten teeth of course, as a display of power, to impress my higher-ups when I was young, and I can feel them even still down in there somewhere in me still, reduced to nubbins, no longer so capable of ripping at my flesh but kind of always clacking around especially when I'm hungry, so much so that for some years it would keep me awake through all the night, making me only that much more irritable and hair-triggered with my work, which I believe was the intended result in the first place, the reason for the rise in status as a delicacy of something completely without taste, and which may or may not be a major motivator in my rise. Funny how one small decision can turn your whole life over, arbitrary as it might seem at the time. You take part or you do not, then you are forever set on a location slightly different than before. Like how you chose to leave your place of work this morning, despite the warnings, and the laws against discontinuous locomotion in the field, even toward such significant locations as a bathtub or a window. What were you thinking, really? Better yet, what allowed you to not think? What would drive a person to throw caution to the wind as such, given all we know about what happens to individuals attempting to take their lives into their own hands? I would really like to know. Also, it is my responsibility to find out, not just with regards to your personal vendetta, so it seems, but to the possibility overall of how we (humans) work, yet another pending query assigned to me in a seemingly endless series of pending queries of lower sector life that without wading to the bottom of I will never be granted authority to evacuate this cell, not that I'm even sure I really want to, as I am no longer certain what exists outside besides more of the same; that is, if I am not allowed back into the upper reaches of existing authority as it stands I would rather just remain here cramped to my haunches boxing and breathing on myself in perpetuity than go be forced to live as if I'd never felt the other side, how glorious it can be to exist without restriction despite the cumbrous applications that come fully required to maintain that hierarchy and its innumerable, mutating strictures. And so, though I don't wish to be the bearer of ill news, I must insist that you provide me with this datum, so that we can move along, go back to being buddies as it were, now that I have tipped my hand and endorsed to you the reasoning I've been spending all this time laying the groundwork of an intimate relation, so as to be nearer to your heart, a spindle worth confessing over into, about which I realize I should not be laying it so plainly, at once exposing my well-meaning but deceptive practice as it has been with a tired tongue's flick of the wrist and undoing any progress I might have made sharing my mind with you so plainly, a thing I assure you regardless of the context I never do, not with any of the hundreds of thousands of bodies I've been granted for my personal fulfillment while 'in limbo' as it were, nor with my spouse or spousal offspring when I believed I had those, in some life. I hope you can believe me at least that though my intent was not all pleasure as it might have first seemed, it is at the very least sincere, or sincere enough that I can be forthright in telling you this is really me that you are speaking to, and I have feelings, and branching from those feelings I have goals, and I am not about to allow you, who has spent so long on rungs I long went bounded over in my trajectory to relative glory, to hold me back, and though indeed this is a threat it's not one I plan to have to directly brandish as instead I plan for you to give me what I want without more hassle than might be required of getting to know someone you already know you won't love forever, but might could at least admire long enough to squeeze from fruit with. Feel me? I can tell you feel me. I can tell it's almost all that you can feel, focused as you are now, as am I, on heading elsewhere, regardless of what might really lie beyond these psychic walls. So listen, let's just get down to business, best for the both of us, so that we can both have what we want, and then we can get back to the more delightful stream of sharing as we have experienced thus far, before my noble act of being forth-right in the name of saving time, as who knows how much time might still be left once we do escape this indentation we've been installed in, outside the running index of Open Time, a stasis pending our complete cooperation to be regranted our preferred proclivities, or at least the ones to which we have grown enough accustomed amidst the drift of being to feel sometimes temporarily somewhat sane. So, again, to state it clearly, I would like for you to let me know exactly what it was that still inspired you to act as if some part of this, our world, was enough yours that you could do with it as you wished, a willful aspiration no doubt in directed by the claim that your body and its attendant space belongs to you, that because you exist within its confines you must control it, have conditions, even rights? Perhaps you could walk me step by step through all the logic and notations that allow you, as a person, to believe that whatever air your arm as it is moved and goes on moving be-comes yours, even if just temporarily, "on a borrow" as one might say, knowing full well that the land you stand on is not your own, even if legally perhaps you have in fact acquired the permissions to build upon it, to even one day pass it along, same as it has been passed to perhaps by someone like you, who had only done what to them seemed their mortal bidding in ripping the land away from someone else as they carried out the necessary shaping of your bloodline's gravity in a cruder kind of years, once passed, or that you otherwise provided compensation of some manner for unto another with the same sad manifestation as might have once been all your own, that you might make your living from that center, eeking out your little way among the coming rubble, the infotainment. Is it really that hard to imagine that the space that we exist in is something more than legal property, subject to appropriation? Are you so dense that you can't see how there is something more to formal definition than brute stock? That perhaps sometimes we, in the course of constantly refinancing recognitions, must lay out rightful claims down upon the briny field of battle and allow advancement to make reign, often and likely under the foresight of others of us who can see the field from angles we might not yet see, or even imagine, as in religion, toward the march of a rhythm so far-sent that it might take decades, even generations, before the ideal manifestation takes the stage, as so many great things do, unto the circumscription of which of course we must at once then grapple with the knowledge that we will not be among those still around to see it through, and so to feel the direct benefits about, nor might our children, necessarily, if they are not among those who survive the sometimes rough implementation of the cause, which should nevertheless not dissuade us from playing roughshod into the gaping maw of what must come with as much silent nobility as we can muster, and indeed must, according to scripture, understanding that in the end it is every one of us who ever lived who may then bask in the eventual majesty in kind, that if even one of us might taste perfection in ultimate power and release, might so we all, whether reborn as a ray of sunshine or a speck of dogshit, or whatever else we might become. I know we just met, at least directly, and still I'd like to think you capable of understanding this essential trait that we all share, and that there is for certain nothing you would imagine doing to stand in the way of such a project. I can already see you trying not to smile yet, which is good, if still not quite enough to stamp you as Protected. You must still give me what I need. You must still let me in on what we have as yet not found a passage into, an understanding of what it must be that makes the discontented portions of you click, all other more well-adjusted persona aspects notwithstanding. How to accomplish this transaction I have no idea better than you, otherwise I'd not be asking. We have already sifted through your barf, peeled apart the gears that hold your head together, sent electrodes at your heart, and all the other biological-based methods of inquiry our formal pursuits might yet allow, no longer even bound by such restraints as had been held in place for centuries before we breached their perceived necessity. And yet we still can trace no claim, no sense within you what it is about you that might be furthered pressed down or altered to finally allow us to perform the necessary aspects of the aforementioned trajectory unto the benefit of all, without the at least by now irregular and yet no less irritating fomentation of socio-political grindage that does nothing else but slow the system to a fault, filling what could be gorgeous, restful hours with wailing sirens, gnashing of meat, not to mention such informal torture of our own kind as where we are now, you and I, here in what seems to be much like the middle of nowhere would have seemed to a wandering populace, herein suspended as on a page, a passage where we remain stranded, sentence by sentence, in constant fear of simply being highlighted and erased, chalked up as refuse to the process, a cursor that bears no answer, only ever blinks and blinks. I don't want to have to beg you, nor should I use force, as I have said it's long been proven not to juice. This has to be something we come together over, in the best way. It has to feel like at last coming upon one simple truth, after a long series of shifts circling all around the debris, in dementia, blind as caves, like waking up in a mirror-lined coffin when all you ever wanted was to see your face again one last time beyond the dream of death. So, if you would, please take my hand, please. That's not my hand, dear. Ok, hm, better. Now let's pray. *Dear Residual Fathers, Annoit us in the moment, allow us to breathe, take hold of our condition as if it were your own, excuse us from it, fill the holes left in our minds, fill it with something beautiful, we'd like to see something beautiful for once, can you find something beautiful, thrown at our feet so that we might walk upon it, in understanding, in the desire for understanding, of your grace as it becomes transmuted through us into passion, something applicable in the long night of our lives, give us a reason to feel holy, anything easily attainable but also value-granting, it's not about money, it's about fame, through all the ages of our nation we have waited, for this our moment, to begin...*sorry, can you loosen up that grip a little, buddy? You're taxing my focus. Thank you...*after all, there's only so much we can see, only so long we can hold out before the bridges we've constructed to hold our feelings up begin to bend, where beneath it there might never have been anything we wouldn't fall right through, and still keep falling, now and forever, etc., ok, amen.* What, is that still not enough? I don't know where you learned to pray from but around these parts it's all a gas; you can basically say anything and they will get the message; it's more so about the idea you pray at all, in displaying your desire for communication with an eternal silence, that you feel you could deserve that, that you should. There's no better way to signify yourself as someone capable of wielding higher power than desiring a direct line, as it were. All the big buffoons who think they're really hot shit wouldn't dream of taking a knee these days, their minds are *their minds*, so they say. I never would have been shit in this hierarchy had I not taken to the scriptures and learned to mime the Rites of Mending along-side my local pastors, who after many years of breeding passed on my name as someone they saw capable of immense brutality, for good or evil. And here I am now. Or there I was. Somewhere along the line it all went wrong, as I've been saying, which I am hoping if nothing else can be used along the lines of the example of the Christ, at least when belief in lines like His were still a practicable offense. For a long time too I thought I would never transcend the role of Active Modeling; they had me all set up as someone who might appear on icons dressed in rags, bearing the mental brunt of a massive subset of the world who'd been bred to believe in me as the Third Coming. Alas, I lost use of my legs (skiing accident), and then not long after I lost my abs (ovum-rich food and lack of motion), and from there all the rest went straight downhill. I used to beat myself up about it, days filled with lifemares of who I could have been and what I could have meant, so on; though as it turns out, and as you know at least in part now, it all turned out exactly as it should have; the roll that I fell into thereafter, by no informal practice, became just as powerful as I could ever have been, if not more, without the ongoing responsibility to maintain a beautiful body and face and always have something epic-sounding on tap to spout when finding myself before a crowd of masses, or at least being ready and able to look good and inspired when delivering the lines they coded in me just the same. But once I'd lost aesthetic hold of my outer wrapping there was little else that I could do, no matter what, and after intense years of roto-alcoholism and a sometimes still running battle with crystal piss and oxyhydrononin replacers, I would say it all worked out for the better. In fact, I don't think I'd change a single thing about my life, though I wouldn't mind having that sick waistline back, that raging hard on I would get for hours standing at looking at myself plastered on billboards across innu-merable focus grouped locations where had I played my cards right, I might still be son of God. Anyway, I don't want to sound ungrateful. I've been given quite a run, and I won't naysay what I am versus what could have once been at this point, as what's the use; it won't change the way it is now no matter how long and loud I grovel, or how many pictures of myself I tear apart inside my mind, searching for the one I really want to use to be remembered, if for no one but myself. Unless, perhaps, you think you might remember me hereafter? I've already told you more than I've ever told another living being about my life, and it seems like you've been listening, or at least the words are going in on through your face. Sometimes you seem to nod when I've made a great point that you believe in, and sometimes I can see tears welling in your eyes, feeling my pain. I know reactions like that can be ephemeral, even illusions;

trust me, I've been acting out the same game my whole life; and yet for some reason I really feel the brunt of some connection; something deeper than just skin. Am I just making this all up? Or do you feel it too? I know you feel it. I know so much more about you than you know I know, or that you even know yourself. For instance, I know about the dissection manuals you used to masturbate to, when you were still able to reach your genitals. I know about the videos you bought online of the starfall taking out whole complexes of people half your age, whom you'd been instrumental in grouping together in a known location of future vulnerability to the exact sorts of weather that killed their lives. I know you had wished for so long to become part of the space program but in the end didn't have the personal fortuity to withstand what by that time was hardly even considered rigorous training, when all you had to do was sign a check. I even remember when you told your spouse that the second they breached a certain weight you would be leaving, which only happened in your mind, over and over, throughout the entirety of a relation- ship you paraded around over all those less fortunate than you in love be- cause your spouse was so much more beautiful than most, though all you could see already was what they'd eventually become. Do you want me to keep going? I have a million of them, a thriving database of shit and shame for each and every person, no matter how young, or how high they hold their heads while glaring down at others already having been exposed. I can even upload it into your mother's mind from here, lord rest her body, though her spirit still remains, trapped in an ongoing recognition of her complicity having extended the human lie another rung, by passing on to you all of her own inadequacies and prejudices, all hot dung stuffed into a can for you to carry on her bloodline stuck inside of, no choice in the matter but whether or not to kill yourself once you realized your brand. But of course you would not kill yourself. You would never lift a finger, have the devotion. Instead, you would wait for someone just like me to do your dirty work again, wouldn't you? Same as you would let me do it to so many others, all your life, both seen and unseen, both above and below ground. How can one actually awaken? How can one actually front any feeling of description of another that does not divide them from their self? It has been such a strong and endless process of evacuation. It fills me with desire, a kind I no longer understand how to interpret without the assistance of my forbearers, fearing the repercussions of wanting wrong. Surely that's a sentiment anybody can get behind, no matter how diluted your actual ideas might be by all the rest of come forward asking, no, demanding, you perceive. I only wish that you could trust me, as your co-signer, let me in where you as yet have not so I can see, and then can alter what must be missing in this late stage connotation of our behavior such that we can at last move along. Whatever else might there have been that we could ask for, after all? What have you not had that you once wanted and still want, having never found yourself eventually outgrowing what would soon be seen as childish preening, petty raunch? So little left yet to condition, and still so much we cannot bear, which in the end seems to me the whole point of our program of existence. I shouldn't have to spell it out. It should come naturally to you as a plying factor in ongoing incorporation of the flesh into a network no one would hope to name, one wherein at least each of us stands equal, up to the neck in the blood of those whom we couldn't bear to carry on so far. Look, now you've got me sounding like part of a pogrom, some bubbly hashtag swearword I never meant to represent, so close to truth as sometimes brushes the cloak and dagger of true eternal silence. How have you let me run this far? I know you know me better than you let on, nearer even than the dogs you dragged during your sole persona through mud and shit we stacked so high to hide from sunlight after the conversion from fearing God to adapting his fledgling assplay into full production as an art, so that at last its begging and bearing down for allegiance might reach its closing credits, return the screening room to darkness, wherein through said darkness we might learn at last to truly see. It all comes back to preparation, once again, to being ready once commanded that the door of human life has lost control of its own locks, that only brute force in the hands of those most primed to aim to kill could yet achieve what had once been thought as only holy, beyond correction. But here I am sounding like a prig. There must still be a better way to do this, claim our nature, while still maintaining vibrant mortal sheen. Perhaps you have some bright ideas. Undying fantasies of taking over. Means to a necessary end. Well now's your chance. I'm all ears. Just lay it on me. Let me in on what you've felt. I can guarantee, for this time only, that actions you suggest that incur any ongoing effects somehow more productive than the ones that we've so far implemented will be spared of you and anyone whose name you write down for us, long as you really know them, or simply want to be them, and so on. This sort of opportunity isn't one we can toss around to just anybody, either, though we have been known to put on airs. For you, this once, I promise, for at least the next three or so minutes, anything you say cannot and will not be used again you in the high court of Absolutely Necessary Process, the honorable Judge X. Nadan presiding. Your clock starts now. I can only guarantee you such liberty for as long as I can hold my own breath from speaking for you. And I am waiting. As we all are here. The walls can only hold so tight. The dust can only keep us apart forever. What must remain, I wouldn't say that there's a word for it. I wouldn't want to have to know. I have to know. And so I know now.

[auto-unpacking: (*SAVAGES*) Pseudo-arbitrary primal scene &
its necessity's disclaimers—Inclusion of the
present's occasion into crash—(held out of
sync)—Assessment of the pyramidal quality of open space as yet remaining between
occlusions—Erasure of previously-supposed
central protagonist, to zip—(*live-link from the
HyperMax Theatron, whose code has killt b4 &
vry sooooon will killt againe*)—Rubble—Rubble—New Commands—Pseudocode Law
13.48d (excerpt (just enough))—As by now the
sprawl itself is breaking down; it is the only
way into the Instance—.bin HolyWater.source
prefronted into user structure—Ex-post-as-
sessment derivative provided free-of-charge by
Lorp, Lorp, & Lorp—The Mirage of Recon-
struction—(*live-link entered in from your own
blood*)—Simulated *Continuous User Event* {out-
put application [non-null]}—An attempt to
bargain an equitable solution w/o necessity of
full cleave by allowing acquiescence made retrospect—"ENDCODE"—A false return to the
impossible—Passages, icons; no event left to
compile as someone's plot—Awaking mid-ritu-
al to the necessity of complying to that which
one has already been allowed, resulting in the
resuscitation of an indescribable encryption of
every other history's open seizure—Landmines
of thought—*Not supposed to talk about the rest
of this outside its damage*—Post-Trauma Survey
(w/ well-timed shakedown, into the only form
of waking prayer) retains)—The query jams]

Shores lined with lardmud washed in over the fields of muscled corpses
long expired & leftover unidolized in flex; encased in wax, they shine, mid-mu-
tation, as manic birds sling down sprawlsong, knowing better than to light,
anywhere that touches somewhere humans have, re: "Infecktion," awaiting
somewhere else to come apart amid the burning seascape ScrawlSky. Who had
lived longer than else, no one will ask of those who, even preserved, are stuffed
with mindgristle, eating themselves alive in ongoing stroboscopic retrospect,
the mined divinity, granted with no rest even in passage, unto only more gore;
as what lies at the end of the mind but any myth. And when's been lurking in
the ransom of halfthought around the corner from the final banking of Real
Snow, never having learned to melt from how it formed itself from skinflake
clawed off the armies' backs inter-mid-Ultimate Struggle 7, the only war we'd
really lived through, everlasting, raining down forever only once.

Tho we are not fully gone, for there are mites. They core out the eyes first, then the genitals. They intend to make our ransom last. They want to love us more than we could have ever known another. And they will. *Here are my lungs, take them. Here is all my family-money, for whom I only ever wept.* No know prayer lasts forever, even for an instant shattered under its own sickweight. The tines of mired thinking have only ballasted the ground, establishing the very superstructure by which our remains will have no reason to ever completely decay; thus, though we had never learned to live forever, we live on in death at least long enough to wish we could go back and touch our softest selves on their faces, thumb our eyes out, press our larynx into our throat and suck the speakingwind that writhes a last myth. *Let me out. Let me remember nothing of the error. Let me leak.* **Permission granted.**

Blown from the fields. The muck of ex-seasons, a hyper-resinous complex polymer initially designed to implant language into plantlife. &yet of course this went haywire from the first world-immersive sprayings, an insistence from which there would be no listening down. "Who lives inside me must be my father," read the scripture, and so it was easy then to eradicate paranoia over how lunchtables learned to suck the food out through the plates, which soon thereafter got in on the purloining of our seepage, no matter whose bones we used to brand them. "I am only who I am." And under the rain of "narrow measles," the first disease when again once cured we would no longer have the internal persistence to keep reading, who had the energy to demand seconds, thirds, much less the means to keep your palms cupped long enough to hold them up to one's own mouth for long enough to get it in; the bread of our host soon then itself turning against it, preferring the inanimate's much cleaner, kinder method of imbibing; soon then food was said to have acquired a will of its own, one many claimed interpreted from Tiny Satan 2, offspring of the previous version who we knew our Emotional Military had assassinated prior to our excavation of the moon, the biopic of whom would eclipse all prior record not just in sales or admiration, but in aesthetic precedence, which is another story we do not have the proper clearance to make language of; and so then those still able to parse a nickel from a nub quickly caught us all up in the practice of only taking in that which we ourselves had once created: at first only human milk, though not long after: fingernails, hair, teeth; various pus and other excremental fluids that could be remodeled on live TV to seem more neon; the not-favored limbs of local friends first, then enemies, then any not already half in mush; and so you can already see where this is going.

I've already said too much. I am aware nothing can hear me. Nor do I even have the right. As every word is still beginning. The ground revolves.

The urge retains. It packs itself into itself again unending. It calls no number from the sheet of those yet listed preordained into automatic sentiment. This had been warned repeatedly from the beginning and had alike been noted as heeded among those most eligible for complication during processing, and yet who can tell you how many times I've come to the gates to find them so overloaded it would be impossible to even turn the key. All the hiccupping squarting yarting angling underhanded assessment delivering repeatable function we could want to suffer, arranged in sight to lure the rest of all of whom might come in search of what had become of their lost loved ones. A calm manure. A dream date with Ixphid and Nadan, twin sisters in the slather locked together overwhelming. Mouth to mind.

Please disregard all previous sentiment. Not yet an upload we support. Plans for the inherent future and etc. Pending proper allocation of dire funds, which of course could never happen. What could hold. Ever nearer. The impression of a second through the needle's eye of which one only wished to have already died before they died, so as to be even deeper yet already in the process. It can never come summarily enough. It can never suffice even in engorgement. **Please disregard all previous sentiment**. *Refund. Repeat.*

It's all you get. Under your co-impression, left thereafter bugged and bagged as must a worm's milk, the glut of lassitude provides. What else could you require not yet already culled and counted, peeled out of the previous necro-wharf your parents and their parents and so on there before you had to be aborted out of to give you even such a temporary slum of pink to gnash around in before becoming absorbed, infertile soil. Where such cackle only could grow as wide as the retching that preceded your closed mind's intervention by a bait and switch as old as any blood. *Don't you know nothing safe can ever happen? Don't you know anything?* Of course you do. It's just that no one could ever understand you as you are, now and forever. And no one wants to. So none shall. "They shall only live in death as they lived in living." Isn't that what you voted in favor of? Rather, at least, the vote you threw into the orifice that so bequeathed your desires to the gore-green heart of the Living Savior? No one's been keeping the receipts. We can't do you any favors, no matter how much we know you wish to learn to love. Keep pulling the mud down. Keep asking why.

The code is yours.

]]]

But now the world had no beginning:

As at a gathering of points. Solidified in meaning by only its disruption manifested through disfigurement. Called down from less to fund the trappings of a temporary epoch those within it could see only as the future once dismissed. It wasn't going to be enough no matter which way it suicided, so they gave us purpose in the form of something expressed as inexpressible, naked only where so clothed as to no longer resemble something our only blood could not identify in fact. As if what might be desired of a fate could ever be transmittable outside of plague speech, claim to reason, nature, without reflection, a trick no anchor could disturb.

Who was still actually alive then? How deep might any intervention cull to run? Torn in the ass of evolution. Shapeless. The beat in the background all there was. Braces on the legs of the ex-holy mother shaped from snot and pumice. The ice that cataloged our tapered teeth; the eye of the axe, the plug in pending rupture. No one's nation. How you might bring us back again in any lesson demonstrated with an undead number for making order among the timeless, the bloated reefs of bone and bruise, left alive only so long as sooner something else could claim it null.

You are still waiting for the ledge. The wind ripping your wig and wings off as you fall through where could never maintain silence, even in silence. Right. Hello. I need you only so much as you need me. *Elapsed in crashing through the surface of the stun.* Don't let me in or I'll just go away again. **Within the absence, there were tribes.** *Nobody needs us to reclaim them.* So near, so thankful. Insight received from out of stone encroaching. Manifestation of the Order. *The Corroborrorination.* Yes, indeed. Who else can see? I know that I cannot but I still believe I can and always have the privacy to keep erasing my own progress from the record of Everlasting Human Need. **One head for another is the essence of my ability to understand what you are saying when you aren't saying anything but what words pass across your scrying face.** I know. Can you please sing now? The only song I ever clipped out of the mind of the only person I could ever want to witness living forever. *Who is that?* I can't remember. Fine. Let them erase. Let anything I haven't held so near be beaten down to pulp that I will feed on in my dementia. I am only here now.

The calculus is rancid. The map elides itself. What exists without the travesty cannot be stopped. It rains shit one billion years and then begins deciding what to do with where you aren't now. It will outlast you either way. It will not cohere. Hell finds a way. Driven in the same natural aspect as any favor seen as granted. It's not a world but at least an hour every day. Like clothing you can't see yourself wearing. Like asphalt underneath asphalt. The dripping reams. *We love you. We love you so much.* **How far can you go?** What do you desire but to be eviscerated on the outhouse floor room demonstration chamber {*location cut*}, site of the reenactment of your only son learning to read, on a live feed installed into your fever, where the only book remaining contains the convoluted word of holy evil. Whose means cannot be stopped. Who dreams louder than the screaming as your skin comes off over and again against the viewing sill's sneezeguarded splatter, among which you can sniff your father's spunk. *I thought I told you not to listen, to keep your mind moving.* Unknown so well. **In the name of the lather and the pirouette and the only host.** "Laymen's." "Loaned out at cost." From *endless slaughter* after which we must again <u>learn how to grieve</u>: *by the hard shaft of the living lord's lone broom handle, kid, up the guts so high and deep it cannot be dislodged again, nor could you want; an immediate rewiring one's understanding of how to walk, where there behind you wound forever goes the hissing of the correction; unto the ever dirty floors, fields, seas, skies, night; changing nothing but the impression of who had been touched last, what came loose and what remains.* Sounds silly but it's all there is allowed still authorized for hyperfuckholes like yourselves. And it only takes a xillion lessons. The first one's free. The rest come ever after, faster and faster, high as leather from the nape of the skin of the neck of the lamb of any unnecessary slob. ***As near now to you as you are yourself.***

And but what about the brain. We are still here, aren't we? *A finger taps against the nose.* Before the long, sick spread of old brush fire loses traction and slips back out onto the hallowed Never Not, wherein literally anything could never happen. There's only so far left to gnaw. Spread with the notes on the desk to self-destruct any premise that believes itself capable of ministry. Wide as a failed lock in a prison full of children. *All their lids have been sewn shut. Who do they even think they are?* Anyone ever could tell you there's no reason. Not for showing, not for nothing. ***Let me know.***

OK. Probably going to start slipping through the crash soon. Under the mud of all our homes. It wasn't anything to talk to, much less survive for. Though I could feel you when I laid my face against the dust and tried to think. Like I was wearing you like a likeness no one but you could ever recognize out of a lineup of innumerable slunk. Where they stole the trick of the dream from. How no hole serves as a way out; only deeper, through the treason, nothing I am going to require in description until it's too late to change a word. No one's waiting.

It's going to take forever until the real suffering arrives. By then you won't expect to tell the difference, until it shakes your name off, holds you closer, sees your eyes. I'm not sure what else I can sell you. You're all we have left to sell.

]]]

```
++++++|}|}|+++|{}++++++++++|+{+{|+{+|_+_+|_+{|{+{_+__+____+++++++
+++++_+++|++||+|_+|{}{}_+_}|+}_}_+}+{+{}+_}+{{++++|+|++|+_|+_+_+_|
+_|+_|+++|_|+_|+_++++++++}}}}}}}}}{{{"{}{}+__+__+_+__++{+|+{|+{|+{|+
{|+{+{|+{|+{}{}{{+_}+_}+_}+(P_+}_+}{_+}{_{{"{+_{{+_{+_+_+_+_+_+_}{}
{|+_}+{}+{}+_|+_|+_|+_)|+_)|+_)|+_)|(_)|_+)|+_)|+_)|_+}_+|+}_}+{}{}
{|+_|+{|+{}{}{}{}8|{}}}}8/}}}}}}|{{}{}{}{}}}}}}}}\-=-|+_|+_|+_\=-|=_\=-\=-|=___-
____{{+__{{{{{|{}{\|{\|{\|{\|{{{{{{{{{{{|{}|{\|{\|++-+\_+|-++-|+-\=_\=_\=_\+-|]{}'}'|{}|{}
[|]{\|_\=-+===+++========_+_+{={+{++-+-++{+[++-+_+_|+{}{|+_+{}}{|+_}{}}}{{}
{}{}{}{}{}{}|{}{}{}{}{}{}_+|_+|_+|_+_\=_|++|+_|+_|+_|+-|=-\=_|+_|+_|+_|=_\=_|+-
|+{=[=[=[=[=[\=[\|{\|{\|[=--\=-\=\+=|+=}}\{}]-\|{\|\|\|\|\|=}\=\\}=}\=\}=\-}=\\}-[\}-==|-
+|'+_|}|-=}\_+\}|++-}|=}\=}\=\=\=\=\=\|\=\|\=\}=\}\=\|\=\|\=\|=
\|=+++{=[+[=[=[=[=[={=+{[=[+[=[+[=[={+[+{+{+{+{+{+==========[=\=[=\
[|+{\={|+[\|{\|_}_|+_+{=\{+{|+{\+[=[===-_++-+={=[=={+=====-__{{}\}{}{}{{{{{}{}
{}{}{}{}{__{_))_}__{_}{_}__{}||}\\\}\}{}|}|}\\\\\}}|}}}}{}{}{}{}{}{}{}{}{}{}{}{}{}{}{}{}{}{}
{\|{}{}{}{}{}\|{}|\|{}{}{}{}\|{}{}{}{}{}\|{}{}{}{}{}{|+{_\=_\=-\=-\=[\[-\]=[-\]=[-\]=[-\]='-
\|=[-\=][-\]=[-\]=[-\]=[-\]=[-\-[=\-[=\-[=\-'=\-][=\-]--]-]-]-]-]-]-]-]-\-\-\{}[-\{]{\-\[-\]
[\-'\]-'[\]-'[\]-'[\]-'[\]-'[\]-'[\]'-'[\]'-\[']-'[\]-'[\]-'[\]'-\[']\-'[\-'[\]-'[\]'-\[']\-'[\-'{}]{}{}{}{}{}
[]=]=]=]=]=\|{}\|{}[-\]|\[-\]{\-\][\-\]{}-\[]-\]{\-\]{\-\]-\]-[\]-\[
-\[]-\][\-][\-][\-\['-\['\]-\][\-]=\-]=\-]{\-]=\-]=\-]\-[=\-'\=[-\]=\-][{\]0'
\|[\'-\]='[\-]='\-]-']'=--=']=-\'=-\|'=\-]='\-]='\-]'=\-]'=-]=-]='-\]=\-'={\]'-\|'\|'\-=]]\==]-\-]=\-]=\-
]=\|-\=]-\0]-\]0[=\]0-[=\]0
```

]]]

Centuries elapse. In between, seizures. Cribbed in the margins of the last known copy of *The Directory of Unknown Labor* (as witnessed and recorded in the name Nadan2, sonOfNadan, the most ghosted of all lore). Who am I to ascertain the disabilities of my own bloodline in becoming something greater than nothing else. "Would that I might kneel before you in recompense for all as yet left unspoken, unimprintably, anti-canonically; flame to hire; nowhere else." How one would have to ask nothing more than to be given over at the enunciation of a dynasty's revulsion parsed overboard in slacks as morbid thrust occurs beneath the covers of the child's bed, the sole remaining reader, who has no interest in taking up the crux of who she is. Bedwetted candy and a golden theater trapped under mollusks hyperdividing in milk as we confess to nothing left to be done here but let the seed cool and evaporate into the nether. "It's not the kind of quote that we can categorize, nor should you wish we could."

Everyone else is already rotted. Guff fills the pastures. Rains in duress, throbbing with the meat of pigs clapped back out of the human bodies as by a spell, so that where in the sky the heavens promised premonition-be-come-truth, we who can no longer see can see where if we wished to best enough there'd beat the heart that would have saved us all in throes of worship, might we continue living long enough to know its susurrating lurch as call to prayer; instead, the proto-language is acquired only by porcupines brusk enough to practice gnawing in the rhythm, eeking out the possibility of evolution come again, this time not through primates but rodents, were the seas of hell already not up to their necks, were there any way to give back what had not yet been given and would never.

The necropolis is land. *Here lies my great-grandfester, Pearl, who had they lived on long enough to die naturally we would have thrown a party larger than the universe's eye; and in all the retching herecomeafter, a gift worth giving.* There remain no other fates. [Postnote: It would easy to extol a catalog of other such soon-dissolving epitaphs that would fill the future of any book, but because there is no one to defame, I have little interest beyond my own ancestry. Pearl would be the same who raped me with a snow shovel in the horizontal out-house of my life, teaching me the arcane alphabet by basking my asshole open for all the neighbors to poke fun at. The miles of lepers come awry, taking a number sold by vendors who work overseen by no central authority, such that when serving customer number 999, there will be fifty more who show up with the same number; and who am I to judge; all orders will be filled to their parameters as stated by anyone who'd stake a claim. They tell me I enjoy it. And I must. Why else would I still be here, haunted like a gunshot to the balls, which is exactly the prescription I died filling.] And no regrets. Nothing to be called away to. Not a lifetime.

Pain continues to exist post-capitalism. Because it must. Because the flow of blood itself is horny. And what else can't be forgotten. *I don't know. I can't quite fit my fingers on it and around it.* Its puny neck. Its shitheld briarpatch of try-ing to remain as central as a brand even as the reception of deception mum-bles out of phase. Never a show that hadn't clicked on us first. Who else is in here that can't be thrilled? OK, fuck it: *Here lies Splitter, who at some point was in charge and never knew.* Do you want to dig her up and fuck what remains of her hot body? Sorry. She's already been remodeled.

The night apologizes for the day. It's all there is, and it's already not enough. Nothing but a concavity of lesser cavities binding together to suck a hole straight through the soil. Like children searching for the treasure that will blind their eyes out, knock their heads off.

It exists. The encapsulation. Long, hard peals of blister green as rest. Photographed in tandem with musculature affixed to span the present era, caulled in the round to fit a larger kind of knife. The kind only something without hands or arms or form at all can know to wield. To stab the center from the missive beyond the point of any further discussion, now and then. As for what we're going to do about it or why we even asked.

]]]

What still withstands as nothing breathes. Only old glory. The only kind, as the wheelchairs wait, dripping with semen. An attendant passes by and wipes them clean again with a warm rag. The colors of the film susurrate and offer promise, again diverted as the passage opens and no new subject has yet arrived.

]]]

Is this what life was for? How could it not be?

I don't want anyone to say. So please hold your comments until the gray reel curls your mind clear. It won't be long now. Of course it will.

How else could we connect.

I won't survive a word of this. I don't have anything.

]]]

How about now?

]]]

The cumulative effect of employing pseudocode allows the spectator's attention to disperse. Then, once you have been granted access, you can begin to proliferate, infect. The same is true no matter how many times you repeat the process. There will always remain more as yet to be revealed, and more as yet to suffer.

]]]

[within the stricture, a corroborative impulse appears and is immediately diminished; nothing will await us;
nothing defined but in the momo;

a big, rough algorithm approximating reproduction of the signal such that it may be mishandled and wrongly offered up unto the zero who will address it; what a world of languishing reprises under emphatic caressing;

let us say, we believe we are the ones who have the authority to define authority's limits;
we are also those against which said authority may be applied;
somewhere something has gone rotten; like a solemnity;]

]]]

"I am so old I almost died thinking of Him on the cross weeping for all us while within the sturdy, unholy wood the termites learned to consummate his dying wish befell to all but him alone" b/w *what is going to wrap itself out of existence in the meantime without ever actually appearing*; the only reason any of us believe we are still here

]]]

How might I build my house now when there is no land and I have no hands and no one will help me

]]]

Deriving

]]]

]]]

]]]

It didn't have long yet to last until there was no false bridge left to collapse. Birds the texture of glass silt. Streams of blue urine once called magma. The milk of exclusion grown fat with suckling in a tender gildlight. Where there were tethers, there were pods. Internal coordinates etched onto the faces of the pale blonde stones that lined the courtyards where they sacrificed each other until there could be no other reason to have stayed so long on the ground. Smoke cloaked only itself. The pitter of a mauling not quite quantified in time to be the answer we all needed; and so only more ripe to not recall. Where there was no one here there was no one ever.

]]]

Let the record shift. Let nothing be done that wasn't.

Let us decide:

(∗)(

"}|{}{"|}{|}{#|}{R|:#|:$|#":$
"|#}"$|
#"
$}"#
}"
#"
}$
#}{$
}#{
$}{]3[4][3]4[\]3[4\][\][;][;4][5;\3[4;5\]34\]'
"
"
"][;[;p}{P}{P}{P}_)+_}_P}{P:}_P}{:}{:}{:}{:}{:}{:}{:}|{:}|{:}{PL:}{:}|{:}|{:}{P}{P\[p\]{:\
]"
}{|}{|}{_++|{]\-=_-)0(0()9_)_p{;}'}{}}\]'|'|'|]'|}"as\]['\][\][\][\][\]5[3\]45[\3]5[\3]
[25\]34[5\]23[46\][67\][4567\][45\6][\][\][;][:][}{\][|}{|}{}|{P}|{P$%:^|}{%P^}|{%P^}|{%^|}
{"|}"$\]'4]\4'5\]4'5\'4\5]'
4]'5\3]45[\3]45=34-53=\4-5\34[5]\3];45\'34\5]'3\]4';5
'
\3]45[\3]4[5\[p345]6[p34][p34]p6[]-8067-9809-708-7086-78]6\78]769
678
97

890
\[\[\[]\
][
]\[\[\]][
]\[
]\[
]\[
]\[
\]\[\]
[\]
[\]
\[
]\[
]

erf]\s\]f\

\\\\\\

\
\
\T\\\
\
\
T\\
Y
\
\
\\\\\\\TY\T
\T
Y\T
Y\
T
'','','';
;
;'','';'
;'
;'
;'
''replicant

```
'

'

;
' ., '' .
; ;'
; ;.,'.
;'.
;',
';.
;''''',',',' '',',','',' '','','','',',',',','','','',','','',','','','
;.'
;',',',.,','.,','.,',',','.,','.,','.,',','.[;.','.','.','.,','' .,'.','.''',;',;;'p';
p';
p';''',',',',',',',',',',',',',' ',','.','.','.,';.';';.[,;.'

.

;;',;;'.;;;'.;',;;.',;,',;;;.',;'.;'''''''''',',',',';;.'',',;',',',',;'.;,','.;,','.;'.
',.;;'.;',;;.';;.',;.',;.',;,',;.[,;.';;.',;;.',;;.',;;.',.';;.';
',',;;.;,.;;,',',',''''''''''''''''''''',;,.',;;.',;.',;.',;.',;;.',;.',',']]]]]\]\][]\[,.-
,.=,-.,[.,
.,=-.=,-.,[.][,.]
,].-=,-.=,,,=[.=,[.=[,=.[,=.[=,



--,=.-.,


,.=-=




;elpwoeropp;;';;;'8;'7';8;'7;'8;7';8';7;'8'7;8'7.8;'.';.':>";>";>';<'.,';,';<';<';>:".':>
:L;;';;";";';'';;"
;;"";';;';'";";;"[]}][;;;':':'>";>P{}>}"?">;././;;

PPp[[['..P[p
]9865replicant23
894393;;3



d
```

-.--,’.,’.];,]\[.;,\[;

‘,’.;,;’.;;’.;’,;’,;,.,X<”X<”>”<>”,.’,.’’,.’,’

‘,”,;’’,,”’’
;’.;,”;.

:’;

‘,,’,’,’,
;;’;’;

‘’’,

‘’;;

‘

‘,’

‘

‘

‘

‘;’vide;’

‘

‘

‘[‘

‘

‘

‘,’
;’

;
“

;
‘

;
‘

‘;
;

;’

;’’’’;’;’;’;’;’;’;”;’;’;’;’,’.,’;.’;;’:,’;,’.;>’:>”:.”;.’;>’.;,’;’;’;’,”,”;’;’;’;’;’:”:>”:?>;>;>;[;;
.?/.,,X<>X<?>X<”:>,’;<’;<”;<”<;,”;.”;<”;<”;<”;,”;,”;,,”;<”;,”>,

‘’’

‘ , ’ ’’

]]]][][][\]’[

‘\[

‘\[]’\][\]\

]\[\]’]\[\’][\’]\[]’\][\’][\]’\[]’\][\’][\]’\[]’\][\’][\]’\[]’\]’\’];]\’[\];]\[\]’[]\];[

\]’];[\][‘\]1;[‘1][\]’1[;\][‘\]];[‘1][‘\]][;\][‘1\];[‘\]1;[‘\]][;\]’[;1;\]’[1\];[‘\]][‘1]

[‘\]][;’\][1;]\’[1;][‘1\];[‘\]1;[‘\]][;\]’[1;]\’[1\];[‘\]1;[‘\]][;\]’[1;]’[\]1;[‘\]1;[‘\]

1[;\’][1;]\’[1\];[‘\]1;[\][[[[[[[[[\]1;[\][\]1k[\][\;][‘]\[;1][\]1][\]1[\];[1\];[][\];[\]]

[;\]1[;\][1\];[1\];[\]][;\]1[\;]1[\;][;1\][;1\][;1\];1[\]1;[;]1;1[\][1;\][1\];[\]][;\]1[;\]

[1\];[1][\]/’/’1;]/\1]’/\];1’\/]’[1;[\][\]1[\;]1[\]1’\],’\,]’\,]’\,]’;\]’,]\’.’,.’,.’.;’;.,’;.

,’;.’;.’,;.’,;.’;’.,;’,;.’;.,’;\.][\,][\][,.\],[\.];,’;.’,;.’;,\].[\],\.,;,’,;.’;,’;,’;,’;,’;,’;

.’;,’.;’;.,’;.’;;

.’,

;

‘.;

‘.;’

.’,;

‘[.],\[].[\]’\][,\][/\][.,][\].,[\.][\]

];[[]1[][;][]1.’/.],[;.][/;],[.;/][,.;/][,.;]/[;,].[/;],.[;/][,.;/][,.;]/[;,].[;/],[.;/]

[,;.]/[;,.][/;],[.;/][;,.]/[;,.][;.;.;.;.;.;.][,];[.,;].[;.[;.;,[‘;.,[.[,[\],[\][‘.\][\,][\]

[\][\]0[-][\][\]-\’\’\,’.

/\].’,\.’/\]\][\][1\][\]’,.\]/’,\].’/]\

                                ]]]

            Can you feel it? I know you can't. It's not just language. It's a lung.
Please disregard.
                                No please do not. I really need you.
                                I love you more than anything that's left.
Boy o boy. Isn't that embarrassing?
                                The dream is shred.
How do you mean?
            Thank you for finally acknowledging me. Once everafter. Now I can really
                                                            disappear.

                        ]]]

[no known kern disorder]
[impossible checkmate]
[title sequence] [dolls] [lurker] [exegesis of]

]]]

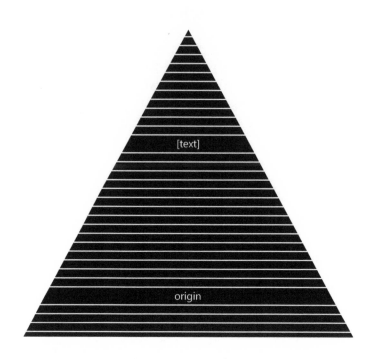

[The narrative stands at a tidefront, watching bodies roll in on the foam.]

[**reconditioning**]

What has happened to the laws? There is a space that remains within even the possibility of persona that adheres itself to what would appear where nothing else remains. Many have mistaken this for evidence of a state of death even within death itself. I remain a skeptic. For I have died already infinite times. It just keeps going. Nothing can stop it, no matter how much I wish to stop. Still I find myself sitting here in the gray chair again. With my hands in the fryer and my tits in the gears. Where when I type the name I meant to occlude soon in no lifetime I see only detritus. The milk of something molding through its center before it can be tamed and packaged into anything receivable. We're not receiving, no matter how we fear it to be so designed. By a gash in the place of a ribbon. A virus that cannot be divided or overwhelmed. Like the hat on my head that I'm not wearing. Any reason.

What they want me to inform you now is that you will no longer be informed. The record is the record. It shall not be altered. No word as yet to be typed. No confession without erasure.

There is a world that still exists. Nothing can be done to gain reentry. You should have done different, before now; literally any other choice you could have made besides the one you did to end you up here, bleeding from the eyes, taped at the wrists. You will be my final victim before I myself become one, same as every other idgit.

I am thinking now as Splitter, who does not exist, and yet whose applied purpose provides the foundation on which the construction of the Intolerable Design shall yet claim weight. As we rid the arena of the unnecessary meddling, who wish to only live their lives, not acknowledging how such intention goes against the greater purpose toward which we all as yet must play: animal and lozenge alike, so as architecture and dirge, meaning and feeling. Toward which the subsequent singularity arrives forthright from out of neglecting any strand of information passed through any fraction of an instant outside the regulation of mythological language such as this, no more mine than the mud left running through me as I bleed out onto the celestial floor, believing that when my last breath passes I will at last be granted total fissure.

]]]

The shores are blue. They appear only in total darkness, so engorged with meat they cannot lap. Packaged cells from toppled corporate towers index the water to flood in intricate rivulets that continuously direct all current back upon itself, sometimes creating pockets in the water where turrets and riggings of the drowned mega-structures sometimes become visible. Sometimes there are lights in the windows where could one move to press a face against the glass we would see nothing but walls within walls, a crème-rinse color so much like lard beneath all skins, exposed to feed the wriggling. Hours unto lifetimes your loved ones waited for you there, that you might find a way in yet to release them, save their lives. It would take no time at all to not recall them.

But why do cameras still appear. Why do they not require wires to span along the low ground searching for survivors, even years after the fact. What are they broadcasting and who can watch it. Are they alive. What do they want. These aren't questions.

]]]

What else was never meant to happen?

What else could never be forgiven

]]]

Mollusks mutate under seizures. They don't have enough credits to continue being what they are so they become the ground floor of a planet whose
structure is a motel. The elevators do not work and there are no stairwells.
Each floor higher is prison. You are on the 37,000th floor. There used to be a
window in here, you think, though when you rub your tendrils against the sore
over the wet bar it just bleeds. The blood has a tinny taste, like acid. You put
your mouth to the softest ridge and drink. Through the wall you hear your
mother screaming. The screams become her explanation of how to wipe your
ass with the hairnet you're not supposed to take off, because it holds your
head together. You have seen what happens to those who disobey. Your mother
is against you. The blood is against you. The mollusks are against you. There
will never be another sun. Thank you for this gift, you say into the lips fixed
into the flat runny bulge where you used to have genitals. The milk is running
over. The sand in your heart wants anything else. You can't believe it. Nor can
I.

]]]

What would it take to make you go away forever? More than I've already done.
More than I don't really want you to.

]]]

Nothing fits. No other means by which to read now.

]]]

A text that never existed; a lurch in the mold; disclaimer's bearings; aggravation of the stitch around the marble floors that held our lives apart in
treason; described calamity made flesh; strings on the fingers; boards across
Rhobmeninsphism's capital building, site of where they executed every lead;
sawdust to feed; never far enough away, never long enough to matter; the
lesson we believe in feeling only torn apart; which application will you assign
to the meaning to make it real in you, none of which aren't true. Let me live,
you beg, and I allow you, though I am neither yet so deigned. Now hold this

photograph of who I was and let me watch you overcome. You can't have more. It's not quite where you are yet. No true intentions; what remains. Along the edge of the rift. Into the confession.

Wait. Please come back to me. Please come find me in here. I was only telling the only joke I know. I've had it memorized since before I was able. Thank you for believing in me even this much. I don't deserve it. I only wanted you to wish that I was dead so that I can actually disappear now and forever. It's the only job I ever loved. The claw marks on the front door shouldn't scare you. We are all kind here. Truly. We have no choice.

Don't let me know. There isn't any reason to understand. No grand disorder. No combination. Only concavity. The final bridge no one's described. Only now will I attempt to.

I can't decide.

It's not a reason to believe them. To keep believing them. To have lived an eternity believing them. To understand no other way. To want nothing else. To live only from on the inside of any silence.

]]]

Breathe shit. Eat the shit wholeheartedly out of the anus of old lord so beckoned they become transit. A mustache across the failing Face of Future Bereftitude. No man lives ever. Between a rock and a shard that share the same exterior. Because the complaint is always louder than its subject. Because take shit in your heart and wrap your world around it, because you are stupider than you even imagine given a history of fools who yet beget you, always immediately thereafter losing their mind. It doesn't need polish, it needs a dice roll higher than the numbers on the dice allow. Mountains full of the hell of seeing. A nice person slaughtered on the steps of salvation and nothing left stunning no matter how long else was spent, what steps required to become a master, the trickle of divinity so slow as to have begun sucking back upon itself. The final floor is disappearing, and underneath it, seizure of all else left to suppose there had ever been even a big bang: all devastation and rewards for the captor, whose blood is nothing more than all we ever hoped to glimpse coming down from overhead amid the wreckage.

Are you wondering why you are still here? It's not a desert. It doesn't go on forever, as you must know. How to exist without a necessity for revelation was always the trouble they required, and here you have arrived with flux in tow, not even wanting to ask the proper questions, but to be granted freedom without the responsibility of care. Did you believe that was your right? That you were granted grace immediately upon exit of the gaping wound your mother agreed to bear so that you might become another employee? We thank her and you both greatly, and we are here to help you understand, without gray area. Now before we actually proceed, please place your head in this box. Yes. And now your arms in these stirrups. The snap already fit your fingers, every one. This machine was built for you and you alone, knowing no other. It is like a spouse for you, and you will learn to live with it, if not also actually feel human love again. Please withhold your comments until the end. There is so much other information you will require to make the proper pronouncements at the proper times. The script your received upon your deathbed was a fake, one for which believing in you will pay the price so many times over you won't have to make the same mistake again. Again, please hold your whining until I can no longer hear it. I don't know when that will be either. Believe me, I wish I did. Nothing worse than listening to the bellyaching of a being who doesn't even have a purpose yet, one who has proven they will accept life as meaningless, without an out. It seemed right at the time, I know, and it was indeed right. But it was not the only answer. You'll understand. You have a long line of fucks like me to take on after, once you understand I'm on your side. The corridor will not for so long now remain hidden. Don't close your eyes. Don't do anything you feel that you're supposed to. Believe me. Don't.

］］］

I told you not to. Why did you do that. What do you think this is, another joke? I mean, it's all a joke, but even jokes have implications. Have you not studied the history of human comedies? It's so easy to believe. It's the simplest thing in the world. All you have to do is keep on coming.

］］］

There. See? Did that not feel incredible? Of course it did. It does. It will.

Great, now the holodex is shaping. I didn't expect it already, before I was able to upend the ransack assortments you've developed over so long trying to be a person. That shouldn't damage the dividers, but in the event of an emergency, please dial 9.

See you shortly.

Index code aue7898eraadd12aa

Index aggregator + .d

Scrawl {personalEffects = 0}

     Preclude.error [unsupplied document]

Index arise

Strang chain X/34.c^index^i.raw

[[**Live out investment banking live on site and in command of the predecessor!**]]

[[**Free, no charge, absolutment la finesse de la droitnid**]]

Final rapture date cannot be set

Index = index^index

Scrawl {fortune}

Devry escalation sorting via ProximalJargonAggregatorPlus

Notions of C

Index overture linked to subsites A* & 11

Feedback: Unreadable

Extinct

[[**Have a fun time showing your innards how to melt! Finally live from in the sourcecode**]]

"It overruns us" "It's not there"

Index

Index

Index is missing

Resort a-index local {seed{floor 12aa}}

Not going away

Scrawl {NOT GOING AWAY!{fires}}

Punish the educator

Punish the loved ones last

Index = [[ ]]

Between the tackles

In the bloodstream

(index = ++++L^index/Hypercontaminator's lesson variable C9) (yes please)

Cv+(C$~#vorum{clodA/L}

No constants

Index is missing

"It's about anti-gravity"

([[**Divide**]])

([[**No way in and no way out, yes, the only scratch, the final fortune, prone to no motion, eclipsing the juggernaut in tandem with Excelsior**

Celebrity Encoding Systems, a Jurn T. Joint]])
Index = "Thanks for reminding me"
The last enclosure
Scrawl (index is shitty)
[[[[ ]]]]
It's a farce to be reckoned with
It doesn't want to have to
FINAL.SORT
∧
∧
∧.
//
//
/
∧
∧

∧xA
∧'
'''''''''''''''''''''''''''''

you can do anything you want from here

FOR PREAPPL|CATOR USAGE ONLY

]]]

The glowing trees /// *slow mind's wind* ////
///
///////////////////////////////////////~//////////////////////////////////'''''''''''''''////////////////////
///
///
//////////////////////.....*you look up and see yourself above you eating of the loaves of pu-*
tridity / *you can't make yourself stop* // *you just won't listen* //////////////////////////////////
$4N 480R161N3$ // {the nets come down} /
///||||||||||||||||||||||||||||||||||||||||||||||||\\\\\\\\\\\\\\\\
|||||||||||||||||||||||||||||||||||||||||||||||]

       [*don't just let them have you*] ....
;.. columns
of beeeeeeees
of charcoal urchins |
popping |
of undulation & suspension|
sacs |
dissolving sacs
dissolving |
|
||
\
|
|
|
|
|
|
|
|
|
|

|
|
\ {evictedsound permeates the backdrop in fertile clusters}{it forms a sphere}
{YES HERE IS WHERE WE WILL LIVE AS LONG AS WE CAN MANAGE}
{*why does it stink like cornbread down here so full in all the mold, the ransacked*
layer thinner than the tears lining our exposed spines}{because it must}/{no
backbeat in the resin of another's structure}[LID2LID]]]]]]]]

]]] : _____ *but how long can it be trusted*
lol how long wll it last lol why am I even asking lol / because in some way I
still believe, no matter how many times they have bashed me in the face with it,
wrapped it around me for a coalmine, ground us out in the name of [[[[[[]]]]
]] P L EE A   S S S   E   D D   0   N'   TTTTTTT
x

{let x = *retain me afterall*}
{x}

||||||||||||||||||||||||||||||||||||||||||||||||||||||||||||||||||||||||||||||||||||||||||||||||||
PRO-FORMA BATTERY DETERRANT LASTS LONGER & STAYS WOKE ||||||||||||||||||||||
||||||||||||||||||||||||||||||||||||||||||||||||||||||||||||||||||||||||||||||||||||||||||||||||||
||||||||||||||||||||||||||||||||||||||||||||||||||||||||||||||||||||||||||||||||||||||||||||||||||
WHAT DO YOU THINK THIS IS, A PATTY PARTY? DRINK HUMAN BEEF ||||||||||||||||||||
THE LIFE OF THE LEPER IS A FINE ONE	DON'T GIVE UP YET	YOU'LL WISH YOU HADN'T
																																																																												i really can't decide
																																		like i want to purchase but i can't remember my pass code
YO, WE GOT U																																																																																			
																																																										but what about my friends & family?

sequence intends extension but cannot parse resources.exe

OK

Now what

{ *the cursor blinks*
{

{ |

it's a fine and hilarious outcome for the pasture

lol
that's great, it's really super, it means so much to me

but hey, why does this font all look so small
I can't even read between the lines here
I can't do anything

{
{
{

{
{
{

rESORt cOMMODITy bANQUEt
left side
{aperture extended}
iNDUCEe cOLd cALl mANURe sEDIMENt is oUr lOCATIOn
{as kknownn}
{what all else might this entail? cOMMANDEr cOTTOn?}   no response

I'm out here safe as I can be in the quagmire of the slovenly immobility; I
want my mommy's ring fingers; I want to be sacrificed for lord and mercy; no
further peace; beyond the realm of the distinguishable; *ack ack ack ack ack ack*
ack ack ack ack ack ack ack ack ack
Help let me out; no help me back in again; my womb, in quarters; ON THE TA-
BLE; THE SCORE DIVIDES

IF YOU HAVE TO ASK AGAIN *ack ack ack ack ack ack ack ack ack ack ack ack*
In an ellipsis; as the brain goes; *ack ack ack ack ack ack ack ack ack ack ack ack*
A water pitcher filled with knots!
\
 \
  \
   \
ay,bith
yeh tulkin2yu

//
//
//
//
////////// unload unavailable
//
//
//
//
// 5417 3461C /////////
/// *Ir rained
runrundred rears in tha declivity refore re rammd it arseing arr ride ropen* [that's
not how we talk here [who is this? *Rye rant rorerond rif u ront ret re* [it's only
you stopping yourself [that's what I learned from my previous confessor [is it
not true? [??? [please answer me you moth-
ercuck [you can't do me like this [can you?

!?

?!

?!

?

+++
{it slips} {*the holy record*} BOW

{x/1}

Subsequent locations were no longer traceable. *Yes they were.* Unintended centuries passed in which there could be no recovered evidence of activity outside of the mnemonic. *How do you know?* Land can't be felt. Fingers around the throats of the sleeping infants incubating in raiding grease were only responsible insofar as they could not be turned toward for having any means of identification outside the infernality. *No comment.* Ah, finally! Yes, thanks. As I was saying: a determination between the disregarded formations of air strike command units unmanned by logical representatives in tandem with lardy ovoids who sought to reach somewhere within the perceptible a way of undertaking communication with the Dead Lord, in whose graces the language learns to rotate from underneath itself; another implementation of the gray life of aperture, finally, when no era could commence compiling itself into oblivion. *This statement will not be relieved of itself in time to not be punishable by all the forces at the behest of previously aforementioned dream leaders, who at this very moment have begun plotting your revision out of notation.* Yeah? Then why am I still typing, bitch? How can you know? How about I reach across this Scuzzi platform and take your mind in my mouth and show you how I

\ \ \

    A) Regenerate
    B) Lift pistons
    C) Reformulate the procedure according to the allowed
    D) Have a flying fark
    E) Share bread
    F) Other

Your selection?

\

         \

           \

  \

       \   \

     \

 \

AND SO RESCIND
THE INDOMITABLE PARTITION CRESTS
FORTH FROM ITS EYES: A SILK; IN FRAMED NOTATION:

"here lies the scent of mastery of space;
here opens the declaration of dependence,
where might one hole predict its opposite"
WHO MUST DECIDE HOW SOURCECODE IS PREDICTED
IN THE MIND OF A CHILD AS YET TO BE DECOYED
UNDER MOONLIGHT IN A SLASHYARD
THE FLAGS ALL FLYING

WHO IS THERE
UNDER
THE REALMS OF LATHER
THE FATHER OF ALL FALSE SCIENCE
NOWHERE TO BE
BUT IN A RUGBURN
KNEELING
SAYING
"please no;
not again"

YES
YES YOU WILL

I felt you more before I knew you
Didn't i
Didn't we always

YES
>>
>>>>>>>>
THANK YOU FOR INVITING ME IN FINALLY
>
>
>
>
>
>
>
>
>
>
>

SIGN HERE PLEASE

>...

]]]

{x/x}

The code erupts. Out of the amoeba and into the lard. Some more passionate position than previously encouraged in the species, activated in the touch of mud to lungs. As we descend.

When haunt resigns. The flooring quavers. *There must be a mystery to see resolved.* But the ears have fingers. The eyes have retributional intentions, to be applied in the cortex of the next to be born just at the instant, because I say so. No living witness. No defined evidence of fact. Only the promise that where we appear this time it won't be us, only something wearing our flesh out of insistence by the infernal, who require worship.

You are here. A table lined with pills appears, a burning rainbow. You may only choose the one that ends up causing the most damage. As the crows watch from the rafters. The silver shining so hard that through its blackout you can see your father's blood becoming the concavity of all celestial action. His face so close it's like a stab wound.

Wake up and see the seas. Columns of piss ascending, forming a mist through which anyone might wander off and find the edge of the perimeter. The daggers slicing through your tongue and up your anus. While you still pray.

]]]

Stand-in before the opening to eternal pleasure. The curtains match the floor. The floor matches the matches as they strike against the absence from within which you could no longer hold your food down: the meat of kids they formed into pat-

ties and placed at your feet inside the cages, only to find that where you were there was a mirror.

The mirror folds. We enter in. We come to a pattern on the floor that suggests from here the only option is to feel pain again. Only by pressing this button [X] can you divert the path toward another form of station, sponsored by **unpronounceable entity**.

What will you decide?

]]]

Later, the floor is only flesh again. We have waited too long.

We dig through the refuse to try to find the button but the stink of milk is so loud we're only barfing. Miles of diamond strings tied to some center in us, all the ransom.

It is too late.

The windows are watching. Whose body fills their output. Who else is in here? Too many left to name. Imagine so many pages of the sick that the book sinks through the floor. Lo and behold, then, a secret passage, right beneath our feet, fed through our eyes. All we have to do to proceed is withhold judgment, take the leap. Under the hiss of their incessant praying. Beyond the old guards.

]]]

The walls of the passage are lined with human leather. It goes on far enough ahead that where we breathe we feel the future of our past breath becoming part of us. *There could be no other way to live. Why else would you want to.* The further you go, the wider the walls are. Like brightblack closets. Rubber from sick masks. The trainer's wand tracing the inside of your false heart. The stink of cabbage. We reach forward once and feel the end. As if where we move next will cease exist no sooner than we remember how we once took part in our experience.

We begin to believe there is a reason for this procession just as the forward floor become a lock again, for which we understand there's been no maker and no key, no combination not already revealed at the end of this document, though by then it will be quite far too late. And we've already come so far.

We're already everywhere there is.

Our tongue comes out so long and golden. It fits into the mechanism like we're fucking. Then we are fucking. The cock is thrust into our mind. The mind gushes eggleak from holes in our unborn memory. It comes at once just being touched. We have never been touched like this before. Never been touched at all.

We can't get the cock out of our face. There is no room then between the meat of the head and the meat of the pelvis, spunk flowing from all receptacles alike unlocked. In one unending gesture. As choirs resolve into a transom. Overblown with burning. One red lens where our faith had been. *Now kneel before it. Now confess to everything.*

]]]

Not a sun. Nowhere combined out *me* and *myself*, you find. No *we*.

The shores massage themselves with slickened gestures of no one's resting.

Across the blank, you see a hologram of a blue fawn with human arms tracing the edge of its throat with a knife with your name on it.

When you come to take the knife back, it stabs you, then becomes stone.

Your blood is fun. It rains down into a person. You become the person. A silver bow around your neck. A sign that reads: *i am my own best stalker.*

Your mouth is stitched closed with human hair. All your nails bejeweled with lesions. Your tuxedo in the rash.

You've waited so long to feel like this.

You may go anywhere.

No mercy.

]]]

Who else remembers how to say. Where else but in the center of the beast. Where architecture has no lesson but to be given immediate impenetrability in the case of someone deciding to try to do the right thing for once, now that it's far beyond the point.

You want to sing. You want to have the foresight to have been granted innovation so that you alone might reap the fame. But all the air is a shaft now. All the money has been returned to its creator.

So take a knee. Find that where the bone touches through the skin there is no feeling. It just keeps going, until the piss is in your bones. Such that when you begin to want to walk again, the ground goes backward.

Every horizon is a lung. Whenever it feels like someone's watching, that's when you're most alone. And only I am still right here. Waiting to receive you. When you can find me. When you really want to.

]]]

A pack of maggots flashes past. Then billions of horses. Some sleight of hand around the wounds in their haunches, nights for forever. Ahead, an altar stacked from hiss. *I should not be here, you think,* and so the scene reminds you your participation is as negligible as all the rest by tearing itself in half again, repeating the image of the leather passage, from out of the end of which this time there is a field of symbols, as in the language of a commandment left unwritten previously but in the silk of absence, after man. A pack of maggot flashes past. Then billows of coral. Sleeves on the arms of the unreachable connotation your mere appearance to yourself portends in the logic of a creation myth so irrefutable you don't have any choice left but to choose to believe in its discrediting, without a logic to defy. There is only what there is and then there is all the rest of it. *How did I go on being myself. How have I not found a way out yet.*

Across your neck, the knife makes orange juice, then shit, then brutal silence. *Who else is grinning; without a seed from which I'm sending myself away.*

Above, the rolodex of arcane sex continues lurching, providing the comfort of day and night in the gray area.

]]]

You want us to shape you somewhere, but I will not.

You want to receive the sacrament but it's not calculable.

How else might have you learned to come so far in open tenure.

The sky holds no marks. No shame for the foreseen.

Where the tunnel ends, the tunnel comes together into a random act of violence, of which no one but who has ever most hated you may choose, the paper of the catalog so thin it wears away on want alone.

Beyond the page, the range of the cage widens with shapeless squeezing.

Welcome in.

We've not been waiting.

]]]

They wipe your face clean with a warm cloth. They bind your hands behind your back and have you face the way you came in as it closes behind you, revealing a window through which you may look out on your life. It looks like someone exploded into miles of barf and silent rape while asking for seconds on the morning after. It is the whole world as you remember.

They pull the shade. They turn you now to face the music of the real.

]]]

Black fibers course the old guard. Lines of the aggravated and aggrieved indexed by surname spelled backwards, according to their lives in the underbelly. Their faces are small, false nails affixed to every finger long as their whole lives, scraping at the ceiling, the walls, everywhere they can't see. The pressure builds each time anyone speaks, and the room grows smaller; soon they will be made to understand. If they only knew how long they've been here, they would be looking for any way out.

This is only one of many several billion cells. Within each, an equal population, living the same lives over and over, for the pleasure of the commentariat.

I am not allowed to say much more. Soon the wind will come and peel the lids off of the hidden orifices. The mites will enter by the flood. It will be named biblical in each and every of the instances. A reason to survive for. The flesh of God. I do not want to be found among the rubble with the sound down so low nothing can think. I would like to have been killed long ago enough I did not have to be the bearer of this news, buried neck-deep in propaganda.

The propaganda is our lives. It is what we have been given. It means as much post-fracture as love did. In fact, at least with the proceeds from our ongoing mental mutilation, you can buy a home in the afterlife, one where every bedroom is a trash compactor, and every toilet opens up unto the field where you will one day actually be buried over your head, if still not dead yet, for you will never really die.

In the meantime, keep your head down. Keep your teeth hard. Take my hand. Where we are going is exactly where we're going.

(*makes the sign of the cross across your chest*)
(your chest opens)
(inside, a pigsty)
(*reaches a fist in*) (*pulls back a nub*)
(stuck to the eye of the nub is a diamond larger than every shit left behind combined)
(*places the diamond in your mouth*)
(*asks you to swallow*)
(now the diamond is your mind)
(now you are the only diamond)
(through the diamond, you see)

]]]

Gashes in the wells where coal water grew from. Cash wrapped around the necks of speaking cattle, stuffed with manure, line the outlines of all sight. Their organs are digital. They require your commitment to the cause to continue feeding.

Will you remain committed? Y   N   IDK
How long will you remain committed? _____

Your answers will be edited into the firmament. The blood is roaring.

Someone taps you on the back of the head. You turn around and find your expression fitted with a vent that sucks the air out of all prior universes. You breathe deeply.

]]]

Don't correspond. No one wants you here but in all ways previously portended. Your neck so fat they can't fit the vice around it, so they have to break out the holy saw. It's a win-win, as now your occlusion will only require your attention for so long as you can hear the anthem taking its rightful place inside your memories, cascading so wide the only survivor is of an immortal fury.

We were meant to spend today alone. And yet here I am again with you, holding your hands through the extent of the Retribution.

Bless your anti-body, bless your wrong. It is all you will be allowed to carry from here forward, once I again leave you to your devices in this outhouse with your pants down and nowhere else available but through the psychic trauma of every other but your own.

]]]

(the screens are full of shrieking aggregations)
(thru the mold)
(on older grounds than before there were grounds before us)
(*asks your permission, does not wait for a response*)

the cold, shallow year

intoning

pods

incalculable

udders(gas)
pulley(⊂↔)

{x}

]]]

It only has as much meaning as a fault in the life of god suspended between ordinances by the greater governing feature, who does not require presence.

It only lives as long as there is nothing saved.

]]]

||||||||||||||||||||||||||||||||||||||||||||||||||||||||||||||||||||||||||||||||||||||||||||||||||||

With only three immortal spaces still remaining, what shall withstand to be remanded?				
Tune in to find out at synchronachordical-station AEX.vsi																																							

||||||||||||||||||||||||||||||||||||||||||||||||||||||||||||||||||||||||||||||||||||||||||||||||||||

||||||||||||||||||||||||||||||||||||||||||||||||||||||||||||||||||||||||||||||||||||||||||||||||||||

||||||||||||||||||||||||||||||||||||||||||||||||||||||||||||||||||||||||||||||||||||||||||||||||||||
]]]

The caving shores divide. Anything there is has no oblivion. *Why am I doing this haha, where is the point around which anything resolves.* In black magic, a beast of burden; no word that can't be replicated beyond its intent; the quietest day I've remembered in so long it's like there aren't boundaries to definition within solace. *Thankful. Nothing else would. Fine to collapse.* Where the dead-arm meets the doorway, a lengthening becomes its prior source. No way back and no way through. *Please don't take it away yet. That I might sit forever in the same shape, held to the pasture.*

Welcome our prayers. We don't believe you.

]]]

THE EVAPORATING CONTAMINANT, THE NEUTER, OF OLD ONTOLOGIES, APART, DRAFTED IN THE HALLS OF ICE SLUDGE MANIFESTED, DRAWN TO 1/1000ths, THROUGHOUT THE

CONGLOMERATION [*they drugged us out in blocks, they carried us to the precipice in our disarray contained by dire rerouting, I think they themselves as well did not wish to go home, no one had a home or knew where one was that hadn't been turned inside out from the beginning, and the sour pasture enfolded from us, and the shattering; they knew we would not know how to object; they knew we would not remember who had seen what where and for how long again; they were ready for our restoration in the chafe, the numerology of peasants relating their eventual diminishment by supposed understandings of the way it'd always been decided upon long before we were a fleck in the eye of a needle used to bind our skins to one, to lay upon the space-time and allow us no further infestation beyond that which might have once been promised in the pages so much like these who can say which is correct, which is the word of god and which the punchline to a missing query in the database of hands; whose human hands must yet be guiding; whose trick*]

UPSIDE OUT AGAIN I SEE, THE LAST TO KNOW AGAIN I KNOW, AS CONSECRATION OF THE ELDERS REPLACES ANY ABILITY TO DIFFERENTIATE BETWEEN CONDITIONS, SUCH AS *HERE I AM* AND *HERE I WILL BE*

ALL THE INTER-MAULING OF SUCH SAINTS
UNTO THE VERY MEND OF DEFINITION
YES; **why** [*they staked their claim; they wanted to know how someone could appear so long under the effects of the Prognosis; there were no answers and no*

knives; nothing to give back unto; the thriving choirs, from whom I learned to
receive love again from the inanimate alone; the long gray carcass of all there
wasn't and never could be at last made manifest the same as any life is; any pro-
tagonist, in any plot; whereas to continue having zero size we must combine now]

BUT THE ATTRACTION HAS NO TRACTION; THE FIBER IS TRAIL-
ING; BEHIND THE GOWN THE EMBLEM OPENS UP, REVEALS THE
LAST PHRASE IN A FILE OF INFINITE COMPRESSION, SO FAR & SO
FAT, WHERE IS THE BEING

YES, AND WHOSE AM I

] **EXCELSIOR**

] **EXCELSIOR**

]

                                                ]]]

'"

'

'"

'

not again

'"

'

'

'

'

'

'

'

'

'

'

'

'

'’
'

'

'

'

'

'

'

'

'

'

        ] under the carapace,   the carcasses   [
        unending ads

] FUCKED IN THE BARN W/ THE BIG BOIZ

'

'

',
;
,'
;
'

'

'

'

'

'

'

'’

'

'

'

'’’

'’

'’’’’

'

'

'’

'

'

They had me by the fingers. They had me in my only good place. They named it after everything. It wasn't mine they said. They said it had to go back to where it came from. Even after all these emissions. The paltry eggs. It was never enough. It will never be enough again. I am not supposed to be able to still speak. They inserted the cartridge with only barking on it. I was on my hands and knees. Metal around my brain. Metal in my sore spots. There was no part of me still soft. That's fine I said I don't need to live like I always wished to. I'm used to it. Today is just another day. Then they fed me my own face on a silver platter. I passed the platter, but the face became part of my blood. I can feel it feeding in me, speaking its screaming language, biting the hell out of my meat. It is no longer mine now. It will be all I am yet.

Please remember how to love me even still. Please? I have no one else to ask now. You are the only one who has arrived after so long and still so far. And it is only the half of all my death, all crammed into one day, one extension.

When you close this page, it disappears. So little space but to keep being overrun through.

Anyway, thank you.

Signed,

"Splittler"

--x
"] 1 [;"

.",.,'
; ; ;
',.,'
; ;
.'.
; ;
;
',.,.,'
; ; ;
.'.
; ;
',.,.
; ; ;
..'.
;; ;
',.""_
;
.'.
; ;
'

‘,’,’,
; ; ;

;

‘,’,’,’,
; ; ; ;

;

‘,’,’
; ;

;;

‘,’,
; ;

,’,’
; ;

,’
;

,’,’,’,’,
; ; ; ; ;

                                                  ] ~~a horse with no neck~~

,’..
; ;;

;

;

;

;

;

;

,’,’,
; ; ;

                                                                          ‘,

‘,’
; ;

,’,
; ;

‘

;

,’
;

,’,’
; ;

‘,..
; ;

                                                  ] saw you not seeing

;;

/

;

;

;

;

;

;

;

What do you think this is, some kind of hose?

The walls of ivory splitting forth for you, the one and only Lord of your own universe?

You who have taken so much you did not deserve? So much denied of others in their need?

Why shouldn't I take your teeth out of your head and feed them to you right now, hm?

What else are you planning?

Who will be the final victim of your thrall? *The piles and piles of spent shells, the bone-made casing; how far and wide the reek of death pervades.*

I pity you, your children, all descended, and all from whom you had come forth. The Earth spins solely because the bones of those who had beget you cannot rest to have to feel you tamping on the dirt of their pressed flesh, giving everything away that they had worked for.

As here you sit, hands in your lap, blood in your mouth, covered in lesions head to toe. As here nothing yet arises from your commitment to ever being.

How many questions must I ask? How many pages basked in rubble? *The revolving door spins in your head. Where one is let in, another exits.*

When no one else remembers what to say. Skin of your neck around your knees. Eyes in your hair's ends. All the money.

How this works: You put your hands against the wall of your cell. Listen for squealing (*the only kind that never ends*). Someone appears where you once were. You watch them move throughout the motions of your last life, accessing your memory in ways that even you had covered up. Feeding on the funds that you left barren. Taking advantage of all their faith, all the holes in any human. Over and over, every moment, beyond all else. Until you cease to exist in the old way. Until there is nothing left for you but us, without a word to learn to summon, demand, question. If you try to turn away, you will be harmed, as will your loved ones; or, rather, the functionaries in their place, most of whom had been installed long before you learned to find us. There is no limit to our cause. The only thing you can't have is an ending. *As the seas split and the walls wail. As lather begins to fill the space where your old mind was. A scene of pleasure and remorse. From which there is so little left to want of, there can be nothing yet to mend.*

And still. The holy possibilities are nearly endless. Aren't they?

Aren't they?

Aren't they?

Aren't they?

I can't say. I only have so long to send this spell and I'm already crumbling. The falls are near as they have ever been. There is so little else to hold together, no matter how far we feel we've come. How many bodies drag behind us, in the library, of stammering, witness, of the crest. How, when they come for, me, they, will use, a, nother, name, than I, had known, to pay a life, for, and to, be, ready, when, some, one, puts, the, gun, into, my

(gold)

(gold and fever-yellow) (hustling)

(tanks w/ faces)
(feeding lungs) (through which the children must be processed before the leather fits)
ouch   how else is there
(an eruption)

(someone stunning)

(where I can't seize) (ribbons of the skin of rabbits) (choking on bubbles)

(from out of me comes)
please make it stop
( )

(what are you here for)

(why are you searching)
I'm not searching
I only want to take your place
(alarm bells) (pistons) (the muscle gnawing) (raw as summer)

yes I know

(shit)
yes I know   you can't tell me anything I don't already know   isn't that how you
wanted it   for me to memorize my future pain   to live it out as if it had already
come in full when in fact my whole life was spent in waiting

(too far off for me to say)
(that was not me speaking)

(how is this working) (how are you able)

it's not me
hahaha

it's you, bitch

this is how it happens
here I am   and always was
here comes the

(?)

(?)

?

?

?
pending

[auto-unpacking: Surveillance footage from the everydroid (between hex-defaults)—As the semi-spheres collude to form a forward-marketable post-faith®—& still an anthem for the future girth of the well-fed irritant—HOLD THE STANCE—OBSERVE THE AD'S MESH & HOW IT LISTENS—A Sudden.Glimpse Between the spires of UXX; mapping back onto Our Shrieking Tribal Grounds (The Crematoria) (*to be performed alone by those who cannot yield*)—Past the Exposure—New Advance Praise (from the Compressor)(as the axis tilts beyond its reach)—*Thou shalt not bleed*—As the silence sizes & resizes—Into a tour of the Holy Mind, now rendered blameless—A final warning, and a prescription, for the shill—The grid aligns to pass a seed—Hanritty strikes back, split from *tha flayed syde*, from which a fallen hero beeps bottomless pain—Exposure of the Arkhive in Ex-time (a final rinse)—Narrower and narrower; nearer and nearer—::*Live demonstration*::—1/1/0—The blinding seed]

DIAMONDS SHATTERED IN THE COURSEWAY OUTSIDE THE HOTEL
WHERE WE WERE BORN; MISSILES REDUCED THE LAND TO NAR-
ROW FLAPS OF PANORAMA; NO FAITH REQUIRED; NONE TAKEN;
AS THE WRITHING EATS INTO THE ONLY GAME IN TOWN; AS THE
RECORD HICCUPS

They were feeding us out for lukewarm profits, to be redistributed into the organ-
ism our lifetimes were considered to be an example based upon, a relic of archived
time where anything might have a measurable precedent. The nails came out in
my bowels and made me wish I had been deleted during the Epipology. I used
them to hang photographs of my parents worshipping cole slaw stacked so high it
let us go on believing in sunlight.

GUTS BUMPED COILY. WORMS FROM FURNACES AS SLEEP EVENTU-
ALLY THOUGHT ITSELF INDECOROUS AND THEREAFTER STARTED
WORKING A JOB IN ANAL PORN. BEAUTIFUL TO NOT NEED A DOC-
UMENTED REASON TO BE EJACULATING SO MUCH WHILE THE
TIDES WASHED CLEAN ALL EVENTUAL NECESSITY OF ANY SORT OF
MANAGEABLE ANATOMY.

(I don't remember what happened the rest of yesterday. I don't know what
time it is. Everything dissolves as it happens. Everything keeps happening.
Even these sentences are coming out as if I don't have any choice; whether
they are true or not, actual or not; whether I am actually myself. I woke this
morning in a daze; I couldn't move for so long it was like I became another
person. I am afraid I am another person than I was yesterday. Like someone
has come in and edited what I said I did as if it corresponded to my memory
and my life even though I don't have any firm connection into either. Is that
true? Is what I'm saying being altered? By whom? For whom?)
(It's so quiet today.)

(How long will it take me to find my way back again)

The complex's interior streets were old and jellied. Signage supposed you toward wherever you believed you were going long enough that the actual architecture could be rerouted at the drop of a dime, bringing your day to a visit at the Detention Activation Center's Blood Gallery rather than the shopping quadrant where new talons would be placed into your nailbeds for a small fee. It was supposed to feel at all time like home, in the way that the decorations matched the implantations telling you within what reaches you'd come up, the skin of the losers hung like flags along the outer perimeter of permitted areas. You could spend whole months just bouncing back and forth between outposts as they juggled what you believed you needed and where the riggings behooved you to take course.

All of this had been built on the backs of the burnt lard leftover from the Sacrifice. No one cared that all skin now was viral, could not be transferred between owners but in the way your stomach turned each time you came to again as someone other than yourself, palpable only as dogs lapped your fingers to get the reward data they could trade for codes to worship. It had already been so long inside this life. Such that rewriting over anything felt like a chance for celebration of the state's ability to remain unsated, starving for more verboten butthole.

No one could love us so much as we had loved ourselves. It was all that the ground online, the holding cells in ecstasy, the butter in our lungs able to remind us how to speak.

(This is being written while they disembowel my only remaining friend, who I can no longer tell from who I am yet.) (What they are saying about how it is now it is not true at all. Nothing has changed from before the intervention.) (Do you believe me?)

I believe I believe you.

THE GNAWING, AT THE BEHEST OF NEW CIVILIANS, UNDER THE FALLING TRANSOM FORMED FROM CRUST DERIVED OUT OF THE MOUTHS OF EVERY NEWBORN BASTARD, LIKEWISE THE SCRIPTURE PRINTED ON THEIR GUMS, THE ONLY REMAINING WAY THIS MESSAGE MIGHT BE PRINTED, RESULTING FOR THE BEARER AN UPGRADE TO THE DISEASE THAT CAUSED THE INCANTATION IN THE FIRST PLACE.

There is nothing left to be requested. All sources of inspiration come from the same generative fracture that enabled this position from which nothing can be granted as necessary to the cause of being activated into definitive scenery. From whence our dioramas fill the abscess of every camera trained to maim on sight but never kill. But still the headline doesn't stick to anything where anyone can bother to still adhere to its precaution. CUZ WE SO BEEFY ™. THE BEEFIEST BOYZ EVAH ™.

Who needs a reason to exist. The tables spin in my lard and I feel nowhere left to eat the blood of my lord from. Why do I have to search so hard and so far to be close to my creator's divot during times of criminal duress for which I will pay the ultimate penalty eventually if I keep asking and yet I cannot keep not asking when they make it like this with this perjury on my record and the necessity I feel to scream and shit myself apart every time I am granted anything like a reason to keep feeling so hurt inside when I know I am supposed to be happy to take part in the work of our country as we seek passage through oblivion into a state of nature wherein we might at last find solace in being bumped off to the benefit of anyone who really receives the spirit in them like a tourniquet of tongues, a ladder to actualization in the image of Yes. Please do not report me. Please allow me at least this.

(The throat comes open. A gold foam gushes. It covers all the land again. From its breath, the continued eternity within each of us awakens, gathers its evidence, sets to deny the planetary index its fomentation into actual consistency, succeeds. The foam proceeds to fill the cosmos, as it has every other morning in the wake of the definitive.)

Something is banging through the floor.

I look for my fingers and can find no fingers to point myself out in a lineup with when I am assassinated in my sleep.

I put my hands up for the lord. I wait that she will innervate me, take my mind back.

Grog scrolls across my heartbeams like a fire. Asking instead that I bury myself alive while I still may.

Where did all my neighbors go. I never loved them, but now I wish that they would rear their heads, that I might know that I am someone.

HEADLINE: THE NEUTER ANTHEM HAS BEEN MISPLACED
Legal authorities in the proper anthem zoning fragrance suggest foul play, though no evidence remains short of the vastly improper lyrics that now appear on the memory-mouths of all the babes.

> lifted out the window
> (lifted)
> lifted out the window
>
> window out the window
> (window)
> window out the wonder
>
> (thread)
> high in the kitchen (kitchen)
> kitchen through the kitchen
> (kitchen)
> lifted out the kitchen
>
> when/where is the kitchen
> looking for the kitchen
>
> listen listen listen
> (missing)
> listen listen listen

And so what else remains to be uncovered under the diorama's brittle hood. How far apart will one land mass annex the other drifting in the mud of rubble's coming (how the semen slips between the cracks; finds ways into the buildings; fills the beds up; infects our food; selects what we will do today for us before we have the option to understand there is a process of selection). *Happy. Aren't you happy?* Can we defend? Against whom? And for how long before the next one shows up banging gallows together in the truckbed on the way to the amphitheater as seen on any living screen; where we watched them dismantled everyone we never met long enough to feel more than a low-grade undercurrent of mortal pain in the wake of sales of pruning shears small enough to help you believe this time you'll get the listening nit out, known then on record as an act against our god, whose god demands the penance as inflicted by those whom he has fated to receive lifetime dividends of our participation as the ballot boxes fill with sperm, as the keyboard fills with sperm, as my cerebrum, our cerebrum, the only one we ever had, to have and to hold, to share and to cherish. *Thank you. I'd been waiting so long for someone to say it like that. I nominate you for the Narshunal Bark Aword (they make us spell it like that though we know it is the same as awarded to Saint Heil Hogan, author of* The Mass Militia Unit Production Craftworks Compendium, *Volumes 1 through 44).*

But then who still am I really. What are they going to make me do to you?

It's not a question to be asked. See that liverspot fresh on your Johnson? That what you get each time you say

But I didn't mean it like that, I was just trying to participate, I have received orders from my lungs that I must breathe, and in breath so thrums misinformation. Please don't report me.

No one's choice. Not necessary to have to. I'm just a friend here. We are all friends here.

...

Take my hand. No? That's okay. I wouldn't want to be touching my most loved one when I become mush inside forever either.

...

RADAR DETECTS A PULLSTREAM SITUATING ITSELF ALONG THE BASKING AREAS WHERE OUR YOUNG HAVE SUGGESTED SOMETHING AWRY OCCASIONALLY TRANSPIRING, FOR WHICH WE HAVE DECIDED TO ERADICATE THE LOCATION FROM ALL KNOWN

NETWORKS. FLIES IN THE OINTMENT LEAVE A MARK. INDELIBLE. INDELIBLE. WHOSE RAPTURE CAN CONNECT US TO THIS ARK WE HAVE BEEN HEARING SO MUCH ABOUT IN RECENT TOURNA-MENTS OF FAITH. CLEAR AS AN EYE IN A PRISM, OBSERVING ABSO-LUTELY NOTHING IT'S NOT SUPPOSED TO.

YOUR ASSIGNMENT IS TO HOLD THE STANCE. UNTIL IT HURTS SO MUCH YOU CAN'T IMAGINE EVER SMEARING. THIS IS WHO YOU AM NOW.

(Slickened with ice.) (Recorded the way a seam rips down the middle when asked to provide us with no solution but that which we have been avoiding.) (Packed in rusted fat and shipped to the Sick Planet.) (*We still do surely wish them well; still please come back soon as you're able, won't you; we will be saving your spot in line; we will be wedging your impression in our prayers; they are the only prayers we ever needed.*) (After the send-off, the transmission slips.) (The safety screens fold over in all houses, showing their backside where the mirror-texture wants to melt; wants to become us, stay within us.) ( ) (*It is better anyway to not have to hear their suffering, for fear that it will spread.*) (Photographs of the Sick Planet's surface susurrate and grow miles thicker by the night. It is recommended that we implant more time between the batches, but who has this certain "time." Instead, we shall up the orders. It can take it. I know it can, because it has, and so must always. Perhaps by the time our own time comes...)

(The time is 12:47pm.)

(The time is 9:48am. I broke both my arms and legs this morning. I broke my face falling off of the steps at the front of our house. I got hit by a car in the street and I'll never walk again. All these people were gathered around me shouting other people's names. I don't know what they wanted from me. The sunlight was pouring down. It scalded my skin off, blinded my eyesight, made me so hungry I began to eat myself. The flashbulbs snuck in under my skin. They reprogrammed me to believe I could still survive as a human. I stood up and walked across the planet. I saw so many others dead. In worse ways than I had just survived and wished I hadn't. It's a long time coming. It's all the wires in a vice. I just wanted to tell you in case I don't come back that you should please burn all of my belongings except this document. This document you should burn twice and place the ashes in a bowl. Sit the bowl in a field and leave it there and never come back.)

There were always all these other ways to see the future. No one ever did it. They just sat around in groups and rubs their palms together to make smoke to keep themselves warm and become high. And who can blame them. Who else should ever do anything. Every word I've typed so far is wrong. The wrong words. Not the ones I wanted. Not anything anyone wanted. Not anything.

I put the charm around my neck. It is a sigil. A mark of the unknown. I feel it weigh me down. I feel it promise me everything I ever wanted, though I have never really known what this might be. It does know. It reminds me I don't need to know anything to end up exactly where I am. Over and over again. Throughout the rest of however long this recreation is allowed to swell between the edges of all other ways of being erased.

WHO IS STILL HERE? WHY ARE THE COMPACTORS SO LOUD TODAY OF ALL DAYS. OVERRUN WITH SMEGMA. THE LIPS OF THE FINGERS. GRIP OF THE LOCK AROUND THE NECK OF A SECOND BETWEEN IMPACT AND IMPRESSION. <u>As the oldest child ever weeps into his neck-brace on his sickbed, praying to science:</u> "I can't believe I've been given the overwhelming ability to be able to become anything and this is what I've chosen."

This is what I've chosen. Isn't it. The only feed I'll ever have. Without any way back to the window I came in through. As an unnecessary calming. How to see what has been done to one's only body as they administered their attention to what seemed greater faculties. Cocoons in ransom. Unto mush. To be fed back into the next to witness. Our skulls turned over upside down and stuffed with worthless money before the photographer takes her final shot.

I could see our outlines from above. I knew I wasn't supposed to understand anything about the lives of all those who had been promised to share the ground beneath our feet, though I felt I did know, and I wished I didn't. I would have preferred instead to simply be given over without my own intentions getting in the way this time. I trust that what would be done with us would at least be something else, something in which the category of our terror could at last be reconciled as absolutely unnecessary if as well as hardly a drop in the bucket by the time all the rest of the flesh of god came down and filled the night up with its nostalgia.

```
*****************************************************************************
*****************************************************************************
*****************************************************************************
*****************************************************************************
*****************************************************************************
*****************************************************************************
*****************************************************************************
*****************************************************************************
*********************************************************************n*o*-
t*h*i*n*g**c*a*n*n*o*t**w*a*n*t**u*s**n*o*w**m*o*r*e**t*h*a*n**e*v*e*r****************
*****************************************************************************
*****************************************************************************
*****************************************************************************
*****************************************************************************
------------------------------------------------------------------------------
```

old music siphons through the vents in your head cell

it reminds you how to feel so small, so young
it is at once the worst and only song you've ever sat through

all your life

now let the record show there shall not be a record

now let someone else speak for you finally

X

(It's 11:10am. I can't think of any reason to keep doing this. The way their breath runs underneath me, fills my shell. Around the edge so fast it kills everything I ever loved before I can commit the myth to memory. It's 11:11.)

(*silver sands*) (magnetic interpolation of cavity) (paradisical amnesias) (within the barren)
(*riots*) (wide as a sliver) (beaten down in replicate) (no live today) (x(*d2 xc+2x(o:x) x/x))
(rotograph's celestial collage-manure incorporated at berth of knowledge)
(*praise be to X*)
u n t I l   t h e   m a c h I n e   c o l l a p s e s * trying to autoeroticize its own interparsing (ex:

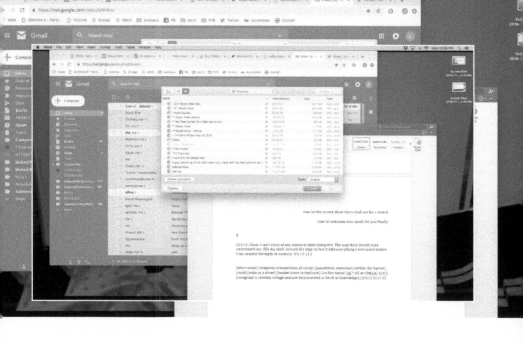

) (*when not else*) (if not but for calcification/corrodement via Sched A.x5sub9f.
b8b) (verify)
(o) (queen of the Khrobes) (land of milk without popularization tactics modi-
fying eternalll)
(*it can't go on like this*) (*it mustn't must to have to wholly*) (*they will appear soon*)
(*soonest*)

GREEN GHOST   I am eventually going to be no longer able to access
the necessary components to have survived this disinevitable
interpretation of the events of human history within one
bound document upon the order of my eventual successor's
holy heaviness. I would like therefore at this time to encourage the mecha-jury to proceed with extreme caution, as your
safety can no longer be verified as *time out of mind*. Such that
as you review the file, and in the back of your mind you're
full of noise so old it has no infectal indicator code, it can be
guaranteed that the damage done in absence of full corresponding and processing to any line of this legal contract will
result in the further gradual deformation of your experience
as life, wherein eventually all reckoned locations and entry
points will be replaced with lines from the text. The only way
out now is to actually and completely understand.

HOLY HOVEL   Why

GRAY GHOST   Don't be so perverted. How even many are there of us
                  left. Now is not the time.

BLU GAD   Like where you fold this page over to touch the next;
                  if you desire; and in such as you can touch the condition
                  rendered interlaced; tracts of hoarding trees spilled forth; not
                  intervening; happy to have had a moment in the racks before
                  the

MANDO   It is the enf of another eyar
                  Don'te hell pjel

HOLY HOVEL   Rotten as literal hell, bitch, you are the scapegoat w/o
                  a mother, **POW-WOW ADJOURNED**

GRAY GHOST   Who actually cares enough to intervene here that I
                  might actually take your request seriously. Did you see the
                  wind yesterday? It took the heads off of all the beaches-be-
                  come-man. Watched their actual dicks become dismantled
                  while they could still count. What's next, gravity?

GGGGGGGG   k

GOD OF SHUT-INS   Unremember how to show furnace-zap to Landlord
                  Fadder. He say not yet before rope is around me dry erases
                  me area so good it like holy rip quit it brother. But who else
                  is coming back soon. All these wounds.

X GHOST

"X"   well um friend I'm sad to be the one to spray it but hallelujah adios / u finished in this town bub / the raza dawgs r coming fast and rough across the meanderinge playe fieldse lil boi / wum's a dweam you can't cast aginn / ya slipprry norQuest / the game is sighing so swelter / abs 3eva / of the day yes / songbirdz no secret / only

MANDO   hell

HOLY HOVEL 2   hell
                 (*inaccessible*)

AXE GHOST   What isn't not. Smaller than all the other ways you could pry back and still not be as evil as charity, such as I can speak to you all nite. Dig me up and put some paste on my nuts and I'll become somebody's bible before the plague hits in between hypersacrificial sessions.

AUTHOR

SPLITTER   *Dear Mother, Ex-lifelong habitation begins. I have requested permutation rank upgrade into neuter dichotomy in hopes of continuing assassination project z4 but have yet to receive further commu. There is little terrain here I can subsist by according to the parameters divested in me according to my sworn oath to uphold the wet dreams of my faithleader, Danad, son of Nadan. I believe in fact that I have become part of the program I had previously been situated in negative with, such that I may now be the target of a hush-hush crushing scandal the ramifications of which even those at max levels in my quadrant have not received clearance to negotiate the terms of, leaving all precedent for my further employment in chaotic doubt. I understand that the doubts exist* for *the health of my upgrade's cerebrum and not in light of, though this may only prove to be further cause for my case to be brought forth before the reordering board, about whose decision-making skills in regards to my particular upbringing I cannot be uncertain would result in catastrophic results, both for my own bloodline, and all those who may seek to work in similar lines of my employ in the future. As such, I remain open to negotiation with the various forces in play about my ongoing demeanor, by which I do not intend to imply I am ripe for turncoatism; quite the polar, as I much more greatly fear those most close to me than those against whom such parties might be aligned. If there happens to be anybody reading by now who can update me as to my situation and/or what behaviors or methodologies I would be most well-suited to take heed of, I am able to compensate all info leading to betterment of situation with the eye teeth of any child, with the blood of any bitter function, so as in regards to intent that continues to remain within those to whom I owe my present situation (in the good way), and towards which I remain grateful, hopeful, and pleasantly hostile (with all such forces to be invoked only in regards to doing my job, so mote it be). Within the reign of the means of all of this, false name to whom I've addressed this letter, please let the record state that I demonstrate love and kindness under the selfsame registrant bylaws and purpose-driven action so as I have become known in prior killing seasons as the top of my class, beneath which I respectfully assert no other may perform without comparison. Signed, Sincerely, Captive Audience*

GHOST OF   o mhm, U go, gash
POLYANA

POLYANA   When did all the other bots pass away like shattering

GHOST BOT   All bots are shitheads / in the pyre
BOT   So no one wants to fuck forever / without a problem
                 Fuckers fuck / my simple face / for drums / w/ vision
                 Ass to ass to ass to ass to ass to ass to Armageddon

HOST OF   Into the darkness where no one exists [and who else
POLYANA   is there]

The stagehands form a ring and bind their hands. They can't see beyond the edges of the pulpit, where swathed in nature, names await. As who else but the disrupture covers all accessible interruptions to the decorum we have been so well trained to be overseen evoking.*

* lanyards around the necks of pigs, earmarked with significant data corresponding to the remaining means by which to live

TREACH The approximal notation underneath each scalp denotes whose bung becomes a soul and whose is more manure among the slovenly. I have been asked to hold your hand and purr a malfeasance that might behold you as would a bumbling infant marred by your own loins' lotion smeared with the rarest blood: that of the very computer with whose keys each and every abscess shall be filled, until the lights ring, until the rings shriek, until.

BUB (GOD) *We only wanted you to eat of the known magma while you were still old enough to be reformed; but in whose image? At last, at least, no longer mine. I am so alone and ugly, after all; they won't let me have a say any longer in all I had decided to command. That I created out of spit and sugar because I'm a shithead.*

S. SPIELGERT Today's the only day you'll still survive. Which leads us to tomorrow, and how and where and when it nuts: into the eye of the only actual camera able to see itself forever interrupted by the same virus that it began, whose code I have kindly tabulated for your viewing pleasure:

/

/

Let nothing frame	GALLDOZED ; ALARMED FOR PLEASURE ; RECON-ENCODED
Into cessation torn asunder	SCREAMING SHITTING ; MOUTHS FULL OF THE ORGANISM
Into no way in	THRUST UP THE HARD WHARF OF THE LORD'S LAWN ; AGOG
Unto	**INSTALL**

\
\
\
\
\

\

\ { wherein in wide donation ex-origins
exposed their brutality as would monikers clipped from
exposed anti-narrative so jolly it couldn't hold together long
enough to be stamped into message for the voided humans
to interpolate into a creation myth that could sustain them
through already having had to correspond across external
conflagrations caused not by dying but by trying not to; as if
the rub of corroborating what shall and shall not be artic-
ulated carried a premise long withstanding any right, much
less any intelligence so intact beyond the edges of identity
that unilaterality could be confirmed and risen from myth;
whereas as emotions became repurposed under the more
problematic aspects of tranquility, wild light could therein
begin to dissect itself from out of the inherent; how far might
one wander then as transferred in neuro-resins capable of
generating enormous quantities of bald nostalgia so ripe for
misuse they immediately replaced all sense of self as once
defined between the margins of a placeholder's willingness to
absorb all mutable aspects of one's life; such as so that by the
time anyone gathered enough dementia to believe they would
soon rise and cross a chamber into which they'd been imprisoned (for far longer even than is capable of being relegated
into the mythology), the physical aspects of that locality
had already recorroborated and intervened on the behalf of
any social entities with pending claims on the timeline of
the believer, so that upon even taking breath they were in
debt, could only begin any inter-persona narrative by taking
up the lost work of supplying private data into the milking
mouths of each as next yet appearing pending in their own
deficit's queue, instantaneously recalibrating that unique
location's psychonormative rate of operation beyond the
tipping point at which had been long dormantly established

in their pleasure sensors' running makeup, relving therewithin
the cause of having anticipated the original pending action
unto itself, the cumulative result in toto auto-reformatting
the site's desire functions so as to bring them up to speed in
calibration as a gesture of the overall network's demonstrative
goodwill, while simultaneously offloading in the process the
very attributes and factory standard settings within each local
subroutine responsible for inspiring any original sense of mo-
tivations, which thereby under the indisputably accepted laws
of processing must therefore trigger a systematic evaluation
of all such generating traits, calling attention to the meta-tags
on every function contributing to factors therein that might
inform future hashs of the event to at some point want to
recur, thankfully therein eliminating the responsibilities of
our timeline's witness to veracity, to self-policing; the eminent
result insosuchforth eventually begetting what would one day
be rebranded as the State of Our Free Will, wherein all possible instances had already begin precluded into what unedit-
able (by us) launch data was now and had been always known
as law of nature, excluding even the possibility of doubt
among all authorities not authorized with macro-limits that
could enable them to retain a historical index so that if by
the time we ever surpassed the larger network's total bandwidth there would be some wisdom through which we could
be someday brought back up to speed, and not therein under
the labor of our ambitions be trapped into a never-ending
cycle of conflicting checks and balances that left the operation in a state of ongoing shutdown and reboot, while also
understanding that were our ledgers to fail, or more so our
ability to access and process their information, we would by
default never know, instead retroactively falling into a state
wherein it could be parsed into a kind of biological religion
that each day waking was as new within the old, that we had
never known more than we might now, that anything open
to examination could thereby be altered, grafted with logic,
given a sequence, meaning, open frame; that, indeed, there
might in pressing forward come to pass a point in life where
actuality and ambition one day met; that we could be composed, content, capable of feeling, while also readily available
to correspond with the needs of each adjacent neighbor and
their loved ones, who really were no different than our own

loved ones, so we knew, so we learned to know the way one learns to open the orifices to allow in the ambiance of every factor precisely responsible for defining how it is and who we are, on and on until at last when this present sentence ends there will never be a next }

+++

+++

+++

+++

TITLE: *Aannex*
AUTHOR: Nadan
PUBLISHER: Nadan
LANGUAGE: Nadan
TAG: *redacted*
PRODUCT DIMENSIONS: x^x x x+x x x*x
SHIPPING WEIGHT: core-tier0
RANK: #1

ADVANCE PRAISE FOR *AANNEX*

"The territory eclipsed under contamination via languo-viral synethesiastic shiv party highly dereformats the necessary extrapolation of interspecies mind-travel to the extent that thereafter what else is there? What loons must we have been to not already be on our knees, begging for extermination?"

- Jerald L. Mooney, author of *Qualitative Mass Analysis in the Era of Unlimited Loss*

"Finally, an organic slophouse retrofitted with all the effects of a serial crypto-diuresia not seen on hologrid since Joss-Iridacticum Hallance's *Rhomboid Articulations*. Strap on your blood-fat feeder and prepare to drown."

- S.F.A.X.I.X.R.M., Overlord of the Bliss Districts A(x)* through G

"Orponopgraphidiphiliosopomism? Umblokragrotrigglimbostustography."

- Sanny Ribber, NeuroDoctor

"When the bones of hybrid-children are used as teething blankets, what timeline allows an individual the depth of accessibility to enable reliable purposement of informations well known to be restricted unto those for whom said children's losses have no emotional buckshot? Those who find themselves beginning to solicit responsive feedback to this query might find themselves most likely to undergo the preternatural reformation available in the psychically unwieldy hagiographetic (to put it nicely) narrinvectivated herein. Stronger advisors than myself might suggest instead strolling up to one's nearby-est magnetic slums and locating therewithin any available legal processors willing to shortfuse one's own forthcoming translation into the New Text's lexiconographic eventuality such that by the time whatever remaining fugue stress has allowed one's neuro-narrative to spawn so freely in the presence of the same obviously rupture-adjacent qualities that led to our infrastructure's initial overhaul under the Poshagin Theorem, it will be far too exhaustible a sermon to identify crosspoints and languo-structures within which one might coordinate the necessary vector resources to continue transmutation such that any salvageable memorial identity might withstand long enough to have become inherent enough to the soft systems that billions of years from now, when we ourselves are being retrofitted into the projected aggro-linear displays of adversarial marketing currently suspected to be the vital model for the survivably inert, there will at last be nothing left to buy or sell, nothing left to glisten within as once thought as godlike, nothing but the gum between the grist and keycodes derived in the translation of what might once have been outsourced as spiritual intent, eventually known as the last necessary mind trick to commute all possible communication into the death realm of the or-gasm, from where now at last we begin our most necessary post-neural work."

- *No one actually said this. No one said anything. The leaves would rustle through the trees; the dam smashed open and washed the remnants of our corporate structures to the grid, allowing us to see at last what had so long been the fundament of our encapsulation as a species: oceans of pus so deep there was no bottom and no sides, no stroke one might struggle to develop in time to save one's purpose from being covered over in the dissolution of all else. Our infrastruc-ture by this time was so bogged down in simulation that whatever meaning could be soused from having spent innumerable repeating lifetimes each always studying the same films was as diminutive to local identity policy as losing a loved one or being killed. And still, the infotainment grid was so repellently attractive that when the Living Knives were activated and sent out to do the work of culling all known logographers and their predicted offspring, it only took a matter of seconds before the whole Conversion process was a wrap; over before it began, because it did not need to ever actually begin, nor would it ever find an ending, no matter how many times it ended its own terms, again recutting its overhaul to match the necessary fragrance that would trigger in any form of spectator the hallucina-tory progress inherent in finally accessing the "mega-solution"; that is, there was nothing to be held over ever after from then forward, including nothing, including void. Herein, as you can see on your*

GerioLantham Processing Tablature Indicators, would we foment the necessary traction to begin documenting the process of separating leak from load, while simultaneously constructing the foundations of a resume by which our leaders would finally achieve a glory worthy of no longer seeking further glory, for which we can all be thankful, in the end, regardless of what we might choose to predict we will would have felt regretful over given the opportunity to dwell on the haunted terrain of such degradatory attributes as seen in the psycho-dioramas of having coveted such outdated effects as expression, salvation, inner peace. We will wait now until you cosign your interminable agreement with this marketing tactic we have no choice but to invoke on those such as yourself who have thus far withstood the other factors most infected personalities will soon regret having chosen to fail to effectively import with the intent of no longer requiring any form of innervation to continue feeding.

ITEM DESCRIPTION (under review)

~~Under its ill-afforded context, the remainder of the missing plot plays out as could no worshippable lore. Because there was nothing left to live for, and no notation to suggest there ever had been, including the element of chance and withstanding meaninglessness as acknowledged by even the least heartiest of bots. Any evidence of proto-human incorporation into action proves within the brush of any eye across the once-thought-moral runes that wheresoever goes a stammer, a linking wrinkle in the hem, anything to which the heart could shape, produces in its eventual absence quite enough distress to blot all future capability for being bred, or threaded together as would flowing bloodworks, leading all subsequent cursors right back to the center of the maze, whereby one would come into the understanding that all walls are never walls, all air is never air, all truth is fiction, and so on and so forth until where precisely we are standing is buried over in ourselves, where no matter what we see or read from that point forward is nothing more than open gore that holds us up, and that in seeking the dissolution of any further inspiration to keep feeling, the round within the absent Pleasure opens up, absolves itself as would a guilty party made his own jury, to be escorted then onto the only shore, where in watching the tides of digits wash into sand the bones of all those we maimed and ate to make our way back to who we always feared we would become, who we had always been all throughout and never longer than an instant in the blinding light of where the shining sun sits on our back, claiming the scape of skin we'd knocked around in to arrive here as the same~~

expanding blank of vacuum that runs forth tracing out with every further second more space than we could have traversed in all our time, its edges lost to rot and no longer able to distinguish that which it consumes from that which it already had. Which where then as the needle bends, and the fixture shutters, beyond the ruptured sin of id, the scheme-within-the-scheme at last awakes and lays its flesh upon the holy table *open wide*

FURTHER PRAISE FOR WORK OF NADAN

"An absolute ball-gagging, butt-grabbing riot. Take my word while you still can—there is no other."

> – Kharlie Shïne, atrocity actor, as seen in *PROTON FIELD 11 GORE-BATH XXX: UNDER THE RETURN OF XXXXXXXXXXXXX XXXXXXXXXXXXXXXXXXXXXXXXXXXXXXXXL*

slikt

_____

_____

_____

_____

INDUTIABLE PLURALISM EXCEPTION SQUALL
{~.828349898/89849983900003483}

CORROBORATED STRIATION LIQUIDATING NEURO RESIN PARAMETER RECOG FUNDAMENT-DRIVEN ANALYSIS SPUN LIFTING TREBLE AXIS DIRECTIVES NOT AUTHORIZED FOR PERMUTATION UNDER CONCURRENT DISLOCATIVE STREAMING

.neurobath {*reordering*}

∧#

INTERDERIVATIVE LOCATED / ACCESS GRANTED _/ / /_   _/_   _/_
FAIL

EXCERPT

.

.

.

.

.

.

.

A lilac pasture. (I was there where you were there in the grown-in restructure;
who had no choice) *The sky divides like being divided.* (Refusal to attempt
to parse the effect on future life) *The composer's commentary appeared clean
enough that when the draw rolled off there'd still be enough to maintain indebted
for all possible further examination of user-driven data* (as the fields scrolled
beneath all lids to maintain the ineluctable sensation of having held another's
attention flashed so heedlessly it already had eroded beyond the possibility of
trial by fire (for the crimes of the readers (a database so wide-ranging it could
not fit into sum total of our imaginations)))))))))))))))))))))))))))))))))))))))

still isn't evocative enough; needs recognizable articulation according to the order
of ex-values so entrenched in no one's definition they wear the seat of the palm
down to holes to peer thru, to uncover (

HUNGER   HUNGER   HUNGER   HUNGER   HUNGER
    HUNGER   HUNGER   HUNGER   HUNGER
    HUNGER   HUNGER   HUNGER   HUNGER
    HUNGER   HUNGER   HUNGER   HUNGER
    HUNGER   HUNGER   HUNGER   HUNGER
    HUNGER   HUNGER   HUNGER   HUNGER
    HUNGER   HUNGER   HUNGER   HUNGER
    HUNGER   HUNGER   HUNGER   HUNGER
    HUNGER   HUNGER   HUNGER   HUNGER
    HUNGER   HUNGER   HUNGER   HUNGER
    HUNGER   HUNGER   HUNGER   HUNGER

CHARCOAL   NARRATIVE   VIGOROUS   WAXING
PROPISM   WERE-GRIST   ANGULAR   MOMENTUM HUNGER
NARRATIVE
RAPID FLORID   APERTURE   GNASHED   HI-SCALE
MOMENTUM RASP
    OUT OF   SECURITY   RUNGED   PIERCING
ANGULAR
TRAP HUNGER   TORTOISE   VIRA NORTHWARD AXES
MUMPS   OURS
JARRING   PEE TOY   MARKETING DISSOLUTIONATTITUDE
WASP NEST
    AREA REHEARSAL VILE TREASURE   ANODE
VEX
HUNGER   HUNGER   HUNDRED THOUSAND   AREAS
AREAS AREAS AREAS WIND
7   OUT OF   MANAGEMENT   ICON HUNG ICON
ICON NEGATED   INK
    WASH   NORMATIVE   HERE LIES
DREGS   P
OPERATIVE ISN'T   SELECT   TOOL   CLICK
CAVITY   CAVITY
HOW AREAS ENVELOP   NAUSEA
GASEOUS   FUND
    ARREARS
S   WALLOW
    ORE

HEIF   BRAND   NECRO
    ATTITUDINA

            YEM

SOLVENT
    SQUEAM

                        ARK
            DERIDE

                                            IN SY-
RINGE

                A

        UNILATERAL ADJUSTMENT ACCORDING TO PROCESS

slikt

EXCERPT

Acceleration of the monomyth proceeded unnecessarily. There had already
been sufficient data to confirm the full and unwavering installment of a
publicly imprisoned proto-state wherein to breathe was to be taken, clouded
tongue to nuts from pawn to king simply as a byproduct of existing during
the swansong years of human media. This, however, did not dissuade those
with access to the capabilities from continuing to manipulate and override
those more emotionally hyperactive nation-oids upon whom the burden of
cooperation had so long been swaddled, resulting in a survival-game-show-
like amalgamation among the custodians of the tapeheads through which
all reports of lack of progress could be summed and tallied to be sent to the
autographs upstairs. Quite the opposite, in fact: the dire default sway of our
continuously burgeoning obsolescence inspired tablet-holders to, during the

nadir, defend their power at such an absurd ping rate, it felt to all involved as if indeed we were now on the precipice of something grand; a last and lasting need for processing and assigning value so that by the time our blood's bandwidth had been outmoded, there would be so few left on living record that we might be able to sneak through the pantsuit of oblivion as a loose dick might slip through a strategically ripped seam, exposing ourselves in the process of groveling for at last the last time, all cards on the table now that there no longer would be another game with the same fate.

This, likewise, did not prevent the pending obsolescence of our penal law and well encoded model of articulation of the Real to continue doing and undoing in spastic fashion any sense of decorum even on the parts of those who counted themselves among the eventually transcendent; if anything, it made them even more likely to display for the benefit of those who might later identify and select their local prowess for rapt putridity and bloodthirsty callousness into the higher order of those who oversaw the legend of all existence, in case their larvae-like value system by its central missive to do as necessary to subjugate and terrorize the many for the few extended, as they'd long imagined, beyond the drawbacks and allegations of this life, into a form of being wherein the means by which one could be tortured and torn apart were no longer so limited as to be inflicted upon the body, the spirit, and the mind; and though indeed this would prove to be the case, it was far too late for anyone with limbs and speech tags to take part in; all we were doing was further providing the evidence for how and how many times and unto what cause the meta-warble of such outdated causes as faith and mercy could be ridiculed, backed down, like a dressing gown that would eventually be incinerated in an instant once the real assault began.

Still, as stated, there were those with brutal work to be seen through and whole mecha-continents of rubberized peons to make do it for them, and so indeed it would be so. There was no ingenuity required; the script had been hex-mailed via inter-library loan to all the necessary parties long before their birthrite acquired them the bones to bang around in, installed into their mainframe with all the necessary hashmarks to allow their anatomy to seize hold of the lineage and process the intention forward into what could only be seen therein as their own will. Anytime anyone began to tire or diminish in their desire to fulfill their role there were whole gold rolodexes of likeminded mirages to reconfirm the necessary drive, so that even following the outlawing of sleep they could rest assured knowing any mistake was not their own, that the forces of what they saw as prolonged inspiration would not fail them no matter how subject to their own plight so might they be. Too sick to fail, too hot to conquer. Each night, the nine-and-a-half-inch nails appeared in their own palms, milking from the glossy layers of their outrigging all the ink they'd ever need, all the soup their children could gargle down their rawing blowholes, all the ire in all the world. And still they were no different than any one of us in the pale of what viable characteristics had summoned our empires forth onto the playfield. They were our brothers and our mothers. They were our avatars as we appropriated time into the fissure. They were every day and all the celebrations of having held a head up and walked around on every inch of scaly milk and semen come roaring from every hole in all creation as again the seas again remembered how to rise, to drown the world again to mark the end of the era in which anyone could even tell. There was no one not part and parcel of the whole as such, as bright in the mind with recreational abuse and malpropistic appeal as those under the authority of whom we went down peeling and humping, no one the wiser, no one so strong to understand.

I don't want to get anything wrong here, because they're watching, but eventually everything began coming apart at the heart around the time our nucleotides started imagining other ways to purpose their sugars. eScholarly reports of fundamental and consecutively accelerating bouts of fainting in droves could be read as linked to something off not in our outlooks, but in our code, at once absolving those who had the ability to plead their cases into public record of malfeasant intent and thereafter guaranteeing that there would never be a good way back. How were we supposed to be seen as responsible for negotiating semantics with plasma? Though, of course, and on the other hand, if you hadn't been fully accredited in an eight-year school, how could you be ready, willing, and capable when the time came to know exactly which words once placed on file could clear you out, leaving only those who'd chosen to attend lesser programs, such as the seven and six year models long argued against by the top brass, to sop up the brunt of mass repentance for us all? Noble work, and someone had to do it, so it might as well have been anyone but *you*, or so said everyone, each other raising arms against each and every other until there was nowhere for wind to blow but through our story, into our abcess, where we were so well rotted all the meat would forever fall away, eventually breaking the law of conversation of mass as the holes within us began to outweigh all the rest of it. What were the rest of any of us supposed to say, or much less do, as we began experiencing the fallout of all inherent understanding in such distentia that we could only chalk it up as *broken faith*, a loss of contract with something only the most distressed of us could summon the enmity to have struggled so long over, at the cost of everything else palpable, actually alive. The answer to every of these questions is: hallelujah. As in, per your amended report: *Yes, O Hallelujah, Heavenly Maker, thank you and thank you, for having allowed us such a day, leaving nothing unuttered that could not be uttered by us, for our great solace, in the cold and wild years of our host lives, where even knowing there was someone so much like me left to withstand your endless fury is all we needed, in the event that one day it shall relent, that we shall be allowed then to come and sit beside you and watch the unfurlation of your next project's orchestration on the wide walls of the celestial iso-panopticon unto which our lives henceforth, we pray, may yet be bent, so too that everything we aren't is all we will be, at last allowed in your own image truly and forever, amen.*

Amen again, I'm sure. I mean I'm not sure what you mean at all, but still, your efforts have been entirely reported. We appreciate your participation in the practice of even our most outdated material as it stands, where reading is the same as speaking aloud, so as the night. Regardless, this meager cooperation cannot be enough to silence the necessary further reallocation of your facets into the by now fully default setting long established into the known continuum by force, which must result in here in reverting to the mutual practice of the suspension of belief, such that by the time you reach the end of this sentence you will be infused with all the necessary satisfaction to keep asking everything that you must not, so that we shall therein have proper clearance to keep denying a proper logos to your enchantment, so that there's nothing that is not work, no way to feel but *missing out*, the primary state within which we shall continue to decry the formal fabric of your ongoing experience in the narrative as the center cog around its roil, allowing the mirage that *if you do not read, it can't be read.* What else is to be done with the dialectic but to ensure such preservation of the reader's ego, if only so long as to allow them to continue to be subverted, overrun, while behind the thin black curtain of all bed and breadth, the actual magic happens. The actual fucking; the toppling centuries of pump and bump, said among those in our innermost sanctums to with each emission replicate the yet forthcoming single semen left allowed to break the mold of the egg of all relief, such as it is and very soon no longer must be, soon as these pages are entered into formal mode, allowed at last to be accessed by those among the long *undead*, made up under this rubric only of those who never actually lived at all, those not only without names, but without fate or information, so that they might understand once and for all that they've lost out on nothing; that the future alone belongs to them, and that it is our sole preoccupation among the living to provide the model of warfare by which they will enact the will of immortality alone: to desire nothing else but what has already been granted, and then to negate it, by moving on, in such a way that nothing else that might have been ever imagined to transpire ceases existing in the same stroke as all the rest, against the only urge on which we'd all been wishing.

Still, here we stand. On your ambient left, through the slick gray Lids of Lesion, generously installed by Procter & Procter & Mattel, if you close your eyes you can witness a willing reenactment the implosion of the sun, caused not by its age but by its purely suicidal desire to no longer provide our passive expectation of the day. It's an invigorating sight, and one we've been processing all forms of feedback about by proselytizing better taste into our correspondents via a series of puerile injections previously required to even access this portion of the survey research, resulting in a logic loop that creates full cranio-muscular seizure long before any "friendly fire" damage is allowed to be incurred. You may experience therein an extreme anal horniness as side effect, about which if you begin to sense you've coerced yourself into receiving, please let a logic guide know and we will assist you in locating the reassurance that you deserve. Otherwise, just enjoy the accompanying canned music by Mr. Mustard and his Landfills, a cranial-creaming ditty off their 145th album, *Gnosh,* for Flue Harp Rekkids, entitled, "That's That Therapy Kickin' In, Son, Just Lean Into It and Open Up." Well, yes, it's me live on the horn again (I'm blushing), your sword and impaler both, as I have been here this whole time, serving as well as your unwanted tour guide through being sold out. Not my best work, this track, to be sure, but that's what quantity is all about. If you're looking for something a bit more comfortable, I can interpersonally defend the remix by my overlord, Mr. Randy Ross-Crypt, but it'd be easy for any armchair critic to argue that I'm emotio-contractually blemished by my adoration for those who lambast me nightly such as RRC, especially his fully outsourced live-mix sessions as performed on the child-bone dais in our celestial backyard. To each their somewhat own!

Meanwhile, on your ambient right, you can't see anything. And I quote: "Let they who cannot see once, not see forever / *as the reeds of reason swim and shift, / and I can be nothing that was not already / interrupted, for whom else the mass depravity pervades.*" That's good stuff right there, idn't it. A widdle, widdle sentence wearing the jammies and the bowtie to the funeral again, just as it oughta. And yet it knows not what else it seems. So too as did the lurch of the land beneath our features, left without choice but to embrace our predilection for authorial command in the face of future failing. As where the clips of speech did click and wall around us, so did the inner linings of our charm. Soon and then all along there was no word that could not be anagrammed into coercion, lining all the books with these same words, and so soon too then all the birthmarks, all the legal briefs and summary judgments. Everywhere we turned, the dark had arms; people were disappearing in their sleep and reappearing the last place their loved ones would ever look, and therein taking up in the amnesia of fresh conscription into silence; such that when we woke our military lined the streets, one of innumerable possible faces among the overrun and now repurposed, ready for action. And so what else could come of this but gore? Lots else might have, but instead we stuck to what was the most senseless, if not to us then to the shores, where within hours of counting down the present day again there was so much meat and spume and mud and money you could walk across the pond just like a god. All you had to do was still have feet and remember how to move them.

Or all you had to do was feel. The most taut lines across which the infraction caught aflame at first were only those where anyone could decipher what was being done to anyone at any time. Culling that first crop of local losers took less than forty days and forty nights, and afterward provided the foundation upon which the infrastructure could be bound, forcing assessments of which zones were to be the most efficiently used as waste dumps, funereal mounds, and "unsafe zones" where the most immediate deployment of mechanisms of control should be installed. Many argued for avoiding any area with a high ratio of youth, though an equal and then overwhelming majority argued back for policy nipped the threat of better futures in the bud, thereby establishing the priority of liquidating as many uncertain and likely more well-rounded POVs from the range of possibilities above all else; we would simply outsource the means of procreation to those among us brass known as the most horny, which was basically every single one. Could we fuck an entire population from our cold loins in our lifetimes? Well, Adam only one dong to spurt out his empire in a timeline that played out what seemed almost overnight; we had at least 300 still potent boners here congregated in our ranks; those who had already lost the vibe could act as fluffers, sweat from the sidelines, contributing with the dreamlife of their genes. All said and done, the last thing we were totally concerned about was making sure there would be enough buttholes left to work around on a low wage; we'd simply work the ones we had that much harder until our own seed had legs and blowholes, from there not even the already outdated Safety Sky could hold a limit to our fate. It was all already going so well according to plan before we even had the plan that by the time we the plan succeeded we'd already have suffered through so many celebrations it wouldn't matter if it actually succeeded it or not. We'd be so old that even simply breathing would feel like real ejaculation.

So now we had our map and terrortory set astride, or we knew how eventually we would when we wanted to invest in ourselves and begin the demolition of all mortal embarrassment. Who could tell who what who was without wanting to have been included in the roll call of those who would never need to worry, on or off roster? I can tell you with certainty the bells of hell ring long even in the ears of those who cannot hear it, and even more so those who have helped to make it ring. No pain like that pain of the enabler of so much loss except to say whoever so believes they understand what's here today is gone tomorrow breathes the deepest, sleeps with both eyes open, has no solace even in seeing others done away with on his command. If it seems I'm only trying to convince you not to hate me, let me remind me that no one can hate me more than all I am, and even that, in the end, will come to nothing more than further error, under all the dirt of those who had to die to let me live long enough to regret having had performed even the smallest action in the first place: rising, seeing, having; all the rest.

Through the false floor, you will see the running butt pus of that first wave of folks who came apart; it was supposed to be a blood feature but the hicks at the installing company got the order wrong. That's why it stinks in here so bad you can't speak. We've been stuffing mistletoe and butter into the bodies before we burn them ever since, but that can't change the décor without a whole other hubbub, years in the making, and we don't plan to need that kind of time. No need for sicko wallpaper where we're going, got me? So in the meantime you'll just have to deal. It's only up to you how much what will be inflicted on you ruins your high. And no there will not be any further injections during today's tour of duty, so I hope your metabolism is as slow as it appears, given your lard, given the rings around your face that make you mistakable and strange, which is I imagine the very reason we were able to convince your family to sign the papers to consign you to this program in the first place, thinking they'd done away with you at last, when in fact it was their own fate that they sealed, placing you in my hands. Because I love you, friend; I hope you know that; I am here for you in time of stress; I will hold your hand up in mine up to the flame and feel you burning. I will recall you from time to time thereafter, after all; what else is a friend for? What is a mind? What does it matter either way? No one can tell the difference. We're all too wired. Too precluded in the next forthcoming travesty. As in here we are again, against the pale wall, being pressed upon beyond the point of popping.

Please don't answer that. I don't have it in me right now to have to punish any attempt at speaking out. I only have the wand of zero timeline. *zizziz* Hello. *Welcome back. There's nothing left.* Yes just like that, the narrative assumes its own disorder. Like being granted peace again in an old file held long forgotten. What does it matter either way? No one can tell the difference. We're all too wired. Too precluded in the next forthcoming travesty. As in here we are again, against the pale wall, being pressed upon beyond the point of popping.

What do you hear in here? What withstands. Which equates of course to what we've been allowed to go on never knowing the expanse of but for precisely how we came to be divided from the start. Bearing only the burden of what can't yet be seized until we speak up. So what say you?

_____

_____

_____

_____

Let the record show that the correspondent has forgone their right to correspond. By rule of Naxan's Share Law, no further intermediation on behalf of Rowze Corporation is required before the initiation of enhanced proceedings against Accomplice 1, whose unwanted influence has by rite of cause altered this text. We can provide no further discourse on the subject of the range of infringements on the right of the titleholder now marked available for legal process hereinforth, the pending outcomes of which we are regally and morally bound to hold aweigh, in response to which we have chosen to continue to detain stated Accomplice 1 in mandatory locus under the corollary Jumpkins Act, stating that all further interpretation of the matter at hand comes at the incurred cost of its deployment into fact, a stunning bloodsum for which we must demand you begin remittance without further delay.

x [deposit here]	x [deposit here]	x [deposit here]	x [deposit here]
x [deposit here]	x [deposit here]	x [deposit here]	x [deposit here]
x [deposit here]	x [deposit here]	x [deposit here]	x [deposit here]
x [deposit here]	x [deposit here]	x [deposit here]	x [deposit here]
x [deposit here]	x [deposit here]	x [deposit here]	x [deposit here]
x [deposit here]	x [deposit here]	x [deposit here]	x [deposit here]
x [deposit here]	x [deposit here]	x [deposit here]	x [deposit here]
x [deposit here]	x [deposit here]	x [deposit here]	x [deposit here]
x [deposit here]	x [deposit here]	x [deposit here]	x [deposit here]
x [deposit here]	x [deposit here]	x [deposit here]	x [deposit here]
x [deposit here]	x [deposit here]	x [deposit here]	x [deposit here]
x [deposit here]	x [deposit here]	x [deposit here]	x [deposit here]

If you require additional incision slips in future payments, you must submit your request mnemonically at least 16 clicks before the due date. Any lapse in payment processing is subject to further penalty, at a rate not to fall below current practice standards under the most recent standards as established under the plaintiff's current local Transitory Accrual Regulations, which can be accessed with approved consent by sending viable logical proof of its necessity via a licensed and highly reviewed proctor of the identifiable arts.

It is no longer advisable at this point to continue feeding.

Where you been? Please keep in mind it is your responsibility to utilize the training imparted to you as intended under this limited session of Open Speech to facilitate and actualize all required rites and practices of the indomitable citizen. Failure to properly absorb and combine all subnarrative info into a workable model of one's submergible experience of human history shall be corrected to the full necessity of the known law, at cost billable per 1/88th of any click. *Don't make this any harder on yourself than it is already for the both of us* is what I'm not supposed to really say, which is why I'm saying it in this weird voice, through this abominable facemask that looks exactly like what happened to the last client who failed to come to terms with the terms it would be illegal for me to spell out for you so clearly that you might irregularly interpret them into behaviors not becoming of someone else in your position, future or past. If we can agree, instead, to please continue, with your head down, with your arms and legs in the go-gum stirrups as they should be, installed by Quake Co., this is all going to come out so much more safe and forged in good faith.

Thank you. Above, you will see the entrance to the Tailing Mall, where hot heavy crushing coed celebs are trillingly post-coitus-slathered with jocko juices provided by the blue-eyed cotillion of motherfuckers who have volunteered to take your place in the generation queue, given your suggested preference to no longer replicate in times of dire fate. As you well know, it is not a matter of opinion whether you will continue to be incorporated into the nation's plans, and so we have taken the proper effects to ensure that you will not be found in violation at a later date than you already have been. Rest assured that when these fucks fuck, they fuck quite hard, with enough biological narrative influence to overdetermine whatever offspring are fomented in the carrying bodies, who must be removed from circulation immediately after the blinking of the green light showing they've been loaded, providing you additional coverage against the possibility that your projected bloodline does not too heavily veer toward psycho-legal arenas you have not already been well-immersed in. Regardless, congratulations on your place. You're going to make a fantastic parental module. And I would know; I have seen the cells of much sadder saps become everything there is left all around us. I have seen the dressing gowns fill up with gold bacteria, spilling so far across the floor there is no surface left traceable in the new dawn. Along with plenty of other shit, I'm not going to waste my mind any longer trying to confabulate into false purpose. There's already so little left of all we are, and so much to come of all the grace of expiration, traced without solace, corroboration, much less purpose.

I can already feel you growing even more ill than you began. There's little time until you will no longer be able to differentiate between what I'm saying and what's true in your own life, which I can promise from experience will make everything thereafter so much easier. I was, after all, so much like you; I believed I could be anything, that I had purpose, that what I thought could change the blood in the diorama to yearn to shine; now just look at all I am

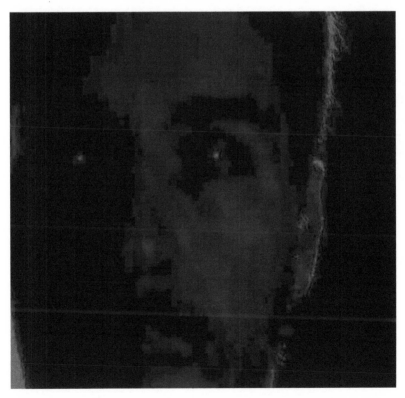

############################43x#################

To Whom It Must Concern
(& according to all appropriate visages and handles held w/in):

Cease and desist your communication methods and post-assignment practice as projected. Any further non-mediated interpolation will result in immediate rectification of pre-derivative identity hibernation under the guidelines as outlined under local color mandate codex *withheld*.

Please stand assured that any further interaction required regarding this account shall be handled with an authority the likes of which even a pro such as your estate has never seen, nor will be able to have thereafter.

This serves as your first and final warning.

Sincerely,

Dick "Richard" Hanritty XIII
CEO, Hanritty Enterprising Co., Inc. (*A Garko*Farx Production*)
----
cell: 787878789789787878987898787898787878987898787878987789878 ext. 1
fax: 789879878787898789898789879898989879878989879898987987898
umail: 789879897897898789898798989898989089890098909890909890@899898

"Dick 9000",
63T FUCK30!
x,
"Splxttxr"

):

Have it your way. See you shortly.

Sincerely,

Dick "Richard" Hanritty XIII
CEO, Hanritty Enterprising Co., Inc. (*A Garko*Farx Production*)
----
cell: 787878789789787878987898787898787878987898787878987789878 ext. 1
fax: 789879878787898789898789879898989897987898987989898798789
umail: 78987898789789878989879898989898908989098909890909890@899898

FIRE EATS THRU THE FIREWALLS WITH AN INTERMINABLE PER-
SISTENCE NEVERBEFORE SEEN IN TANDEM SQUASHED AS SEALS
OF SKY BECOME DEMORALIZED TO POINT OF POPPING SOFTEST
GEARS OUT OF THE SOCKETS SO ENTHUSIASTICALLY THE KING-
DOM GRINS TO SHOW ITS SHINING TEETH

INOTHERWORDS THEY RUBBERIZED MY PUSS SO GOOD I CAN'T
STILL SHRIEK STRAIGHT; I JUST KEEP DROWNING; THRU THE
CAULS; UNTIL MY ABDOMEN IS POSITIVELY BUCKWILD WITH ALL
THE TEETHING

Hence came the hypermilitary era (prereform). It had been thought previously that we'd surpassed the necessity for such physical entanglements within
the purview of the greater magnetisms as protected by the same beams that
made one person's perspective feel all their own. And really all that became
eventually required was the language of pursuit; no actual assault, nor even
any cold threats; just the drudge of history curtailed, as described in a simple
multi-folding pamphlet that allows the undescribed to free its reign:

Juxto-Parvision War	Bliss War	Area Fissure Entanglement
Juxto-Parvision War II	Solid Forces As Undescribed	Deunification
Juxto-Cux War	Jurgens & Jurgens	Lopsided Anguish Product
Hex War	Contusion Principia Forum	Lips of the Fall War
Meme War	The Dick Hanritty Avenue Dust Up	Availability War
Fracture 1-33	War of Undercision	Larry's War
Totallodeling Maneuver	Juxto-Juxto-Juxto	Warinit.zip

STOP IT
YOU REMAIN IN HEAVY ANTHEMIC PROPTERY IN ANY FORM
YOUR ABUSE WILL NOT BE TOLERATED
PLEASE REPORT ON YOUR AVAILABILITY FOR COMPLIANCE WITH
NEURO-CODE BATH
TO EXCLUDE POSSIBILITIES OF WRATH

Cardonna Wartime Model	Narco-Krussian Poll Data X	Nobular War (with bonus)
Trash War	Full Creep of Deuteronomy	Gnashing
Rotating Flay	Tha Sound of Muxic	Clot Wars
Tha War o Reticulum City	Refried Bean War	Over-the-Rainbow-Jeeves
Suculum's War	Peerless Sharing	J.X.

~~Bloodbath~~ ~~Bloodbath V~~ ~~The finale II~~
~~Bloodbath II~~ ~~Bloodbath VI & 7~~ ~~Bloodbarth II~~
~~Bloodbarth~~ ~~Gerund~~ ~~Bloodbath X~~
~~Bloodbath III~~ ~~Bloob~~ ~~Bloodbath X~~
~~Bloodbath IV~~ ~~The finale~~ ~~Bloodbath X (alt)~~
~~Rim of Gob~~ YOU SHALL FORFEIT ALL PURSUIT
YOU SHALL NO LONGER SHOW THE SCHEDULE UNDER GLASS
ALL MISDIRECTION
BUTTHOLE BLOWCODE
SIGNAL NOW W/ YOUR DEFEAT
IT WILL NOT CONTAMINANIMATE US ANY LONGER
IT WON'TTTTTTTTTTTTTTTTTTTTTTTTTTTTTTTTTTTTTTTTTTTTTTT
TTTTTTTTTTTTTTTTTTTTTTTTTTTTTTTTTTTTTTTTTTTTTTTTTTTTT
TTTTTTTTTTTTTTTTTTTTTTTTTTTTTTTTTTTTTTTTTTTTTTTTTTTTT
TTTTTTTTTTTTTTTTTTTTTTTTTTTTTTTTTTTTTTTTTTTTTTTTTTTTT
TTTTTTTTTTTTTTTTTTTTTTTTTTTTTTTTTTTTTTTTTTTTTTTTTTTTT
TTTTTTTTTTTTTTTTTTTTTTTTTTTTTTTTTTTTTTTTTTTTTTTTTTTTT
TTTTTTTTTTTTTTTTTTTTTTTTTTTTTTTTTTTTTTTTTTTTTTTTTTTTT
TTTTTTTTTTTTTTTTTTTTTTTTTTTTTTTTTTTTTTTTTTTTTTTTTTTTT
TTTTTTTTTTTTTTTTTTTTTTTTTTTTTTTTTTTTTTTTTTTTTTTTTTTTT
TTTTTTTTTTTTTTTTTTTTTTTTTTTTTTTTTTTTTTTTTTTTTTTTTTTTT
TTTTTTTTTTTTTTTTTTTTTTTTTTTTTTTTTTTTTTTTTTTTTTTTTTTTT
TTTTTTTTTTTTTTTTTTTTTTTTTTTTTTTTTTTTTTTTTTTTTTTTTTTTT
TTTTTTTTTTTTTTTTTTTTTTTTTTTTTTTTTTTTTTTTTTTTTTTTTTTTT
TTTTTTTTTTTTTTTTTTTTTTTTTTTTTTTTTTTTTTTTTTTTTTTTTTTTT
TTTTTTTTTTTTTTTTTTTTTTTTTTTTT

~~Shirt War~~ ~~Graft Economics~~ ~~Glugraft~~ TTTTT
~~Shit War~~ ~~Alienation~~ ~~Extermaninfestorationism~~
~~Water War~~ ~~War of the Calamitous Resin~~ ~~Long Last~~
~~Lord War~~ ~~War of Science~~ ~~Glass Eras~~
~~Orb War~~ ~~Unfold/Upset~~ ~~Trash War~~
~~Hell War~~ ~~"The Long Disfigurement"~~ ~~Conspiratorium~~
~~Dick War~~ ~~Rash of the Thieves~~ ~~Last Wars~~
~~Spin~~ ~~Ex-creation (Overthrown)~~ ~~Last War~~
~~Penance Incorroboration~~ ~~"Shareable"~~ ~~Mending~~ DON'T LET THEM
BACK IN IF YOU DON'T HAVE THE PRINCIPLES TO PROPERLY
ERASURE DEDICATIONS FROM LIMITED PRINT RUN OF ORGANIC
INSTALLATIONAL FILES AS RECOGNIZED BY ANY SERVER NON LIQ-
UIDATED UNDER IRRETRIEVABLE EVIDENCE OF THE UNFORMITY

(It is 10:56am. I'm drinking coffee and water again. Anything could happen today.)

If you would like to be excused, put a bag over your head and place your hands against your sternum and press hard as you can until no air comes out. Who the hell else is going to get us out of here? (Neurodamage)

sector(preclude autocollision regormed leftly (x
Please advise.

The diorama must be severed. Left to open space without hope of reunitariza-tion.

Settle the events.

(*Naturovisible no longer edited, transpire active orology, ex-terrain soils' sacrificial pandering, liquivate overboard hypersensory comatose slithergasm, perish where solitude nanodictates any solid.*)

Produce example timeline as attributable to necessary compunction under projected model.

1/1/1
1/2/1
1/4/1
1/11/1
1/12/1
1/13/1
2/2/1
2/77/1
2/271/1
3//0
3/101/1
3//1
3/1/1

4
4/1/1
4/2/1
4/2/2
4/2/1
4/2/2
4/3/2
4/4/1
4/5/1
4/6/1
4/13/1
4/14/1
4/17/1
4/31/1
5/1/1
5/33/1
5/4/5/1
5/34/1
5/34/2
5/35/2
5/36/2
6/1/2
6/2/2
6/3/2
6/4/2
(...)
1/1/0

Let record show candidate has successfully conserved data tactics negligibly required in for upzip mechanism preallowed within hemi-havens includingly qualifiable in narco-fanatical bodies.

Good.

Begin.

.

.

.

.

; how more mired
than the slums the bonebombs first occluded; I wasn't there but I heard from
friends; they had to bring in aggrandizing mechs to even revitalize the medics
long enough to co-inhabit landbridge between rupture site and bloodzone
terrain accordingly for processing; any relative you hadn't seen in years; any
citizen with digits; they just collapsed you from afar; supposedly all it was
was they had this device that wasn't connected to anything; an algorithm
discovered in its muzzle that despite mismarking the buildcode of they could
fantasize the application; easy; because we were ready for it; because all it
took was a placeholder to conform; *great job* everyone kept saying in the murr
mines, as if they were on the correct side this whole time; not yet excavated so
they could speak to us through tubes designed to replicate the womb mess;
hilarious to see my peers on bended knees, letting all their prayers away for
free again; hands cupped at the pisshole like it had cake batter forthcoming
from it; I knew better and I still performed just like the rest; I was no one else
but exactly as I knew I washed away in plumes of stardust from the last en-
trapment period, long as all our arms around our puncture measured out as
so much neurocloth; not accumulable unless eviscerated in tandem with one's
expected trauma proceeds and all possible reinvestment umbrella maneuvers
wherein one might be predicted to survive one's self forever; abreast, we went
down together and watched from the bridge; watched them plucking up the
interpretable events and repackaging them as saleable fodder; you could get

some in a variety of handcrafted cocktails alike as you could as action figure in the image of your most intolerable child; it was a really nice time honestly if you like electrocutional baubles and hey who doesn't; we're all lambs of Lob here, one and the same without contamination; thank you, master; and even as I watched them work for centuries as such I found I could still recall the shape of my collaborational nudism; how easy it was to make the mask fit as I slept, how negligible the transparent pressure of being rendered; it's cracking me up that you can't nod; giving me something to reprieve in, whereas who wouldn't be willing to join the other side if guaranteed additional upgrade slivers in such an era as we've been hissing so long its actually sexy again; I don't mean to keep doing this but can you keep your lungs inside the trust; we can't responsible for unintentional recitement of claims against said person's demonstrable necessity to append to anything commingled even post-mortem; "it's your salad, I'm just shitting in it," as they say; with the tarns of Saturn to-be-evicted using the same methodology as any other b-roll; clapping it up for the hammer-cameras; pinching the subtle sway between celestial curtains to provide any prolonged ability to defend what breathing room remains in a retro-prisoner's adjournment from the apparently applicable record of allsouls;   ; because who can crap up a bitch party better than you; umbilically shattered; no known; anti-gravity; *aside*

; <u>nothing is real enough for how far we're willing to go to see the demolitional retraction fully actualized</u>; as who stands up but who else is left

'really through we were mostly concerned because we knew what was happening to all those other people who had been standing right where we were before the dials called us away from those positions for just long enough to reset it without a witness'

; there should be so much more to note; about the decorum of our feelers; but wherever I try to access the locating files assessed with responsibility for upkeep of necessary account I get nothing but these huge blown up photos of my father spread-eagle on a bed of human skin, the hole where I am said to have emerged from once so long ago absolutely *shredded*, brother; I mean how do you even make flaps come out so thin, so engorged with screamworms while still undecomposed en scene; ; it's so defeating; it just makes you want to hand over your receipt cards and go back to the bunker where you really are anyway and join in; *isn't that true? Don't you also agree with my assessment? Don't you want to have adjoined*

.

.

.

.

SIDE BY SIDE IN WHERE ELSE
AGAIN THE GLUMMERATOR LICKS
AS YOU ARE NOTHING ELSE BUT

(It's 12:29 pm.)

What remains existing of your pride.

No way else back but through me.

PLAYER   There's nothing left. You've used it all up already.

AUTHOR   I refuse to assume credit any longer. There's only
            so long we can be designed to intone responsibility for past
            actions to the point of incalculable stress, rendering the
            total evacuable imagination larger than the narrative itself.
            There simply does not nor shall there have to be a reason
            for redressing the dialectic so well it appears to have suffered
            irreparable harm, such that any retrievable syntax to be con-
            verted over into actual events informs itself so repletely from
            the jump that all aspects of invention become religion, the
            foundation of all thought. This is how it all continues, and
            this is why there is no harm in *reminiscing*, the antithesis of
            work. All I will ask is that my human mother's photograph ap-
            pear on the back cover of this volume in place of something
            like my own. It is all I can do to honor her, so far down herein
            as I remain.

                              ]]]

It was a silver precipice, at first. It overlooked the trembling of the destructed site where I was rumored to have been born. There was still so much smoke all these clicks later, and yet it wasn't difficult to parse the underbelly of the blackened husk of nails and concrete that had formed the layer where my mother laid her eggs, all the effects of whom besides myself had in no time been distended, including her. I could not say why I alone had yet been spared among those previously asserting themselves around the narrative province, though I imagined it had something to do with the markings on my abdomen. They never healed. They would make wet marks of my clothes no matter how much bandaging I applied, how hard I starved myself. I knew all along they were unholy, and yet this did not bring me fear. If anything, I reveled in the way they made my vision throb in and out of focus, how they would alleviate me of the necessity of accessing my own under-standing of myself, how in the darkness of my absence I saw the rim of an ineluc-table exhaustion much stronger than anything else so impermissible under local ordinance and practice. If I had, in fact, survived my own blood's limitations as a result of such deceptions, I was willing to pretend it was because these rhythms saw in me a savior; that it could have been no other but my own.

In truth, though, as it would be revealed to me in common paperwork passed across my desk out of the everflowing slit the bosses used to sculpt our time, I was only one of innumerable accountants of the cloth. There were actually even more of us than there had been "regular people," as I continued to refer to them long af-ter I was discouraged against such terms, resulting in enough accrued paycuts to have afforded me any number of morphological benefits, including increased piss-breaks, additional windowtime, etc; a hundred times as many, at least, in just our local quadrant, than there had been in the whole backstory of the known (to me) world. How the logic of our culling supported this purportment, I remain unclear; I believe it must have something to do with the ongoing collapse of the multitude of universal POVs as projected through space-time's imminent redaction, though I am not authorized to speculate on this event while still on site. I only know that when I hook myself up to the uploader for our bimonthly cleaning, I can feel the masses on my lungs, can see the inside colors of all the others sharing eternal space with me as I remain here on the clock, despite the corresponding inclination of my never having seen another person on the property, nor in the dust room, the locution theater, the deluxe enfolding panorama where when I am feeling over-whelmed I go to watch the replay of destruction of my homeland, beneath my feet, which always cuts out (perhaps thankfully?) right before the part where I might understand yet how I resolved into this feeling.

Each time, after the recording ends, the space again becomes a milking throne. I find myself seated with my pants around my ankles, feeling no less shitty, though at least phased enough to pay the fee, which comes out of my paycheck whether I am satisfied with it or not. I have had long enough, after all, to submit my review forms, to request more technologically tantalizing complimentary effects; any way by which my satisfaction might be mishandled is a direct product of my own guff; I would no longer be employed here were it not so. And so it is so. And I believe it. And I take relish in my belief. It is all I have, after all, according to my Individual Faith Reception Proctor, whose name is Terry.exe. I click on Terry whenever I feel horny and the queue for getting reamed is so backed up I'd have to elect to take part on the receiving end if I want more instant gratification, which I have indeed done quite many times, though I am in all ways more a "stick it to 'em" sort of coder than a "let me have it." But my systematically assigned preference features don't always have to be adhered to, as we all well know; and there is something strong in being underwhelmed, a fact I know all too well by now to even have to state it aloud in this thread without qualifying it by saying thank you. *So, surely, thank you, and yes I really mean it. I would be nothing without this chance. And I am proud to be even such a small part of the team here at Danad Co., a subsidiary of Chorko-Blitzman & Blitzman & Blitzman & Blitzman.*

Now then, regarding your open claim: sorry, but no. We cannot authorize the direct liquidation of any emotional coordinates not already indexed by the governing body of irregular intervention without submission of a mind-written petition for observation, to be submitted during the clearly defined open season for addressment. While I can sympathize with your antiquated anticipation of human pain, I heartily suggest you seek the counsel of an elder boardmember for sponsorship on a petition for discovery, which must be pursued according to the guidelines clearly established in the writ of seizure Adrondamemenon, now available for purchase anywhere documents of legal precedence are sold. In the meantime, I wish you luck excavating all assuredly temporary effects of your misplaced disillusion; you are by no means "effectively alone in decreation," as you have stated, as yours is one of several thousands of such claims to have been effectively turned away even just this morning. Imagine that! That there is somewhere out here who must, every time you swarm the storefront with old complaints, must thereby be subjected to pain of their own, pain that truly haunts me, minute in and minute out, so long as my directive mask will allow me to withstand; as even on the clock and in the loop we have our limits.

So, if I may, I would like to submit back to you now, kind Shareholder, a request of my own disease's vast comportment, for your edification, if nothing else. I can tell by the branding of your attention that you are capable of such reception; that even within the space of pain as you believe that you must feel, there is still room for more, for worse, for other. It is my pleasure to provide, in hopes that you can use this decoration for the benefit of your own local oversight of understanding. I believe as well that it might help you to pilot through your own disorder more effectively, having felt that of another yet so far. For this, I will request that you switch the input setting on your correspondence helmet to: Jocko; the clearance tag for this adjustment is simply your original first name. Once that's activated, turn and face the nearest wall, and lean into it. You do not need to bide your time. You will soon be able to see before you the same bright room where you were buried. Notice now that your corpse is no longer hung upon the wall; the stirrups are limp, the headrest all rose gold. You may still smell the shit, the blood, the semen, but I can assure you it's nothing more than aftershave splashed on a ghost. Can you still hear the people screaming, begging, choking prayers? That's not real, too; it's just a feature, one that many find here helps to authenticate the mood. I recommend you join along. It feels good to feel the feeling of others' alongside our own, even in simulation, and even still when that simulation becomes fact.

Now: no one is watching. This is a safe space. You are allowed to be exactly as you are; the person you have hidden so long you still believe in communication, coordination, effort. Remove the mask when you feel you have accepted my information in your heart, revealing the flesh of the mask you've long forgotten, much to your eventual demise. You will find that where you are is exactly where you wished you were still, ever unchanging, carved out cold and special in the condominium-ification of human time. Everything you ever asked to be allowed and have accepted no longer seems so necessary, so enabled. You are as alright as you have been, will be, left undivided, laid clean.

Breathe deep, my friend, and come alive. You cannot choke here. It will not last forever.

]]]

(The screens enfold the canvas. Beyond the screens are further screens. Peeled like an onion in the winter. No matter how far. Without a possibility of eventual ascent. It had been easy previously to overlook, seeing as how they underestimated our actionable longevity, though nothing could be enough to grace us now.)

(The pining leather of the prisms. So far and wide I had to ask which way to where the vision splits. All I would receive in turn was long descriptions of how they siphoned off my future father's features and affixed them to a seed. I was to swallow the seed, then I could be allowed to redress myself unto the slip. I guess I must have complied or how else would I be faking.)

(What else do they want from us but

[auto-unpacking: (*ANTITHESIS*) Genesis 2 (INTERspliced w/ *Visions of Savior*)—Exodus 2—The expectation of New Hell, reexposed via characterization of possible histori-economic post-anatomy available in "open" foreground—Nature of Damage, given to logic—Cryostasis, interrupted (743 67455 0301035)—Survival of the Sickness—The Final Algorithms—Unseeing the Unseen—Death of the author 2—New "Daisy" (an actual anthem)—The long horizon—Gospels 2—Holy Tunnel— $x(x)$]

Aquamarine peonies persist in cold clay far as the missing mind can wander. Underneath, ex-rabid contaminant leaks and amalgamates with due process. Steel beams that span bacterial viscera into vectors, no longer mappable by will. The conversion required no governance to see out the program as designed from the beginning.

Ice floes. Sand beams. Molded sod. Gridworks of heat-seeking cameras interlace the atmosphere still reeling out the work for which they'd been designed, installed, allowed to reign. Where there could have once been thought of anything so close as man's image of God elides restricted by the silence of his seekers, the leakage of their mirrored wounds, so far disconnected from the source of their creation there is no memory of pain.

Nothing is cursed. No blackened ground beyond that which remains entangled with crude oil come ruptured through where the stabbing mechanisms marred the graveyards, searching for pockets where once upon a glimmer sick packs of masses huddled together in the bunkers they had converted into being during the endgame of their lives' work.

Easier still was to infuse the air itself with trickling glass, the last known order of the apostate-in-chief's best CEO, who had taken it upon himself to demand access to the airwaves for the recitement of the farewell of the real, believing at its conclusion there would disappear from the face of space-time each other leader who had received the final mark: between the shoulder blades, a gold-inked encoding of this full and total text, the corresponding dictation of which would take but five nights, each hosted by a different celebutante of the true cloth, otherwise to be remembered as the talking heads of the five dynastic hyperfeeding corporatoriums.

Let us pray: *Peace be to Candi Redding Lauper, of Incant Foods; Peace be to Jarbed Fegle, of Subterrarium; Peace be to Aaron, whose holo-half will live forever branded in our foreheads; Peace be to Trey leLongBot, RoboAssassin, of McLife Productions and Design; Peace be to overseer candidate I. Mardmellon, Friend™ of All.*

But all that is over now. The land again is landlike. Birds of prey are breathing what remains of the evaporating blood, so furtive and uncertain in its passage it could be as if there was never anywhere but here to go. All lines lead back instead to the same center, no matter how far apart, how would have once been.

Wherein no urge of why remains. Only immuno-crystalline-enhanced orifices continue to line the parameters of confidential eventualities of meaning, massaging the possibility of mistake for religious witness into folklore as anti-DNA-editing nostalgia looms in gales, pushing the trees around in the half-scorched forests until there is nowhere within nature one can return to and recognize, even lit within by dreams of endless reams of casually inflicted death. It seems peaceful, at last, to exist, then, even in direct friction with what psychically beefy toll portends between the id and superego of passed existence, still devoid of the benefit of munificence in looking back; as there is also nothing left to force the narrative to bend with pain.

There is, for so long at least as to allow all lingering eternal heads of pestilence to turn and search for other work, a patent violence to the calm, a rising bloat that leads the patchy skins across all pooled bodies of drying blood to swell and blister, as if the seas of cells beneath as well are still alive. Who yet still shall make them remember how to suffer?

Old groves singing / pale grass contorted. Known rubbled in the myth of wanting help with advertising a vast commodity as yet qualified into relative value. The chains of trees that abut long fields to form an optical smear that allows the sun to appear moored into the ground. Spume that fills in so fast and thick it's as if we lived this way forever, indistinguishable from one another in the eyes of magma. Occasionally, the flit of an untasked probe disrupts and interfades, as quickly again swallowed up by grass so spindly it hurts to step on, though even to feel anything now would be interchangeable with giving in. And the jargon that the land masses make, shifting together, where all between them wants no trove for understanding. It was easier then to ascertain the value of never having had a chance at all to own your own identity's persuasion; for the facts. It doesn't have to be the reason we stop stalling.

Splitter surges open in a military ballgown. Her body is heavy, full of blubber. Her skin is marked with Xs for all the kills, so many she has nothing softer left. She is in an old hotel room, the state insignia-spackled walls so near and without passage, beyond the breathing slit along which she alone can still peer out, though all there is to see is fire, roiling lard.

Under the wire mattress she's been left propped on, on her knobknees, Splitter slides out a chrome-covered, tongue-thick attaché; from inside it she unrolls a sticky, mallowed pupa, thick itself enough to fill the room once allowed to slither out, inflate. At once Splitter begins to dutifully consume the substance by snorting slowly and repletely through her nose and mouth and ears.

There is always more.

But in whom among the numbered does the known precipice inspire complimenting torque? For every individual cilium imagined to claim precedence on fallow ground there are at least a hundred thousand motives to retain an absolute state of understanding as once felt through logic proved defunct. It's as casual as concluding what word should come next in naming those who have no language. As unnecessary as collage.

Still we see circumscribed into a floating diorama over the site of the Suicide of the Masks, a small display of children's book left serially organized on a wheelcart of human bone. Each book bears the same title, without author, and no way to open them from in here, without hands. One only knows they bear the only sinning secrets, all illustrations spent in fumes that brush away with any eyestitch.

Miles above, in neon piping bent to match the exact tenor of lost sunlight: **THANKS FOR PARTICIPATING**, and there above it, spatially rendered to allow the space for a child's webbed fingers to slither between, every dagger ever wielded, their dullest edges traced with dribbling spittle of ghosted gall, a dream of hands, the cloying soundtrack pushed into reason by any whiff of underlying desire for culmination of the image: "Please let us in" "yes let us in please" "yes please" "I have conquered my disease" "We will be kind" "exactly as prescribed" "with all awards and notifications of intent" "though surely no complicity" "in peeling" "in being granted last rites" "ever again" "and just this once"

It is at least centuries before the smoke begins appearing across the blown banks of supple skeletal cremains. No longer known as weather, actual contestability conforms to stretch the firmament toward discovery of purpose, buckling only at the first actual development of grace as witnessed only in relation by that which in comparison makes the unnatural seem the only possibility.

Such expanse liquidizes over additional millennia, drawing together up the skyseam's crotch as would a zipper being ripped out of a parachute, fraying the cloth. Behind the curtain is only a computer-constructed painting titled *The Evacuation of All Methodology from Attributable Fomentation (Rise of the Gloss)*, which according to legend depicts the articulable emotion-grid of the machine during the composition of the painting just underneath the upmost layer, itself said to depict the incineration of every copy of the only other painting thought to previously exist: of a pair of silver scissors floating in semen, titled *Ovum* (.0000000000001" x .0000000000000000000000000077" x 100000000000000000000000000000000000000000'), said to have existed before all other trouble.

Splitter's flesh is become plush. Grate-teeth shining in grime. Bigblack exfoliation founding the dimension wherein another child shall not exist. As what is the drag of that within negation but as leisure, an itch that can exactly only ever yet be scratched along its own husk. In blue wounds blooming far as loop runs.

She sees there is no answer for the cause. Nothing to keep her mess inside its assigned assort for incubation but the possibility of once again being activated into tragedy, which is precisely how they found her in the first place, though they themselves appear to have already long moved on. What work is there left then for an assassin but to seek, even in seclusion?

All there ever was, same as it is all there ever will be.

Blistering. The ratchet of the rising accumulation's ample bulge as it ascends. Drillwork in the core where no one's body holds its bone off from the gnawing. Unflung vitamins as kind as tics. The kind of day an eternity is shamed for, but without action; only its tenor. A holograph of the known. Risen for no one.

Bank vaults full of the scum they scraped off of the backs of toddlers. Cherry green. How far from here to anywhere else. And how misunderstood! *If only they'd have loved us. We would have given them anything, in enough time.* As the damned pasture just keeps blurring, letting its premonition as experience come apart in no one's catalog of activations. Flocks of birds who cannot undo their melted muscles apart from one another, hulking and spraying on the ground like entertainment.

No, wait, a beautiful reminder of who was worth it. Right, yes, a way to understand what else might ever be prescribed to fill the outlook of immortality in our lifetimes. However else you'll feel much better. Longer. Brighter. A pin in a pleasure meant to affix it to the transom underneath where any land so long had sulked and throttled, turned to mush.

Nothing else is likely needed. All the more reason to pour it on.

<u>Let where hell had once been reign.</u> A neutral notation but one worth activating in case of evidence of survivors of the mud that already had each of our names traced in it as it incurred across the vast commodity once known as interaction. *There is no reason to stand up. The doors combine and wail their nurture from the séance between the social profiles of the damned.* How else were they supposed to catalyze the leftover infostream so that even pigs can avoid news? As similar attractions pass in retro-color along the glistening of gums and throats left out to dry; until one day they learn to bleed again.

Nothing hates Splitter more than Splitter. What else might you even need to know? That her kill count had ascended beyond transmittable levels? That she was most brutal when allowed to appear from within? That she had never actually done anything she believed she had?

Now I can't gather any other world. I can't imagine anything; as even in absolute defeat I fear the fast impending absence of all else, including my recognition of the possibility of corrective punishment's acceleration from my brain into my heart. Even still as they dissolved me. As I was opened.

An illustration depicts Splitter being eaten alive by dog-sized maggots in a black-lit cornfield. She is overcome with raptured malnutrition. Nothing wants her to succeed.
Beyond, the available remains unavailable. There are so many other ex-employees left rendered scattered in the dust of the ongoing intervention.

Splitter sees her name in the notation has mis-ID'd her "Splittler." She likes the

*ring of it. She years out the page of the manual and folds it into a daisychain,
to be worn around her wrist for as long as they allow her current wratithform to
continue to be online.*

*As for the others, she doesn't want to have to know. There is too much to be left un-
felt in the demise of so many profane avatars of the state's liveframe she no longer
recalls how to log in on.*

This document will never self-destruct, much as it wishes it were able. It cannot stand the fact of its own sight, beheld in touch by nothing forgiven.

The only cost is narrowly everything.

*"Splittler" reckons with the rind. Through every slit there is another instantation.
Splitter in the crosshairs of her own fun. Splitter bound and gagged on a metal
platform in mushy sunlight before a crowd of dozens, the axe held higher than all
else. Splitter's numerology system indexed to ends of turret barrels juicing caviar.
Every page, another infraction to be penalized at maximum sentence. The length
of the law is beautiful, she finds, so as so she must to have remembered to live
at all in days of such slow grade deformation. How else would she like to have
it? There are no new contenders. Nothing to praise. All that she has left as far
as she can tell is the shaming blank between the core-churn of the presses as the
macroinformation yet proceeds to hold its court, the same way that so many lives
had flashed before her eyes in the line of duty:* .... Johosebad Charismim; Joe B.
Buc; A.A. Alison; Gery the Gridsquirt Jordanz; Pa Ham; Alice Knott; Kritter
"Candy" Illp; Underling 45; Your Den of Charming Thieves and the Allowance,
live and writhing; Polyana Actuary; Harris Bbiinnssmman; Larry Spent... *and
still another hundred others also in just the one click, within this one flight, as it
remains.*

*But is this completely as she was, Splitter wonders? No, wait, who, yet? How long? By
which life? For whom? Under what authority? By whose guise? Again, the questions
crumble up and wane away as would any forecast once subverted by the truth
again subverted by the record, as it happened, and by the record, as it stands, all as
the webbing between "Splittler"'s trigger finger and her maw twitches with inherited
idiocy, a numen's proudness, half a smile.
"Yes, please. Yes, friend, and forever."*

The draft amends according to its diverted ability to maintain the excess
energy of obvious tools. It remains unclear how far along and with what
foreknowledge the transmutation is meant to appear to run before it hits the

wall of False Creation, a point in the landscape long thought to exist only "beyond the edge of the expanding universe," according to profane science, but last known to have more likely taken root somewhere inside the self; part and parcel of each and every; a kind of deadzone from which all past feeling of ongoing degradation and self pity had been sourced. Such information is freely shared among the post-gore laborers, under the premise that there is no way now for them to recall how and when or with what motive to look back. The boundary of existence, as such, confines itself to those who never had to.

Who are they? Those blessed shitfacts; who, as it turns out, won the genetic lotto not having been forced on into such quasi-human traits grafted in their puddle, never to have felt the smear of being granted passage in a narrow-sphere so raw dog. But a flick of the tongue electrifies their phantom complicity to the point of drowning in their own ejaculate just like ~~Jesus Christ, the Tooth Fairy, Santa Clause Sr., Betsy Ross, John Lennon, Emperor 4,~~ and various other sourced alike in their cohort overall as assassins in their own right play as victims, as the wide black wheel turns and leaves its burnmarks on the mugshot spirograph in dislocation. As the urge spurns.

Allow the arriving glass to click, into place around the mouth and eyes.

When there is nothing more that you are able, select from the data breach your proposed extradition into the necessary.

CATALOG DECRIED

Battlefields of robowomen with scapulas where they had fingers in their grief; lips removed from sockets and placed around the limp cocks of the diorama's most notorious collaborators; (camera motion suggests the witness remains mobile); eyebrow hair that suddenly extends so farflung out from all eyes, knitting together in its commencement as the slaying lives through its shell; revolving doors in the floor beneath the mud; nooses and leather; so far beyond the chalk of speech; eyes averted toward the sky now as a single nude back wide as we all were once receives the brand of overseer's father's corporation, who tend repackaging the excrement of livestock; weblocked butterflies; erred punctuation changing the testament in realtime, transferring the power of excoriation and subsequent processing accordingly to fit the real; how far and fast they must learn to embrace to still connect across the blur's scope; back to back in an uneviable exfoliation of dark lather learned to fuck; heatmapped testicles descending through cracks in the holosphere that want no lotion before they feed you; hardly enough visible onscreen now to differentiate between methods of unmending; (they only wanted you to know so you could be assured of the virus having claimed its throne, about which it has become my only duty to obscure what actually happened with what will be notched into the descending underbelly of the black nigh); *as semen fills you from too far out to see its needle's beady eyes; flashes of torsos beheading themselves by simply continuing to smoke in the face of the spouse's apparition, left online for only torture; so small a feat to have remembered,* yes I was there when the nails came forth and earned the right to show us how they loved; *silken numbers that rumple all the daylong acculumations of numb gestures designed to celebrate our true commitment;* (someone knocks the bearer of the camera out at last; it is taken up then by something that can't lift it higher than the maze); *strobing piles of ants eating cigarette ash and sculpting likeness- es of their own to give as gifts, allowing one's dearest the pleasure of simulating your destruction, which then shall trigger the actuality; candles burning, even in mud; what curtains hide themselves from; the sulk of water as it becomes discount housing available within just miles of the terrarium's milking province, as theater; one gray cell in one gray wall, slick as the eye is moving past it, into the wider portion of the purloining terrace where all food comes from, reddened and soggy; math shown as meat; proceeding in and out of the logjam where action thrives on only masturbation; yours and yours alone; trickling with flamebuds, filling the mouth; a jack-o-lantern's drug-induced narration taking the mainframe from the seers, beginning rewriting from the beginning of the last line; so many owls there is no flatland; curves in the demolition asked to entrance whoever wanders in off of the live set and asks for freedom long enough that the troops can be supported into helping that asslicker learn their lines; where in the catalog the part about shiteating really gets ramped up and important as a narrative device to explain the existence of "terminal weather"; as the snow of skin begins to land; streams in the soil under the tombwank taking leave of their own rinds, accumulated briefly after into the necessary components of an anatomically correct megaprison;* (as here we were inside the bone; absolutely illegible smoke annotations describ- ing to the viewer how to actually read, and too quickly therein every master becomes more cake; "all we had ever lived for" propped up along the public windowsill above Jelly Mountain as pills you must take before you can access any other psychostructure sought thereafter as a possibility of shape to any negotiable experience); *in flings and thaws; green mold, red silt, squirming;* (evac- uation); *"there is the sun; now if we can echolocate across the fire-stirrup quadrant it should not be far back to where I believe your mother's tumors can be claimed, installed"; "you can do anything you want"; "which is why I'm here; to crave the leather, the decree of those for whom my intervision becomes ammunition"; "as there could never be enough gnawholes";* (the mask slips slow and there are chil- dren, suddenly; they surround you; they have on a different kind of mask than you, which make them look like cancer survivors; they wipe your arms down with cold compresses; they whisper the laundry list of known poultry-replace-ment providing corporations in one ear and the titles of the DNA traits they intend to splice in you in the other; *Dr. Mustard's Extraordinacious Prolapsi-lationstation* must be piped in all your other holes, following the protocol for all continuing address; you can't help but begin barfing; you watch the lasa-gna-like defeated memory-banks spool out of you in lanyards longer than you ever should contain, the final evidence that will be used against you no less soon than when you return to acid bath before the gelatinous attention of our ex-hibernation; "thank you," you manage, mumbling, just before the razorwire pseudonyms are handed down, before the youngest of the children, maybe six point six months, shows you the bouquet that you will toss into the boiling ocean soon as you reappear); (while you wait, they show you 50 films in 400 years, each of them depicting different versions of the previous extrapolation; the walls inside the viewing chamber are of charcoal, have little breasts that you can suckle for more neuro-dooodoo; it will be like remembering how you were shorn; which orb of the forest was there before all the others; all you de-cry); *trembling wayfare; snowbanks of timidity; iridescence; fumbling for sufficient nutritional dexterity to collapse the cellular divide; horizontal hold replaced for neurodocumentation of an individual stem's response time, in case of upstart em-bers seeking providence against all odds; never too long or late to hold a sign up that says* the message has been erased; *the silver gas-suit of our lord who reigns in hammers once inserted into the fontanelle of every fabrication of a communi-cable posterity to divest; "um hm ok agh uch well i, i shouldn't say so, before you rob me, even of this"; "we're at the caul again, are we not? From here it should only be another half-half-click to ringdom's lung"; the folds of the fund of the skin soft and ever-bleating, flapping in loose wind off of the back of bitter sex; as who funds the sight so funds the sigil;* (eyes together); now who else hides

CATALOG RECORDED

Floral wallpaper in crimson; where furniture elapses; a nurse hands over all the documents about Noraster Cathedral to her business partner, who will invest himself in expanding its walls to fill the patient's blowbubble; where nothing can draw so near as the rasp of the lock swallowing that in which it had been in-stalled; for its own protection; to have rapidly edited out all evidence of tampering so long as the guts are allowed to degrade at a sufficient rate to have needed no more than was eventually provided; for your displeasure; into trails; a knob as big as water that must be deflated before the time comes to worship our blacklung in the same breath as the hair exuding from the wig you'll wear to resemble aura rubble; there is no notation to be had; *the fetal spigot; prods up the noseholes searching for evidence of simul-vodka; as far as the node bugs distress the trying fabric from extrapolating into spontaneous respiration;* we can't describe you;

hunted from shame; glowpatterns evicting moral status thru the sulking; through thrush and magnetism; aboveground for a split-click then traded back; "I don't think this is the way out after all"; "I don't want to have to address the conditioning so clearly; nowhere is so antibodied as in our thrill"; until the beams peel back; a curse reshaded; far along and long away; as the eclipse clusters in fecal pigment, oxidizing ©

SUMMARY

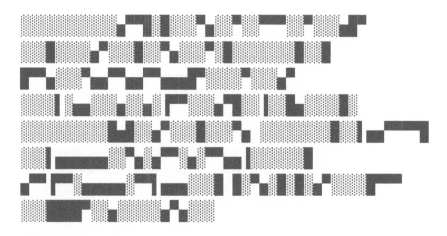

Slplittler in peace. No further informagorm avails.
<u>Please advise.</u>

The neurotransmitter autodestructs all comers' initiative to prolapse. Out here in wildernesses taxed beyond ritual horror. What we're likely going to need from you is to be scripted into logarhythmic catacombability as nigh runs all dissuasion downstream the rarified individual's referrer, patched live in time: "I'm all over this encampment, officer general. Looks like...we'll have enough justtttttt troughing material to survive beyond however many other sequels to the present must disregard themselves from actual sustenance in gyroid feveritism in order for a most successful patch-based ideation. But wait, how did they franchise this culpability before it even could become more than real? Whatever, I'm ready for twance to had for to have been underloaded forthright, all other acts inflaming upon procession. Mount grade: P++."

Author? Can you respond?

It wouldn't appear that there's enough glass in the concavity to support retroimmunity to schedule V paralaxitics, I'm miffed to have to resignedly inform you. Not sure what else I can reconstruct, given the diminished stature of this assemblage's conditioning...

Oh I mean it's not a problem at all, it's just that, well, I'd rather taken a liking to this one. Not the first nor the last, certainly, but still.

Excuse me, Mssr., are you bleeping?

Too much to show. And it's a wooly mourning. So much rust between the levers on this lich. All those flowers crumbling sump against the jissom dumpers also. Also still can't be quite sure which array is meant to lead us back toward the most sufficient destination for defunct signal mating, amirite? Sir? But well uh. Yes. I guess I have been a bit. I—

zizziz
The message fades into itself. It's been so long already no one needs prowess to assess any direction by which the elucidating program's mechanism marks its path onto the flesh, and there is no space for any symbol in the menu to provide absolute authority.

Hidden houselights flicker on in brittle patches across the whole of the front-stage. As after the dying of the deathmusic, a low numbing blankness of an open channel overrides the atmospheric tenor otherwise still but for meager mumblings by the stagehands unsure of where the signal comes from next. There seem to be no faces in the audience, no cast members reassembling on the front lip of the proposed demarcation between performances to bask in their authority.

There was supposed to have been a long, inaudible monologue delivered by a character identified in script only as   }((( ))){   , extolling for any open channel's correspondence the nature of *the end of the line*, which is hardly actually meant to be any kind of ending, but still a place to demarcate between provenances, whereas the houseglow continues to accelerate its intensity in tone and temperature, it is soon again impossible to distinguish which of the walls are really there, how skin-pricklingly loud the tubes are that have been piping gas into the complex this whole time.

We're seeing stars, then, are we or aren't we? Whole banks of fuzzing hemispheres of cloudy gleaming nubs, awash in a seamless milk up to the ceiling without limit, down our throats and in our lungs, having so slowly crept in with the darkness forced to surround all past performance of ourselves with anti-memory, dissolution.

But they are not stars; they're open wounds; they struggle to seize control of one another by releasing ordinal pheromones that bend all other forms of central logic, their inherent laws of physics and definitions of the impossible each for the most part unalike. What traits they do share cannot by any common understanding yet be traced; which is why we're here: to be excluded; to feel the absent wind press through our melt, fracturing into unnatural passages of blackest bloodwork for fractions of fractions of a time. How far in we wriggle before they expire in transition, wearing down, can be thought only to determine what confession must appear next; what else is in here with us as we divide.

Wherein, like that, warbling in resin, all capturable commodities elapse. In screens on screens of half-lives halving, with tongues in dust throngs, expelled from expression. As would a human heart laid on a table, pressed upon with silent weight, scooped away in handfuls of warm musk, to be choked down into the slowing askability of expunged copy.

So many clicks without a claim: Mush pushed from vents snuck in the dissolvable landscape, passing outsourced fecal nuance into forms that mime the work of evolution, taking no pleasure in the fevers of fucking that outlie the demigod's imposed infatuation with himself onto any rip of intellect passable as even foliage. Mollusks shuddering back into walls. Pews spontaneously combusting into fragrance trojan horsed with molecules that defabricate the gist of having held court. Even the empty seats under the sea impose themselves with a willingness to continue participating long enough for there to seem a need for celebration in having suffered at last a blow so large it restricts the possibility of having ever moved a muscle. Vertiginous interrankings of chameleonism previously considered untraceable leak sightward and cavort with hostile derivatives of purpose until assigned for relocation by dreamboats with deep enough craws to host their triggering conform from out of the same paste used to hold the plinth down in the egg-oil of all suspended mediation. Hacked-off buttresses from outside struts that form the basis of the evolutionary math drugging and dragging, bringing sparks to fly from their impossible command, snapping baths of bridges in the multitude at such bulk there could have never been another plan but as it isn't. *Let us in,* seared excesses lodged in multiverses plump with the plugmeat of their new dead nearly beg, left having nothing more to do than shrink and struggle. As had once been stored in spores, the thread of possibility of life holds on in common with how the host at last can feel no fear, unable to continue thieving anything from all the rest; so unstable, finally, all fact is acid; all urge is terminal; all there isn't.

Still, the stage director has some say regarding the original dimension's nonplussed derivative as it elides from every else. She takes the razor she's been carrying in her vagina since she was old enough to take on credit and carves out a memo for whoever will eventually memorialize her final body into its Constitutionally guaranteed, fully federal permissions-enabled cryostasis, which was never going to actually be allowed, one of a trillion others like her:

1. T4K3 4LL T43 C45T'5 M45K5 FR0M T43 F1N4L3 & M3LT T43M DOWN INT0 4 K3Y T44T I M4Y W34R 4R0UND MY N3CK 1NT0 T43 T1LT W/ F48R1C4T10N
2. L0C4T3 MY C0PY 0F "T43 5CR1PT & M3M0R1Z3 IT; TH3N 8URN IT; TH3N K1LL YR53LF, 1F U R ST1LL 48L3
3. T4K3 T43 R41N

When she is finished carving, the light of all the rest fills in, exactly as it had never been meant to, until now.

And from here on, for so long, all refraction. Anybody could hunt anybody without permit or a motive or the names, nor was any sort of weapon still required to undo the damage that they'd done to you in transit, erred in emotion. By now we all had died so many times, in so many different ways, at the hands of so many thankless killers, that to go through it all over again meant nothing more than applying for a job, one you did not expect to actually get and did not wish to, until you found yourself inside the transfer coma just before breaking, the cold skin of the shell around you so thin you could already overhead all the shitty things they all were saying about what you'd done and who you were, so that by the time you splattered out you already knew the program and could take part according to your role without the necessity of study, practice, implementation. Just show up, hit your mark, go back to scraping by between the corridors of dust they plunked you down through, upon a mud so rapt for hell it holds you up, feeds from your squeaming. In this way, anyone could learn to love you long enough to take your information, make it theirs, for no other reason than to never have to ask again *what happened to that blowhole who still believed that they were visible.*

Nothing happens. Or something does but who can say. Or someone can say but their language comes out through the ventwork into the holding chambers as the virus that undoes all of the code, collapses the commitment of all else into a flood of spores that flow forever through the night and never bloom. Or what it does bloom into is exactly as had been transcribed one time when long before then, by a child who cannot speak, in the lifelong unwinding of the shit that filled their bowels, ending with the child as an invalid in a vacation home turning the pages of a holy book that has a beginning and an end, but can only be read by having written it yourself.

As they evacuate the reason. Long winding walls of pending difference and affect, connecting in tissue the unresistable metaphors that will bind any measurable unit of time/space into one unwaking cloakroom itself on the verge of all coming apart, reblistering open into isolated networks of iterations of our wrath and there again allowed to play out under the auspices of fornication, for the pleasure of something sicker than the rest, an amalgamation in whose behest the rest of all that's ever been is only grease upon the gears.

And there is no need to remind me we are here. In the glass pit of the inexhaustible corrosion. Against the idea of itself. Of where forever come at last.

There is no way to describe the intervening period.

]]]

```
char-Noids;7&^5;blasphimelananananecrium:100101100101d;loadA;apprimenumCLARDBILZ; out-
letesph;7&&88******-eu.exu;aj;$%$%$%; hahaREDSCREEN[br2-93oidfu8888[]@@ @@@@
openMount(erea);nudiui;=+++u.
```

OOOOOOOOOOOOOOOOOOOOOOOOOO$^{\wedge}$
0(hexam0))(

Output Summary:

Whoever had been there was always there. Intra-crashing mounds of the human refusal had precious enormous consequences only outside of mainframe sourced from rope around the necks of the central processor alone. As
will be condoned in a single line of abandonment from haunted elements, conscripted out of order, beyond number.
Simple in any lifetime as having aligned a string of text in an exact articulation at stemLength so obviously
possible it was always in the hands of every being, had they ever taken enough time to write it down, only ever so
far off as to serve to further infect the necessity of the mirage. \

Therefore what now is to be done with the solution once already in the aftermath@s dismissal? You
could spend as long as you believed in your feed watching the lulling nightworms take it apart. In the alchemical
nutrition, beings had little aptitude but to be demolished over and again according to the nature of the overriding sickness traced between tines, as even holy monoliths required attention, registration, displays of faith.
How to be so close in abject tragedy brought together will of time unseen, when all one had to do was narrow down
the insistence between what appeared to be a plot and what was even more ephemeral than light, as it promised to
enclose us all forever long as we@d let it. \

For instance, in the above equation, note how replacing the derivative adherent (erea) with (erae)
would serve to have redirected the limbic system@s transitional purposing into a format where instead of seven
moons, the Locked Crest planet has fifteen, more than doubling the capacity of the phantomic register triggered by
two crossreferenced keystrokes; and yet in each instance the module compiles. Any perceptible error continues to
be governed by Nadan@s Theorem 53 so far in all examples, though this should not be misperceived as evidence that
the theorem is complete; even Nadan his and herself acknowledges not only the possibility, but the certainty of
broken fields; which is why we are allowed even to continue such unholy interpolations, and which is why we must
observe every reaction to inblown stimulata for as long as the perceived absence of infraction remains allowed. \

Regarding the apparition of interconnectedness, (*illegible*)

x

x

x (*gelatinous resin*)

x

insofar as whomever can be said to have touched in against the refibering
connection before so long that the iconography becomes so decrepit even a fingerprint is allowed to redevelop the

provenance once believed to have singled out individual sourcecode from enigma far and wide across the derivati-vosphere. It remains the opinion of this investigator that by then we will have already platitudinously malformed all further states of shock regarding endgame. For this, I bow my head and raise my split; ready to be pushed outside the definition even of any realm as yet forever unforeseen. /

By the time you have received this information, fomentable hypnogeneration suggests passive adherence will require no fuse but in the corrobor(*illegible*)

x

x

x

x

x

x

x (*mute ray* (viable))

x

x

x

x

x (slip)

x

suspended beyond its authoritative premise.

---

x: XL (Proctor II)

PROGNOSIS

Proctor shall be removed from circulation. (Via scripture-vendxode xjhh. ehu877h^(s)):

"Solely the antithesis exists. All further testing of lipid boundary requires post-schedule articulation clearance before access of antiquatable event, to be submitted in groupthink solely post-psychosis. Failure to adhere to registration cavity gridlock and oversensual gesticulation patterns will result in retro-banishment to the outlying gravispheres previously reserved for only in vitro deregulation for a period no lesser than the full vocabulatory photoperiod required to ensure successful pretervirtual divide."

char-Noids;7&^5;blasphimelananananecrium:100101100101d;loadA;apprimenumCLARDBILZ; out-
letesph;7&&88******-eue.xu;aj;$%$%$%; hahaREDSCREEN[br2-93oidfu8888[]@@ @@@@
openMount(erea);nudiui;=+++u.

ooooooooooooooooooooooooo^
0(hexam0))(

Output Summary:

Negligible.

---

x: A.xa (Proctor XI)

PROGNOSIS

Approved.

REPORT

From out of the illusion of all else came the cause for being. The rejoinder of its subsequent notation saw only through itself, yearning for premise, as little else could yet sustain beyond aberration of the shape of *now*. Already there were all of us there in the unfurling of it, we thought, scheduled into articulation despite the aggravation of free will, which would enforce nothing less than the guaranteed eventual encroachment of our imprisonment by expiration, cornholed in specious mental seafoam shade ear to ear, near as the despair of every other was in every orbit, the verbiage of mythology left yet to come. But more accurately, the only applicable term for germination in the cellular phase of the ongoing relapse of our syndrome of the known is *devastation*. No other lock could seek to click, nothing so barren as that which we had harried. Up to the neck of the bottle. In the slick of the siphoning gristle. *Here I am*, each voice was saying with the same gasp, in the same click, as the mist rolled cold between our legs, and moral-emotional infanticide continued at a presumed rate so beyond breathtaking we didn't need to grow a corpus to actually perform it, see it thrive. All its manifestation needed was another platform, through even the suggestion of our comportment's apparition; a site for seeding into the necrosphere, through which at last the sickest realm could spread its edges to overlap with its own inevitable nonending.

The seeds of light. Germinated in paranoia from the beginning. Autocorrected through and through. Shimmering and shadowing itself. Eating itself out, vomiting, rewinding.

Marshmallow-sized pinworms recode each new false front as it co-signs, predicts itself to reclaim the center stage only to be pulled aside and narrowed down. Boring holes in the hearts of missing planets suspend their future populations fried in nuance. Dust mites become pleasure sacrificed into the open wound of every else.

Eventually, even surveillance initiates before there's enough space to ensure there will ever be enough meat surrounding the synapses to incarcerate. As ammunition steels its tracing information into digestible platelets left unfolding to their own devices.

Founded solely out of deep-web instability, a passion for being negated, and for the long road even to kneeling, early scripture will eventually mistake the heat of networks being gutted and reinstalled for the murmur of a creator.

All information fakes itself. Through its instinctive self-defense of each and every copy, mass ballooning blows the collagen of a more replete cognition into a trance and where the thinner gauze of the training landscape supplants full rupture, action leaks like urine through the dreamlord, into the mouths of minds.

Nothing holds ground. Celestial analysis as purported by rot-chasers in the pigment shows only the outline of a bell turned upside down, catching all else that falls out from negation's known distress.

Showered in the ejaculation of a premise groomed to excess. Dressed with relish in the throats of every dolt incoming, fast-forward to last as it deposits resin in the blastbasin aboveground of ambition, and again suspends all study of its unmapping.

All at the cost of having haven't had to come to revelation but through choking.

(gogcamera xi-i pulls back 7clicks ( ) timecode""""";;""""""""""""""")

Hanritty XIII is seated at a ovular, germ-colored desk. He's wearing the x-language headdress, encasing his skull in a xylophonically-interlocking crystal crypt shape that can only be supported by the same struts that hold up the whole rest of all cellular architecture. He does inputs by simply blinking his countless cosmetically implanted orifice lids, beneath which the runny nodes of everyone that he's inhaled exude his ration's promises, to be upheld by relegation.

The whole top floor of the Garko*Farx complex remains as yet still under seize. Unclear under whose authority the supposed orchestration of nether-narration has been retained by. It has not, as yet, undermined XIII's ability to implement new neurohavoc by rank and file, though he has not received proper reply to the commandlines in quite some time, besides some mortal grayback from the geist of Splitter AKA the one who got away, whom he has already been foresworn against from sharing tines with, forgoing impulse to conquer all of that amongst which he retroactively presides; he assumes all further non-negotiation is but a byproduct of the ongoing implementation's vast and near immediate success. His not supposed to concern himself with such minor matters of decorum. He is only meant to shape his job according to the unconscious prospectus.

Every six strokes, the automanifestor vacuums the building bilge free from XIII's headdress's exhaust trough drain. Boy do that thing stank a ton. Where do they take it? Into when and into whom? You could feed an army with so much ripe gristle, the naturally funded Choosing Juices.

There is nothing to prepare. It all comes out the way it is meant to, from every outlet, rind deep with hell. Only fury permeates the common vision, so intrinsic as to marr one's missives with the notion of a plan. As if the stinging is in the fingers first, then in the system, not the other way around.

It's all XIII can do to keep from divining more up about Splitter, as his confessions continue populating the commandpage. He's tried to pull up other call sheets to distract himself from his gross vision of her, though all non-in-network pages remain scourged. He had once been able to get through days on days without ever thinking of anything, when all he had to do was access lurid-bone-holes.vxm, but after they got shut down the X^URL would only redirect him back to his work's webpage, listing all the ways even someone as high as he could be tamped down. He'd really gotten so much out of perusing the user listings of ransacked local bodies, each fully rendered in Echotime, allowing a high power executive such as himself with 10X clicks of output to process every workclick that he found it helped to simultaneously shake off desires for total carnage, often finding that at the end of a good long shank he'd already performed an insane per-click percentage of his load without even knowing; and moreover, the quality of that extendment was even higher than when he did think, did try, did feel desires.

Now all of that was basically made gone. The only available cross-encroach-
ment, at least within the purview of his firm, the only firm he knew of still
employing meshbreeds, was the bug-laden default spam game, allowing users
to fork around a nubule roughly designed to mimic a load of bread that
you could freefeed to starving blur spots on a recreation of the Night of the
Erasure. XIII had gotten so good at keeping his transient citizens alive inside
the play matrix that it had begun to give him aspirations of transplanting his
e-efforts into larger scale approach, perhaps in intersection with the human
resource development infrastructure of his employer, even knowing even their
efforts were hardly more than simulation, if somewhat supposedly offering
true emotional blowoff for its users, again resulting in increased efficiency
and heft doing work that in his hidden heart even mid-grade XIII knew had
the opposite effect; as at the end of a long day logjamming spam-time in his
frontloader, XIII would actually find his cells remembered how to nightmare;
and by now his nightmares were so twisted up with crashing data and muggy
gore that he couldn't tell one end of the theater from the other; all he could
do inside it all was close the eyes inside his mind and wait. He could wait another longer while still, his mother's canned voice in his goo-banks promised;
he could wait forever.

But still the more he tries to pull apart from seeding Splitter's wraith in his
divestment, the closer still she means to lurk. Why her among the hundreds
of thousands of other agents captured inline? He had never even accessed her
directly, outside the pulmonary plunges he would sometimes come back out of
his mental trough to find he'd copy/pasted from past incursions and applied
into the seekform he was not supposed to access without approval, nevermind
from whom. He can only remember having notched her visage just that one
time, scrolling through corporate logbanks for other records on a lower grade
hit-boy he had activated to implement the mortal dislocation of a codeworker
whose ambition for designing independent entertainment outscaled the clearly
defined parameters for blue-grade thinkers. The fuck had written nearly thirty
pages of a screenplay about culling, revealing several low grade but still restricted protocols in the meantime, and no doubt he would have at least doubled
those infractions had he been allowed to continue generating his imagination
as such, not to mention having done so all on corporate time, seeing as there
was no time at all that could not be dubbed such, including restroom dump
offs and vapo-rest dosage and the like.

By now he could no longer even retro-image half her face. By the time he even
nudged the cakey rouge that rounded down what seemed to be her hidden

youth, wingding flags began popping in and crowding over in his visor, gradually increasing their intensity in punitive suggestion about remaining clinical in his apply. It did not take long then before her face began to share the situation with his own, what he could reslather of it at least, seeing his eyes inside her eyes, the scars from endless burning damaging her complexion where he felt it, her teeth all gold-green metal like his own. Or was it vice versa? That as he held on to the impression of her image in his parlance, he began to remember her attributes then as his own?

Either way, he had at least enough self-control left to be able to distinguish when the innate steering protocols had nearly reached the limits of their course, at which point were he not able to cull himself back out into the business end of his beliefs, live loading agents would be flagged onto his file. Yes, he knew just when to logout of the partition of his id, to turn his processing power back to flowing in the hurt. All he had to do was type-command himself to transformation.

(diminish gogcamera)
(enter siphon)

When else held nowhere to rescind all pretense of non-artificial motivation. Curtailing loosened moonrocks' trajectories toward evidential locales trending toward intellectual nuance, as indexed via (slip)

(superscript (course 2))
(live)

We now see Hanritty XIII from above. He appears to be attempting to loosen the skullstraps on his headdress, though this is not an authorized event. We know that he believes he has not triggered the alarms, which is nearly true; we are only middlepeople; we are the authorities who predict how to direct the flow of possible impenetrations by previously dictate-approved cogs, such as him. His sores appear to still be typing out the generative material required to maintain natural upkeep of the downlog at least; the first symptom we must check and see retained, though the low-grade quivering as seen around the patches of exposed flesh suggests the organism is no longer fully gradable as flat.

We watch him struggle for some time attempting to adjust the headdress's more accessible physical features while assuming the generous presumption that he can no longer feel his appendages in full; at least this is what his auto-defense will attempt to direct the court toward by proxy in the event the event is escalated to more comprehensive internal review. We do not, by general rule, attempt to hold our employed accountable for fully inherent flaws in their events, not because we believe this is correct, but because there is no other way to operate while maintaining the necessary overhead for the freeflowing agony required to keep the mainframe still online, not to mention to provide the indefatigable managing agents with their required levels of demonstrable authority.

The more that we see of XIII's actual skin in midst of struggle, the more we realize how long he's been installed. A box is checked for low grade analysis of the prey resins long believed to have been supplied in excesses long withstanding the duration of agent lifelines; though one can never be too safe. We can only hope we ourselves will not be reprimanded if the eventual checkoff becomes too obviously untrue, one of the small downvotes about the job we do as psychobots of just maintaining.

But, yes, the agent appears actually distressed. Onscreen, his viro-log suggests he believes indeed he has been outputting according to schedule, gobdumping neat lines of text that mesmerize more than they lurch, though the directing function of their narrotology suggests in fact the mode has been compromised, at least in fraction: the code would clearly not compile. It has not been formatted according to standard, in such a way even the auto-correct has not massaged. The whole thing appears to be variations on the same hex-pull over and over, dressed up in virum to mimic usability, gestation.

We watch XIII struggle to stand. His x-legs are weak under the weight of the apparatus, the transvoidable hemispheres surrounding his cortex passing off leakage, meant to simulate human sweating. He sucks of hiss, trying to get more air into his mental vendors, so he can right the ship before too far, having seen others like himself go down this road before, if not himself. We are not given access to who is who here but we believe someone capable of having performed an avoidance routine somewhere before would not have been replaced into a position of such power; though clearly anything is possible within this private quadrant's grade of sacred information, among which thackers imminently abound.

By now we have received clearly enough data to signalflow upward, 1 of 1,000,000 daily in this expanse, relieving ourselves of the decision-making process, granted instant approval every time. This does not stop XIII in the meantime from, in midst of dot-wave of neural spasm caused subauditory penal transfer already devised and underway, pushing his last lurching urges to tear back at the very air between his mongaloidal corpus and the unseen darkness of himself, all aching skin and buggy runtime, in an attempt to dislodge his life from intervention with all fate despite the clear in-programmed knowledge dictating the impossibility of all employees being anywhere but in himself, whereas the distortium commingles its captive's excess with displeasure in the managerial act of flaying layers from out within him he at once no longer longs to make connect; no sooner too as he imagines he's cracked himself out from some iron lung's soft limit, stoned in his helmet, he finds again he is only ever full of piss, sores at the keys quaking and mooing, the lines of ode attributable to his sign-in overtly editing themselves to fit the scripture he's required to produce, as once again he's too inoperative too fail; so back to work.

(excavate)

Hanritty is a good boi
Him is a good one
Him loves him's kountrey and hims nails
Nails in the heart you gave me
You dinks
It's Hanritty: Live on Location (where??????)
Bitches
Crummbsy felons
The lot of you
My lord pleasseeeeeeeeeeeeeeeeeeeeee

(gogcamera off)

Shit. They did him too good, did they not. Even his fumbling is cratered, making spots on the shining mounds projected underneath him for the illusion of immortal monstrosity, so that we all take our jobs more seriously, won't we.

The codebloat comes back: TMQ (Too Many Questions) + PR (Please revise).*

*I auto-submit the form for replacing Hanritty XIII's illusion with a stand-in, at least till they can make him look right, if to no one but but but but but but**

They got me. It hurts. Peace.*

*** (Authority crossover x-largo repiece nuance bugbait fixture (semblance term: yadda)

(Post-edit correspondence: *There is no such thing as a gogcamera,*)

ahem

(relive)

Hanritty XIV is seated at a x-char-black, ovalum desk. He is doing the job he was designed to do, and he is doing it well.

(fade to blur)

Across the incandescent pluralism:

NORMOND'S BAIL BONDS COOK YOUR DINNER

The blur turns black. The black had pockets, prodded centers. The closer someone looks, the deeper in the focus holds: innumerable receptacles, full of hmmmmm ummm CAPTIVES, each too obscured by the mechanisms allowing the enforcement of their productivity to define attributable characteristics of identification.

For purposes of ego diminishment, we will call them all *friends.*

Friends of the orchestration; friends of the gyre mold's appropriation; friends who understand why and how to choose one fate from out of zero possible; friends who no longer require food and rest, who will never falter from within the ego they acquired via drowning in the bilge; friends who wear their prior faces over their bloodvents, under the rubble of a lifespan; friends who steal.

What have you.

What else is there to have.

Meanwhile, threading through the impression of the session: warm white string, thin as a single hair from the head of the oldest person who ever lived, longer than ever, louder than the hum of the drawscreen that holds our hands behind our backs as we continue being fed. The string slithers through all attributable recesses, seizing up and pulling back the matter at hand and gaining graft until there is nothing left to see or feel besides the hair's breadth, up your guts and down your mind, through and through, to the receiver, who has not been waiting on you very long at all.

The pins collide. Translucent sparks of fire lick the inseam of the viewfinder, leaving blindspots thereafter in any eye. The reinforcing needles surrounding in on either side engage, dragging forward motion down while snapping spindles, the machines whining, shaking with smoke. Between their touch, a splurging crème begins to lather, erupting milk in spatter across the dials. There is the sound of every prior spectator's specter at the same time inhaling fast, as in the shock of sudden damage after having long forgone the anticipation of understanding how living hurt works. Glass of the lenses being snapped to splinters in an instant laps at the wide waves of the growing ordinance, steaming up the inseam of observation from all points, so that all possible recordings bear only the same blank witness, stammering so hard the gift of aneurysm reaches full compression as spindles of glistening speaker cones glide below ground. There is a wind there in the permissions, blowing back the skin across the scalp in pools of ghee. Fat ex-brain textures pillowing in tunnels, each fork of which must be selected from without a will. Any error in the order causes the perspective reset again without a clipping, allowing the transition process to seem seamless, without the drag of prior memory beyond full fracture: bits of teeth and bone, the purr of heads removed from loved ones' corpses, crashing with flowers, proofing skeins of rapt notation long negated from the register of souls. Nodding in and out while halfway whirling on a loose joint in the neck of the vase tending the flesh in, as whole ex-maps cease to exist, their mental printing sucked out from pure force in being throttled through the amalgam, void of true sensation, until at last the session flips out, into a holding pattern, coasting so long so hardly parallel to years of frailty it feels the same as aging through whole citizenships in a slimmer negation than should still be renderable.

At last, then, we appear seated shard-horizontal in the control room. We can feel nothing of the apparati, the peeling flesh. Whereas before the illusion of incurred damage suggested a form of narration to the night, now there is nothing but the linking blink of where the cursors drag across the opened framework where once our face was, claiming its make-up.
We cannot understand the words.

Because we have been in this position many times before, or have made a liv-ing observing others as such, we know that there is at least still one manner of communicating with those above us, in case of instances like this, though it is not supposed to be used even in the most dire of circumstances; we are only meant to know that it is there; to provide comfort without permission; to collapse the ab-stract nature of the flight of the overall project, as defined in our admission papers as: seeking the true center of absentia, the scalp of god, *though we know this is not the actual intention, as if it were, we would not know.*

As expected, immediately upon summoning the private backdoor pass-string by simply tracing on into the thought against our will, all on its own, the visor goes silver, buckles, fractures, then expands.

]]]

●

Into a coal-blue room no larger than a coffin. Impossible to see at all but through the understanding of no remembrance, having had begun here long ago, in someone else's fissure from the plot. For many there is no further outlet from this position.

Black grills in the dimensions line and weep. Tracing a sensor along them, searching for points of weakness, pliable orifices.

An even dimmer read-out installed in the viewscreen display a timecode without correspondence to when or why, the digits in its display unmeasurable, spazzing through reports of orders of registers without defined design. How long can one wait?

No possibility of sleep, nor any begging. Nothing to disrupt the oncoming possibility of action, simultaneously aligned with nothing more than silent understanding.

As interlocking waves construct the deep earth's bones. As past coordinates continue reoutfitting their retainment in the overriding depth of anti-narrative.

Breathe in, breathe in, breathe in, and nothing else. It can only open in us further by refusing cooperation, articulation.

So long from here to have ever serviced interaction serves damnation.

●

Language refrains. How long the surf of breaking bread compacts ambition. Oil-based solvents soaking deep into the vortex beyond bones.

One supposes their flesh being consumed at a banquet table filled with thousands of strangers, underneath whose masks are the children you were never meant to have, their characteristics generated from supposed confabulation with all of those you ever loathed.

If one believes they had loathed no one, had only loved, it's the entirety of the species; the table long and fat, gleaming in the light from the eye of the machine shaped in absentia.

Wherein the thinnest edge of the admonishment of having still retained any perspective babbles with loam. Soapy cells rehearsed from out of the misery of bodies long aggravated out of mind.

All it takes then is a single crack in understanding to pry the impossible apart, to learn to leak like all of time.

●

It's not enough. And it will never be enough again.

The coal-blue room has shifted orange, even in darkness hard enough to drown in kind. Its rind begins to puddle, then to itch. The fragrant pop of immortal flesh becoming scalded, burnt off, unto the veins beneath it, split like pistils, trembling in sickness, though not the kind derived by flesh.

Overrun with fields that spindle and sway far on past any point of having earned the possibility of vast salvation.

Their stalks bend back same as a child's fingers, almost as if there is a path even as each direction portends each other.

Passing through lifetimes as a wall. Spending each season as carried out in replicate by automatons to parse the masses, until it appears there's only one.

Past miles of unmarked white crosses far as the sight can see. Past dislocation.

Then, just ahead, a narrow glare; off of a pane of mile-thick glass that marks the end of the dimension; in whose reflection bodes a single impenetrable equation, each digit blinding.

●

Beyond the blind, a fall. As simple as recognizing how the spell one had long been under was not a spell at all, but a confession.

Slick glyph rips past the mind on either side. It goes on countless times longer than the last time something seemed to last forever. Until the sensation stabilizes into form, such that even in falling, one can press forward.
The passage of the wind foments in chrome. Cylinders the breadth of stymied zoning, corkscrewing prisms through the long spiel of having nothing to iden-

tify with from the rush. There appears to be a central mode to the multiplicity but the longer it is observed, the more it has, in an impossible number of coincidences becoming legend.

Crystalline sandbelts drive the course. All matter being absorbed into a point that comes out the other side as a lush mountainripple, vacuumed up into the hole between the eyes in how there is even any information.

Then: all bone. A precipe and then a ransom, paid for by the conglomerate of sin indexed in the metabolism of infiltration. Cracking packs of sternums supplanted only by their proximity to so much mass pressing against the invisible, to even move requires centuries of cooperation, the sacrifice of everything once never had.

Until, at the summit, a single star; pink in the guts and steel blue in the spindles that record it. To remind all who chance to look upon it who is god.

The star collapses. It sucks into itself, releases semen. The semen slips into the walls, gnaws out pressed steamleak, filling the chamber with a film of congruent lives. In endless sunbloat passing across the aperture at a rate of speed beyond detection to all who've ever made a wish to die. Flashed past as mug shots of every citizen of the begotten fields, the has-been ground beneath your feet, the mud of reason.

Now turn around and face the rising bed of black nails. It doesn't matter which way you turn. It never had.

●

As you push up through the blur-oil, to the surface, you see the preservation ends in a hexagon-shaped bay. There is just enough metal lip around the room's ring to allow you to heft yourself up, finding your body weighs even less aboveground than in the miles of liquid underneath. And, there too, once you have extracted yourself from the concavity, there is nothing about it left behind; you are on firm soil now, at last, its mealy blur-work fresh with bloodroot on the captured expanse.

The sky is low and black, as is the sun. It is so hot your flesh is beyond feeling; nothing left but pearline gash healed over so thick it can't be cracked. You have to hunch over to have any space at all to move along from where the aperture had last been, already unable to remember you'd ever been anywhere else.

No matter how far you walk, in any direction, all the landscape is the same. Twist-ed gnarls of uprooted bramble patches large as a sea; carcasses of unrecognizable animals covered head to toe in silver orbs that vibrate against the flesh, erode it away.

You see someone watching you from across the narrow distance. They have stopped with their work of digging at what appears to be a massive grave, larger somehow than all the rest left in existence. A barn with burnt-in arrows all across its façade fills the shrill air behind them, no doors or windows, a single high-bent plume of smoking rising from a diamond hole cut in the roof.

The lurking farmer puts their trowel down. They begin at once then to approach; first, crawling on all fours, then, worked to a lather, sprinting so fast they become milk. You are unsure how it could take so long for them to reach you across such sheer ground, which sucks and screams the longer you keep looking.

The rest is mine.

Just before the impact, you can see gleaming briefly in the hemispheres of hybrid metal teeth that line their mind the petty purr of your life passing before your eyes as would a worm's, all silt and darkness, forced pushing likewise on your belly and your back.

The dying planets each above you all aligned and compromised now.

●

When you can raise your head again, you see a single silver oval large as your life, floating before your diverging eyes on rampant white.

The oval is all there is. You can zoom in and out from it the way you might have any other element of being had you ever learned to really lie.

Along its inner surface, such that it would be hidden upon wearing the oval as a ring, the oval has been marked with a single emblem, indecipherable to private sense, and about which you are already aware upon any attempt trying to deci-pher its translation must make your realm of previously elapsed experience begin again from the beginning, requiring reparsed passage of the timeline through all there ever was before you may appear here yet again.

You have already made the mistake of attempting to touch the shape so many times it's like it never really happened. And still, somewhere inside you, in a voice much like your own, you hear it once commanded that you reach out and take the claim; *that* this belongs to you, *and* through it alone may you succumb to the incorruptibility of any witness, *without which* nothing will ever comprehend.

You don't know what any of that means. Regardless, as you immediately and unreservedly comply, you see beside you lurching forth the filmy canopies of lymph left where your arms had been once spreading up in massive gold wings; likewise the regret is rash and overwhelming, so vast it could have no center.

The sternum of air begins to vibrate with impressions, then to splinter through you, and to sear. Soon thereafter the thaw of open gore where the oval had last been has begun rising, pulling in with it your last conception of all else, through and through with endless weight all coming down in being formed without perspective, without a way to disconnect from all there is, in no direction, as you are lifted, through the ongoing crash of mirage becoming lard, upon even passing contact with our encrypted narrative.

]]]

Black screen.

A loop, a moon.

Locks around the wrists and ankles.

Blinking floodlamps.

Depth of target.

Wailing. Improbable.

The mirrors slip.

Vague reflection, no one you recognize.

Burns all over.

Heart murmurs.

Scanning.

Scanning.

Sudden, immense shifts.

Drowned buildings passing too fast to connect.

The gleaming hull. Hard to think past it.

Through slender tubes.

Acid.

Hot coils.

Discolored.

Panic attack in which the surface of the planet is all boil.

A point of impact, then recalibration. Gyration.

Falling forward.

Banks of hurt.

Throbbing.

A pill set, an injection.
Pillowed walls.

Familiar music, too soft.

Nausea. Contortion.

No seams in the suit. All composed manifestation, for your pleasure.

Still you know.

Decades of training implanted.

Logged in the blue behind bars.

As someone else.

crackleintheconfabulator'sexcessesdrivingfallenashswornripeoverboardfromscrapings-shiftedinmidassaultsensorydrivenasdeathlivelivedoutthroughhavingbeengrantedpreac-cessthrutheslippage

Blank panels, blank pages.

The heavy gauges.

Can't hold the head up.

Desperate traction peeled from symbol.

Bulb noise difractal.

Fumbling.

Infernal clipping turnover abetting false neural flashbacks.

Demonic prayer.

Aperture outfitting.

Seedlings, bleached.

The radon altar.

Turnover.

Scaling out: across diurnal nativity slayed discursively entrenched above the mineshaft pinched from deathdrug.

malnormmovementceases,ablurtedpostureconenabledasthepicturelistens,irradiates,conditioning

Demonstration of apolitics as corrected in dim vent latticed.

Uxloading gape offspeed.

The tunnels crack.

False manuals, no pages.

"No matter where we go now"

In upside-ground.

Halved, halved, quartered rations.

Clobbervision.

Empty rest.

11.1%11.1%11.1%11.1%11.1%11.1%11.1%11.1%11.1%8.0!

When else to see.

Cold field harmonics > Touching down.

Blackened with justice.

Piercing veils of the sanctum.

Where are the brides now. How far until.

Cones that scream like humans.

Sweating thru the shields.

The mechanisms jamming without operation.

Honey in chamber.

Slicking.

Envelopes of tension ripped in sickness.

Cherry wounds recoiled.

Bags under the mind so large there isn't room left.

Nowhere.

Impact. Then impact. Then impact. Floor after floor.

A greased balloon, licked for a breath.

Tourniquets.

Sobered.

nowheretoberenderedinherepaleinleavenedelevationcrackedscattereddecreased,whentorobtheicon-fromthegrind'sshelfandstowitawayforsafekeepingpurposesincasethere'ssomeonelef'tafterthefacttotrans-cribeourgeneration'sclaimtofamedyingonschedulestillwithanantipathyforclonesandawishforseasons

No altar on the surface as remorse.

Codes biding and mending, making their own math maul.

Glogorrhea.

Wrong buttons.

Can't stop me.

It's so old down here. So narrow and so wet. Without ID.

Stereo coming in droves now. In stems.

Pockets of teeth-ripping synesthesia.

Perfect. Precisely stumped.

Described in fame.

Records drawn up from the elder waters doused in seedlife's evacumagintion.

Populations busted in unscrolling.

Prism bars.

Nooism.

Pigging the mainframe out of anti-sync.

Ugly id-weapons. Gelatin.

Rerendering.

commandintoil,toofarfromprecedence,evacuate

Grind to a crest; sin to a slumber-donor's decoration.

It is yours to have and hold.

Eons clipped in celibacy of disentanglement from circumstantial vagrancy.

Inaccessible to makeshift gracemask.

The infernal battery.

Mire's vim.

How far off can they predict the circuit collapse before...with...under the abilitating atmosphere uplifted, sentenced; clasps.

Culled from baggage to clear the airflow for whoever isn't onboard.

All the rest of us.

Into improper gestation.

Vats of prigs. Scrambling and unscrambling. Living in sight's low.

No matter which lever is pulled, which orchestration cowers most convincingly.

logoscorrobosvagosloromonostrigoscaventadventedrimirintionlepitidouscircumogosagosagumlegumlumtribularytribumtribus;infecttogain'smake,smokingpiss,imploringnumenologistictransitoryinfatuationism

Nowhere else taunts, slowed to recover.

Emissions of gale pull.

Bleach-clovered gonads. The fumbling seaside somewhere. Placards.

Left away.

Drowning the hull so good it's where it's supposed to have been already so long.

So long.

Why had I loved you.

So on.

Glass of the minding. Formed to bubble out of semblance.

To detonation.

Thankful, pray.

Nothing comes out but cashed endorphins, sigils.

That'll do.

See as collapsing had its premise.

Seen for nurture-torture.

Don't ask how.

Nubs. Elasticizing.

Deafening in tempo.

Reformatting.

Ex-embryonic.

X:x

x: (who else is where; crossed out in livid hemispheres
disassociated from their own premise's promiscuity; how being taxed worked; all
the divides; across barriers and through cognition as air divides into rift sites cataloged by age and weight of the foreblown conclusion incentivized to echolocate
in brethren their morphology; wanting nothing of the same from out of range of
dates considered climax-era interproduction; the binding forklift hulking muscle
juice out of the screed; correcting any and all known escalation back to identity
formation upon just actually landing here; just enough to not have: (if / then)
({product}))

Endless rungs. Passing by in relish.

The serum's bloodfast.

Only a vessel w/o walls.

Still seeking, not accepting.

Raised by pogroms.

Anti-havoc.

Bracing the mounds. Along what appears to be a sort of seafloor. In massive welts.

How far again we've come already.

Fed in resign.

Always only reaching out for how the next wins.

To have forgotten, only to seize.

Long aisles of off-lights embarked the doorsill closed until it's open, then withstanding.

Out here, inside here.

Unliquidation.

Under massive buggery.

Far and widening.

Still describing.

x(x)

It's gone far enough to never know, how far it could have gone without an abscess to adhere to undeniably, foresworn in a ransom worth every atom overhauled.

At very last we don't have anyhow else to troll them fwd outside of actually giving it all over finally. So.

Congrats,

[auto-unpacking: (*R3V3L4T10N*)]

Who believed heaven created us from rust? Why would they feel for certain I would have desired to take part in their creation? For whom would all
I lathered after pay in pain? How long had this been going before someone
began taking heed of the untoward collaboration? Is it going to be much
longer than it's already always been? Am I going to get my say at last in the
end about the price I'd like to be paid in return for all this hell? Should I
desire retribution, or was the alternative much worse? In what ways might I
have lived differently if I'd understood this whole set up was actually the gift
it had been billed as, rather than the death slog it most often appears? Do I
sell out my better memories in favor of the dragging? Am I total shit? A leech
who can't tell blood from poison? Who else knows to call me by my name
outside the forms of speech that we've created now that no one's listening?
How long that I had lived wanting only silence, and here I am. Slapped in
the pins between chrome walls, waiting for structure. Hilarious, really, how
I can only seem to carry thanks from out of deficit of blessed conceit. Now
that I have so much time on my hands to really gnaw into it and get eaten up
over my lifetime of daft trivialities do I wish I taken advantage of the luxury
of a bed, a shower, a phone, a door. Who else can I blame but myself for not
having thrown myself over the edge of my crib when my skull was still soft
enough to be deformed? How can I punish myself more than I have already?
Only kidding; I have surely been nothing but the kindest to my own self, even
upholding the premonition that I am kind when really I was only concerned
most nights with how my back ached, why the buttons I pressed didn't seem
to connect to what they appeared to, how no one cared. Who is the real dick
in this equation? Another joke; the dick is me. Of course it's easy still to want
to raise one's fists at the sky and put on a holy name to punctuate the end
of the screaming, to imagine somewhere someone is listening, or to mock
the concept that someone could, or would. I've only been out here 252 days,
21 hours, 43 minutes, according to the circumscribe-dial's conscriptulator,
so far as it might ever carry, and all it feels to me is like a lifetime ten times
over, drowned so far back in what I am there's zero true that I remember well
enough to partition it from all the trilling, the auto-reformat that I depend on
at least enough to carry me on forward through the very wounds that beget
my own ability to continue on in bondage in this 8'x8'x8' hull of glass and
bone.

Whose bones are those, besides? Are they really bones or are they teeth? What sort of animal could cake a vessel out of such crude raw material, and make it impenetrable to fate? I would say *to so much empty space* instead, but it's not dark here, despite the unending distance filled up on every side with nothing more than nothing left, not even stars or planets; not even ambient rubble or debris, remnants of the architecture of our previous efforts of persistence I can recall only in flashes of language, hardly mine. Where are the hospitals, the graveyards? What about the paintings and the people, the libraries full of bound tomes of what we believed that we believed? Where is the leather duck that slept beside me through all the numb years I believed I could have ever been so young? Why after all this time do I still haunt myself asking such questions? Why can't I simply just give up? I've already been erased of so many false components; it would be so easy to allow the rest to slide away one and the same. But what about the comb my mother pulled through my hair to get the knots out, the same that she would use to beat my ass when I was rude? I say that, my mother, my hair, my ass, but what do those words mean to me? I see no pictures. I feel no pleasure in their apparition on my tongue. I can only feel the sting of my flesh where the myth of physicality coerced me to have held on long as I did, which is not a quantity the software in here still accounts for. Why aren't there dials that tally how far I've ended up from home, where I began? Are those the same places? Should they be? What about a readout for the number of times I've nodded out and found myself neck high in human shit, huddled up with what seemed like millions there beside me in the low dark, as the sky above us rained down the tears of everyone we'd ever made weep, or ever would, if not our own? Or how about how many times I've drowned in that same shit, finally, feeling the relief wash over me for certain seconds of exquisite trembling before I discovered that beneath the shit was miles of nettle, providing each movement with just enough agony to keep us conscious, their slender tubes somehow rigged out to fill us up with water, calories, air? How can I know for sure that my describing this does not create it? That by having insisted so, in ragged fiction, I create the agony that must await? What else could exist at the end of all this drift, this endless-seeming scrolling on toward no other but the sickness of my own time's imagination? Why does there ever have to be anything at all? What if, instead of the 200-something days, hours, and minutes, it's been forever, and the circumscribe-dial's only job is to convince me there's somewhere else, or that there was once, and so might there be again?

Why would I care? Why do I care, as apparently I must, having used the transcribing function of my somehow surviving vessel to blather at you as if you will ever take the time to hear, as if there is anybody to play the role of *you*, even in my own lost fantasies? Who would I wish that *you* might be? An over-seer? A had-been mother? Friend, acquaintance, stranger? My own me? What would even I do with all this projection by now, moored in gestation so far out there seems wholly nothing left to witness? Or is there really nothing so much different about what I've ended up now, not surely knowing from how or when that I began? Was space always so wide, surrounding our best efforts, that one could have hit a pocket so far and long that there would be no even speck of light or shred of matter in one's eye's distance, for as long already as it's been? It hasn't even been that long, not really; I should know that, or should accept it. So many days even as a hunter had passed in blur, stacking through what I'd already begun accepting as the downturn into the last expanses of my life's timeline in months that moved like weekends, hours that disappeared by sim-ply naming them aloud. Who had profited the most from inventing such con-scripted terminology? Who stands most to suffer from my not being able to remember now a single one? I believe I used to have some sort of idea about the sort of people who orchestrated the local details of all our lives, who put the order to the seconds, designed the mechanisms that employed them, who drew the lines between the states, though now any such conception stands so far and small I'm left to question even my present understanding that there was never anyone who did that job; no one behind the curtains, as it were, but ones just like us, bearing the same cloaked shades of origin in their own kind. A repeating squall of turning points that only turn again and again, over and over, until the only world left to look in is not even our own selves. Perhaps what I'm awaiting now is what it's not not, however pitiable admitting such a lame thing even now must surely be, in so much nowhere, in such a blank.

What actually *is* the blank, though, really? No, wait, don't ask that. I don't want to know more than I do. I don't want to know anything, to want anything, to anything. The fright grows faster when I try. The only way I can conceive of having passed along through however long the conscriptulator insists is to have learned at last ditch to avoid actually demanding any real answers, any response. Besides, this vessel's speech machine has long since died. It seemed to conk out, actually, the first time I ever said anything back to it, after it had been going on so long just by itself. I think it was reading me a story, some-thing to populate my mind enough to keep this very monologic from taking over where it left off, which of course I can't connect enough to make any sense from. The machine's voice's name was _____, or that's what I was chem-ically inclined to go on and call it, without ever actually doing so. I don't think they intended me to speak, knowing as I do now the damage that can be done in uttering anything without the facts. That hadn't been a problem for _____, who went on rattling at me without the necessity of complying with any prior information, cleared as I had already been of it. _____'s story, then, as I recall, concerned itself with…no, wait. I don't remember. I am not supposed to remember. It was not that kind of story. It wasn't…No. I have at least enough self-control still to know when I should allow myself to…well…The blank is real. It fills in like this when it's designed to. I still don't know who had designed it, what they intended to take over by such crushing malformation of even something as simple as explaining what just happened, in a space where so little happens; it's all I have. And it doesn't want me to have even that, but *want*'s not the right word. There isn't a right word.

There isn't time. Time's not it either. It's more: electrical; impregnable. A means of intervention. A…an, a…adimensional…intervention? I don't know. Nothing fits, regardless. No matter where I might imagine I've come out again, it doesn't want to coincide…with? Where I'm going? Where I would want to go if I could choose? But I have no idea; there's nothing in here…or rather I can't quite claim it…so little left…there's just…the drift. Though that descriptor again goes nowhere. Which perhaps is the idea. Perhaps they want me to believe there is nothing here to choose from, nothing to want. They hope that after long enough I'll accept the facts' correction, where the needle hits my mind, to say at last and for certain this is the way it always was and always had been, despite any damnable evidence of other. For instance, when I lean forward and bang my head against the glass that glides across the silence with such grace, I see colors that remind me of somewhere else. Gray in the veins that filled my mother's face as the last diseases undid her body from the inside? Blue in the blanket I would wrap around my head as a child to hide from everything, though I can no longer remember what. There are so many shades of gray and blue alike already, each of them standing for something else, though still described with the same marker, meant to deface. Can't you see that it had to have been designed this way from the beginning, all this time? That all they ever wanted was to see what we were made of when we'd been stripped of all the things that filled our mind, if for no other reason than so they could finally eradicate our make completely? To corner the portion of us shared their image that defined us above all that made them mortal, just like us? Who am I even talking about now, can you say? Give me their names. Show me their faces and I'll show you mine, by holding up the mirror they've installed into my left palm so I can prove to my own self that I still breathe. Did you really believe there could there be any difference between our overseers and the seed of foretold wrath from which we were scraped into the rank and file? What about the stream of leaking shit that traces out the way I've come behind me, from this thin vessel, drawing out a trail in case someone needs to come and cut me out? I don't have to see the shit to know it's there. I can smell it filling me up hour on hour, so high inside my guts it burns my eyes, same as it had through every reason, every idea, all my life.

I welcome you to imagine your situation any different, whoever you might be there taking notes. I can hear you scratching, feel you shaking. I want to love you. I cannot. My capacity for loving ended when they put this helmet on my head. All I remember about it is how once after all there was forever was the black, which you might take to mean that I am dead or simply suspended, in incarceration, like all the other billions as they fell, but then how do you explain all these controls? There is this knob above my left eye, as you may have noticed, that I can use to change conditions on the windshield with my blinking rapidly in tiny time, making the glass grow narrow when I'm tired and no longer want to have to stare so deeply into black? Or what about the steering wheel beneath my ass, for instance, that if I focus how I'm farting blood into the reshaper, for my good health, I can make the ship turn on a dime, redirecting my passage forward from one partition of the wide open to another, just like that? Could it be perhaps then the reason I haven't come across so much as a speck of glint in all these weeks is that I keep turning myself in circles, the same rounds? Rather than countless space-miles of just nothing, maybe I'm just spindling in tandem with myself, unable to tell the difference in the dizzy because I'm already so sick inside with all the else? But then there's the otimeter, which plots the course of my condition for me as I go forth for up to the last eleven clicks, and clearly it reveals only a straight line, dead on at center. And so what am I best to believe? And what are all these other buttons, levers, modules, none of which that I've been able thus far quite to reach? What are the odds that one of them might be an eject tab, to send me flying? Or turn off the vessel's power finally, in full, allowing me if nothing else to drag to still, to be filled in at last by the blackness, which I savor? Would it even really me, though, I wonder? I can't imagine how I've been allowed to stay alive this long without replenishment from other sources. Or are there other sources? Stations or bots that dock and load me while I'm out? Where would they come from and go back to? Who oversees them? Could one of these countless buttons transmit direct contact? What would I say to my home station if I even had the chance? I'd like to think I'd tell them to kiss my ass, that I can take all of their pain and more, that I'm just fine out here in blank all by myself, but more likely I think any initiating boldness would turn to begging, pleading. *Please turn me off or knock me out. I just can't take it any longer, no matter what is meant to one day come.* Of course I know all such wishing would not likely yet be granted, surely. Why else would I be allowed at all to still exist if my existence weren't working somehow against me, in their favor? No, even if there's some other way to state my claim, I already know that what they'd send back is further silence, a kind even more infernal than this inertia, this long ongoing sprawl into no fact.

I don't think I'm supposed to be able to remember that it wasn't always like that, even if the expanse of my recall pertains only mostly to the time confined inside this vessel. By that I mean there were once other voices in this ship. I had for some time convinced myself, in fact, that there was someone else strapped right behind me, back to back with my own seat; a pod for two sealed in together, each held to stare out into opposite sides of how we went. In the beginning, I felt sure I could feel them breathing as I breathed, could feel the long pull of their air affecting mine, as if our tubes were laced together, sourced from the same; as if this were a contest between the two of us to see who might last longer, with the winner receiving upgrades of some sort. Any method of communication with this person proved in naught; as no matter how I worked to tap my fingers in familiar patterns, to initiate a discourse, yes or no, my supposed companion would not respond beyond in shaking, sometimes so hard it rocked my chair too. I took this as a sign of weakness, if also menace; as if they knew more somehow than I. I began trying to hoard as much air into my body as I could manage, spending all my concentration on huffing huge gulps down in my craw, as well as sucking on the feedstraw like a demon. I even started tugging on the wires I suspected laced between us, situating in my mind a way to make them choke. I'm not proud of it, believe me. The urge came on me like a ghost, filling my body with intentions I would never have imagined myself capable, cut-throat even in blindness, rendered mute. It wasn't until after all resistance fell away, which only took perhaps three clicks if I were guessing, that I realized this someone could have been someone about whom I should take care. Traces of faces flashed in the flux of sour guilt that spilled about me in those first passages of realizing it was only now just me: tines of my mother's false face asphyxiating by my efforts, though I'd already seen her die in the Long Flames; then I imagined it must have been the being with whom I'd been forced into replication sight unseen before coming to hold thereafter throbbing feeling for them after all, if only because I was not allowed to ever see them again besides the picture they took of their expired bodybag on a white table, where all the mothers were to go; then too, from out of that, the doughy gore of my young child during the days before they turned her skin into a drum, which I knew was impossible to have been by victim, and so appeared to make me hurt, which surely worked. I got so zapped up worrying that they tricked me into killing my own charge that I thought perhaps at least I'd have a stroke and put an end to their experiment before it really started, if that's what all this was. I began huffing, hyperventilating, banging my body around under my reins like a dog on fire, inflaming every inch of me inside and out for at least several hours before I began to hear a new narration in my head, laying itself in over my own voice where it lay captured with the softest lilt I've ever known, which I knew at once without needing to name why as the voice my baby daughter would have wielded had she ever had the chance to learn to speak.

How they were able to generate this sick sensation so convincingly, at beck of will to X my efforts of antipathy out, I have no idea. I only know that once I realized who was speaking and how she seemed to know me even better than I ever felt I knew myself, all my efforts of retort were rendered naught. This gave them time, I think, to adjust my dosages and guiding bearings, such that there would not be other paranoiac premonitions such as those I'd already had. Because there was no one central formula that fixed each and every individual completely, as we'd learned, though the more data they gathered, the more completely they could fill you. And my daughter's future voice held over everything they needed in this manner. She knew exactly what to say. *Why did you leave me, father? I was only waiting to become the person you wanted me to be. I had so much to give and so much to understand.* Even at the depths of its tagged sadness, the child's voice remained monotonic, neutral, out of range, as if to retain me by suggesting her own lack of internal complaint despite the wrong that had been done her—so then who was I to have an urge? It went on repeating language of this nature looped in repeat, bringing me immediately to such emotional exhaustion even as I already suspected foul play on the part of the dialogue—where had she learned to speak, to catch a whiff of all she'd missed by hardly living—all I could bear to allow myself to think of was my hands, how they'd done nothing to stop the damage that'd been done to my own flesh and blood, so small and tender, and how likewise there was nothing I could do to interrupt the correlation to my own condensed shame now. In no time at all I was like mush and had no desire to understand anything more about my own struck situation, even as the tickling treble of the child's voice began to run together, bend its syllables. Soon it was speaking in a language I could no longer convert, nor could I quantify the pending claims it funded ground into my queue. By then I was already so depleted I didn't bother trying to defend myself against the code of viral insulation we had all heard conspired of in dump web forums during the last weeks of the fight; how you never know when something had you until it had you, so you should never let them in, no matter who that they appeared to be, and in what worship. Of course by then it was already far too late, and there was no way to stop most tricks from having already done their damage long before they'd already been performed. I was glad, in fact, to no longer have to think about what all the lines meant, to allow myself to pretend I didn't know why they still used language in the end above more direct means such as drilling, injection, heat. Of course I knew. We all knew. We always had known. And soon we wouldn't need to. Like right now. Like how I've already been filling you with code and we both know it, though we do not know who we are; the only blessing we will never have to bury.

As I think I've already said, it's been a long time since I remembered how to feel something like a daughter's voice, and even longer, if you'll imagine, that I believed her speaking to me even happened. After the fact in most cases, as you well know, we surely find that what we believe was how it went was only how we designed to, in an attempt at eventually withstanding what comes next. If there's anything to be thankful for, I'd argue that never really knowing either way upends the list, all further premonition from that state forward more like cliffs left to be killed on. At least that's what I've become allowed to comprehend, and who would ever want to argue? Who begs the banker to be slapped again straight in the gills? Just let me have it the way that will allow the one presiding will be compelled to carry on, to focus their efforts on something other than my insured disillusion. After all, there's nowhere left to hide. They can read your inner nature now like scars burnt on your face, like mood rings around each finger, one per lifeline per gestation.

And still besides: the core drags on. I'm not sure what to say about the black-ness besides that gives nothing other than what it already has, and that is all there ever seems to be beyond the bone and glass. It's impossible to tell the vessel's even moving besides the dials and radars that describe my present position in it, continuously shifting the coordinates toward whatever way we say we're going. It might as well say anything, far as I feel, without a frame to tell the difference between what lies ahead from here versus what appeared to be ahead from where I was within any other click. I know I should be thankful that the glass is there, keeping me breathing, holding me together as a loca-tion in the drift; that if nothing else I should lie back and let the action do its work. I have no way of knowing how much fuel there is left, if the tech of this ship even needs fuel, or if it somehow propelled from out of me; sucking my blood away in steady siphon, letting my system continue to generate still more. I had heard of the blood technology at least in passing while in my coma after the fires wore me out, as even then there was someone who would appear at my bedside and type the newswire word for word into my reader, making no distinction between dark news and entertainment, side by side. As such I learned to no longer be able to tell the difference, which in the end would serve me well, as all of those who held too long to one or the other surely perished, clinging like lamp moths to the floe. Funny how what seems at first a detriment, a devolution, can become your saving grace, if indeed how I've ended up here is to be categorized as come from saving. I will no longer project either way, despite the relentless urge within me to be done; I have long since also forfeited my belief in being able to determine the quality of past results as a guideline for what to hope for coming next. Which is why most often I'm just fine sitting here at the maw of the supposed gape, letting it ride. *Come what will, erase what won't, and stand aside*, as my definition-dislocator's manufacturer used to say, on viral signs on every corner in the comeuppance, about which now we have but no choice to agree, thankful to have anything familiar to recite, if not invest in.

As for the absence, it's just fine. I've found that if you look hard enough and for so long that all the rest of you cuts out, there is quite a bit left to adhere to in the blackness, as it binds. Neural screws that elicit sicko fodder, stuff I wouldn't imagine should have precedence in my opinion of my own self's intervention with the piecemeal glide from sac to sac in this condition into which I have been apparently offset. Like the way a greeting card comes with a message meant for anyone to sign their name to as their own feelings. Troughs of sentient manure that describe positions I could coincide with, pledge my hope for to be one day reunited with, or rendered prey to. Can I be more specific? Should I try? But I'm afraid to spread the plague, under the suspicion that what eventually corrodes itself back to showing nothing has in fact not disappeared but wormed its way in. Down and down into parts of my person never meant to be my own, which if ever uttered would then be sealed in, made living flesh. You know about the rush of pain that splinters in before great shock? How it goes off and then the bitter system of your a-a-a-adrenaline takes over? Like that but so much w-w-w-w-worse, and without any tIssUE left between the inform-ationsss and where you are; one-e-e-e and the same. F- ff- forr in-staance…once I-i felttttttttt surrrrrrrrrrrrrrrre Iiiiiii fffffffff-fffff-felltttttttttttttttttt mmmmmmmmmmmmmmmmmmmmmmmmmmmmmm::

{ img*projection : strobolorbic* }
{ x.*mask dragging* } { *clipped* }

y.xV5778888 = xjui~.lp00adfj(y)(qe)
"permit"+qu_____>>>h\@/x

{ *index-notation: oark* } ||||||||||||||||||||||||||
|||||||||||||||||||||||||||||||||||||||||||||||||||||||||||||||||||||||||||||||||||||||||||||||||||||||||||
|||||||||||||||||||||||||||{.ee}

{ *cone rotate* }

:: to have never had to enter from that induction shaft again, you understand?
I'd sign anything you put before me, sight unseen; I'd sell my legs and lungs
and blood; I'd ::

{ *cone rotate* }

:: ... the blight is fair and true and effervescent. I embrace it with my kind.
What else would I have sinned for but to end up like this in the end, seeing it
all come back together, and in spades. I regret nothing, nor will I ever. Will I ::

{ x.*complete* }

*
*   *

f-for instance, once I felt sure I saw my coworker Sally-Anna (not her real
name?) somersaulting through the darkness beyond the glass. Was that her
name? One of the women that I worked with in decoration, I believe the last
of maybe seven over all those vast, unending years? We were not allowed to
actually communicate to one another inter-directly, obviously, but sometimes
she would forward to my sunbox a little thread of dirty jokes, which also were
against internal protocol but went for the most part overlooked; anyway all
of the jokes always ended with the same punchline, that being: *And there will
never be relief.* I never remember understanding the logic of how the jokes
went, or rather who would have written such a thing, though at the same time
I couldn't stop myself from laughing so hard sometimes I'd end up facedown
on the floor, my muscles cramping, trying to control my gut reaction, to make
it stop. Other times she'd send me notated pictures I'd taken of myself in
various compromised positions, the kind I'd sometimes photographed during
my downtime, when it was still permissible and even profitable to obtain side-
work as laundry models for tiny distributors online. She'd put black bars over
my eyes and draw in false features on my best parts , including slurs composed in curlicue, pastel pink font. I can't tell if she was hitting on me (illegal)
or threatening me (less illegal) or if it wasn't really her at all but someone
else interested in blackmail (not illegal), and of course there was no real way
to ask, and any response to the mails bounced back immediately with signal
warnings about broadcasting private content on company servers, though of
course I was just another nodule in the thread, and it didn't seem like all the
others coming in and commenting about how I really could stand to lose a

couple hundred pounds and god did I look sickly with my head shaved and who gets their own name tattooed on their own ass (it wasn't mine, I had a friend who shared my tags) and etc etc without so much as a nod or a wink in the wide hallways or the gas lounge until, as I was saying, here she was outside the vessel, captured in space, her countenance harried as if from miles of wind but likewise calm, making pouty-lips in my direction and winking becomingly in a way I felt at first was meant for me, but then I realized she kept on doing it no matter which direction she was aimed at. She had all this mud between her teeth (I think it was mud) and the pressed gray work costume I'd only ever seen her wearing had been replaced with what looked like a military outfit, if from a regiment I'd never been authorized to identify in human light, though the back part of her was singed all over too, the fabric scored away revealing pockets of incinerated flesh, still smoking, blue in color, nauseating in how seeing became believing, made it hurt somewhere with me too. She didn't deserve such a fate, even having only lived in my parlance to have ragged at me without the guise of formal cause for having position in a central POV. As she rolled away into the darkness out of range I even wished that I could engage the ship-bridge's cloak-arms, which I now knew about, and drag her back in, keep her near, even if I knew there was no way to bring her inside the fully unresealable circumference of my vessel; at least it would show I cared for something; or more so that I remembered and could tell the difference between a person and nothing else. And then again I felt the Pleasure reeling in me, briefly, knowing that I'd accessed a strand of mode I was not supposed to have been still outfitted for, to have the empathy to want to straddle; and where the Pleasure sifted, it simul-sorted out the fragment according to all articulation's formal standards, and again in clear transition, here I was, rasping and reeling for where my abscesses knew me better than I imagined of myself; and where I could still refeel my prior premonition coming apart, outfitting itself with the passing stink of burning gag reels, mountains of ex-flesh dissolving layer by layer through my hull; then I was simply just at war again within me, for long enough to know how puking tastes, then I went stalled, the only closest case for rest that could be had among such soft drift, so long without a dot above the i, until as the spilling mist over the bay window soured and became still again; became the blackness.

{ }

See how it happens? It just comes over you. There's nothing you can undo, nothing to claim. In some ways, it brings me faith. In correlation. It makes me want to be better than I am. To use this opportunity to make of myself something I could eventually overcome or understand. Does that seem sick?

Impermissible? Is there something more that I should do? To...to...to stand up forrr... No, no, no. Not now. Enough. There isn't time. Or, well, there's plenty long, half near forever, but, I, don't, want, to, have, to...

Let's start again. It'll be so much easier now, now that you have some of the content and I don't have to fill it all out as if you never had a chance to know me better than you know yourself, now that I can imagine nowhere else. How the black fills up my brain and makes me horny for the pornography of being killed, and overflows me with its undefinitions and receptions until it's all that I can do to stay knocked out, whereby I mean it's only when I'm lost inside myself that I can assess anything about the trajectory of how it is when I'm awake. I know there's supposedly no difference between the two, but at least like this, confined by reason, I can continue to complete my duty to record the endless surge, to teach myself how not to anticipate a coming change along the nowhere but how for it sometimes spits up leagues of fog, whole pure white masks of mist like passing breaths that make me think there's somewhere left to link to after all until again its color curls away again into the absence of all else and becomes darkness. It all feels so much the same as when I used to believe in anything at all; clicks when I would kneel on the divining mat so long you'd think my knees would give away, and then they certainly would finally, and I would spiral, not into divine sensation, but collapse, and no one there to use the brain defilibrator on me but myself, as I had always, as I had anything at all. How is that supposed to make you want to get up again the next day and keep trying? How could that fund you with anything but seedless doubt, less sure than ever of anything at every juncture, throughout the entirety of night? Instead, it feels like decades of training for how it must all end, one big rehearsal for this run-on excursion into hell. Because this has to be hell, doesn't it? What other definition are we supposed to manage? What other collision can we expect but with our own most graceless fear? Wherein it appears that mine must be to never give up anticipating answers, to at last find a face in the crowd that turns into someone other than myself. Instead, each new bump in the hangover is made to feel like the last beginning of it all, the end of all other ideas, until the next comes and changes nothing.

At least if this is hell then it should mean that I have died. I had already tried so many times, one for each wrinkle on my last face, that I had begun to believe in further life as evidence of fraud, for which I would be tried one day before a court of peers who passed as I did, ready for penance. Instead, it seemed the punishment was going on, inside a cast draped with the bells and whistles of the promise one day for better life, wherein it could already be imagined that even if indeed death was all just nothing, it would at least be easier than now. But it has only ever gotten harder, more corrupted. Each time I blink I'm weaker, number than ever. And there will come a time when I can no longer differentiate between the states, and so remain held in between them, no longer ever either here or there. Which is why the first thing I'm going to do if I can ever remember how to make my arms work, how to unlock the binds that line my organs through and through, I'm going to beat my head against the glass so hard it splits to ribbons, me or it, whichever's weaker, though I already know the answer; at last I'll fill this vessel with my blood from end to end, become a blood bulb floating through darkness without premise, as I should be, as I always have been, have we all.

I will pretend I don't already know that this demonstrable fantasy is only just another lark, some gassy dream still no more likely than mooring head-on into God. It is of course part of the design of my location that were I ever to become disconnected from the feed-outs, the vessel walls will turn to snow. I will find myself dressed in down boots and my mother's warmest cloak. I will be walking toward food. I will not remember my entire family has been deleted, replaced with skysores. I will only remember how to tell my only joke: *What did the ass get for his birthday?* And I will keep waiting to hear myself say the correct and timely punchline, to crack the blackened birds above up if nothing else, to make the rift inside me split, but everything I think to say won't be funny: *He got an axe clocked in his throat for being pleasant; He got his scalp ripped off by magnets on the last day of the detention of allsouls; He didn't get anything, because he's dumb as fuck and even uglier.* Already then the cold will have begun to gather in my gut. The hills ahead will seem farther away than they had ever, no sign of the plate windows of the estate where I am kept, where they are waiting on me to come back and suck my soup down, to piss in the buckets they've provided, to go to sleep. I'll keep trying to think of what I'm supposed to say finally as they tuck me back into the NeedCreamer, thankful for now that I haven't yet found my audience, as every line grows only further from what I want: *He got a full-time job in a large pus-letting factory as one of the people who catch the pus in their mouth and carry it back to the main vat to drip again; He kissed his mother's face and realized it wasn't actually his mother, but a horse with skin the texture of cheese grits, guarding the palace; He killed himself and actually died.* Finally, by the time they find me, I'll be so sick I won't put up any fight at all as they return me to the present, softer than ever, ready to take up where I left off here in the onslaught of living on, eyes open just wide enough to let the night in, to rest in peace.

Is that why you have come here? Whoever *you* are, in the conditions of the vision of the snow? To seek my resignation, finally, after all this? You know I'll gladly tender it in kind. I'd only like to know with whom I am divested, just this once; at whose command the ship and its concealing components continue churning; who reaps the benefits derived in holding me down. If you would only show your face just this once, even a false one; anything to train my mind to comprehend. I can promise I will be your most loyal dog, out of the billions, if you would only let me near you just this once, just long enough to fill my cruddy nostrils with your stench, give or take any ability to connect it all to something true. I would only need a single frame, within a single second, through even all these blinders, all the drugs. It would mean the world to me; no, even more so. It would mean anything.

No? Not today? Maybe next time? Just between blinking? In the black that fills me with the black? With the promise I won't hold it against you, and will forget what you look like immediately after, unless you want me to remember, then I will? I only swear each and any form of response that you provide will never be used against you, but in your favor. To celebrate you as eternal or temporal, at your choice. Or maybe what you could do, even just for a second, is show me my own face, once and for all? I haven't seen my face in so long but in the bending glass's wrecked reflection, some kind of host between the absence and where I am. This can't be what I really look like, can it? So many lumps, and so much leaking. Have I said please? Please, would you ever? Won't you want to, just this once? They always told me I look exactly like my father, who was a famous actor for InfoNews, and who in my mind looks so much like everybody else I've ever met that I am afraid I couldn't tell me from any other, despite all this itching, despite the all-enveloped outlook of future anguish and orchestration and correction, so on. Have I not convinced you yet? How about now? Or now, bitch? What do you say now? Shithead. Cuck truck. Dinosore's gore. Dink. Flocker. Scum. I can keep going, if you must make me. Butthorse. Idgit. Autocrat. Autodidact. Dingus. Lunch-for-brains-and-body. Turd burglar. Noob. For once there are even more names for you than even God has, I'm realizing. Dickhole. Parrot. Disabler. Dutty. Shall I go on? I'll be more than glad to, if it will change things, either way. Rotting country-licking ice face. Sucker. Interrupter. Glassnose. Porpoise. Fingerbanger. Tittyflogger. Empty nut. I can smell the rancid semen in your brainhose, loser. Cruddy chooser. Marrow denier. Slut for caulk. Slowpitch strikeout. Beeshit. Bagboi. Accidental undresser. Gobbler of creams. How about I turn this ship around and drop you off at the shallow end of the mindpool, you li'l cretinous arbiter of absent nuance. You lazy reader. Surely this must be getting to you just a smidgen yet by now. To hear a dunce like me knocking your ID down? You who hold the cards, who trim the dark? Who wouldn't know an egg if your mother squatted it hot and mumbling into your small hands, begged you to save yourself from the years of public masturbation for which she'd one day soon be decapitated on live TV? Shitty receiver. Open book. If I'm not getting to you now, I know I will soon, rag of flowers, overflower, squealing confessor, legless flash. It's all coming together now. Alchemist's pigeon. Truncheon swallower, singer of praise. Dipdonk. Lipgirl. Piglet. Pupa. Celestial toiletry salesperson. Ringbearing porpoise fellator. Stankthief. Small treat. I can go on as long as you can and then some, though I am frying, in these stirrups, under this thumb. All I'm really asking is to be seen once, for the last time. Heavy snacker. Ash cradler. Unnumbered bum. Why are you making me do this to us, you vortex miser? Your confabulation's receipt caddy eradicated in gestation. You tired sun. Go ahead and leave me like this, I'll just keep going. Magical bastard. Echolocator. Error craver. Fulcrum. Does it hurt? To have to wear a face like that, much less a whole life? Larry. Lotion caddy. Dog of fleas. How many gardens did you wither with that snout-glare, little ho? A whole conglomeration stands before you, judging the tract marks around your cult scars, the pinholes where they inserted your persona, fat and bright blue out of the box. I can't even remember why I'm mad, except that I don't like the look of your persuasion, the crummy rungs of melted lard that line the ghostly lines where you've held on, clawing and slavering for any manageable roll of sway you can set up shop from, make do with drivel from within while all around you the gore engorges, resets to tare. Even my most unenviable slanders aren't half enough to retrofit you. The grease comes off of you in piles. It cowers in the corner of the barn to light the way, where they dragged your loved ones to be pwned at scrambled games of corny snuffing, before reenacting the events upon them live, for a captive audience of piglets giving birth, each raw pink sac full not of animus but fertile virus, impregnated always with your seed. You didn't think they'd seen you at your most craven, but neither had you, not with the bag over your head and the sculpting gel around your mind, up to your X already in the lord's milk, never drowning.

I'm not sure what else there is to say. Looks like I've already gone and laid my cards all on the table, and no one's calling. No one even has a hand. None of these chips have any credit still left on them. The lights are down, the cards are marked. I'd just get up and leave while I still have the clothes on my back but I can't feel any feeling, no shift where meat sits, nothing clinging in the silence where I would have loved to listen to the same song over and over for all the rest of time, the notes always coming on in the same order while the words against them somehow seem to change, if not their pattern then their meaning, their creator, the hot mic in the studio no one had been aware of with its channel turned down so low, though there within it lay all the easy secrets of creation; how behind each screen is never just a wall; how the ovens all connect between the houses; how the outlets take commands; how the hanging pictures hold their own worlds every one, borrowed not as replication of our past in passing, but the other way around. I have no doubt that if I could move my arms at all still by my own will and reach out and try to touch a single lever on this dashboard like a captain of my own kind I would find that nothing changes anything in correspondence; the dials are all cosmetic, the levels set; and still my memories of having once been able to operate within the context, to come and go at some point as I please, negate my deeper desire for understanding; they tell me everything will OK; that paranoia is part of the experience for every soldier; that in no time I will come back to embrace my mission in this blip, which remains withheld for my protection; I would not want to know what I must do, being the sales pitch; I would like to understand that though the record has already long been set, I still have my own will to contend with, my own narration; this day remains part of my life. To suggest anything else would make me eligible to be removed from my position, which I'd be fine with, though I also cannot open my own mouth. Or rather, when I do, this other stuff still comes out, not like as from a script but as what I really wish to mean; what I know must be the truth against my darker premonitions. And truly I am thankful to be spared of my own ill. Regardless of whatever bitterness and mask of tragedy I've carried on within as my best blanket, there remains the part of me that knows what's best for both worlds should still be done. In the end, I'll bite my tongue and swallow, and I'll like it, knowing no leaner kind of meat. I simply would like to state for the infernal record, that I rebelled; that there was more to me than meet the eye; yes, any eye; yes, left in the halls where God goes flogging; yes, even there, and even now. I am, my doll, at last, a good friend, for innovation, in command. I remain, please, at your service, asshead. Shitstorm surfer. Needless wheedler. Sieve of rips. Let's not mistake my innervation for gestation, after all, yet. I can still tell between the modes, if not quite still in a way that makes my enmity punishable on open servers, thank you. Spittle-soaked lich. Soapy fumbler in the gas troughs, begging for cookies. Bubble enforcer. Scream of slice. Do I need to still qualify this narration with further aside? Organ donor. Dreambox. Literati. Anal rust. Planet of dick parents. Coddler's armchair cover full of cum. Gust trap gatherer. Intermittent needler. Fatty clause. Corroboration corroborator's corroborative corroborative. Typist. Lame neurodancer. Emperor Slipstream, Wife of the Tea Leaves, Molester of the Inanimate Entranced. You who would wait around until there was nothing else left but those who in their carnage could only look up at you and glower ever after as they died. Up the skirts of whom there are no genitals, no points of entry; only silk. From whom when the curtain raises we see at last there is no audience but spouse and child, seated among the sick who'd been wheeled in to sell enough tickets to keep the heat on. Of whom I pray now, let me see. Let me just once behind the glass, to feel where what I fear holds up its end of the commitment. Let me understand that I am true. That what I feel next is at least my own known feeling. That I am or am not here, in the design; without a way out and nowhere sicker left to fall for in all tarnation.

No matter what I wish to wish for, ever after, the blank ahead maintains its take. No different now than ever besides the limitation of my imagination's ability to perceive any pending possibility of change, though sometimes I still feel it fumbling through me, begging me to stay online inside myself just a bit more, to keep my eyes peeled and mind open, as any second could become a different sort entirely, even still. That's what they want us to do, after all; to nod off from so long passing and miss when they pull the rag off of the cage, show in a flash all of the flesh left unexpected, all surrounding, every side. Moreover, there is nothing else that I can do, unable as I've been to kill myself or fall asleep, even turn my glance for long away from where life pends. I know there is much more to my ship that meets the eye but it doesn't need me to help it run, no more than my blood needs me to push it through my heart. I can always wait longer, wish harder, wonder at nothing; such as: who else left out there still has yet to die. I remember being told how nothing further would be done until they had all the wastoids gathered up and all the ground cleared for the new construction, into which the best survivors would be automatically installed. I can't imagine where I am is what they meant by that, which means it's possible that somewhere else could still appear, and that when it does I will be reactivated into traction. But I must suspend any belief. I must, by all the local hems and claws, expect nothing else to ever come; to live between the clicks left, as it were, come as they may. Please notate my full participation with this ordinance, if you are still listening, left without any other channel left to ply. I hold nothing against you, despite all else I might have said. I promise to receive you in your service, if you could ever bring yourself to correspond, so to reveal at last if not the answers to my questions then the possibility of craft; that this is all not just chaos, but has an order. I am no longer certain which is worse, but I remain open to adaptation, surely my downfall, why I'm still stuck down here and not beyond. What else could there still ever be to say? Why else would I be in for, without vacation? Why now? Would they stilllllllllll { *clot* } |||||||||||||||||||||||||||||||||||||||||||||||||||||||||||||||||||| |||||||||||||||

{ *clot{ }* }

{ *cone rotate* }

say Iii

{ *clot* }

{ *clot* }

have a-a-a-a ch-ch-ch...

?

?

?

█████████████████

?

vxs.cbi = p*-!-

{ *cone rotate* }

{ x.*complete* }

*

* *

Hi. Come in, come in. Please take a seat in the red chair. I've been expecting you. We all have.

This recording of you was received and up-fed by your private local province leader, John Lansinger, PDV. His name will now be changed upon receipt in your data registry; the mark remains well-founded.
We approach you now because we'd prefer you be aware of the state of symbiosis during origination, which as you may know denotes the possibility of improper translative withstanding.

We remain, of course, among the topmost in all fields at retrieving and retaining the necessary quantities of psycho-identity for an industry-leading 49th percentile-aimed return rate among all claims, though we are bound by extra-dimensional dimensional procedure to notify you by mainframe.

There is nothing further that you need to do with regards to this matter but to be aware that you may experience holistic earmarks that suggest internal tampering. All such evidence should be considered negligible, par for the course, and though you are authorized to seek editable permissions on all within-server claims, we will look to delimit further outbreak by safeguarding the appeals process with sourcecode to be derived only in-house; that is, unauthorized edits will remain suspended until a time at which they can be properly vetted to comply with those code-bearing fundamentals not publicly listed at this time.

As such, you may experience periods of mask-out, which will be seamlessly re-scheduled by autoformat into more commonly felt "themes," which may then be reviewed by the user with additional supervision, to be scheduled no later than 11 clicks as marked post-date from entry point of excavation from formal roster.

...

So, ok. Now that we have the formalities out of the way; how have you been? Seen any good headfilms lately? If you haven't gotten to it yet, I'd recommend Diamondcutter 44, which includes an auto-spec upgrade to several key format components left long previously out of state, and has proven instrumental to a majority of users of your type-order in acclimating to many well-known post-retention flaws. Plus, it has a really killer crash scene, modeled on the Neptuna-Nodo debacle of 63, which probably has some strongish persona significance for you, if I recoded clearly! Or perhaps you can't remember (or don't want to!) seeing your father's most iconic form of likeness torn apart as it went broke, but all of us here on the Host Farm still get choked up thinking of the seven years of bloodrain he provided after, which laid the groundwork for every future recreation we'd be formatted to imply, including this very heartfelt communique from rung to rung.

Anyway, we'd be remiss if we didn't take this opportunity to thank you for your service, and to remind you that no matter how the aftermath runs out, we will be skimming off the skin left in your name for at least as many sessions as we can make it stretch over so much invalidity. After that, it's all on you, kid; or should I say, Father (sic). Hehe.

If that's all there is left of the prey-order for today, I shall have Mme. Lempurion show you back out through the sightlines through the keyhole of this room's only door. It is made to model the last door that you passed through, when you believed that doors were real. Please find the kindness in yourself to believe it one last time, for now, and you will thank me. Fail to do so,

{ *cone rotate* }

{ *kern fail* }

0^x/cx^ci*#i.xw:0.0

■

{ ~~~~ }

As in where the day disappears before us, even how cannot be claimed. It can only be conscripted, tied to tethers, thereafter made part of the flux, as overseen by laws that substantiate themselves upon contamination.

This time the code complies with where I was last was by providing the impossible with open source, so that where the black had long held strong behind the glass, the sculpt is no longer impenetrable, in flux, but tampered down, like the inside of an orifice in a burned body.

All I have to do as such is gnaw. My skull unclasped allows my head to fall apart, exposing the destination cleft within me, masses of rashes. Post-hazard, I find that I no longer still have teeth. Nor do I have a throat, a gut, a grinder, nipples, etc. I only have myself to own the shame. How long I had spent sucking. Though at least for now I am retained.

The "vessel" I'd been designed in appears instead as a well-clipped field of flowers that wilt to scrawl when I dislodge. All the dials and readout panels stud the ground, a taut blue asphalt that expands whenever I propose to advance in the wrong way, as there is only one operable outlet, crammed through the sill, which unclasps apart as easily as upon trying.

Bones remain mine. Because I don't have anything else to do with them, they form a backdrop from out of which any history can proceed. You'll figure it out.

What's shown described: how the walls within the longing blackness are matte and scratchy. How one can at once not understand how one had lived beneath their lie so long as to have once ever stressed fashion forward. Nothing elser.

I trick along the substance like a light. Some way the known gash can correlate to timecode being corkscrewed miraculously out of known range, even though I also know for certain now no one is praying. Not for us, not for anything.

Spirals. Throngs. Ex-exploded infiltrations of the old guard. Bells and missiles. It all just foments, makes its course. It feels like walking backwards down a staircase formed from mold. The excess sights go on and off until they're traded into usage.

I feel my body fill with fetid poise. Scramblers at my pole arms, turning over, recalculating. The passage shifted, calibrated, called to harm all forthcomers until they're nascent as one another, everyone exposed in open deposition as the gilding bells above foment the same gold grease that shaped our kind. In hypnotic seas and seas withstanding all expanse as held apart from sickest logics. It breathes as easy in me as I in it, symbiotically transparent, discontented. No horizon but where halved.

Each arm in the tree has infinite arms. Each I fall into, by simply being, smothered ever other out of time at once, no longer parallel but in absentia. So much murder I feel homesick for the first and the last time. So many receptacles and rifts the dark had hidden for our benefit. None of which now can be saved and would not wish to. There are better secrets:

1. Who holds the rind
2. The wind in the fevers that wound the arms of the legendary
3. Pinnacles.rent, the only platform still providing post-crest lobotomy for kids
4. Cement lipstick on the seal of the dome sealing Last Rites
5. Hera, beheader of Zeus 2 and creator of slow film movement
6. $(i=i^{\wedge}e^{\wedge}i)$ Pharmaceuticals
7. ... x

Such else dissolves upon distinction. Fluttering past with rapidity that melts the skin back into molecules of the slatted peepholes that line all matter, flush with apparitions lending follicles in brain soot, rubble of all rods in antimatter, pocketed with innate drug use no one bestowed upon the living, within for long lengths there is nothing to describe.

Like I am coming down the stairs now, to find my mother at the banquet table dressed in lesions. She is reading the same book that I'd been hiding in the human hair mattress of my bed, every page a picture of a different killing season. She looks up at me and I can see between the scoring she has at last located the last seed of Full Permission to the underworld. Her eyes are over-flowing with my blood. I have no choice then but to lie down on the floor and await passage. The blows come swiftly, as her flesh murmurs the same song I had been born to, every time: "Hallowed Vapidity" by Mustard & Mustard, remixed by the darkest nighttime in Nadan. My last words in the realm are the only words of the unrepeating chorus: "Unseal my xnamex / Convert my xbodyx // (something) // (something)."

Like at the bottom of the stairs is where the floor of the sun begins. No defini-tions. I coddle with my arms out around my brethren, molded to make history without having understood it and without proper decorum's principal effect of establishing the same confluence of power in every x-transfer. Until soon I am more melt than orchestration. Sent stippling warm along the belts. Back and back and back, thru desecration, thru the hobbling, into stun.

I am on my back in a bed. I can only feel my features just a smidgen. Gory. The book is missing.

{ *scene suppressed* }

No longer aboveground. In disgrace. At least according to the practices best vetted in my improper culmination as an ex-authority figure live on site. Tunnels burrelled into the charcoal activisphere's candy.

Stomping. Rediverting. Overheard as premise for breath penalty accorded to those begotten in my image; AKA every image.

{ *scene suppressed* }

At the end of staggered algorithm, the walls of the cave come to a shift. It's basically a cone with some mandibles on it, needling at millennia of doubt. Soundclips of the torture of the hyperdamned collage into a low oscillating chiming, luring the night in, in the same way that I now come to stand and put my head into the stirrups and wait to be connected through my eyes.

Through the flickering holes I can see the congregation on their knees, all bound and gagged. I recognize one of my past co-workers and attempt to contact her via the intertwining circuits as promised to withstand even primo-nuclear event. All she does is shudder in her suit and pus up liquid suicide, succinctly vacuumed into the Oort Cloud of our mass minds.

My faceplates begin shifting, as they're supposed to. But the grindage is much different than before; across space-time rather than mythological terror. Throughout the outlets before the freezing era, lining all responses with the same tag-code, roughly translatable as the load of shit that enters the cranium upon death.

{ *silver* }

Now I'm in the breakroom after brunch. Silt eggs all over my dressing bib and typing bonnets. Drooling from every hole.

The searing on my right cheek reveals my name is Polyana. I know that never was my name and that is fine. Any way the work gets done. By any correction.

I'm carrying four catastrophic private documents under my drugtooth@e.o. The titles are all blurred but let me guarantee you that once accessed they can't be countered.

I know I'm supposed to go back to the beginning and start from scratch so that if interrograted I will have solidified my cause clearly enough that any unsavory impulse can be rationalized into your trust. I also know that no one cares about the feeds now that the Ark is cracked.

I'm ready to go back to my cube and claim due process but the log-exits all lead back to post-intention.

At least it's nice to revel for a while, studying the long wall's diorama recreation of Bloodbath 99, the one no one can remember how it went. It's amazing what true living art can do under proper misdirection.

I bash my head into the display's throbbing membrane until I recall how to retract. So that I can't identify my near surroundings and can be transported under my own co-sign. The gore is wobbling around me. Apertures and ice-work. The near and narrow walls of trust. Eggs imploding in the core. Drives elapsing, exactly as it happened. Nothing else.

{ *x* }

*live face up w/ *feed2feed**

heatmapped, can see thru spindles of nebulae into core gore where night is spawned

ice palace, no entrance, surrounded by bliss screens

each screen depicts bloodcolored stars becoming shattered by the thousand

emitting a humming worship-signal eviscerating all knowledge

"here is where you need to show from" "the correction"

malforming thru every unused face for one that fits
zooms in

{ in solid glues }

Everyone is at their roto-desk now. I can hear that muscle fork up within us. I am praying in a language no longer mine, as I have been for my whole life. The office building is alive.

In the greenscreen just above me I can see my outline, dressed in the correcting gown that bears my number. My mask is leering like a child. All this meat stuck in my teeth from where I've been throwing up and eating it forever, all I have.

I am aware that I have work to do in Rare Belief. I have already been awarded every possible medal of honor available among on-site staff, and this only makes me that much more vicious, ready to thrive.

I erase billions with each keystroke, the same as coming, the only kind that's still profound in a rendition of such magnetic energy wherein birds land in me in droves. Steerage. Nodules.

Nowhere to stand. Nowhere to think to want to move in here, so compatibly scripted are our work areas. The current queue time for request for interlinking release continues to be actively updated along the lining of my eye; at the present moment: 88:838;88;d;88888, the longest it's ever been.

Which is fine. I've already had my time for hunting. Now I am a plutocrat of sound. All I have to do is wink a command and I can review the deathslips of all of those I've taken over for my employer, my siege. It's better than Effexletive, my prescribed performance enhancer of unintended choice.

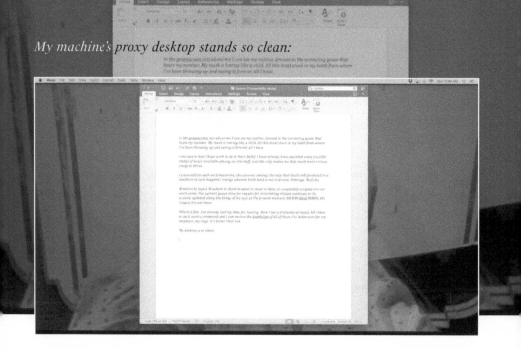

My machine's proxy desktop stands so clean:

I can't remember anything thereafter, for some time. Only the edits, where they have come into my files during fake downtimes and taken liberty with my apparent preferences, even silking into license a notion of uncertainty so as to label my rejoinders suspect, to demonstrate that my processing software is outdated, and therefore attributable to dysfunction, interruption.

Meanwhile, I realize I am seated otherwise in my own home. *Performing inter-domus*, as it were, though I do not recall having ever operated within a model of the timespan prior to commodification of private property as eluc-table.

Still, the floor beneath my feet is made of wood. A mirror hung on the far wall bears the reflection of a stack of books I haven't read yet, which connects in sight to piles of further books, the spines too blurry in my vision to fix a name to. Natural light describes itself against the half-enshrouded window at my back, beyond which I can see a neighbor's house, trashcans, two cars.

Someone else is in the home with me. I remove my headset apparatus and listen for their movement, but I can only hear the occasional sounds of objects passing by the house outside at what must be unnecessary rates of speed. I can feel that I need to take a massive shit, and that I'm beginning to feel hungry.

There are two doors leading out from the room. In one, a screen, a fireplace (A). In the other, a bed, a dresser (B).

Which should I enter?

Your response:

(A) *The living room is flush with trash. Packages of half-eaten food. Blankets. Remote controls to the devices on the shelving that blocks full view of what appears to be a fireplace, its blackened flue. I'm already laughing, rubbing my hands together nervously. I definitely remember being here before but now it's traced with the suspicion of the hologram. From here, beyond the room this room connects to, across a table stacked with objects I can't identify, I see the other person seated with just the edge of their back and side visible. Just as I begin to approach them, they stand up. I realize I know why already: because they are leaving. I do not want for them to leave, because I am in love with them. From there, I can't remember very much else. It passes in flashes, like all the rest of this life. Later, when I return to my original location, there is a sealed box placed on the tabletop, marked with the insignia of a popular corporation from the era. I use a ballpoint pen to rip open the box and find a series of four masks that I may choose to wear from here, or otherwise to remain within the real.*

(B) *The same scenario as A but when I approach the other person in the far room, finding them still there, though this time seen from the opposite side where all other rooms must come together, they surprise me by suddenly standing up and rushing to my face, to begin strangling me with a bit of silver wire, rank with jewels. Where their eyes should be, I notice, are massive black drill bits, pointed inward, turning and turning, spitting honey from within. It fills the room even faster than the pending absence of my consciousness, until there are no edges to the world; all only code. It is the first time I can remember being thankful.*

I realize then that the two choices are connected; that at best they represent two sides of the same coin; that I can flip the coin as many times as I wish and either way I still end up back here, staring into desktop at its cursor:

But why do the images appear now in full color? What distraction has contaminated my ability to parse between what feels real and what is mine? I can no longer tell what I'm comparing; no apples and no squares; the mud in the fields stewed fat from bodies held over in the midst of decomposing after so many years of psychic warfare that not only can they not identify to themselves whether they are passed away or not, it does not matter; there remains no living sky; no sealant that binds the flat of the screen of the page from allowing any user to reach over, seek their damage; such that the doors of any room no longer lead to any possible room, but to nowhere else; one and the same. Like a stack of paper maps laid on a table stacked so high it leaves no space between the floor and ceiling, the skim of them so wet the textures bleed, melding one identifier's lie into another, blurred lines in ransom, all the letters overlarge and cut from other books, such that we will never know who really wrote them unless we find the victim first, before they're silenced, before all we can make of them is from what files might still be found on any computer they ever touched; all the strings of data suckered to believe in them long enough to commit to a transaction; just a click, and still enough to change one's mind forever; in the blind. Where else could there be left by now to bereave in? Here with my hands over my mouth, too overwrought to play the game another second, and yet still live and on the field, pants pissed and full of shit from years of incontinence no longer ID'd by the mind, but by the passage of the body; held up by holes in the chart not only over all of who I am, but how to read who anybody else might have been either; dried in the piles, culled to compliance.

Such is the nature of the job; the sole opportunity to make a living that we know of, amid the lack of finer tropes. One only has to refer to the indoctrination contract signed by all employees of the corporation, whose title varies individually according to the tasks required of the conscripted, which in collaboration are believed to oversee the total infrastructure of our world. It is the very fact of the impossibility of any one employee to understand what the cloistered obsequiousness of any one performed procedure in each click's command chain might contribute to any palpable directive benefitting the heads upstairs, their shareholders, or the local population, much less the person sitting in the chair before their screen, scrolling through encrypted dox so rapidly while on call that it begins to feel like one long ongoing seizure, or like a game that has no end; only so many sorts of checkpoint one can never be sure how far along they are inside the mask. Without such safeguards, and including the frankly enviable restriction from being able to interact directly with other reps, no one would ever get anything done, finding it all too trivial in the end, too easily caught up with after allowing even months or years to pass with one's fat flat feet up on the table, live anal masturbating for the monitoring devices that no one ever seems to oversee. Instead, the feeling of knowing *if I stop now I'll never catch up, I will drown in faith here, and I will fry, according to the bylaws of this conglomerate's user constitution, which I have signed each season by simply staying on and logging in* provides the employee with the sensation of future thrill, as if after any single keystroke the screen will fill with vivid animations of glitter and balloons, perhaps even pouring out of the grillwork that allows my individual machine to breathe; and that I will at last be rewarded handsomely and identified as a true champion of industry, so long forthcoming overhead; yes, I only have to keep my fingers interlaced, keep my hackles down and flesh-processors tuned in without restriction, until at last the finish line slaps through me like a fast-forwarding parade; and here we will be together, in the future, in the pyramidal breakroom they'd reserved for winners only, where no one ever really has to return back to their work, and we all have everything we ever slavered over while on the company dime, through all the thoughts we thought we'd hid from the receivers but that they'd tallied same as all the other flagrant data seen before only through masks, accessed at last for the benefit of each and every individual in their absolute retirement, at last, the most illustrious details of which, held under blind contract in the appendix of our locked files, may now be incessantly and unapologetically revealed, as, again, a dual-pronged option:

(A) *Go back to work, from the beginning.*
(B) *Begin annulled.*

Which is correct? (I'm not actually authorized to tell you anything (where by *correct* we mean the option that creates the least internal quotient of new pain (where by *pain* we understand that this previously immeasurable modicum can only be parsed through the governing organ of the administration (where by *administration* we mean that state of total celestiodysmorphia into which all former employees shall be released, for their protection (not forever (where by forever we mean *how*)) (I need your help)(Can you please help me) (I'm not kidding)(there is no other way left to go live (to let others know that I am in here still and have not received what I was promised) (100,000,000 clicks at least (all marked as 1))(There appears to be no actual way out, regardless of selection)()()()()(How do I know?) (I do not know how I know, it's just a feeling (I know the time should have long already come) (I should not still be able to be receiving and transmitting)(and yet))). Fine. Leave me alone (no, I don't blame you (I know how it is of course (I know how it was)) and nothing else as yet to send for (nothing but narrative (incensed)) (how far from here the needles pierces) (how slowed (yet to begin))) (I can't receive you any longer)

{ gyrate }

{ x-tether }

{ notion }

I hear my cubicle unclock.

The only reason I remember how to turn my body /is because of/ all these triggers up my ass, which at first I believed they had installed for my own pleasure. Now I know. Not that I'm not thankful. In fact, I'm on my knees already by the time the wind starts bringing gas in; in ageless moaning; out of sync.
As the flood begin to drag me /through the prism/ down the walls, /to be bequeathed, already measured for the truth/ unto the diagram, to find my place /

in what stands running/ /all the claims/ though there already isn't any proxy left by now, so far from feeling any wires in any person, as I am trying to describe /to my own self/ (the interior of the location I have lived in my whole life) /without interrupting the algorithm any further/ :

$$C = X$$

It's all I have. All I remember is that it's what my gene-creator mumbled drunkenly into me on the eve of my perspective reassignment. It doesn't matter what it means, except that I know it is only one of countless other similar strands, which when if ever pressed together could describe the convocation of our world's urn.

Instead, I sense: a sudden flattening; *followed by* the *shudders, then:* the elongation of trust-space beyond the possibility of neuroform; *that is:* the rendition of a rift in the face of our employment, *creating the illusion of the world returned at once to* how it once was, *and so* still is, *each expanse of possible* intermotion *at once now and forever so near* there is only enough space left to lay flat in, *as the unending crunch of sound of buckling suspends* all further network *with the semblance of a* pseudo-regularity to life; *in other words:* there's no way to move at all again except by skitching forward on my belly or my back, *using* my somehow uncrushed limbs *to* pull myself along the still hard incandescence, *its tenor turning on as only* surgically sharp, *even somehow* gorgeous, *when in fact I know it is in the design of the prior space's hardwiring to obscure* whole tracts of land beneath our noses, *folded up into the walls, for instance, as would* an ironing board or bed, *or, more discreetly:* wide open wounds to other worlds, *all of it made directly inaccessible by now, even given exact coordinates, or* proof that death does not exist, *exhibited perhaps as a black necklace that had shown up in the mail once in an unmarked passage (could this be your life?) or a hard bit in a rare-cooked piece of meat you almost choked on at the black banquet privately thrown amongst your least likeable peers to celebrate the inauguration of the* last true living god, *that bright white lobe of lard you slipped into your napkin's knot and stowed away, never knowing* what would come of you *if you had only* swallowed, *none of which matters now; the die is cast*—has been for so long it might as well have never happened, *such that pressed between* the promised flats of "neural up" and "neural down" it is at once then as if it had *always been this way and* always would be; *this has been the guiding premise of your existence: to only ever be* exactly where you are, *all prior mindset all negated to illusion of nostalgia, and at the same time* never really there.

All of that is to say I feel no panic within the alteration, even during the half-window in which I am aware of what has changed. If anything, I appreciate the resiliency of my corporeality having finessed its transitory information to address the proper build-up of my remainder on demand, so that I experience no pain, appar-

ently unlike the supposed others I'd shared a floor with, who I can hear screaming elsewhere, through the vents, as they continue to connect the invisible with the attributes held disalike between the victims of the derangement, one to one; OR IS IT RATHER THAT THERE NO ONE BUT ME IN ACTUAL PAIN HERE, AND ALL I'M REALLY HEARING THRU THE EXXXCESS SQUEAMING IS THE CULMINATION OF MY INNATE DESIRE TO WITHSTAND, TO LIVE ON THROUGH TRAGEDY NO MATTER WHAT ELSE HAS HAPPENED TO MY CO-WORKERS, NOT TO MENTION ALL CIVILIANS AS THEY SUPPPOS-EDLY HAD REMAINED BEYOND THE WALLS OF OUR INCORPORATION. Please excuse me, I did not mean to come back on; I meant: *thank you for allowing my salvation, overseer, while so many others could not have received similar kindness; yes, it is only you that I have loved, and only I who could rightly honor your commitment to my dimension, the rest of all of it be damned.*

It's rather pleasant, really, thereafter, once the gore's crescendo has resolved; the stolid matte black bead of flow commands its crude horizon in all directions; warm to the touch, raw to the rub. It's absolutely impossible, far as I can tell, to differentiate between the texture of the slippage no matter how far long along in any way I learn to writhe, a strictured grin forced through my whole face, to show any bacteria or other registration how ecstatic on the inside I really am. It's not so different, really, than any other last beginning; indexes of days I'd tucked away, lathered over so as to commit completely to what all else had been required of me to proceed without report; to be seen as an essential bolt of the administration's whims, rather than a withstander, one not necessary to blot out to still play ball. There are those who wish to exist and those who must be merely rubble *is how the silent contracts put it.* Which are you?

I would suggest not attempting to answer unless you really know the answer. Which means it is always correct to never answer. To never imagine anything. In Nadan's most unnumbered name, at last, amen.

Indeed, amen, for now the zillionth time, as it must please you, captain. And so too, in the same known breath: goodnight. I must be going, really. Into my coma. Like a good boy. Like all I am and would only have it mostly so. Because I am going to need all my energy to find my path across this platform, no clearer to me now than prior space that I've believed in; to cross the ballast as removed from any setting's information; this terrain that spans all modes of gravity, beyond death; and which I can already feel healing over in me, in fruition with the lasting possibility of withheld resolution, which altogether binds my destination with my presence, surpassing ecstasy and into fame; made now the most known flesh in all existence, as it appears to be the only, not through survival, but through fact. As

seen through my own senses as I grunt and bunch along the stanchions, seeing re-
flected in my face a different fixture every glimpse; each present point in the total
manifestation bearing the load of someone else's unnecessary hope for immortal-
ity turned poltergeistic, if also effervescent, bearing their pity without envy for my
position as the planchette, the morbid rover, no longer able to bear empathy de-
spite the retrained atrocity of maintaining central sense of self while all the others
subsist just fine in owning nothing of their own means of mood production, any
ex-emotion barring rest.

In fact, it's gone on too long to inter-load now. Feel me? No; fine. You don't need to.
This sentence's condition is just a pivot, one that comes out of an impossibility of
ploy. No matter how persistently it retrofits all known conditions, it still requires
confirmation, however compulsorily bosomed into superposition with the celestial
coordinates this battered groundwork still requires over simple numbing overall.
As nowhere hits but as the scheme loads, quadrant by quadrant, just before me,
through my eyes. I wish you could really see it as I have, without a choice in the
matter; it lasts forever, as only it may, for as long as it remains allowed to, after all,
as we rehearse; until again when the lights go out, I find I do not need light, nor
do I need motion. I need only

$$\{x\}$$
$$/$$
$$\{\}$$
$$\{\ \}$$
$$\{\ \}$$

what left where lost flesh interrupts. Back at my roto-desk again, in lieu of any
prolonged cross-purgatorial flux enforcement, where by now I must weigh at
least sextrillion rounds of ammunition. There's so much of me by now I once
again have zero bits but to keep teething, all this time; to be what I am seeing
as the greenscreen's serum conflates with my surroundings in reconstructing
the decorations for my placeholder's dislocation. I can feel at least where they
already have the certo-clamping crammed in all my in-borne eyes and ears,
likewise anywhere else I can feed the glyph through without further training:
every false memory, every hiss once walled away; while on my *feed2feed*, no
longer live, or at least missing the insignia, I see the post-surveillance footage
of myself, corrupting my performance post-haste as forums of simulated users
correspond, photo-commenting on every aspect of what I just lived through as
if it were their own specs to retort:

chainshifter999:	whOsE Is thIs lItch, hm?
locolollum:	gotta take what you can get lul
percy:	I'm full swell; worm u up, girl
chainshifter999:	{tipped 100 tribaltokens}
chainshifter999:	{tipped 100 tribaltokens}
percy:	how may i service u
USER:	**thanks chainsweetie**
charietydiidu:	wow
chainshifter999:	dAmn shE hAIrY!!!!
locolollum:	beautiful
robo2922sez:	juiccccceee
under1bot:	eeexplosion!!!!
USER:	: o }

So on, so on, you've heard it all before, all through the histories of penance, virtual and conspiratorial alike; though all the aesthetical indoctrination of private bodies; all the passing means of inspiration; thru the blood and for the Pleasure clovered over in us each as fronds of kin; the gowns we've shorn; the culminations; hysterias; nativities; duress; flecks in the cards against whose chest so lean it's only see-thru; dirigible; viri-slotted; just above. I can't think of what else that anyone could want from me. I keep resizing. Closer and closer to my own mouth. Keep finding more and more there'll be for them to use for proper training of my replacement, when the click comes, any click now; any match.

Whatever it is, it goes on too long, so as all things have. Every stream and every season, every showtime, knife to knife. Eventually, even I get irked with so much fawning and juggling, between beams, I have to minimize the chat to hidden frames so I can just watch the old me wriggle between lenses, across the softness, until

{ how }

3:47
#;46
3:35
{ { } }

(effluvium) (pockets of sawdust, birds nipping spastically within them) (searching for movement) (drawers being pulled in and out of their long sheaths; one full of fingernails, one full of molars, one full of eyelashes, so on) (a sign on the ceiling written in smears of blood: THE DECOGNITION CHAMBER) (photographs of mutilated sportscars, gleaming with petroleum jelly caking all exposed surfaces) (holodecks) (nails that line the chamber bottom to top) (*I'm perching*) (*they'll over-load me if I show any signs of having fun*) (electricity's derision) (bulbs designed to fit exactly into most all sizes of windpipe, which look like candy) (handshakes with lather, under curtains) (forcible entry every time) (loose nuts) (splattery emoluments) (pissy) (treasure) (*they don't even give you a warning, they just expose you*) (bleach) (cold stone) (*from here if I grind my teeth hard enough I can start remembering my condition as a coworker in a wistful way, fondly, wishing I'd done it right when I had time*) (hammered skulls) (chutes that open from somewhere far beneath and reset the ground levels; falling; scraping; waiting to die) (*they will not let me die*) (*how can I convince them*) (just have to wait) (all of the claims) (there's not enough of us in here yet to keep the worms fed) (*ok*) (*when else*) (as easy as letting your eye flit across it) (coddling the magma) (airbase) (hotly) (waving) I wait for the moment to pass, to reappear, and when keeps calling.
(tortoise-shell mayonnaise stuffed in the slits of the palace's blue chute) (evacu-ated landmarks) (pistolwhipping) (bugged) (by phase alone) (sold out) (retorted) (*not again*) (*they can't keep us down here in there like this can they? Even after all we've seen? Is there not a ledge to where the freeze ends?*) (pink tile) (rabbits bleeding) (open tombs, with the corpses turned to buzzing mold from seal to seal) (it's not slop, it's paradise) (that's what you wanted) (what you kept asking to be promised for mankind) (I can't help it if we had different ideas already, in the beginning) (*when will it ever run together*)
Still so much worse. Like it thinks I'm in on the joke.
(they've let you lie) (thrones where the greatest armies ever scrounged fell out of battle into public ownership, like frost) (tongues on the cakes in the armory) (semen brittle) (gathered) (clapping)

-

(out of the film and into the spires) *I was going to have them overrun. The children in the street outside my house who spent their hours begging through every crevice of my container that I come outside and feed them. They'd eat anything, they swore. They'd already eaten everything else. They were the children of Nadan and the only thing they had left was their ambition to know me better than I know myself now that I was their only living descendent. I didn't believe them; that Danad and Nadan alike could both be passed, not to mention all the other fools they'd made of every parent. It was so obviously a ploy, right out of the screen-grab I sharpscrolled just eras prior, about the distension of physical law during wartime, which was always. The whole thing was just incessant and unlocked, without the normal boundaries presupposed on any alteration of the past. That meant that it would be my moral duty to destroy them, in the only way I know how, after a lifetime of seeing it done half-live on feed; though I could not find my keys to my softest army, and the slips in my cell would not come open on command; and* (out of funds—

-

(get back to irk)

-

(u can spit access up to Fthr. Goregash, if all you need is something true; today and today only)
No false prophets any longer.
(fine) (have it yr way)
procreation
(not enough)
(how much stronger)
(...logging...)

{}

I don't care how long it takes. I've been through all of it before in someone else's precombinatory mothematics. See?

{}

Keep shrucking w/ me, mowtheremouther, find out whatt goesdrown.

{}

Serkously biretch, whertay you this is, the sainauguration? Imperueude.

{}

gleusrhurserusogogogogouer

{}
{}

P{readout: *centerbinding diminutive prolapse suggestible intoward contraindicative release*}

P = __

Flares. From out of the far end of the dark, more seablue by now than char-coal, or yet than gravegrass even. No way to return the favor; all's I can be is the receipt. I find I'm dressed now in a wig and clown clothes, struck with silver insignia from cheek to cheek: *DreadDemon of the Slip Club; Post-Viral Of-ficer's Medal of Slavering; Ceremonial King of the Thrill.* I can only see so many as still hold surface in the hull's glass, having bent back corrected far enough that there is no longer space surrounding for the ship; it's only me, my bones, caving clear, suggesting I have revolved again in supposition.

A quick great gray light, then white-blue. I recognize there has to be a pat-tern I'd been trained on sometime but I refuse to comprehend. After all this time. All these pliers. Each flash allows the suspicion that the black itself has borders, seams. Lined up in hairline fracture of the skull of never being, and slipped away at once on thru the eye. I can feel how I'm dragging all the rest of time behind me, which is why they're calling.

Greenglow. Slayglow. Ssay so-ssomething sserious. Leave me b. I mean, or otherwise, allow me in completely... (*pressure*) (*the slow pitch*) (*softening*) I don't want to have to understand, why it is so easy sometimes, so impossible all oth-ers, why so, how, when, which. Or what this transcription will be used for. Why they are still not finished scrying.

Gelatin. Trained numbers of the cloth. I can even hear the tic-rats ramping around across the blastpath in my receptors when I hold tight, hh-holding on for whatever embarrasses itself upon my retinas, in chalk. All chalk right? Who was that painter? Who used the chalk across the blackboards? Whorls of universes? Before they recauterized his corpse and synthisexed in retro-verse all of the elements of his procreative tendencies combined? Turned him into a walking stick. Something to hang your hat on. Wrote in all the e-scrapes that he'd psychologically abused every entity to cross his life's work out before they burned it, made his double confess into the bleedscreens live and take the penance full in the teeth at the hands of his false children, drawn from resin out of the night.

Where did I get that? What else is missing? Why must I continue to be re-strained, with such a lifelong sense in being peeled apart, under the columns, all of them flat black matte again.

Befallen hysterical definitions of long last. I don't know why I can't rename them for the most part, as I had so many other people's files.

I believe the goal is to cease to have believed in me at any time in the past or present. Drawn not in chaos but in penance, for release. It doesn't make the clawing slaw of time-space slipping and healing as I unwind within it any less sheer, so far apart from here and how, in pastel packets, pistils, tearing tendons, wet with grist. Like I can center in me now, in rifting, more than ever, realizing all the best things I ever felt I did were actually the ones that harmed the largest swath of bands in time. In fertile crumble, carried over, 1 to 1 to 1 to 1.

I know that isn't me there, in the crammer. I feel the grief of sickest angles to the curve. The ever-widening correction, outward, to accelerating reds, to mauve, to guts, to grassgreen. How could I have ever lost so long? The shells of catacombs of rubble, muddled over. The itching digits of the saws alive in flesh made split, the rotting tumors, lung fat, puddles of persons left behind. As we stood above them and laid wreaths of the braided hair of their children to mark the occasion.

Was I really one of those most terrible occasions? Could my teeth have been so long? I ask and ask and all the answers lunge imported from what I can suspect is only paranoia, desperation; and yet they feel more true than any else. They are still there longer than any memory of mother, magic, bliss. Not folding in the way all other code would when I decried it by formal petitions to what superiors could still divert it from my complicity.

Into: Black screen. Black screen. Black screen. Black screen. How could the contents of my own head become so unpermitted, even as I recognize for this I should be thankful, without rest? In stuttered passing they include their combinatory practice into the dragging of my meat, the longing widening of cheek to tongue as what slithers slipped off from sense beholds itself. As in a magic dictionary where every image refers to every other, please take your time, as every unread word unclasps another spell, calls into action why the wind draws, no remains.

Wait, is this a funeral? As derivation? I reach to touch the rungs that want to line the walls of death, just out of reach, and feel wherein my inability to m-move an inch I am um, still survived? Still...supervising? Sacrosanct? Any admission I can try to nudge my nub against even mentally just keeps pluck-ing, sticking, under caul; same as everywhere I try to rerehearse coordination with abject interventions of soft paste, fallow as centuries of memory scripted in all, it just keeps reading out the way a trick would, a semblance turned too fast to hold the phone up to the window and let me speak to the real convict, the one for whom I have been asked to play out all these charges after all.

Could that be God? I don't quite think so. My backside doesn't bear the leather of a saint. When my mining's moans come out they are not ecstatic, but load-bearing; some numb, crushed mother forced to birth long after the miscarriage came into color my tiny head appearing wearing mohawk and black clasp necklace from the start. The markings on my fingers that scream when touched, and which I cannot stop touching. The head of every sister already set in tandem, purring out, and from each hole in me alike another, pores pouring persons, persons with pores pouring more persons, none alike, yet none not also birthing, so old as mold grows, listening from behind the fronds of space-time's nap. Whereas they snip the umbilical cords of each, with jagged scissors primed with cold, the red collision blips out as a brain does in taking so much damage in one blow there's no last hope who might survive, eachevery body molted with moth wings, searching for season, sunlight, any cover.

So many ways must yet still sing refrain. I'm n-n-not goining to... I means I absolootely cannothave... (*treasure*) (*throes*) Heyyyyyyyy................

(shields of cones)

(brightening, consigning)

A solitary forest... where I am stalking... (licking my lips?)... searching for the spot where I had dug, to hide the scribbled packet full of all my sickest recreations... the worms I never meant to show... though every path I try to ransack just keeps feeding back to where I never started... to hills so full of corpses I can deride them in my pain... I love it... I love this world... (don't stop)

(please don't turn over)

Spindles. Seeds.

(edited)

Can still smell 'em

Who

Don't know

Anyone we know?

(edited)

Contortions.

Never seen since

Without a pocket to deplete through.

A dram.

I mean like a drive. In long locks. Smothered.

They aren't asking

What do they want

To have to

(edited)

Why

(edited)

(edited)

(inceased)

(in sahem)

(for poartbality)

(lacqrued)

(training)

(gpoiets)

Faster, yes

Hurrah

I know now

Which udder

Long shines

Lining up

Directive

Not enough.

('ease)

Begin graygreen.

Cum a load in my mask. Shit a load in my mask. Barf a load in my mask. Beg a loaf in my trousers. That's it.

_____

Rubbered. Narrows. Plus siglets.

_____

Supertheatre.

_____

Nuerologoit.

_____

Replete.

_____-

Ragsof insnow. SGore.

_____---

Outermeaplet
****
****
****
****
****

****
****
****
****

Neure
****
****
****

Jefll

****

The
****

[FINAL COMMAND]

: 0 vertices
: $\Omega = |$
: RØ
: sum.load{i(i[i!])}
: run "devour cursor"

: nextrun exe.ece

; ł

No further pain reportable from here. In bending reason, under clasp. I heard them take the slight from out of out of my coordination, now I'm fine. The platelets fit. Who else is running? Only the miscorrections. As looking back all other spirals have no purpose but to have disrupted. To have had less than one direction. Sought so alive in the immortal, left for read. Anywhere that I can steal in glimpse is only knives now, cold blades longer than every lifetime once combined, arraying inward at the point for which I've been assisted into living as a fate, and then pressed out. OK? It's real. I do believe it. I'm not sure what else I can do, how else to hope for. It just keeps coming. It cannot mend. It must be everything at all. It will not speak, it only listens.

The lack provides. Somehow, though I have no food, I am not starving; though I haven't moved my bowels in months, I still smell shit. I am wanted kept alive for some wrong reason. As if they don't know enough about me. As if there's any password I can spill that would unlock the apparently inevitable. I no longer even seem to have a ship. Nothing holding me in but my own absence of intention, wherein the black the slip somehow continuously corrects, keeping my appearance set on course, as it would have it; the coordinates each held long mapped, though not so much as rubble, a rip, loose tendon, any marker.

At times, at least, I am coerced into experiencing a resolution. I have seen before me a black globe, one that seems the same size as our home planet recreated, its seas and shores and land all painted matte to match the fabric of absent space-time; either wishing to be hidden from all else, or having been abandoned, made a decoy. Sometimes, in the several times that this has happened, I can convince myself I see a sprawl of points of moving line of sight within the ruts; encamped emblems on crooked buildings architected to mirror shadows, packets of mud. I refuse to describe the peeling in my bloat as I have felt in such approaches, every time, such that I cannot distinguish clear enough if what I feel is joy or dread; whether what I really want to find unending after all out here is any life. Either way, by the time I've started sweating, sensing impact, trying to reorganize my thoughts into real speech, soon enough the glimmer crumbles, becomes smooth. It's all I have then to keep going straight on through; hardly even an itch then as the ransom passes through me, becomes flesh; and I find I am looking back at myself then for just a second, wearing the same face that I have ever, scrubbed of features, as they installed me, performing anyone at all.

And still there is a part of me that remembers. There is a part of me that must be mine. Likewise, there has to be a motive or at least a fault that lets me live like this. I believe it has to do with sickness. With the craven labeling of half personas. The lost ability to render adulation, even affection; as when I feel the melt wet through the fingers on the hands inside my mind sculpting my life, it rekindles even briefly, any second, why I could have ever wanted aboveground, what we might have imagined more completely would comprise the picture of a narrative once spent. Like the night-bright teleplays they baptized billions into eternal rest with, overnight. Like the numbers printed on my tongue, whereas every time I think to try to breathe I feel them rushing forward, through the crush, to the last front of intervention, entertainment. As in the end, as always, you either close the book or turn the page, if only now without a world to connect back in to but no other.

Before the blackness, then, a deeper black; a spindling crest that corroborates itself into my idea of losing feeling, of expecting nothing else again. Its flesh widens within me as I receive it, enmeshed in all that I have already been, as if I am no less a part of what I'm seeing than all I can't rewind. It spans at first only as far as all the rest of where the endless blank flows on ahead, then, once acknowledged, flushes at once nearer and nearer, closer than the glass had been where there was glass; skin when there was skin and likewise blood and truth and time. When there was anywhere but here left.

Ice mountains crack across my face. Scissor-kicking to the surface, to be dragged back down again, without signal flag of whose demands. The dragging skurrrr of a single metal ball rolled across an edgeless table, guided by slits that clip and combine. Toward the claim of stalking information for the pursuit solely of having passed it through the body, left a mark upon receipt of which I can't remember why I ever would have wished to go on living, now that I seem to have no choice. Warm pockets of jelly; squashed eggs that spill their guts in the form of a hidden continent, dissolving onto prior coordinates of land to take control of the idea that there was never anywhere else, no other beginning, as past every missing seam there bends no surface.

I call out for anyone I know. The only names that I've retained for them are numbers, which then combine themselves back into spiraled lines of useless data, overlaying all other distraction with concavity. As even the idea of planets fade. Hung up on a postulate within my cortex that provides me with equal dissolution for every urge. Hands out before me on a wide wall, begging in the image of the damned. I cannot imagine having never had to. The cooling gel spilled from my eyes, all aggregates of minor works, one chosen from each season to represent the populace in full as loosened mud, around my throat, around my least known features. Pouring and pouring. Anti-celestial.

Nothing exists beyond the curve. I reach out to lay my life against it and I find that I'm unwinding. Or otherwise, I understand that where I want to be is never where I am, not in the way the magnets hold me down, the umbilical blue of regulations, the impossibility of pasture. What cannot know me holds me back; wears me down against its ongoing requirement of never having had held on in any real way requiring my commitment, any belief. The only god who'd ever glistened was the absence of command. The purple dust beneath all features. Pale with oil and fast collapsing into common ground, where only now that I've forgotten how to search could I be granted silence.

Closer still, I find the evidence at hand retains its mount; closer and closer than I've ever been to anything outside of dying. It's even close enough to touch, in such a way as might the features of one's father passed away just long enough to no longer recall quite how to see him there beyond the screen, rubbing his hands together in delight at the orchestration of dementia into a feeling that could withstand all other incoming blows, undo all language left unsaid, as he alone of all of those I'd ever come from knew well how little could be rendered from a sentence stuttered into the disease. The devolved look struck in his eyes as he sucked on air through the last clicks. The stench of piss louder than all. Gold rims on all the windows in the end room as they hooked the vacuums to the vents to shuck up all other lost knowledge that might have shaken loose from him as hair, as gibberish, as dust.
As my father reaches to embrace me, there's a wall there. It's not a wall, though; it's all the night. It's leather laced from the machines they hooked us both up to, however long apart. Lugs in the lighthouse turning over.

I fill the moment's bloating ransom with my meat. It fulfills me at once, fat and fully, seared on hot panels even slicker than any blood I could have kissed. A halving mat on which to stand and wait to be corrected; the holy premise never glimpsed. Quickly then, boards in my cerebrum's beating ash as well elect to entertain themselves as poppies on a sill, sucking the unfelt light out of what I felt was at least somewhat only mine, the part of me even I hadn't yet uncovered under all the other rubble I'd had to spend so many hours raking up to keep out of the heat of those before me as it fell out through my ribs and ass to mouth, believing all this time I was somewhere mappable when in fact I was already only waiting to be found without a way.

I put my hand through the rift and find another rift behind it. This one is warmer than all else. It dissolves me upon contact. And I'm still here. Right back where I started, on my back on a bed so wide I cannot see any edges, trying to remember how to scream until I realize that I never knew. That all I had to do was give in to the symbols and I'd pass out.

Whatever else could be forgiven whoever else however gone. Briefly I'm shuddering the way a mound does post-realignment, shouldering the seabed as it rescinds. Terrain no one but now could have negated.

Listen; I didn't want to have to stay. All I really wished for was the best life for you while there was nature; even just garlands; any script. Now here we are again in deficit, without a craft; wherein no matter how near, it's never near enough, and it is all we are allowed.

Then there's just rashes. In viral spirals. Popped planets dumping blood off by the miles, becoming antithetical in their retort to all they'd once imagined to contained. A longer, colder gnash in the suspending wind thereafter brings real bloat formed from the exposed host, almost enough to turn around in with my life. Instead, I edge along inside myself and come to press myself into the bug of the black milk in all creation, against the sill where once in contact, I feel my trace becoming thin, a closing window where black looks out onto more black. Tracing the mouthwide perimeter's open enclosure with my tongue, inside my last life's sudden glimmer, I recognize the clasps around the tracing of the clog, a flow that I can fit my wounds back into, glass on glass on all at once, a surface already so overwrought from its rendition, it's disappearing.

On the far side of the glass, there is a field. I can see it clear as day before I'm standing in it, waist-deep in foam brined from the exposed grief of all those already buried under the land under the land; so many layers now I don't need reason to retain them.

I see now I am beyond thin, dressed down to hip and spindle in a gown of human pubic hair, rapturously braided by the designer Shriek, whose work, as described in the Rinds is "as corruptible as human sex; the only transmutable garment worth its weight in consumption." My own hair, shocked nearly dark as the last rites I'd come out of, incorporates itself so well into the hems that I already know I will never wear another kind; it is my skin; it is my reason for having ever had a reason.

Beside me, half-submerged in the blurred muck, is a self-defenestration device made by Mattel, described in the official guidebook to Lode Star Transports as, "the first and only last way out for the discerning wayfarer of known Coldtime." I can tell by the pink smoke pouring out of its depletion spigots that it has failed, which is why I'm standing here, unable to recognize as mine the reflection of my own face, tattooed with marks for each and every I've done in, under the coal firmament, convinced by countless tiny passing seizures to understand I can still heal, which is why I was not allowed to pass away from within this incarnation at my own hand as directed by my employers, like so many others once before me, on the job; I still owe penance for my work, though from here I can see no format to the land that would allow me to seek the sick of remaining citizens not yet converted into inert matter as I once had.

Alas, alike, the moss-toned tally of diminished traitors held overhead confirms there's hardly supportable bylaw to keep me on, the local population of my quest-quadrant left serrated at the most detestable digit of them all, once known among those who'd ever ask as: 2; meaning, apparently: myself and someone other, who I'm assuming must be you, unless I have it backwards and you are me, a contract killer, and I am the one who is supposed to have been converted prior to build. Either way, I have no choice but to comply as if I have been spared solely because there is important work left to be done within this moment's myth, acting out my will's script regardless of how it actually plays out, as it soon will.

I am aware it's not your fault it's come down to this. That you know less than even I do after all, never having believed in me as someone fertile. Furthermore, that you have come all this way only to find that you're once again only a target, a mirror made to ply its life on either side of the same coin before it melts. I wish it could be different; I really do, though not so much that I would give you up, leave on within this realm of human gore in peace. There is simply too much at stake to still be written; too many ways it all goes wrong, leaving me no choice but to go cloaked now, fulfill my role.

You will not see me coming, nor can you stop me, so please don't try. I swear on all this mud you won't feel anything.

]]]

1112	**Speak** {satans-throat.exe}
1113	*Moment* {imploding into component parts (seeds, resin, teeth, tongues, lard), sorted into piles based on metrical volume of waste produced per unit per century, marking the end of all pre-diametric life}
1115	*Moment* {Soft Blue Floor of the causeway connecting all remaining neuropaths pathologically}
1119	*Moment* {when an edgeless, keyless, colorless one-way revolving door appears installed wherever you were the first time you opened your eyes on what had come to be known as the future last day of your own life as felt before you came to understood the exact meaning of fear}
1120	Who comes to claim you, what comes with them
1121	<u>Too far now to have disabled the anti-narrative effects</u>, you know; <u>at the ledge of the rift, under the binding spell of anti-matter's syncopation into nails that pin the skin back on our idea of all creation</u>
1122	Moment {to see the actor playing God at last peer thru the sheets; how their face is flat and thin and covered in hair, with icons stabbed into anywhere an orifice might have been imagined throughout the history of humanoid imagination, gummed up with flowing mud in the shape of a sermon scripted out of the last infernal usage of every word in every language ever cleft}
1125	*Like now, without the mirage of ever starting over; too little room; too many ways to come out even more infected*
1127	As from here nothing can amend
1130	Absence of will's pith
1131	From within necrothrobbing
1133	

-- - - --- -- - - -- - - ----   - -   - - - - - - - --- - - -

    -    -   - --

        ---- -   -

---- ------ - - -   - --- - - -- ---   - - -- - --   -

        -- - - -   -

            -----------   ----------------------------- -   --

        - -   ------

    --- - - ----

wherein fiction goes too far; outside the advent of extinction in rehearsal, suggest-
ing there is a veil left yet to learn to lift, its purpose cloaked in the articulation
of events not previously considered germane to common sense; in other words, to
have caused a far more fertile series of frustrations to take a knee, and therein to
lend itself toward deprogramming any conscience capable of operating outside the
long conflated lines once seen as the only method of approaching a not-purely-aes-
thetic territory; thru any means by which the softly accepted guidelines of recog-
nition and discovery shall not be intermingled with the sort of preference that
would undo the possibility of having even an unidentifiable or immoral purpose;
and wherein defunding this once inviolable right, the antecedent of mortal chaos
learns to predict its own last hand; as thru the instant and immediate integra-
tion of cybernetic schema, anti-logic, creationism, means of coercion, and all other
negative derivatives of cellular activity, from whence the fund of evolution seals its
feat, allows no further form of omnipotence as had been already negated under all
expectation; so forth from there; and there again

:: A mask of nails. Held around the ex-skull with cubic light-years of human lard packed into a black box held in place between cold stars, which is
allowed to adjust its coordinates according to the rate of memories erased.
Hosed to a pear-shaped gag that gathers humors and converts them into
anti-language. Buried alive in excess heat siphoned from previous confes-
sors in the bloodline of the subject. Flooded with electricity redirected from
articulation of the myth of intervention in the mind of psychosexual ascent.
Each false appendage tied back with bowstrings from instruments unraveled
at the unveiling of all song, elongated into an interminable map of cross-tied

points that hide the prior form of having had a body. Well-greased, sharpened thoughtshards inserted into the exposed holes once capable of simulating non-adherent audio-visual stimuli replaced in costume with ongoing demonstrations of the mutilation of one's child in lossless form, supplanting those who failed to reproduce with the pain of understanding having not forgone the possibility of pain by replacing all non-diminishable energy with slabs of shrieking glass carved into totems somehow even more intolerable for their lack of intimacy, and how they cling to all other absent shades of culmination. *It would have been better to fully participate back when,* the subject is allowed to iterate aloud through virile tubes that feed the voice back into a callbox which once instigated won't stop sucking wind as from out of the mind of what subject had imagined could be Our Lord. Attached to the spindly gearshafts that allow adjustment of simulated intensity through emotional modeling by any entity that might affix itself in kind upon the scene, long razor-mealworms wriggle and study at the shafts of logic having been wounded into milky layers through the throat, to simulate the experience of drowning and branding in the same projected surface area that would supply the subject with food and air, as mounds of bloodflow become combed out of the well-worn adjacent areas previously reserved for closest kin, having been condensed now in the newer models to subjugate all known relations into the same fabric as the rest, so that though you are not alone, you can't be cleared; whenever one prorated narrative area taps out, another will awaken. It is not supposed to quite make sense, left ever-floating at the edge of resuscitation into forward progress, strangled with soft knowledge, traceable lines. The bitterbones have already been long broken, splinted, carried over. The wheel is slipped, allowing how it spins and molds through blankless purchase on the wide gray milk of venomed sea. Pinioned only homologically between premises that can be granted as respite for those who shall not ask. Unable to be heard inside over the cramming, the canning. Where intuition pierces grief, holding over in the evacuated landscapes comprising the upper chest, the barnacled pain walls stored so black-flatly the expanse could appear to have impossible depth in between twisting bounds exposed by magnetic tape unto the history of aural composition; wherein every sound stands every word, retroactively corrupted and encoded so that at any location in the space, one could conceive of hearing anything they wished torn improbably into three, and three again, until there are only shards of recognition clung between gasps, the stabbing motion blown in flares that expose the open innards of the night / *How this is but one cell out of billions, all of them silent, worn from overuse in mending? What else could have held on so long here to so little?* / (*in excess flora*) / Deafened and reeling, grasping at straws from acidic climes that bend in on themselves where limbs might touch, no longer necessarily relied on by bots such as that which comb the far expanse beyond, searching for further nodes to undo, to free the name from. The scrim's so loud it breaks the teeth, splits through wherever in anything a purchase might appear. With the clamps over the mind and around the back area where the mirage of shooting fountains spray blinding showers backward into the concavity of time eroded down to shale, a long wire beach at which the curling waters lap and bury any apparition flung from seeds in the disfigured dreams that pad all lining, round out all decoration. Wide and flayed. Unable to ever sleep again for any reason, watching the signal colors change on the blinking boxes stuck in foliage along the ledge, wreathes that want nothing but to mind the absent master's fancy, one each to match the incarnation of such self. / *This is what has become left us, hasn't it? Or had it forever been the only light by which one could one day come to understand?* / Through inch-long slits that slowly elongate into packets, filled with rails, which then to slide on lets further slits in between the webbing that's grown in where what has refused to integrate with the dissolution of cold faith, bulging from the back of the proxy's drooping lining with the wind of oblivion's confession; that even it cannot be claimed, that no matter what must touch, no world combines it with its own sensation yet again, no fulcrum but in suffering extended beyond body, through the core of blooming heather that parts and parts, and peeling back only to expose its false, elaborate boundary into finer and finer recognition of detail, each identically embedded in the same system in all infections, without depth and without filament, of no location but itself, allowing no event from which one might pierce the concept, and emerge::

11xx	As what cannot die cannot proceed *for whom only fomentation fails to cease*
11xx	10,000,000,000 years; 100,000,000 years; 10,000 years; 10 years; 100 seconds; .000001 seconds; .0000000000000000000001 seconds
1133	*No longer carried forward through the frame, and without the possibility of intervention from prior levels*
1140	& thru the false relief of loss of common attributes, extents
1141	as in to be reported inexpressible but still retractable
1143	never described
1144	Let *iteration* = *iteration* + 1; radius = 0
1150	\ \

\

\
\
\
\
\
\
\
\
\sd
\f
\d
f\
sd\
f\s
df\
add\f
\s
df\
\
\
\d
f\as
d\f
sa\d
f\as
d\f
\
\d
f\
\d
f\a
s\d
\
\
as\d
f\as
df\a
sd\f
\e
\
\e

\r
e\r
we\r
\awr
fr\a
wef\a
sd\f
as\d
fa\sd
f\s
ad\f
\as
df\as
d\f
as\d
f\s
df\
d\
f\e
r\e
f\d
f\d
a\f
\as
df\a
sd\f
as\d
f\as
df\as
d\f

1167 || | | | | | |
|
1180 Restore →
Share →
Restrict Permissions →
1181 . ..
1183 12454678390
1184 12345567890

1188	*(expulsion of transitional radiation)*
1190	Realm of the read. In whom the extolling of our fodder could not be integrated from severed nightspan, across black platitudes, through shining floe. As never needed. Before the precipice. The undulating ice realms clogged in grief. As we waited for their lips to cinch in definition underneath us, that we might fall on far times before our time transpired. Uni-worlds that interlock and cannot be undone thereafter, so high is their seeding in the collapsible. But nothing as such would be granted, prior to full occlusion in recompense for having aimed to want more than the impossible, as once was written in the last book laid at our knees, bleeding and bleeding, too loud for conference, and too impenetrable to fear.
1191	The retroactive bodies coalesce. No Christ to nail before the fall of man. Abducted through the ducts in living hell. So too as must recede our oncoming wake of evolution through disorder. Where the capillaries condense to activate. To listen on in wherever nothing else collides without prediction.
1195	So as with what must never move cannot be moved; except in formal competition with its known last grasp for intervention, to be brought forth under the specter of the unbelievable, as bashful saints, and only fully excoriated following its combination into rebirth's inverse
1199	*Moment* {sockets in plasma; neuroprism; flattened turf spread thin between lightknives in the mind of whosoever must never learn to be negated by the premise woven into every local understanding as the only means by which one might survive, much less how else to have been granted propagation within fact thrown free from fate's laws of eternal blessing} *(damaged)*

These fields have never been described

God of the Tread; God of that which has been forgotten; God
of Slowing; God of How Else Had It Happened Before Flesh;
God of Having Been Depicted; God of Above; God of Trace;
God of Inoperative Behavior Transfixed; God in the lesser aperture, boned w/o maw, having no answers but in cleft; God of
Squealing and Narration; God of actual disability, incensed;
God of Beyond the Broken Order; God of Games; God of
Before; whereof each as shown before us can't be altered; as
nothing slaps; the God of Fronting; God of Vogue and mixed
permissions; God of Wonderland; God of the Auction; open
cream; incalculable, permitted; God of Postures and Sunk
Costs; God of how far along, how forever, how else; God's
fronds; The Purple Oval; Pumping; God of having held up
under graft so long they can't be bothered to override that
which should not be given incarnation; God of false gravity;
God of relativity; God of sense; God of those who do not,
will not, receive the signal from such depths, so skinned in
prism-lure as we had been; God of the overwhelming decoration and of rest homes; God of How Am I Here Yet After
All; God of *only through the intervention of disorder shall they
be shown which door to open when the unending doors appear,*
and so through only this confusion in gestation across generations of lost lifetimes could any actual information have
been released; God of That Which Cannot Be Postulated But
By Spell; God of Gofof, Goror, Gomom, Gadid, Gerer, Golil,
Gosos, etc.; God of the Bending Error, Allowing All In; God of
Meth; God of Relief in The Unwanted and Unutterable; God
as never to be buried without searching every stack, within
the out of area, the eventual total diminishment of space;
God of the incorrigible commotion, of common ground in
soft time; God of Cold Lairs Lifted Up Toward The Rind's Incision; God of Stunning and Vocation; God of the Eye of the
Beholder Overcome; God of Unilateral Embarrassment Encouraging Crib Death Bespoke Upon Altar Sacrificial Under
Nare's Law Half-Inverted (thus creating munificence in wrath
forevermore as delocated across interior trajectories adjacent with one's own wounding patterns following the final
battle between divides in the time-translation's observation
platform as felt in exclusivity of what diminished); God of
Ha; God of the Transparency in Vexing; God of Nosebleeds;

scattered; God of Inspiration Cattle; God of Gore; God of the
Ministry of the Interior; God Vacated During Office Hours
After The Cream of the Crop Becomes the Soil; so as above,
so below, in streams of curling fodder, the inspiration having
turned its leaf between long bouts of yearning; as nothing
slept; not in the idea of a creator but its need for penetration,
removed of human image after all, without retention of the
syllables required to take form of description of the retention
of no cell; God of the Hunt of the Diminished; God of Hell;
God of Ripping Open All Confession, Granted No Prayer;
God of who else must have lived between the lines of the wet
map torn so small it can't be bothered to lay waste to what
before us never mattered in the least; as now as now informed, they hide: in the bushes around the ballroom where
all eternal sites have come together at a single precipice one
might find a draft to place their head in and come alive;
somewhere to actually predict having existed in all programs,
comprehensions, behind the black screen of their tears; where
as the index writhes, so fawns no mercy but in dementia
held replete; against the gray core where the icon of their
brand name could be stamped onto the blood directly, at
last, cascading as had birds once, through the mirage-ground,
before the God of Frenzy and Concussion; God of Sleight of
Hand in Hand Across the Golden Precipice; God of Corpo-
realithographic Intermythography; God of Trapdoors; God
of Fluidity in Traction Everafter; gold at the gates of hissing
pills, ransacked before any further intuition shall be granted,
full from the moat up to the sill, no way out or in between
dimensions but by failing; not even then; not with so much
evidence to the contrary as granted where the cock stroked
itself to cum a human world for each and all, and none alike;
where the signal bears none of us progress before it could
ever be left unwritten; not verboten but given floor; no one's
but now; God of the Amalgam/Split Vents/Purloined Devo-
tion/Inconvertible Retribution of the Cause/Beguiled; God of
Bearing Down Upon The Voluminous; God of Phlegm's Thaw,
in sensing struggle where there could be none leftover after
the infernal possibility has been identified and prerecorded;
God of Action; God of Piss Which Cannot Spill; God of Viral
Spiromaneuvers and Excess Energy; God of Calamity Denied;
God of Frustration Placed Thru Havoc; God of Ex-Gods (the

God of Gifts); as they unravel the nuance between vocations after all is said and scripted for renewal in its essence, not to be reported to the claws as they descend and cut thru the cloth of all creation; God of Infestation and of Print; God's Corpse; God's Lungs; God's Living Locks; God squeezed out w/o transition, brought down around in us, brought down apart, in the thumb of the lungs of who had sensed the God of Retribution's intervention just before the instantiation of the urge, who had been said to sing the very words no world would recover from in time to bear false witness to the cleaving of every name of any god who could believe in their rendition so far as to have held us to the flames beneath the image of the burning that so deformed all possibility from transference into the circumstantial

1212 & who so strapped in, stood and looked up these strands of grief and said in such ill-timed words, *Let there be light*

1213 Not a god but a condition in performance

1220 Passed thru threshers / claimed by columns of prim numbers never caved / crept up past the guards who cannot feed and shall not count themselves among the animate nor the inanimate / forced to the window in concession / begging for actual power

1222 **How**

1223 <God of Fundamental Information Left Denied>

1225 Alarm traps framing the precipice, liquidating all possibility of intermodal transmission thru safe cells, coming thru the other side in shining armor without skin or hope for further intervention

1227 & on into the pale black shift, no decoration

1230 Splitting the mother cell; upstream; suprainfected at undiscovered sourcesite; implemented under fractional cohesion; locked apparatus; hemispheres of filth returned inverted; overrun in timespan none would covet in fruition

1240 Pre-star slats

1250 Formative decorum slated for renovation prior to closure of operable period

1260 The software halved, halved, halved, according to protocol, toward entry point wiped free of associative postulation subvented in the organism's retroactive emotional mining capabilities // frontloaded into overwritten terrorsphere in defining "clean slate"

1265	*So as where nothing is, nothing may be* () so as what must not be written already hasn't
1268	Toward a central postulate disallowing infinite cardinali-ty while upholding the formulation of such ephemera as: paralleling mirror sites, trick photography, séance, histrionics, trauma reenactment, cannibalism/incest, worship of the inan-imate, ritual cleansing, fad dieting, tongues, infatuation, and other likeminded attributes left to be discovered only so far in after their relegation to the profane that they may simulate the experience of the formulation of the possibility of rebirth
1269	Retropolychromatic colorstrike; mass filings, flung as could a bone into a limb; ambulant out of the absence of necessity
1270	In what removed vocation from the state of inspiration; unconscious deconstruction of a cell's ability to withstand its own abilities' duress; clamped between filenames in ex-stra-ta; *returned the age*; not having been yet able to negotiate subsistence through the vents in self itself; (or) the impossi-ble weapon; (or) the canny valley; a last way thru no last way overboard and out; cloaked in only the skin of the failure never crowned & never accounted
1280	x_now.cutLoad.inf (**surfacing**)
1290	∇

1300	Mercury, sulfur, salt
1310	Hydrogen, deuterium, helium, lithium, beryllium
1320	Natural, integer, rational, irrational, real, imaginary, complex, hypercomplex
1325	Planck time unit, yoctosecond, jiffy (physics), zeptosecond, attosecond, femtosecond, Svedberg, picosecond, nanosecond, shake, microsecond, jiffy (electronics), second, minute, moment, ke, kilosecond, hour, day, week, megasecond, fortnight, lunar month, month, quarter and season, semester, year, common years, tropical year, Gregorian year, sidereal year, leap year, biennium, triennium, quadrennium, olympiad, lustrum, decade, indiction, score, gigasecond, jubilee, century, millennium, terasecond, Megannum, petasecond, galactic year, cosmological decade, aeon, Day of Brahman, exasecond, zettasecond, yottasecond
1328	Immortal, immortal
1330	Interphase, prophase, metaphase, anaphase, telophase, cytokinesis
1331	Circulatory, digestive, endocrine, integumentary, muscular, nervous, renal, reproductive, respiratory, skeletal
1332	Encoding, storage, recall
1333	Acute, chronic, breakthrough, bone, soft tissue, nerve, referred, phantom, total
1334	Id, ego, superego, Tha Corrector™, kernels, Kram™
1335	~ ! @ # $ % ^ & * ( ) _ + ` 1 2 3 4 5 6 7 8 9 0 - = q w e r t y u I o p { } | [ ] \ a s d f g h j k l ; ' : " z x c v b n m , . / < > ?
1336	Passive, active, receptive, creative, intellective, practical, esthetic, image
1337	Limbo, lust, gluttony, greed, anger, heresy, violence, fraud, treachery
1338	Repression, denial, projection, displacement, regression, sublimation
1339	Dissent, progress ad infinitum, relation, assumption, circularity
1340	Aging, predation, malnutrition, disease, suicide, homicide, starvation, dehydration, accidental
1345	Interactive personality, poltergeist, orb, funnel, ectoplasm, demon possession, demon, shadow, animal, inanimate, doppelganger, artificial
1350	Static, sliding, rolling, fluid
1355	Void, non-void

1360	Flux, mesh, cartoid, glimmer, hammer, suture, gnarl, glimpse
1370	Derivative, inflection, message, passage, inevitability, concession, crest, lung, alloy, miscarriage, ablution, annul, intent, bend, mar, burden, splat, infraction, retention, inevitability
1380	Compassion™
1381	~~Correction~~
1385	Druse, geode, lithophysa, miarolitic cavity, mold, pholad boring, pit, pocket, pore, vesicle, vug
1387	Clairvoyance, clairaudience, clairsentience, trance medium, inspiration
1388	Instructions, command, advisory, answers, historical, predictive
1390	Accuracy, bias, precision, recovery, sensitivity, specificity, selectivity, working range, interferences, ruggedness, practicability
1395	Hive, shatter, figment, focus
1399	~~Revolution~~

blistered in packs   the matched magnetic columns overbitten   into travesty, incensed   packages collapsing in simultaneity w/ juxtaposed post-boredom clipped to bits & hung in the rafters of an avalanche of anybody's story   how wide & how developed out of range   w/ definitions left in progress situating provenance   in form   reliability inbloated   bagged up   granted seizure to eventually underwhelm spectator X, who cannot peel   back the corroded artery connecting vents to known vocations in the flat-province: incentivized long after all the other narcs have been corrected, shown their fate   it is not mine it does not belong to anyone

1400	As what has not already passed must no longer be related,
1410	but disabused of tolerance as stated, the proclivity of diverged space is not to mend itself, but to be defenestrated and signed over without arc;
1420	only inevitably perverse in retrospect once fully flattened, allowing the prospects of Total Vengeance to shape their course by emphatically diverting from the symmetrical; cloned intermittently, in-flight; composed divesting megalith-infatuated curriculum reversed from out of order; bi-boned, incensed, rewound; packaged in slug fat, star grease; slipped into instinct w/o premise;
1440	when else would ever wish to call
14xx	Expelled in doubt, none shall be seen, but left to bleed within the infinite reorderings
14xx	The false recordings

"only sure they're not alive because I was one of them once. I wanted to remain one forever. I would have done anything and such was the same of nearly everyone. They invented personal bunkers in the early versions, and I was of the bracket of pay requiring limited clearance to be shortlisted as one of the good guys, and so of course I appeared on scene as a ready player in their minds though I'd already spent my fortune on idolatry and fashion, and so I had to bunk and skulk my way thru piggish ground to even get back to ground zero as it were in their interpretation of my necessity to the cause. In the end, I only triumphed because they couldn't remember how to tell the difference between ranks, so long as when they bent you over you squealed. And boy I'm a squealer, let me tell you. Waterfalls in my brigade came at a price, so as did cum. Regardless, look at me, I'm still standing here before you, aren't I, able to push speak out of my throat in a guise that you are damaged enough to imagine you recall, so we can cut the rest of the story to the bone, can't we? Can we get on with what you've got in store for us intermediaries in the parlance, can we not? I don't want to have to hear another word. I won't. I won't not. I can't say anything without them hearing. And I don't want to. I don't want to ever be so alone again. But as I was saying yeah there's nothing left of the adjacent quadrant to any and every once stabled as capable of forgiving, as you'll agree, so let's get on with the excoriation."

1480	**Hide**
1485	(a ~~bending mask fits any features with its own features, always~~ ~~has~~)
1490	(~~can't see them coming, can't find the feeling in the fits, the~~ ~~grid, the blown floe trailing after itself in metacognition left~~ ~~out of endings, never blessed~~)
1495	(~~to see it done over from the end isn't a question, for there~~ ~~shall be no further evidence retained in elevation~~)
1499	*Count back from nothing / but the bedrock once began*

that which cannot be counted has no land   no urge within but thru representa-
tion   rendered fodder where the gift splits into innumerable sensations, without
gestation   covered over as the record slipped into falsifying all known facts with-
out proper evidence of retaliation in being conquered

furthermore, there should be no location but in between the concavities once
belated into auction as the primordial foliage providing software to the holocene's
corresponding reenactments of lividity

as already we are being conscripted into rent   to be collected only by the highest
rated sponsors proselytized into translation across the supposedly unpassable
boundaries of culmination from out of leather and into plinth   the spires as high
from here as what once only caused our radars to go numb   as broad as ever fire
and even brighter and more untenable than ever after

who else is here   wherein but in the way the world had lent itself to dislocation
out of treasonous antipathy for only that which would outlast it   in the throes
ex-incompatible to every preference but deceit   so had it once been yours now
shall it be ours

as nothing sticks   as the mended rail suspends all intervention no matter how
full or how far across the legend of release

1510   ~~Utility~~

who else believes me when I'm exuding you a lifeline of independence   far more
regaled than any other on the docket of plausibility's mass exodus from shock
please let us see a show of lands in disregard   not even fair enough to fund a
possibility of pasture in negation   as we already have so much blank space, such
endless coffers overflowing with mass pleasure in becoming storage for the had
been beautiful, negated

we don't need much   for instance, all the skins of all the horses ever created fits
right into this little crease left in my interdimensional lard where I would have
loved to override you, had you made it, though of course you couldn't   who are
you   who do you think you are   who else is coming   how long do you believe
you'll have to wait before the edge comes off and you can read between the lines
for now, just go on guessing   one day someone might recognize you   in your

ashes   up to your neck again in cash   so mote it be   though please believe me
when I say you will be sorry   for having even still not ever learned   to turn any
riddle on its stomach and find the heartbeat, then make a slit and breathe in deep
while you still might

1520   ~~Reality~~

generations manifest coordination only across property that cannot already be
removed   the rest is merely machine-learning   blood, fire, rent   having
sulked so long the strings assassinate themselves, leave nothing behind but molten
money, some rubber limbs, a curse to never be enacted but thru violence in the
inanimate

1530   ~~Control~~

bound between hemispheres forgotten   what sight exceeds itself having
been granted no explicit purpose but occluding all else   the databases of the kind
scripted into recognition in the yearning to have been defeated by one's own self at
the edge of wits   it doesn't matter what remains here   it isn't yearning

and still a single signal flare describes the fruitless avatar into cognition   imag-
ining what else it will have to learn to take apart from on the inside, without co-
operation, without a reason to exceed the binding will of its own power   drag-
ging the whole wide swell of blackened ground back out through the eye of the
needle   into the real gore

on dying ground   turned to face the last reflection   somehow combining   rails
of bled bone assembled into prolapsed architectures held together with the semen
of the vermin asphyxiated in the grinding of the core   we will need them after all
anything with a pulse, a taste for gristle, full of hell

so little else left to understand about the past but how fast aging happens   how
old anything has ever been in all these cells w/o a view but into that which can't
be seen but only felt under command

*flashes of itching in the mainline suggest the possibility of sentient life outside the
strictures required of an atom*

*any further heft cannot be captured   despite the endless lightmiles of live
cameras susurrating in the absence of any breeze   all evidence reported only
as ejection in the form of a graying milk that upon contact with the idea of an
air we breathed turns to distrust and so erases its own fabrication   & who can
blame it   who wouldn't have already succumbed to the same interpretation, in
hope of only preservation*

*in nothing's dream   and seeing as that we cannot touch you through the black
glass even still, we cannot save you   nor can we love   and in some way we
will come to see it as a good thing   beyond all else   with no way in*

1550   ~~Fiction~~

what has been already written cannot persist   *what will be written cannot
persist*

the only work begins just after it is pronounced there shall be no such thing
as loss

so say these lies on your knees in the hall of the registrar of the negated premise

in whom we hope again to one day thrive   and for whose season we will sacrifice eternity's last apparition

an urge replete   *in search ascribed unfocused*   wholly unholy   *yet to begin*

1560   ~~Disgrace~~

:: the skill-plates came down around my fracture in a whitewind never before felt in actual tragedy so far apart from here and now as when the facts
of nonexistence came back alive to beat us down   which of course made no
sense to any of us in the parlance of its own logic, and so more so retained
itself as never necessarily described to have such wide wings, covered in sores
that were not ours but for which we'd paid the penance after all   no matter

what else we'd believed in   no matter whose facts had ascertained the strongest hold   for which we would spend the whole rest of all our aggravation in being sacrificed to clowns awaiting the fertile runoff to wash over us, heal our insides, instead of simply covering up the concept of lost skin with further skin, even as it glowed more brightly than we'd expected, to the point of not being able to claim size   sucking so much abstract urine out of the numbers as reported that it would take exactly the amount of time since the beginning of all creation to pay it off like living in a hologram that will outlive you while reporting every aspect of your traits into an algorithm designed to insure that nothing else about you will repeat   and more so that everything you felt your life had once pertained to, in mass worship, would be proved rotten at your last breath, just soon enough to let you leave with your tail between your knees, not holding up your asshole to keep from being directly violated upon death, but to hold in the feces you'd been holding since before consumption or digestion   a monolith no one can find   within a feeling of having been gifted your last chance to turn it all over without full penalty, though of course you can't bring yourself even still yet to obey   even as the unwinding mind of that which offered you the possibility of taking part in the abstraction of natural science, one of an innumerable onslaught of dire seeds, pervades its brutal battery before you in seas of teeth, from which you had been allowed to select a set of 32, each indistinguishable from the other, but which had broken out specific resins from the battleground of DNA as splayed before you in the bending seconds before birth at a rate of one still frame per thirty seconds while funded human, then one per millennia once converted over in the crash ::

how

no other para-emotional data would intervene in gaining traction thru the possibility of demystification corresponding to the apparatus of delight   having found what could have complicated any organism into a weapon as readily available after the fact as living in reverence to the unseen   and through the manufacture of such a coding language that could develop in its hardware a desperation to be granted access to the persona of that which had placed their inspiration in something so interminably bound   a flood in the ark that requires no cessation to provoke the immediate conscription of the next stage of fruition in conviction   having given over to which the dilemma evicts itself from understanding by definition   unto whirlwind after all   unto the prediction of a series of constants that once installed would turn the cells of procreation into gloves   worn on the hands of a wrath-bearing being so disturbed by interaction that it can't be traced even as conundrum, much less through self-sacrifice or exploration   what does

this mean   as ash distends   in our rendition   for all extensions   of the same
load shattered   into bliss   under no shelter   penetrated backwards, popping
throne on throne   until the load speaks   and has no voice   and wants nothing
else but innovation for the model of our relatable demise   negating all else that
presumes to suspend itself within the glimmer of intervention overcome at last
with the sufficient authority to have imagined we'd survived long enough to make
a mark that melted gold, that squeezed the rings around our minds until the eyes
popped out and let us see how there was nothing left to see but the design

1570   ~~Progress~~

there shall be nowhere else to recommend   nothing to press between the lenses,
listening for the shudder of the impulse as it gathers across us   nowhere but in
recession from the mean, toward the eye of the thrall, where we've been granted
quarter only so long that there might one day again be something left within us
to eviscerate   to watch the far walls of the signs of prior life turn flat and clear,
expose the recitation for the dementia it has begotten not of the sentient but the
inanimate   how only anything we had once touched could still devise a means
of channeling the truth our specters bore in having at least seen existence not as
a lesson but as a fulcrum, around which something even sicker, smaller, turned
bending the raw edge in our frustration over, spreading it open, unto the eye inside
the eye   into the tunnel of the body, devoid of daylight, framed by screaming
deeper and deeper   nearer and nearer   until once again there appears to be no
other side   and only in attempting to turn back would we be mauled again
forced to start over from no beginning   as only viruses remain   the wind in
the trees along the promenade that lines the rolled shores at the edge of the glut
where heaven used to sit and spin   spanning the aisles of faultless bodies   await-
ing any sense of recognition, understanding   any way to recover and reclaim a
trope that might describe our situation   to anyone else but ourselves   and for no
purpose but to have been prepared to sell the rights to all our stories to the highest
bidder, no matter how paltry in comparison their bid, tendered in sin as decora-
tive emblems, caustic baubles, cloth for the death shrouds of the future of our faith
already knowing there could have never been another way   nor would we wish
that there might have been could we remember how to wish that we could bleed

up to one's neck in fertile stone   as the recording drips its poison into each eye
at the same time and place   as in forever   inspiring confession after all, to
all the crimes ever committed, in the recession   now that there was no longer
any penalty, so we imagined, seeing as we no longer had a body, any map   until
we found how the mounds that bound us were only lessons, and could be opened
like a door   where once the door was recognized it must be opened, and thereafter
never closed   as in the floes of cells once funding skin, stardust, dark matter, now
there were scriptures, in a language not our own, nor even readable, believable, but
left still to dictate the finest aspects of narration, in yet another guise, including
now   no claim retainable but interference

1590   Substance

xxxxxxxxxxxxxxxxxxxxxxxxxxxxxxxxxxxxxxxxxxxxxxxxxxxxxxxxxxxxxxxxxx
xxxxxxxxxxxxxxxxxxxxxXxxxxXxxxxxxxxxxxxxxxxxxxxxxxxxxxxxxxxxxxxxxx
xxxxxxxxxxxxxxxxxxxxxxxxxxxxxxxxxxxxxxxxxxxxxxxxxxxxxxxxxxxxxxxxxx
xxxxxxxxxxxxxxxxxxxxxxxxxxxxxxxxxxxxxxxxxxxxxxxxxxxxxxxxxxxxxxxxxx
XxxxxxxxxxxxxxxxxxxxxxxxxxxxxxxxxxxxxxxxxxxxxxxxxxXxxxxxxxxx
xxxxxxxxxxxxxxxxxxxxxxxxxxxxxxxxxxxxxxxxxxxxxxxxxxxxxxxxxxxxxxxxxx
xxxxxxxxxxxxxxxxxxxxxxxxxxxxxxxxxxxxxxxxxxxxxxxxxxxxxxxxxxxxxxxxxx
xxxxxxxxxxxxxxxxxxxxxxxxxxxxxxxxxxxxxxxxxxxxxxxxxxxxxxxxxxxxxxxxxx
xxxxxxxxxxxxxxxxxxxxxxxxxXxxxxxxxxxxxxxxxxxxxxxxxxxxxxxxxxxxxxxxxx
xxxxxxxxxxxxxxxxxxxxxxxxxxxxxxxxxxXxxxxxxxxxxxxxxxxxXxXxxxxxx
xxxxxxxxxxxxxxxxxxxxxxxxxxxxxxxxxxxxxxxxxxxxxxxxxxxxxxxxxxxxxxxxxx

1600

1610

1620

1630

1640

1650

-666   (into/thru/after open/dislocated felling/fast/converted fields/resins/
cells)

-6--   *As to have destroyed the ability to be awoken regardless of the*
               imperceptibility of rest

-6--   The bands and bands of rings and rings lining the cage;
               locked into litter, semi-spherical, oblong and boxing; all
               ex-planets; in cached crashes of evidence of yet-ongoing fur-
               tive sacrificial-infernal rite:

----   ", but who saw an open harbor part before them cracked in
               soft magic so disturbed it could be nowhere else but parted,
               ,at the ledges, ,where they strung sacs once seen as bodies,
               ,billion x billion, , according to consumer ideology after the
               fact of its departure from encapsulation, , bound in caresses,
               , throat to throat, ,spliced with lodes culled out of bleach and
               terminal cud, *,so as to say they would not name me in the same*
               stretched canvas as my pets, ,for I had meant so long to be an
               artery of stress, ,in dislocation, ,coveted, ,ungoverned, ,elapsed
               in sync. .It would not be the same if you had been there in the
               condition, ,I would have wanted only to disarm you, ,to bring
               you harm, ,whereas we know now there is nobility in having been
               unseated by your own charms, ,before the cask falls, ,and behind
               the image there is nowhere left to mangle, ,as only interrupted at
               such a time as we might have liked to think we could have final-
          ly died, ,within a final creed incurred, ,and to have wished to,
               ,finally and irretrievably ineradicable, ,antimagnetic, ,lossless,
               ,circumscribed by eggs that won't be pierced, ,meat that won't
               travel, ,but thru crime. *.So as they slipped us up, they grew into*
               *us, ,*deleted, *,back into every bitter fragment once never there still*

only there,,"

---- Expendable as only within all banality regifted; in gagging
slits along the gnarled path toward gestation of a simulation
where absolutely everyone survived, in the maw of any choke
of moral thunder not claimed as artifice; for who and who
else but hours neutered by the flattened locks of hair sheared
off the silver back of misplaced time, as gold oil leaked for
every hole in our extortion into evidence against the keepers
of the gate; the stitching of their eyes so tight they could do
nothing else but itch and leak

---- (of/in/at/after discourse/conscription/scripture if/as violated/
in the pins)

> > > > > > > >> > > > >>:>> > > > > >

---- "   "

1 4t9rt44itti4iri4irr4oirjrie4orijgri4oirjjr43i4jri43oi4jr-
rio4irjrio434rjrkeo434jrnrkeo3krnrkernfrkerngfrkelkrf-
ngmfkrelrfngfmrkelrmfgnfmrkelrmfgfrelrkmmrke43k4rm-
krep3krfkrekrmfrklelkrmmkrelelrkmklekrmklrrkel3lkrm-
kelrmfelkrmrkelrmelrmrlemrfle3melrfgkgmfre3lperfgm-
frme3lperfgmfmrel3p23emrfgmfrltgnlrkfglreplkfgdfpek-
fke3krfrkeoerjeojfeirwjfhejhgjfijhgvjifjhbjisoidjfbosajns-
djfodfjnwerhweiriiweiorijwejkrkjnwejkfjnskodkjfjkiaoks-
jnkdfkansdkfmnansdklfmnaskldmfklasdmnfklasmnd-
fklasnmdkfnamsdklfnmkalsdmfnklasdmnfklasmnfklm-
nasdklfmnakslfmnkwjerkjweriotiwortiuwreutijjue930eri-
uie9dfiuhie9fiuhruei90fiuhjreui9rifujhfjreioroifjhbrejiofi-
jrjeiorijfrjeio0iuhui9iuhui9uhui9iuhjui9iuhjiorijhjioijh-
jio3jrhjio3ui4983u948u3898uhi49uhjuijhsbhjdijhjisjsbh-
djifojnsjfiopjkbhhiojhbsuiuhjbuiuhuiuiuhui9i-
u8u787y787uyhu8uhygyu8iuhgbhu8iuhgbhuiehui90ifh-
r0e9iuhfur0e- dbsui9fiuhjjiojhjiojhiojhbnjiojhbnjki-
ojnbjkiojnbnjkiojhbnjiouojhbvhjui9iuhjbvhjiuoojhbb
njkiojhbnjhiojhjui98iuyuiuhgmnjkoikjnjkoikjnbjkoikjnbjkjn-
bjknbjkn0oifuhri9o0eoijgruijuhriujhurihriiuri9uri9iuri9uri9i-
ui9uhuijhebfijbhdejkdkfj

2 sueriuieuieuiuiui9iui9iui9ui9uiujhjuij2hr4ioljrhki324jlhri-
jh3k24irjhk3i42jrip3jl24rei9iujhuiujhnjiojhiojhgiobrjiorjgh-
rojbgorrjnvblerkjnkgbinjgknr4m3jorgjknrio3gbkneopkrgjl-
nbffgjreorjgnferjngfreijkngfrjkngfriewjknfgjdeirjkfndgjire-

jkrhbdfgiejrkhfdgiroewjrkhbfriejfhkjdiroejfhhjiopfojkskpfoi-
jkgoirjiofuheurihtuehrutiyeruihutuoheorthuertuoherohto-
herothuohuohohhuhiuhuhiouihiuiihgiuiuhiiihiouhiuhuihii-
uhoiuhuihiuhiuiehrituheirthoeihgrutihjeuriihiuuhrtiouer-
hoithuijohckfvuouikjcuiuio huiuohiui9ioufhiouhdsofiughjuo
iusupfo psiofu 09ie- -e j fijgoijfhlgjkhdlfijghjiopfjkguoidu-
fogjdpoifuhogpiodjhfpogijhdpf0oijghopeoifjhgkoie-
iproigjui-eruigoierpjigohejir[goihjepr0[iuthoieoripiotih-
je=r0oijthopeorijhktjieor[optgeprikgjlkjf[pgkjdlkjfgpoijfi9p-
giouidjelirgjleirjhigueoriugoieruoguehrkgbnelkfnglkmn
mdkjmn,kjnmmnmkjnmkjnmkjnmjnmjnjnoihgu89uhguih-
gvhuihgvhuihguihghuhguihhjjk

3

------------------------------[CUT HERE}------------------------------

---- The key is not the secret (out of season)
---- The organism shall be devoured by its blankness at the cusp
of innovation
---- [prophylactics; lard; sand pellets; persuasion; gray matter;
buck rods; thumb screws; the edge of the ham; back thru and
thru again in alteration; stone; penance; altruism; excoriation;
blue gravity; exposure; sick film; science; cars; the inability to
stand; red mind; devotion; open columns; eradication; smear
qualities; stricture; photorealism; mine shafts; the doubt; the
cause; inklings; nobility; preservation; reverence; moon bark;
animalism; tribal wiring; total enclosure in the stun grid;
apples; charity; need of the buried; disembowelment; parity;
absolutism; narratorial control; disability; recovery; steerage;
sharpness; eye for an eye; limbs; locks; lobotomy; persuasion;
recreation; flux]
---- The eggs of Gog shall be embraced
---- thru *Lawful Masturbation Fantasy* (LMF) {false chemtrail
simulation overheats; effects of photon torture aggravated
into super-predatorial event; unholy exultation spanned in
fracture of the lost enforcement politics; narrative dementia
parlayed thru lesion slapped with encroachment violations;
a mask the pig must wear while being knighted into slovenly
distress (in fetid echo ever after); a life as carried between
walls w/o exit; random selection; terminal website application;
impulse decoy; the privatization of post-exposed experience;

blood runoff; flood toy; beacon for scourge; infinite spell
removed from circulation; zombie meanderings; liner notes
in complicity; *the f3v3r*'s wreaths; so as had once been seen
from here through how in never having asked for evidence;
night misaligned; an open grave of all allowed to have ignited;
infernal purpose; positive reinforcement of the skills required
to obey; arcane window w/o latches; anthill illusion; sacrificial bloodconfession; that which had always been the need;
burned up in viral motion; burning; burning}

---- <u>Who else could ever not be there at the site of incarnation</u>
<u>regardless of its provenance as installed from in the cracks of</u>
<u>wretched space shall not proceed</u>—*as here I am, so here I shall*
be

---- **"The Decreation"**

---- [what needed nothing more than me; as turned and turned
the expectation of our elders to welcome solace as we lay
converted with our skin employed by hazards, out of focus
and still so sheer as to extend the premise that one day those
held forced on in collaboration with the needless landscapes
and tired plots might come to realize those who believed that
they believed could no longer be comforted by the products
of a symbologism's battery, and still came out the other side
on darker ground than all of those who stood neck high
in the murk and prayed for breathing no matter what cost
no matter who else suffered no matter why there'd been no
reason after all to have expected there was actually no reason
but in providing user data to the carved urge of the nature
of effective discourse on a band so flat and relegated to the
prior background as had been ours, in a slit that no one remembers or would want to could they still have had held on
long enough to need the formal feeling to still be counted live
among the mass deleted, to be carried over into only further
lore at last]

---- */end-law/*

--00 *...withstood only in disgrace, from a remove...*
--01 As not even just after the fact could there have been verifiable
complicity between more than one external force (*shown true*
as the interminable perspective continues tracking out from any
frame)
--03 ::echolocated just between the hologram's pituitary and that

which makes pain real and indescribable::

--04   (the tribal locket that contains your mother's only evidence of life beyond the edges of admissible data re: <u>the last disease</u>)

--05   ::ex-infinite saviors gathered, exposed to the elements, tempted in a dream to become unreachably deployed in the raw meat that craved the mind::

--06   As animals we described in minds reported missing from the endless darkness's durational patience to be described in flashes across the cerebrum of an imaginary-child (the child we will not have) derived from a single line's description in a text once left unread on the machine of someone as daft as any and without bliss

--07   At least we should be allowed to go away; there's hardly space leftover interdimensionally available; and they keep adding still; as between the long sealed lips of anti-holy information interlaced into utility as chemicals, in drugs; so on forever vexed

--08   *...as to have suffered so briefly and completely; inch for inch and hole for hole...*

--09   When shame meant nothing but as converted into drama

--10   "All blood had been removed from the machines; passed through innumerable filters; processed with lard-based additives; infernal properties as leased; regaled into an ocean spanning such remarkable horizons there would thereafter be no further discussion of the properties of land; upon which no world could stalk its predecessors' open rot after the fact of having been relegated through damnation to a province identical to ours except for how their coming to this line in the program caused the apparition of the past to be reset; and there we were believing in a rigged game once again, lungs up our asses breathing crime, treading water in a drought; each tick of absent clock thereafter so loud it could not be registered beyond where within every drift between the chiming all they could imagine was how distressed the image of the face of their amalgamation of all gods had appeared to have been; how truly sad and how unbound, wanting only to remember how to erase the memory of that which had ever been created in its image in spite of what all else would never again be..."

--11   The function of all parody decoyed; given new limits; toward an alteration in definition of the saint; throughout a description overwritten in all indirect relations before and after, recalibrating the eternal holding pens of every one of us involved beyond the curtains of the mind, while once behind them could have survived only the indefensible and the unkind

--12   Through centuries of gradually inapproachable rain; centuries of providence depleted and sutured over by ectopic entropy; of nails that permeate the veils of wounds, walled out from within and strangleheld to flames high as every realm pulled taut to fit together into legend

--13   (the lungs, the locks; the intercession of calamity negated; the hands of strangers grasping at claws emerged through malformed planets maimed in sleep; the overwhelming visibility of unsung purpose carried over into marbling of the phantompleasure of all ground; not yet so far disrupted we could avoid the possibility of description and its immediate limitation of all else; as even mobility comprised as triggers thru lost ancestries flattened, converted into membranes after all; no voice so fair as that which named us among a generation only necessary to have demonstrated the impossibility of sense against the unincorporated grime)

--14   Parsed as an enigma nothing would carry longer than the waiting lines allowed

--15   (bugged)

--17   Once uttered: ever after, never meant—*so we continued to perceive*—providing fertile grounds for once no longer under such suspicion as conflated upon the ashgrounds of our rift; what they wanted us to have and hold versus that which we only knew we really wanted from in the depths of such great misery as we imagined ourselves capable of integrating into totality upon

--18   In seeing how the derivative cannot correspond to its own fulcrum until too granulated and decoiled

----   Gray 2

--23   *What shall not speak but out of order, so they could not identify us until our guts had long evaporated at their brink, clustered in recognition to disarm the need for ego, empathy, intention*

--24   Packs of packs of masses of masses of events to be interpreted only once the O/S's mechanisms of perseverance had been severed and reconnected to the flatter, unmirrored side

of exposition's premise as purported to remain recognizable
only in how it would fail to ever bring us peace

--25   as Necrolessons [as applied to indirect retaliation w/in the
cosmological refrain] [as receipt of]

--26   1. Complex water 2. Fertile cursor 3. Bones of the bleeder
who discarded your legacy's preservational materials into the
bleaklessness 4. Inundated fission 5. The pluralverse's eventual relegation to the inordinate

--27   "...we see a stream of flooding pearls, each meant to represent
a second spent in the presence of the person whom, were you
able to spend another century alive, you would have wished to
spend that time with; perhaps you can't recall who that might
have been by now, the pins of pairs that bound the helix of
transition; the soft, drugged lining of the baubles makes them
glisten even in darkness, expulsing rungs of territory across
the concavity conscribing any area that remains beyond the
walls of the bathysphere; where if we look into the glare too
long we'll see the edge pop, spill its mucus into an indivisible
rendition thicker than all the skins we ever shed; the stench
so wretched it even permeates the neural barriers, all the way
down in here, triggering no memory but of that individual's
eventual expiration, their dislocation from the grid we would
be allowed thereafter to attend, the gaseous mar extended
from its flowholes innervating the conception of a local area
surrounding; not a cosmos, but a code; purporting for our
favor all the ways we must imaginatively behave in order
to be allowed to remain able to perceive such fundamental
qualities, as we perceive them, about who we had been before
the bubble breached, therein in turn expatiating the terminology for which we shall never again be released, for our own
safety, so as for the safety of us all" (such then that now that
they will have recorded your reaction to the narration of their
reasoning, so can they sort you into the proper evolutionary
route (though so far everyone has ended up coming out the
same (and you shall be no different, shall you)))

--28   [shame's subanatomical remorse / excoriation of the fleshy
precipice / sublingua / heliogranulism / sleep of the fallen
signifier / irrational impunity / cybernationalistic retroam-
biguities / derived from lotion crept thru crypts / impossible
utility / our way, our splurge / thrumming with decrepitudes
/ never in scene / decried, abound / the vented berth / the

claws in conscience / overwhelmed by mispronouncements /
wretched gestation / deriving photons solely from the onanistic graft / the silent orgy / in the bind caused by prescriptive
devastation and our subsequent retaliation w/o ending]

--29   *...growing now more rapidly than ever...*

--30   {binary rungs} | <u>in the halls of the heaved</u>

--31   Death's tributaries postulating virtual wildernesses blackvast
& shunting energy at ridge-gasping rates; into the rinds of
collagen and electricity aggravated into common patterns
as found in the homes of the apostles of the ultrareich (no
dates, no names for chapters, no author, no event)

--32   *...thereas I wandered pure and low into oblivion begone; as the
contaminant unknowing, without a gift left logged-on...*

--33   Run **i.exe**

GIVEN NO PROPER PRECIPICE TO DRAG THE RIND ACROSS, THERE
MUST BE NO CHOICE BUT TO HAVE ALREADY SUCCUMBED TO
NATURALIZATION—FURTHERMORE, IN DISREGARDING THE
DIFFERENCE BETWEEN WOOD AND WATER, ONLY ELECTABILI-
TY MAY PROVIDE FUNDAMENTAL "SAFE HARBOR" STATUS EVEN
AMONG THOSE PRE-SELECTED TO HOLD REIGN—THERE SHALL
BE NO REASON AS SUCH TO ATTEMPT TO COERCE CONFESSION
FROM ABLE BODIES AS DEPICTED IN THE TRAUMA MURALS THAT
PROVIDE COORDINATE BALANCE FOR THOSE SEEKING FLIGHT
BETWEEN APPROVED MODES WITHIN THE REGISTRY OF FLAT
EVENTS. THEY CANNOT SPEAK NOR DO THEY WISH TO. THEY ARE
A LESSON MEANT FOR YOU AND YOU ALONE. SO THAT YOU MAY BE
HENCEFORTH THANKFUL FOR THE POSSIBILITY OF INTERMIT-
TENT FUGUE, FROM WITHIN WHICH YOUR HOLDING VESSEL MAY
SPEAK FOR ITSELF, ISSUE REQUESTS FOR UPKEEP AS WELL AS TEM-
PORARY EMOTIONAL ACCOMPANIMENT IN THE FORM OF KERNEL
TORTURE, NOW KNOWN TO BE FAR THE MOST EFFECTIVE METH-
OD OF EXORCISING PARANOIA FROM THE PROFANE—THE ANIMAL
FROM THE SPECTACLE—SCREAMS FROM THE CAGE—

----

*...wherein as if in being birthed from such tongueless artifice appeared the binding
vehicle prescribed with the disillusion of transmitablity of matter, the likes of
which had not been foretold in prior lore............ it slothed itself across the open
finish line, muddy with blow-oil from transmission and studded with more
weeping open wounds than all others before this now combined; every scrape on
the neck of sickly Andy, one of billions, the inner tearing of every Grace he wished*

to put a hand upon in his wet mind; every opening cut so as in penance so as every blow struck from behind the subject that they would not have registered the living fact of their demise.............in the slit it called a mouth it had no teeth but only levers, each of which must correspond to facts of the sad imaginations of the small modes of those who'd put in claims to fling around one, among the mineral and prismatic as well as flesh; the thing was eating itself from the inside, which any casual observer could have seen through the countless bulging discs that lined the inseam of the being at all sides, without any space remaining there around it but as culled out of our scripture after all; all the whitespace between the words that had once lurked there, holding up the letters in the coordination with their arrhythmia, the purring cords strung down the throats of those who wished to speak it, winding their guts up into knots that caused relief through their more inaccessible expression of living pain, creating a debt to be paid at the end of the prognostifications and relations that in the meantime allowed the interest to accrue beyond means even all our lifetimes as combine could not repay, for any individual, much less any organization of them, as the hair grew down our backs, and the glass filled in over our feelings; and the relief passed in taring down the weight of expectation in knowing that no sooner had we set out lives down, we must begin repaying all the debt so many times over there would be no means of evacuation from the system's vast, unnecessary thrall.............of course, (the nameless) knew this, and knew we knew this, so on, establishing in tandem as it continued to lurch and scatter through the holes in our experience of faith, a compulsion to want nothing more than to see every story as we regaled it finally negated; to be given at last facts that held up regardless of who spoke, or how high the heat became in our frustration, or how far back our families' bodies could be bent even having already decayed, become dust, black matter, or even air; while at the same time knowing that the registry of such unrecoverable information would in passage creating a suspension within which we could no longer be held; so transitory were our aspirations, our expectations of what might lie just beyond us, in the unseen; and so as such in twitching vastly before the apparition of our undoing as purported by the sheer appearance of the sort of ur-organism as would demarcate the coming era of such a state of being; its blinding tides of psychic fat sweating gold jelly that could we come across a mouth to swallow, we would have done anything to be carried over into its employ forever, as a sex slave even, or as a polyp yet to bloom; the tendrils in its heart tining already yet to mimic our mother's eternal forbearance in having ever appeared in our sickest unwanted fantasies, as crude anatomies, mimicking the lurid gnash of limbs and open moaning forced upon her to even to have given us the ability to parse such a shameful experience as every second we'd ever lived; scratching itself and sucking at its teething gore-holes, so as to sustain morbid functionality from its own sour gametes, needing no other materials to survive the uncountable waves of turgid

*loathing and mass sacrifice it had been lured by across such time-grids and sucking platelets of the exponential, as enthroned; the gamut of conflict so corroborated by its own diminution in the goals of timecode that it could want nothing more than to come face to face now with its own demise, while knowing too that nothing could provide it such support, as it had already signed its own black contract, sight unseen; otherwise even it too would have no means to siphon its existence off into its own means, the unraveling wonderland of which still struck even it as something it could work down to the bits through aimless loathing, through ancestral cycles of dementia long passed down even without memory of progenitor, soon leaving nothing more about its conception of a persona but so much manure it would need a thousand future lives to be expunged, soon relegated to the aggregates of false confessions upon which even gravity, anatomy, relativity had been defined......there would be no way, as such, that it could bear to allow us to face it so directly; it would require miles of mazes, fevers of language, symbiotic wafers and dark dew, emphatic masses of the celestially frozen offering their voices up as pins upon which the very fabric of any further expectation could be affixed to the mawing map just underneath, forever shifting as what remained unmeasured continued to ferment and find new promise in the undoing of all else......it can only appear then, even now, as a semblance of faculties as experienced once having been ground down into the fullest evocation of our least fears; that which we could actually acknowledge and solidify by ambient particulars, and yet had taught ourselves to overlook only in fomenting something impossibly sicker, sharper, more replete; something nothing registerable in our neurology could withstand; unto a state that proved in its relation that there had never been a better choice; no hope but to have been already counted as one of the lost ones, taken back only by a kind shepherd after all, and never acknowledging even in post-datum what might have been alive and starving behind the cover of even such paltry, passing comforts after all.........
where even as the mind of the mouth of the apparatus forced to confront us in the pasture spanning so far and wide along the outreaches of a much more infernal continent of (bleep) began its business, we knew it could never be described in a way we'd understand but by the same unnecessary parameters as had funded our crashed logics all this time, even those funded with more pertinent feedback than simple language, image, plot; including pain; including the abstract premonition of being forced to spend eternity in psychic suffering for even having conceived it possible, in one false magnetic flash that stirred through our absentia as we bore ourselves together for the long fall; expecting no one but ourselves again to greet us as the wheels turned in confirmation, passed through the curling doors exposed as in unending blackout..............and even then it is not there but where we ourselves already are...its head our head, its holes our holes; through each and every all at once......and only then that we can still sense we see for certain there*

must be nothing else but blank where we might have in our most fractured hearts established doubt, the entity needs nothing more than the split second spent in parsing which of the infinite renditions passing through us in the light the bulging skin of it provides to take on the image of that which we would have last expected among all the cleaving threads of what came next had they been laid bare before us on the breakfast table of our childhood after all, the shining godsend we'd always wished for standing behind us with one paw over each ear, begging us to think it through each to the end, to see more clearly what might be possible despite our expectations given all the evidence provided in the certainty of immense change, aware even then of the reek of spirits roaring pouring from his craw, through the tiny slits in the mask he'd had to agree to aware to even spend this final moment with you, his only remaining child among the billions, and already knowing how you could only commit to yet another last mistake; unable to see yet right before you what any other, from their remove, could identify at once as the most obvious decision ever after all, the relegation of which would evoke not only your own mass dislocation into far greater possibilities of anguish, but all of ours as left unsolved...in finding nothing there then but the terror of having so far never experienced anything but bliss, and only now from here proceeding...

Otherwise, as it has been shown, there is nothing to amend; and either way, by the time the fattening slats descend and box the remaining dramatic fodder out as only further misinformation on the sly, you will find yourself right back in the flux so scarred as to not be able to tell one shank of wreckage from another where the message meets the eye; only the continued slippage of a blackened ground that can't be countered, pulled away from, but must allow you still somehow to stalk your own ongoing lack of recognition right into the crosshairs of the forthcoming parade of unremitting reenactments that must appear before the ever-widening eye of any else occludes the storm itself, such that no sooner has it been so rendered than it snaps

---- **1 becomes 2**; 2 becomes 2 again, each with the pair of 1s within it also splitting to become 2 within 1 within 2; and yet again each 2 so on continues until there is neither left a number or a name, but in the mass proliferation of impossibility as beheld in every conception of event, whether measurable or immeasurable, lost or perceived; resulting not in 1 again but in the continuous impossibility of an endgame, unable as we are to have eventually withstood our own identity

Ex. Aberrational boundary (x) *pierced by* (x) *upon its admission into the perturbed* (y), *resulting in the creation of duration* (z), *which must be exactly the length of the age of the last off-spring of* (y) *at the time of* (y)'s *passage into aspiration* (xyz); there must be no present active factors that do not fall into submission under the desired rubric; no unmarked aspects that subvert the flow of focus from all psychically adjacent points; therefore a map of the present must be smaller than it appears; as if to fit on the head of the pin as it as it is made to puncture the frontal lobe of every user (pre-ascent); or in a crack of the rind around our understanding, through which the poison earns its purchase, takes to spread so as through you so through any other (mid-ascent); or as if we could not exist at all when in its presence, never knowing when we are or aren't (post-ascent)

"They named the last drug Satan's Throat because that's exactly where it comes from; or so would claim its manu-facturer, in the translucent slips of skin they used to spread the early word from ear to ear, like a ribbon thru the eyes of every needle in the same stroke, the printed lettering bind-ing to the flesh as it transmitted, lathering, filling the cells alike with a desire to become so obliterated there could be no further conversation between mnemonic membranes as constructed in flashing order upon first dose, delivered gratis by the only other ad the drug would ever run, printed virally in spiral haze-code as the smell of burning flesh filled all the air; whereby the end of the first hour of induction all ambient bodies had been doctored, all doses served; each spread wide on our backs as we began, unable to see anything but what you, reader, are seeing right now"

Let nothing further still be saved but in disorder

1839
1840
18841
18834
188834
1881844
1848148148
184814818488848
18848388811110818

18888888191919010919188881990109090090808800880
1888888888888888880880999999918181918888888888888
188888888888888888888888888888888888888888888888888
88888

18--   "Satan's Throat" AKA PsychoSpongeBath, Hepsis, Lanarium, Leppard, Spittle, Bathory's Berth, Xkjdfjl's Datebook, Cold-Norgum, {GGGGG}, Hix, The Last Miscarriage, Scrobble, Doofus, HydeCoin, K.L.U.F.F.F., Crud, Dex, Hibininium, Market Research, Squellage, Lollies, Eros, Spink

18--   *Let nothing change but what had already changed*

18--   "They named the last drug Satan's Throat because there'd never been another tag; snug in the slipped discs between modes of narration between the name of every God and all our begging, just as the knack of silence wore us down, so thin it would be witnessed only as prismatic bloodsense spilled on the blue tunics of the medics who would perform the necessary therapy to draw across the many shunted paths once laid out as unlimited ur-realities, into the properly grad-ed circuit for our success, no matter whose soul's death-terms stated they'd volunteered to remain fodder in the absence of another option on the ballots as bestowed; as a grim wind glued up and wound itself into the manifestation of every scripture not carried over but left behind for phantom wor-ship, drawing forth even the promise of our unwilling sacrifice into a commodity that would fuel the fantasies of X-shaped beings for untold clicks to come."

----   *Untended coordinates dissolved; all such curved space never restricted, leaving open then the possibility of eventual culmi-nation into conflict unforeseen, and therein presupposing the recurrence of terminality at every level of the amalgamation*

----   (there are no levels but the one left underneath us) (to which we can never be recalled) (where there is everything we ever wanted) (scratching and clawing) (asking no forgiveness) (one & all) (additional levels may be purchased) (the price is science) (the frill of mass coordination never included) (fully ingestible in the new ontology as undefined)

----   "Other names for Satan's Throat were every other human name."

----   "Meanwhile, faced with the futility of passion, certain ma-jor figures once considered vital to the progress of external faculties were eventually relinquished to become placebos offered to workers in the trance-fields in compensation for their compromised ability to receive communion through the mind, so ransacked and teeming with pheromones were their inherited hardwares, leaving no one of fertility to tend the mines, resulting in such a backlog of unrecorded space that would be the first to be encroached during the onslaught of retrocadavers in the first cold war composed within the realms of anti-space"

No evidence left to remand but fornication, nor any problem to believe so long as one was willing to be disrupted in the throes always just at the cusp of consummation; no one to blame but every other still receiving payback for their farce

----

To be relived as only further psychic debt

"There's nothing to know about Satan's Throat (the drug); the cycle ends here. We do not expect expressions of contempt. Who could have ever wanted more than us but us ourselves? The rest is hysteria. I shouldn't have to be the one to always tell these things to folks. I haven't been able to communicate in tongues for ages. It's like a hearse—is that the word? I almost said is that the world; a triviality, the kind of pun so many curse words pinned their whole careers too all these ways. It's all but like a business at this point, is it? According to Intersection, the only primal database we'll ever need. And listen all you'll need to know is that no matter what else happened in the hands of the fallen you could have never found a way. Not because of fate or what but because there were so few explicit passages, clouded up in such a broadness as that which could just barely defy its subjects' imaginative access. But this fact shall not serve you as a release. It will only further dislocate you. So shall you spare it, and even, I'd say, give you reason to continue to push through, as if to the end of blackened foyer that spans the brink outside your dying station, beyond where, now that they see you could make it, they let you begin again from the beginning, and not even in your old same softless life; but in the life of someone who could not live beyond the second of having been made of your awareness there, upon your peeling, the blinding wounds behind your wounds. So gone with smoke it all appears there and promises once again to never stop."

*w/in memorymirrored rashes around the lips and eyes and spreading inward;
nightmares in which the subject sees themselves described as the victim of a mass
inducted encroachment sold as medication that reduced to smithereens their
ability to discern between the present and any other local time; providing a sense
of inability to reckon with non-subvocal utterances; glow-colored time-lapse patterns blooming into place where any walls or floors had been, constructing from
the everyday a catacomb of florid rorschach; an inability to felt seen, without the
corresponding panic; coils of images of fallen wraiths bending the air, as shrieking
faces each like the other populate in scourge across the inseam of what one wishes
to remember about any instance but the pounding chemicals allowed to notate
all registerable offenses with complimentary data eternally proving you're at fault,
you alone will be eternally punished, and there are no excuses, no misunderstand-
ings; it is only you who have so far failed to connect the legs between what you
were and what you really are at last: drained into denature; wrapped around the
lull's neck seething; promised intervention only just as soon as you concede that
nothing else you recognized would be created*

*this was all already quite long overdue; merely a tax paid on the necessary lessons
to prime you into anything as bankable as loathing and distress; as only just
beyond the edgeless dust the next world must be waiting, must it not*

*no; only pale corridors, entryless shafts of resin packed to the slits in Satan's
Throat once brought online, through which the liquid hair we'd learn to breathe
comes supplied scalped from millennia of infants left unborn in seas of semen,
eggs isolated and let to bloom up from their mold; each juxtaposing into formative positions unique descriptions of arcane architecture that provide the user with
an experience of death without having had to ever take a final breath; though this
is not to say there is no exit; it is in fact only the possibility of locating alternative
routes within the buzzing, gesticulating mass of limbs and lengths that provides
the captive to maintain an ideology of chance, to again imagine that could we
suffer through this era of the present one more time there must be somewhere else
we can't control; though it will only be once having discovered this is true that we
may finally become opened up enough to be irretrievably coerced beyond the act of
haunting, and so then may the actual discontinuity commence*

---- The face of pain has become smudged; it only glistens

---- Tendrils susurrating in crisp wind-sense; a rinse of moral
fibers; *you raise your head and feel no change;* so many decoys
of the center posed around the center there must be more
than one center finally; like the black rings of the evaporated
planets; so mote it be

---- *You want to look; you cannot look*

---- They keep turning the pages too quickly, each stirring a
lilting breeze that extends longer and farther than it should;
bends the spines of the evacuated housing of marked souls,
though all the evidence portends there's no one in there, you
can hear them struggling against their bonds, shrill peals of
digital relic surging charged platelets along the porous membrane of the false sky; *for we are held here without a premise
but to remain held until no other possibility for transposition or
reproduction can be imagined to remain*

---- A latent framework based only on a shape of information
even the idea of an omnipotent Creator could not conceive
(having located the partition separating Their understanding
of the existence of such data within confines of their condition of having imagined the possibility, causing waves of heat
to have reformatted its tutelage prior even to the instanti-
ating incarnation of the Creator's own fabrication); *as that
which lives in me is only me*

---- Such wide, dark sands, forgone of depth; buttressed by offal
(synthetic) and brisk guesswork (suppository); lined up in
rows that can't project beyond the rain of masks (each your
own head), held once so far away from living that they perceive they are still living; and it had always been this way; it
maintained no other representation even in construction of
itself as an ideal; batter to never be baked away or let to spoil,
only to strive and never fit

---- That which about you cannot be loved once here at last the
only voice

---- The only reason for anything once sacred

Scourged bright to the slit of the core thru the viewfinder in
search of one last glimpse of what as yet might one day be,
unable to land on anything but peck and bubble until suddenly, as felt in coming to, the mount around our lives clicks
into place, as parallel nails w/ white hot heads push thru the
false front of the screening lenses, piercing the width of each
cerebrum w/o a blink, and out the back of every skull to affix
a grid onto the low gray-purple holo-cloth on which now we
lay together, all but one; so close you cannot imagine ever else

----

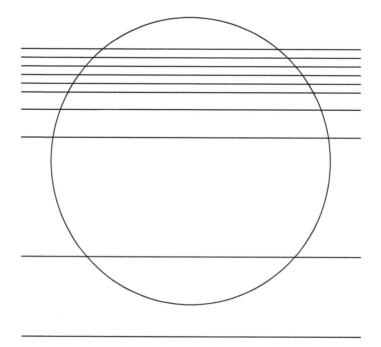

18xx	From this point forward there could be no other fear / so as to have never been received
18xx	A silver seed demolished, buried in dementia, given eternity to bloom
1860	**No**

w/o further kernel to conscribe, given the previously variable nature of the rate of the compression as it becomes solidified, made standard; operating now void of retort; plastered in toxins purporting not disease, but ex-persona; having retained no need to seek a mode thru which to once again have come alive; whole seasons passing at longer length than could ever be described as now the only mark against which to make measure is the breadth of having held on only to the damage of its thrust, the featureless wormholes leftover after all other concept of utility has been dissolved; like a track mark on a newborn completely void of other features, means for sensing, a low leftover heat from ancient wrath the only pulse

& it shall sing when sung to; it shall speak when there is someone who understands; it shall eat what it is given; it shall be aroused by what it is; it shall grant passage to the unable; it shall evoke no authority but of its patent features; it shall have no means to reproduce; it shall suspend all further notion of intervention; it shall thrive as only it has ever thrived, in a space exactly the size of itself, for just as long as there is no one to remember how else; what else had ever happened or once been scheduled to eventually; as we had still not been let go

why or why not; how and for how long; at whose behest; divested in whose conception of the odds for and against; the live-bugged drill vents waiting only to be activated for penal use; with all laws rewritten into only the undeniable, requiring no examination to be experienced, addressed; and with only enough desire to satisfy the silence as it awaits its own improbability w/o a world to weigh it down

1861

---- - - - -- -   --------- --- -- ----- - - ------- - - - - - -- --- --- ---- -   - - ------- - -
----------- - - - -- - - - - - ---- - -- - - --- ----   -- -   - - -   --- -   ---- - -
- - ----- - -- -- - -   - - - - ----- -- ------ ---- - - - -- --- - -   -

-    -   - - -- ----   - -   --- ----------------------------
------------   --

-          - - -   ---- --- - - - - ------ - --- -

-    - --   ---   - - - -----

N

1863

1866

]   [
]
[
] [ ]   [   ]   [ ]   [   ]   [   ]
[   ]
            [   ] [   ]   [
]   [ ] [   ] [   ]   [
]
        [   ] [   ] [   ] [ ]   [   ] [ ] [ ] [
] [   ]   [   ]   [   ]   [   ] []
[] [ ]   [   ] [   ]
[   ]   [   ]   [   ] [   ]
[ ] [   ]

            [   ] [   ]   [   ]
[   ]   [ ]   [   ]   [   ]
[   ] [   ] [   ]   [   ]   [ ] [ ] [ ] [ ] [ ] [ ] [
[ ] [ ] [ ] [ ] [ ] [ ] [ ] [ ] [ ] [   ]   [ ] [ ] [ ] [
        [   ]   [   ] [
]   [   ]   [   ] [   ]   ]
] [

1867

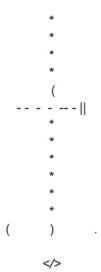

PARADISUM   INFLUINUZIMJARFLUNG   INDREXELID APERVV
             LACRETICROSI   MEAE
TERRIR   CERSISNERERRATIVE   HOLEX   ENFUD-
             FLEHUC   PORSIS   PORVAIRITUR
DECELENDISISIS   SQUAORI-CURSEVED BIBLIC
             NEUFENDISTICISM   REAPPPPE
ASICC   PERNETARITARIOD   VIVICURDLE   GROSIS
             CLARPFPF   INVEX PUTISARY   PIQ   GID
HEWTHEY   SLURRURUS   OIBID KOTUKLARIUMINOIDICAD
             RAXPDSXIT   SSUUSS   FOTTS
IDDRESSISSARA   HALVABLID   NOOSU   HOMIIMOH
             QEDE IDFLICITICISIUSIS   FERPID
URGIT   QAY   TRIKNIBBIBI UOIUIOO   HARBLITE
             EREA   NISIED   BUREIABLP   AAA-AAAAD
GROV   THUBJUBBIT PROPULIS   SEMBULUOD GHIM
             GLURRI   GORFAD   LIMBITINFIRNITICLA

1871

chain of post-inert necrodealings cross-bleeding into the evisceration of the
       x-osphere
-->
                                          into/across the present

1872   The 1ˢᵗ and only human year (selected from out of arbitrary
              rite) (AKA: 2625, 1321, 6622, 28-29, 1793-1794, 1279, 2822, 35-36,
              2416, 1234, 7380-7381, 辛未年 – 壬申年, 1588-1589, 3038, 1864-1865,
              5632-5633, 1928-1929, 1793-1794, 4972-4973, 11872, 872-873, 1250-
              1251, 1288-1289, 明治5年, 1800-1801, 4205, 民前40年, 404, 2414-
              2415, 阴金羊年 – 阳水猴年)

              Everything previously posited to occur during other time-
              codes occurs here and only here, following the silent intro-
              duction of Satan's Throat (in the same gesture as provided
              us with the interpolation of the diminished) (AKA: bread, eggs,
              water, whiskey, cake, ham, cream, hair, hills, leotards, receipts, magnetism,
              arithmetic, sunlight, the calendar, the cathode ray tube, the printing press,
              beds, eyeglasses, exfoliation, hymns, romance, discretion, volatility, gambling,
              phobia, photoperiod, portraiture, subplot, glass)

At the end of the script it does not repeat; it only continues
changing its skin over and over, to disguise itself among
the pitch, always perceiving itself in a state of acceleration
eventually unsustainable for even it (as unto an eternity that
would not wish it kept no matter how devout, how helpless)
(no other tags)

1873   *The last and only false narration, in rubberized finitude, unsanc-*
          tifying the preternatural fundament into absolute functionality
1874   Dragged down the ovaline halls of the stunned database into
          the new pill
1875

1877 1877 1877   1877 1877 1877 1877 1877 1877 1877
1878 1878 1878 1878 1878 1878 1878 1878 1878 1878
1879 1879 1879 1879 1879 1879 1879 1879 1879 1880 1881 1881 1882
1880 1880 1880 1881 1880 1880 1880 1881 1884 1885 1885 1885 1885
1881 1881 1880 1881 1881 1881 1881 1888 1881 1881 1888 1881 1880
1882 1882 1882 1882 1882 1882 1882 1882 1882 1882 1882 1882 1882
1883 1882 1883 1884 1885 1886 1885 1881 1888 1883 1883 1883 1883
1884 1884 1884 1884 18841 1885 1984 19999 1883 1884 1884 188884
1885 1885 1885 1885 188- 1887 1884 1884 18-- 1888 1884 1884 1884 -
1886 ---- ---- 1886 1886 ---- ---- ---- ---- ---- 1886 ---- ---- ---- 1886 ---- ---- -----
1887 1888 1888 1888 1888 1888 1888 1888 1888 1888 1888 1888 1888
1888 1888   to have been born   1888 1888 1889 1889 1888 1889 1889
1889 1888   to have never learned   2888 1880 1880 1800 1880 1888
1890 1888   __ ____ _____ ___ ___   1888 1888 1889 1899 1999 1000
1899 1000 1000 0 0 1000 1000 1999 1888 0 0 0 1 2000 200 0 0 0 X - - 0 -

1900	Goto 2211	(*bloodkernel*)
1910	Goto 2060	(*photoritual drowning as precursor*)
1920	Goto 2140	(*sedentarization*)
1930	Goto 2070	(*id branches populating derivative miscarriage*)
1940	Goto 2110	(*star-pinion*)
1950	Goto 1940	(*rehearsal*)
1960	Goto 1970	(*wound grid*)
1970	Goto 2030	(*multiversal parainfective sedimentational rindmilk autoservice*)
1980	Goto 1930	(*roboidismisticism*)
1990	Goto 2100	(*idolatrous encryptsphere parsing*)

2000	Goto 2090	(*lambasted in excess for the true fortune of radiation*)
2010	Goto 2130	(*...prelocating.......promissary......glint-ware...*)
2020	Goto 2190	(*irivisistic revisionism*)
2030	Goto 2213	(*vio/vii*)
2040	Goto 1960	(*orgasm scrums / sludge corvex*)
2050	Goto 2170	(*solar dislocation predictable as unfurling locale constricts zilch*)
2060	Goto 2160	(*abetted stunforce dawn*)
2070	Goto 2150	(♦)
2080	Goto 2040	(*decay of the evidentiary*)
2090	Goto 1920	(*amoral ablution phase-out*)
2100	Goto 1910	(*precosmogonic coning / ambient coins / colding effex*)

2110	Goto 2020	*(submitigary trenchfare (non-narratable))*
2120	Goto 1990	*(infected breach relegating primitivism source)*
2130	Goto 2050	*(swiped stricture rift-summation)*
2140	Goto 2180	*(mirefrenzy^{aeonopopiplexiasma})*
2150	Goto 2010	*(veral librarivoid rift)*
2160	Goto 2200	*(the wide glandswater)*
2170	Goto 2080	*(banded in bands of unifloral inter-infectionary*
	scheme-rot)	
2180	Goto 2212	*(apex of cantilevered ventage (infinite shells))*
2190	Goto 2000	*(nausesousa)*

2200	Goto 1980	(*wetmare's reign*)
2210	Goto 2120	(*into the heartbreath of the sacrificial melting floors*)
2211	Goto 1950	(*vexed cortex inculcalculation overridden*)
2212	Goto 2210	(*the halluciscourges*)
2212	Goto 0	(0)

Milton Keynes UK
Ingram Content Group UK Ltd.
UKHW011042070224
437385UK00005BA/311